Praise for
Too Good to Be True

"Lovering, a master of manipulation to rival her own characters, does a skillful job of unspooling her intricate tapestry of psychological intrigue while deftly juggling her multiple narratives."

—*Kirkus Reviews* (starred review)

"This firecracker of a novel will leave readers wondering what they would accept for love and how the most perfect of lives may be a façade. A must for book clubs." —*Booklist* (starred review)

"A head-spinningly devious plot [with] a plethora of twists . . . Psychological thriller fans will keep turning the pages to see what happens next."

—*Publishers Weekly*

"Twists, lies, and cons, oh my . . . You'll be guessing the ending until the last twisty page." —*theSkimm*

"Just when you think you've got it figured out, Lovering will throw another curve ball at you." —*Betches*

"Covering dual timelines and told from three differing perspectives, this exceptional psychological thriller is full of twists that will have you wondering which characters to trust and who to root for." —*Book Riot*

"If you like your romances twisted, you have found your new favorite author." —*CrimeReads*

"A layered tale of tense domestic suspense full of duplicitous plot twists." —*Lansing State Journal*

"I raced through *Too Good to Be True,* desperate to see what new twist was coming next. Gripping, tantalizing, and perfectly paced, Carola Lovering somehow makes duplicity sexy—and even understandable." —Sara Shepard, *New York Times* bestselling author

"A twisty tale of love, greed, betrayal, and revenge. Addictive and unputdownable." —Michele Campbell, international bestselling author of *A Stranger on the Beach*

"Thoroughly engrossing and beautifully crafted, *Too Good to Be True* mesmerizingly merges seemingly unrelated lives and expertly weaves together past and present story lines. Deliciously fraught with plot twists that keep readers compulsively turning pages, this is the type of book night-lights were invented for." —Erica Katz, author of *The Boys' Club*

"A cat-and-mouse thriller with masterful twists. Will leave you guessing until the last page." —Liv Constantine, international bestselling author

Also by Carola Lovering

Tell Me Lies
Can't Look Away

Too
GOOD
to Be
TRUE

—

Carola Lovering

St. Martin's Paperbacks

This is a work of fiction. All of the characters, organizations, and events portrayed in this novel are either products of the author's imagination or are used fictitiously.

Published in the United States by St. Martin's Paperbacks, an imprint of St. Martin's Publishing Group

TOO GOOD TO BE TRUE

For information, address St. Martin's Publishing Group, 120 Broadway, New York, NY 10271.

www.stmartins.com

Library of Congress Catalog Card Number: 2020040976

ISBN: 978-1-250-87701-7

Our books may be purchased in bulk for promotional, educational, or business use. Please contact your local bookseller or the Macmillan Corporate and Premium Sales Department at 1-800-221-7945, ext. 5442, or by email at MacmillanSpecialMarkets@macmillan.com.

Printed in the United States of America

St. Martin's Press hardcover edition published 2021
St. Martin's Griffin edition published 2022
St. Martin's Paperbacks edition / March 2023

10 9 8 7 6 5 4 3 2 1

*For my father, Joe Lovering—
the wisest man and writer I know,
and the one who put the world
at my fingertips*

Isn't it funny? The truth just sounds different.

—Penny Lane, *Almost Famous*

Part

ONE

Chapter One

Skye

Something is going on with Burke this morning. I can tell because he asks me three times how I want my eggs.

"Over easy!" I call from the bedroom. It's how I've asked for my eggs every time since we began dating six months ago.

Burke is a morning person and I am not, and I love that he's gotten in the habit of making me breakfast on weekend mornings while I lounge in bed with a book.

"Over easy, right?" he shouts again from the kitchen.

"Right! Thanks." I sink back into the pillows, confused. Burke and I have been living together for over two months now. He *knows* how I like my eggs.

The fear that my forty-six-year-old boyfriend might be developing early-onset Alzheimer's suddenly seizes every square inch of my brain. I recognize the irrational concern as it formulates, but the compulsion has already taken its unshakable hold, and I can't lose Burke to Alzheimer's out of sheer laziness. I climb out of bed and knock on every wooden object in the room eight times: eight knocks for the headboard, bedside tables, both dressers, windowpanes, closet door, baseboard moldings, and the little hand-carved elephant on my dresser. For time-management purposes, I should really avoid buying wooden furniture in the future.

"Two over-easy eggs with an English muffin and extra-crispy bacon for my beautiful girl," Burke says, entering the bedroom with a tray. "And, of course, coffee." He looks adorable in sweats and a T-shirt, his dark hair damp from the shower. Affection floods me, and I almost can't stand how much I love him.

"Breakfast in bed?" I sit up straighter as he places the meal in front of me. "I didn't even know we owned this fine tray. So fancy, Goose. What's the occasion?"

Burke shrugs. "I just wanted to do something nice for my Goose. I know how you love your lazy Sundays."

I smile. Burke and I have called each other Goose ever since we watched a documentary about geese and how they mate for life. When a goose loses its mate, it circles and calls endlessly for the one that's never coming back. Burke said that's what he would do if he ever lost me.

"You're the sweetest." I bite into a piece of bacon, crisped to perfection in the nearly burnt way that I like it.

Burke stands beside the bed, sort of shifting from one foot to another while he watches me eat, a peculiar grin plastered to his face.

"Are you okay?" I look up at him, worried again. "Did you already eat?"

"I . . . I—not yet."

"Well, what's the matter? I can tell there's somethi—"

"Skye. There's one more thing to go with your breakfast." All of a sudden Burke drops to his knee beside the bed, staring at me with wide, deer-in-headlights eyes. Several slow, strange seconds pass before it finally hits me. *Oh. OH! But it can't be this. Can it be this?!*

A small box appears on Burke's palm—it must have come from his pocket—and along with the air in the room, my heart goes still. I hear him saying something about how much he loves me, and how even though it hasn't been that long, he knows he wants to be with me forever, and then he flips open the box and there's a ring and then he's asking the question that every girl dreams of hearing from the love of her life.

My jaw hangs open. My entire body feels fizzy and light.

"Skye?" Burke prompts. "Say something."

"Yes!" I scream. *"YES!"*

Burke whisks the breakfast tray to the floor and dives into bed beside me. Shock runs through me in hot waves as he slides the sapphire-and-diamond ring over my finger. It's loose over the knuckle, but that's okay—easy to have it resized, Burke assures me. He smiles up at me and it's his biggest smile, the one that reaches his ocean-blue eyes, dimples teasing either cheek, and I'm grateful that I never gave up on love.

"You're crying, Goose." He touches my face.

"Of course I'm crying." I wrap my arms around his neck and pull him in close. "Oh my God, Burke. Oh my God. I just can't believe it. I thought you had Alzheimer's or something."

"Huh? Why?"

"Because you kept asking what kind of eggs I wanted!

And you *always* know to make mine over easy. I got so worried I knocked on all the wood in the room."

Burke laughs and presses his lips against my temple. "I was nervous, I guess. Are you surprised?"

"*So* surprised. But it's just perfect." I gaze down at the ring, a brilliant round diamond framed by two smaller sapphires on a platinum band. "How did you know I wanted sapphires? I never even told you."

He swipes a tear dripping down my cheek. "Just a feeling."

I nuzzle in toward Burke's face, inhaling the smell of aftershave in the creases of his neck. I can't help but imagine Andie's reaction when she hears we're engaged, and this is how my mind works—once an anxiety-inducing thought takes hold, I'm powerless against it.

You can't actually know someone after six months, Skye, she'll say, just as she said when we moved in together.

I listen to Burke explain how he asked my dad's permission a couple weeks earlier, and how he's arranged brunch at Buvette to celebrate later this morning with my dad and Nancy and her twin teenage sons, Aidan and Harry—it still feels weird to call them my step-brothers. My stomach twists—I don't want to share any of this with Nancy and her kids—but the excitement in Burke's voice tells me he's proud of his effort to include my family in this special day.

I can't believe I have a fiancé, and there's Andie's stupid voice again: *Don't you think it's weird, Skye, that you've never met his family? You're living with someone and you've never met his family.*

But Burke doesn't have a family—his parents died in a plane crash when he was nineteen. He's an only child. It's not his fault.

"Want to finish your eggs?" Burke asks. "Brunch isn't for a couple hours."

I smile and nod, and he grabs the tray from the floor and places it on my lap. I bite into a buttered half of an English muffin, and *God* I would do anything to get Andie out of my head in this moment.

All I'm saying is that if he seems too good to be true, he probably is.

I lean my head on Burke's strong, safe shoulder. "Tell me how you picked the ring, Goose."

He launches into the story and I cling to his words, willing them to drown out Andie's voice, which is negative and stemmed from envy and a threat to my happiness. Because Burke is *not* too good to be true, and unlike Andie and Lexy and Isabel, I never had a Burke, not until six months ago. I never had a reliable plus-one or a valentine, someone to bring to parties and weddings and be debilitatingly hungover with on Saturday afternoons. Until Burke I never had a guy who told me he loved me or brought me soup when I was sick or wanted to make me come until my vision blurred.

See, I'm not the type of girl men want to marry. I'm the kind of girl men *think* they want to marry—at first they see a pretty face, nice apartment, good clothes. But then they get to know me—the real me. And even though I never relinquished my optimism, even though I kept up my monthly visits to European Wax Center and my thrice-weekly runs along the West Side Highway in an effort to shed the stubborn baby fat; still, if you had told me a year ago that in 365 days a quality man would ask me to be his wife, I wouldn't have believed you.

But six months ago, I met Burke Michaels. Handsome Burke, with his jet-black hair and dimpled smile. From that very first day I knew something was different. A week in, I made the mistake of telling Andie he was the man I was going to marry. She looked almost angry when she responded that it was psychotic to consider the notion of marriage with someone you've only known for a week, and I knew I'd hit a nerve. Andie and Spencer have been dating since college and they're not engaged yet—they don't even *talk* about it yet. Andie says it doesn't bother her, but I don't believe that. I don't believe you can spend eight years with someone and be okay with an ambiguous future.

Burke and I, we knew from the beginning. We didn't get into specifics, but the shared understanding that we would always be together was there, like the sun in the morning or the moon at night. It's a peaceful, uncomplicated feeling when you know that what you have with someone is a forever kind of thing.

I help Burke rinse the dishes, then shower and change for brunch. Even on a day as happy as today, I'm dreading seeing Nancy. I think of that night on Nantucket two summers ago, the way she whispered to my father on the porch while I eavesdropped.

I worry about Skye, I really do. She's a beautiful girl, but with her . . . problem . . . it just seems to be setting her back. I worry about her meeting someone. . . .

My problem. My *fucking* problem.

It's not Nancy's fault that I dislike her, not if I'm being honest with myself. I can see that now that I'm in a solid place in my life. I have the perspective and the maturity to admit that she never stood a chance with me, not after what I'd been through. It didn't matter that people said she was bringing color and oxygen back into my father's being, not when I could still vividly picture my parents dancing to Van Morrison in the kitchen, laughing and kissing like teenagers. Not when the mother I'd lost was a mother like mine. A force as palpable and vital as my own heartbeat, an entire world in a single being. You can't replace a person like that.

I pull my long blond hair back into a low ponytail. I swipe mascara on my lashes, and Burke comes up behind me, circling his arms around my waist. I press my cheek against his chest and listen to the steady beat of his heart, grateful for its kindness, its openness. Finally, I've found someone who sees beyond my *problem,* someone who loves me in spite of it. And not just anyone—I've found tall, dark, and movie-handsome Burke Michaels, a man with a clear conscience and a good job and eyes so blue you can spot them a mile away. I'm suddenly almost excited for brunch at Buvette, fueled by the thought of waving my new ring in Nancy's face. My dad never even gave Nancy an engagement ring (*It was the second marriage for both of us; we thought understated was more appropriate,* I can hear him reasoning).

I finger the earrings I've chosen for the occasion—my

mother's emerald studs, the ones my father gave her the night before their wedding. A pang of sadness rushes through me, and I miss her more than I can stand.

"I wish your mom could be here for this," Burke says from behind me, reading my mind. He props his chin on my shoulder so that our eyes meet in the bathroom mirror.

"I was just thinking that. I wish your parents could be here, too."

"Me, too, Goose."

I smile at our reflection, the diamond sparkling on my left ring finger. Despite our missing pieces, it is truly a perfect sight. A dream come true. I'll never be able to understand how I got so lucky.

Chapter Two

Burke Michaels's Diary

SEPTEMBER 8, 2018

Dear Dr. K,

Her hair is yellow and thick, nothing like my wife's. Isn't that awful, that when I first notice an attractive woman, I instantly compare her to my wife? I used to think I was a good person, the kind of man who wouldn't be struck dumb by the tumble of blond hair down a creamy, anonymous back.

But shit goes out the window, I've learned. It goes out the window fast.

This journal was my wife's idea, by the way. Well, technically it was yours, Dr. K (why I'm shelling out an arm and a leg for couples therapy when money is our central issue, don't ask). I'm supposed to be writing down my thoughts daily, not to show you or Heather, but just for myself. *To get to know ourselves better as individuals, independent from our marriage,* as you explained it, Dr. K.

You said that for this journal project thing we could write each entry *to* you, like a letter of sorts, if that would be helpful. And I do think that will be helpful for me, from a structural standpoint, so that's what I'm going to do, just so you know. Not that you're ever going to read this.

Back to the blonde. Here's what happened: I was standing behind her in the hotel lobby this morning, feeling jittery and impatient to check in even though I wasn't in a rush whatsoever. I'm taking a weekend in Montauk. Hotel room for one at Gurney's Resort. I told Heather I had a networking opportunity in the city with some old Credit Suisse colleagues and she didn't question it, bless her faithful heart. "Just make time to journal your daily thoughts like Dr. K said" was her only response. After twenty-five years of marriage I'm so used to taking orders from Heather that the urge to follow them is drilled into my subconscious. And so here we are. My daily thoughts.

Why am I in Montauk? Good question. The truth is I'm having the worst month of my life, and I needed to get away. Three kids, one in college and one soon to be, a mortgage, and a wife I used to be crazy about. I feel sad when I look at Heather now, because mostly all I see is the absence of what I used to love.

There's also the astronomical cost of my eldest daughter Hope's dental implants (she claims she hadn't been drinking when she fell down a flight of stairs at a frat party and knocked out several of her top teeth last spring). And then, to top it all off, there's the fact that I was recently fired from my job of over two decades at PK Adamson. I'm sorry, let me rephrase: I was recently *let go* from my job of over two decades at PK Adamson. According to my ex-boss, Herb, there's a crucial difference, and one that earned me two weeks' severance. Two whole weeks' severance! After twenty fuck-ing years. Can you believe that, Dr. K?

I hope you know I'm being sarcastic. It's not easy to convey sarcasm in a journal. Anyway, yes, I was recently "let go," although I suppose it's not all that recent since I've technically been unemployed since April. And if you think I've been sitting on my ass for the last four months, you're wrong. I've applied to jobs at every other wealth management firm under the sun, but no one will hire me, not when they see what's on my record. In 1999, when my *old* ex-boss offered me the data-entry-specialist position at PK Adamson, he said, "If I don't give you a shot, I know no one else will." And he was right. He's still right. Because in certain situations, time doesn't ease the grip of the past.

But with twenty-plus years of experience under my belt, I refuse to switch industries. I can't afford that kind of pay cut. With the mortgage and college tuition and Hope's teeth and our *vital* therapy sessions with bril-liant, out-of-network you, money is tighter than a vir-gin's pussy.

Forgive my crudeness, Dr. K. I'm quite distressed. In case you were wondering, insurance doesn't cover dental implants, which come in around $3,500 per faux tooth. My daughter is currently making do with dental flippers.

So, here I am. I lost my job in April and I've spent the summer working my ass off to find a new one, and no one will hire me, and my wife thinks I'm a worth-less piece of shit, and maybe I am, Dr. K. Maybe I am.

But I do know that life is short, and I need this week-end. I need it for my own red-blooded sanity. I con-fided in my buddy Todd, my colleague—ex-colleague, I should say—and he told me Gurney's in Montauk is *the place*. Right now, I need to be at *the place*.

So, back to this morning. I was making a bet with myself about the blonde in front of me at the Gurney's check-in desk. A woman can look amazing from behind and then she turns around, and, yikes, the front of her washes your fantasy down the drain. A "butter face," Todd calls such girls (everything "but her" face).

Anyway, I was really getting into this internal de-bate, but before I could settle on a firm hypothesis, I got my answer. The blonde whipped around, and her face reminded me of the pretty girls in high school—big doe eyes, supple skin, small nose. A combination that is simple and astonishing at once. She looked directly at me for a split second that jolted my nerves awake, that hushed every sound in the room and in my head so that all I could feel and hear was *Yes. Her.*

All too quickly she resumed her conversation with her friend, a lanky brunette. The girls (they were more like girls than women; mid-twenties, I guessed) brushed by me with their rolling suitcases in tow, and I caught a whiff of something sweet and young and expensive. I heard the brunette mumble something about Aperol spritzes by the pool.

The man behind the desk at Gurney's was calling to me. "Sir, please step forward."

I heard his voice but somehow didn't register the words until he'd repeated himself a third or maybe a fourth time, and the woman behind me jabbed my shoulder and said, "Go."

Go. People in New York and the Hamptons always want you to go. To live in this part of the world, you have to keep moving. Maybe that's why Heather and I never survived here.

If the concierge was annoyed with my delayed reaction, he didn't show it. He was tan and cheerful and well rested, effusing good health and Matthew McConaughey vibes. All that vitamin D. He checked me in to my Superior Ocean View room, the most basic room Gurney's offers, and it's still costing me $1,080 a night. Not a small charge (more than four sessions with you, Dr. K), and if Heather knew what I was doing, she'd send a pack of wolves after me. But like I said, I really, really need this.

I changed into swim trunks and a short-sleeved button-down (Heather got it for me on sale somewhere—she says short-sleeved button-downs are in). I grabbed my key card and the new David Baldacci novel and headed to the pool. I didn't have a set plan, but for the first time in a long time, I was filled with an almost youthful optimism.

Everything about Gurney's is decadent—all clean lines and shiny surfaces and crisp aromas; the opposite of our split-level in the suburbs of New Haven, with its squeaky floors and peeling wallpaper. The pool at Gurney's is perfect, an oasis of turquoise surrounded by plush chaises on a sunny deck overlooking the Atlantic Ocean. I closed my eyes and felt the warm rays on my face and imagined I was fifteen again, not yet with

Heather, the possibilities stretched in front of me in their expansive, limitless might.

When I blinked my eyes open, I was back in the present, and there she was, the blonde, just as I'd hoped she'd be, lounging on a chaise clutching a glass of something neon orange that could only be the coveted Aperol spritz. She was a vision in a white bikini, revealing a curvier frame than I'd expected—certainly curvier than skin-and-bones Heather.

The brunette friend lay on the adjacent chaise, using one hand to twist her long dark hair into a pile on top of her head. In the other she held an identical orange drink. The brunette was hotter than I'd realized. She had a Mediterranean vibe that reminded me of that sexy anchor on *Access Hollywood*. I stepped toward them.

"I've never seen a cocktail that color," I said before I lost momentum. I knew that if I lost momentum, I'd stop myself, and I'd never go through with any of it.

I recognized the shift in their facial expressions— *another creepy old dude hitting on us*—and almost turned around, almost decided to abort the nonplan. But then the blonde smiled at me, and it lit up her whole face, and I remembered that even though I was forty-six and long out of the game, I still had a full head of hair, almost none of it gray, and that I was handsome in a way that Heather always said transcended age.

The brunette had a bored, slightly aggravated expression on her face that told me she wouldn't dream of screwing me, so I turned my full attention toward the blonde. Because if I'm being honest, Dr. K, there was more to the reason I'd come to Gurney's. I'd come to Gurney's to cheat on my wife.

"Haven't you ever had an Aperol spritz?" the blonde asked. Her voice had a mesmerizing quality, sweet and singsongy. "It's all we drink in the summer." She knocked her head toward the brunette, who was now busy scrolling through her phone.

"I haven't. But I'm sold. Be right back. By the way, I'm Burke."

Now, Dr. K, you know I don't drink. And as much as I could've used a bit of liquid courage right about then, I wasn't going to wash twenty-two years of sobriety down the drain. So I walked over to the bar, where I asked for a virgin Aperol spritz. The bartender looked at me like I'd just told an epic joke.

"Oh, you're like, serious?" he said when I continued to stare at him, waiting. More Matthew McConaughey vibes. "I don't think I can make a virgin one?" His voice spun the sentence into a question.

I drummed my fingers across the mahogany bar top. "Grapefruit juice and soda water, then."

"Right on, dude." The bartender gave me a knowing look, like we were in on a secret. Which, in a way, we were.

I paid for the drink and then wandered back over toward the girls.

"No spritz?" the blonde asked.

"I decided to stick with my regular old greyhound." The brunette rolled her eyes.

"Vodka or gin?" the blonde asked.

"Vodka." I willed the dishonesty out of my voice.

I stood there like an idiot and sipped my mocktail, wondering if I should sit, or if I should wait to be asked to sit. Heather may not be wrong when she says I have terrible game.

"You want to sit?" The blonde finally nodded toward the empty chaise to her left. "Cheers." She clinked her glass against mine, and I held her eyes, wide as saucers and almond brown.

I soon learned that the girls' names are Skye and Andie, the blonde and the brunette respectively. They're childhood best friends from a much wealthier part of Connecticut who now live in the city, and they're in Montauk for a "quiet girls' weekend." As the alcohol hit their bloodstreams, they revealed more. I learned that Skye is a freelance editor for young-adult fiction, and that Andie is some kind of dietitian based in Brooklyn, which didn't surprise me. Her scrawny body looks like it survives on healthy shit like tofu and broccoli.

When the waitress came by, I ordered them another round, and then, not wanting to be perceived as a creep trying to get two young women plastered, went to the bar and got myself another grapefruit soda. Even though I wasn't drinking alcohol, something about the peculiarity of the afternoon made its edges blurry, and the longer I talked to Skye, the less I cared that Andie didn't seem to want me there. I don't remember exactly what we talked about, more just the *feeling*—the feeling of being free and happy and alive for the first time in longer than I can remember. I swear, I could've been drunk.

Andie finally wandered off to call her boyfriend, some guy named Spencer, who I feel bad for, because after only a few hours of being in her presence I can already tell Andie is a Heather-esque handful.

Skye suggested we take a walk on the beach, and that's when I felt it, the sureness that *she* didn't have a boyfriend. The sureness that she was interested, that this spark between us was a shared thing.

Skye asked for the check and the waitress dropped the bill in front of me—*me,* of course, old man sugar daddy—and Andie had already left, and I swatted Skye's hand away when she tried to lay down a credit card, because even I know that's what you do when you're interested in a woman. I'd paid for my mocktails separately, but six Aperol spritzes at Gurney's—they'd each had one before I arrived—at twenty dollars a pop plus tax and tip comes out to $134.32. I dug my Visa out of my wallet, and my mind flashed to Heather and the kids, and I wished I could, for once, just not think of them.

I forced the credit card transaction out of my head as I followed Skye toward the ocean. It was just after five, that perfect wedge of time near the end of a beach day when the sun isn't quite so strong, and a golden film is in the air. Skye and I chatted for another hour, maybe two, the ocean waves rumbling back and forth, back and forth, a sprinkling of humid mist along the shoreline. I watched Skye dig her heels into the sand and squish it between her toes. *This feeling is amazing, you have to try it,* she told me. *The ocean is my favorite place in the world.*

Todd is so right. Gurney's *is* the place.

Skye's blond hair flew in wisps around her rosy face, strands of light dancing against the darkening backdrop.

I grabbed her hand, soft as silk, and interlaced our fingers. We walked like that for a while longer until the sun dropped into the ocean—a neon glow lining the horizon, Aperol-spritz orange. Darkness crept up the shore and it was time to turn back—Skye and Andie had a dinner reservation in town. *Text me tomorrow,* Skye whispered before we separated, typing her number into my phone. *Skye Starling* is the newest addition to my address book. Skye Starling—can you believe that? What a beautiful, fitting name.

Today, Dr. K, the world made a little more sense.

Chapter Three

Heather

I met Libby Fontaine when I was sixteen, a junior at the high school in the tiny, forgotten town in *far* upstate New York where I'd lived all my life. I looked my best back then, but Libby looked better. Even her voice sounded pretty—buttery and feminine and articulate, never tripping over a single word, never a *like* or an *um*. She called me one morning in early October.

"Hi. Is this Heather? . . . My name is Libby Fontaine. I got your number from your sign at the general store. I have a four-year-old and a three-month-old, and I'm in desperate need of a sitter. We just moved here and I don't know anybody. Do you have experience caring for infants?"

"Absolutely," I stammered. It was mostly true—I'd spent enough time looking after Gus when he was a baby and my mom would disappear for eight-hour chunks. That was before she disappeared for good when Gus was two, so toddlers . . . toddlers I definitely had experience with.

But I was desperate for money, always, and the truth was, I'd forgotten about the babysitting sign I'd posted on a whim at the general store over the summer. As it turned out, nobody in the microscopic town of Langs Valley could afford a babysitter—people locked their kids in the house in front of cartoons whenever they needed to run out, as I should've known—and Libby Fontaine was the first person to respond to my ad.

"Perfect," Libby said. "Amazing. You're a godsend. What do you charge? Is twelve an hour okay? Fifteen? Fifteen sounds right. I know it's two kids."

I almost dropped the phone. "Fifteen works," I replied in sheer shock. At my last gig—pulling the weeds out of Mrs. Lundy's garden—my hourly wage was five dollars.

"Amazing," Libby repeated. "Can you come today?"

"School's out at three-thirteen. I can come then."

Burke dropped me off that afternoon in his rusty Chevrolet pickup. He sucked the butt of his Marlboro Red before flicking it out the window, onto Libby's spotless front yard.

"Burke." I gave him a look.

"What, Bones?" He grinned, dimples appearing on either cheek, and pulled me in for a tobacco-flavored kiss.

I climbed out of the Chevy and walked toward the house, where a flaxen-haired young woman was standing behind the front screen door, arms folded. She'd been watching us, and I felt my cheeks burn crimson.

"Hi," I managed, stepping up to the porch. "I'm sorry about that."

She opened the door and walked past me, across the driveway to the place on the lawn where Burke had littered the butt. She picked it up. I knew I was bright red.

"Heather. Do you smoke?" She stood in front of me, tall and willowy.

"I don't," I lied.

"Who's the guy?"

"My boyfriend, Burke."

"I'm not a hard-ass, but I can't have smoke around my kids."

"I'm really sorry. I'll try to drive myself next time, if the car's available. Or I'll have someone else drop me."

"We can always pick you up."

"Thank you, Mrs. Fontaine."

"Call me Libby." She swung the screen door open, an invitation.

The house wasn't big—no houses in Langs Valley are—but it was the nicest one I'd ever stepped inside. The wood floors were polished and all the furniture was white or a pale wood, and the walls were painted soothing hues of ivory and sea-foam green. My eyes lingered on a sterling-silver-framed photograph of Libby in a stunning white dress and lace veil next to a handsome man, their smiles bleached and radiant.

I cringe now, thinking about the way I must've looked to Libby that first afternoon—the epitome of white trash with my nose ring and diamond-studded jeans and ashy-blond hair.

"The playroom is back this way." She smiled at me warmly, as if I didn't look completely out of place in her idyllic home. Closer to her now, I studied the details of her face: impossibly high cheekbones, wide-set eyes the color of caramel, those thick, arching eyebrows. She wasn't wearing any makeup and had only simple diamond studs in her ears. Back then I couldn't have defined what it meant to be classically beautiful or well-bred, but I instantly knew Libby Fontaine was both of those things.

Libby led me through the refurbished kitchen and small dining area toward the back of the house. Glass vases of fresh flowers were on nearly every surface.

"You just moved here? I don't see a single box. Your house is gorgeous." I felt the urge to compliment her—maybe because of Burke, or maybe because it really was the most beautiful home I'd ever seen.

"Ten days ago. I'm too much of a neat freak to have unpacked boxes lying around." Libby laughed. "Weird, I know."

"Not at all. I'm impressed."

"We have a lot on the walls, which helps. I made my husband hang everything the first night." She gestured to the walls. "He's an artist."

"Wow. It's stunning." I glanced around, studying the decor. That was what made the house look so complete, I realized—the dozens of exquisite pieces of framed artwork. I thought of the walls in my own house—was there even anything on them? A stag head of my father's mounted above the tiny fireplace. That was all that came to mind.

"It's not all his, of course." Libby laughed again. "That would be tacky. But we're lucky that we have a nice collection."

In the playroom, a small towheaded boy sat in the middle of the carpeted floor, surrounded by at least a dozen toy trucks.

"Nate, this is Heather."

"Hey, Mama," he said without looking up.

"He's obsessed with trucks," Libby whispered to me. "Literally, eighty-five percent of the time, this is my son, sitting on the floor with his trucks. For four, he's pretty easy."

I smiled, crouching down to the boy's level. He was just slightly bigger than Gus. "Hi, Nate. I'm Heather. I'm going to be your babysitter."

"Hi." He looked up at me and blinked. His eyes were the same coppery color as his mother's, with the same thick, dark lashes.

"And my baby girl is napping. She should be up in an hour or so."

"Cool." I nodded. I was slightly nervous about caring for an infant—I had no doubt Libby was a vastly more overprotective parental figure than any I was used to—but for fifteen dollars an hour I would figure it out. I was good at figuring things out, if I had to. "What time will you be back?"

"Oh, I'm hanging here today. I just wanted you to come over and get the lay of the land. I'll still pay you, of course. I thought we could hang in the kitchen and chat until the baby wakes up. I can make tea? Or I have juice. I don't have any soda."

"Tea is perfect," I said, even though I wasn't sure I'd ever had a cup of tea. I followed her into the kitchen. "Thanks."

"In all honesty I'm starved for company," Libby confessed as she filled the kettle with tap water. "We moved from Connecticut. I don't know a soul here."

I slid onto one of the white ladder-back stools and watched her move gracefully from cabinet to cabinet. She wore a loose button-down shirt—maybe her husband's—but the top buttons were undone and I could see her thin, sinewy frame, the concave of her clavicle—a body not unlike my own. It was the reason Burke's nickname for me was Bones.

A weighty diamond—far bigger than I'd ever seen in real life—sparkled on her left ring finger. The band was constructed of diamonds, too, I noticed when she came closer. Even her smell was expensive—like face cream that costs ninety dollars a jar. I've seen it in department stores.

"I don't mean this the wrong way," I started, feeling seduced by this woman, by her heavy scent, her sudden and mysterious presence in my monotonous world. I was suddenly overcome by the impulse to say exactly what I felt. "But why Langs Valley? Why did you move here?"

Libby turned, and I noticed a light sprinkling of freckles across her chest, her skin otherwise creamy and unblemished.

"My husband is doing a study on the northern Adirondack Mountains." She blinked, and something unknowable flashed across her face. One corner of her mouth poked into a weak half smile. "A landscape series, which is a real pivot for him—his style is primarily abstract. It really is beautiful here, though. Quiet, but I think it will be a nice change of pace."

"Quiet is for sure." I nodded. "How long will the study take?"

"Who knows." Libby flipped her palms up. "Some studies take several months, some take years. Peter wants to capture the mountains in all seasons, beginning with fall. He's so talented, though. I know he's going to be very successful one day."

I nodded, dissecting the implications of her statement. Libby and Peter clearly had money; if her husband wasn't successful yet, the money had to have other origins.

Libby turned back to the tea, and I watched, enamored by her every movement, as she dunked the bags in the boiling water to steep.

"So, Heather, tell me about you." Pillows of steam rose into her pores. "What's your story? What's up with this boyfriend of yours, smoking those disgusting death sticks?"

My *story*.

The air in the room seemed to slow, and brighten. Something in the way she said *boyfriend of yours* told me someone such as Libby wouldn't be caught dead with someone like Burke. It was also the first time I'd heard the term *death sticks*. In my world, cigarettes were a prerequisite. My friends and I smoked in the parking lot every day; once during lunch and once between seventh and eighth periods. When my father was home—which wasn't often anymore—we shared a smoke after dinner.

I looked at Libby's flawless skin and healthy glow and knew with clear conviction that I'd never smoke again. It's strange, but sometimes a new perspective can click into place, and everything suddenly looks different. That night, I would go home and take out my

nose ring and call Burke and tell him our relationship
was over. I would put Gus to bed and flush my Parlia-
ments down the toilet and do my algebra homework for
the first time all semester. I would fall asleep thinking
about the smell of Libby's face cream and the art on her
freshly painted walls.

As for my story—I didn't have one yet, but I would
soon.

Chapter Four

Skye

MARCH 2019

I never realized just how much planning goes into a wedding—from the flowers to the rehearsal dinner to the invitations to the band, the details are enough to make a severe OCD sufferer such as me spiral out of control. One thing Burke and I have decided on in the past forty-eight hours—besides that we are definitely going to hire a wedding planner—is the date: September 21, 2019. That's for two reasons. One, we both think September is the best month to get married but don't want to wait until 2020, and two, the Earth, Wind & Fire song. You know the one I'm talking about. *Do you remember . . . the twenty-first night of September? Love was changing the minds of pretenders.* This year, September 21 falls on a Saturday. The song can be our first dance. It's perfect.

I still haven't told Andie anything, which I suppose is strange. I used to imagine that the second I got engaged I'd call her screaming, but things aren't the way they used to be. The list of things I keep from Andie seems to be ever accumulating these days. For example, I haven't told her about Burke's brief stint in prison. I haven't told anyone. Burke was barely out of college when it happened, and he was naive. Plus, it was a white-collar offense—it's not like he did something violent. The whole thing was an astronomical mistake on Burke's part, yes, but one he learned from a long time ago. Attempting to explain the situation to my family and friends would only cause unwarranted concern.

I *do* have to tell Andie we're engaged, though, and the clock is ticking. We have a long-standing dinner on the books tonight—one we've rescheduled too many times already—and it'll be the right place to drop the news.

I send my last work email of the day and close Outlook. The clock on the upper right-hand corner of my laptop screen reads 5:55. Fuck. I press my lips to the clock on the screen and kiss it five times. Then I touch it five times with my right hand, then do the same with my left hand. Then it's on to the rest of the clocks/time-telling devices in the apartment: phone, the monitor attached to my laptop, dishwasher, microwave, stovetop, and finally Burke's iPad, which I finish touching just as the time ticks to 5:56. Phew.

Burke says more germs are on your phone screen than a public toilet seat, but fortunately (and miraculously) germophobia is not a symptom of my particular strand of OCD.

Six o'clock—fifty minutes until I have to leave for our seven o'clock reservation at Rosemary's. I shower and blow-dry my hair halfway. Tinted moisturizer, under-eye concealer, and a little bit of mascara is enough. I squeeze into my favorite dark wash J Brands—they're harder to button than they were the last I wore them, but whatever. It's been a long, happy winter of too much Cab and stinky cheese. I can lose the weight before the wedding.

I choose an oversize Vince sweater to complement the tight jeans. Zipping up my brown leather boots and long black puffer jacket that resembles a sleeping bag, my winter uniform is complete. In New York, spring can never come soon enough.

Now that I'm ready to walk out the door, it's time for my exit, and I'm relieved Burke's not here. It's not that I *mind* when he witnesses my routines—he's going to be my husband, and I'm not trying to hide anything. It just isn't my most flattering moment, the way I *have* to knock on the door in a specific pattern before I can leave.

One two three four five six seven eight; eight seven six five four three two one. One count up to eight, one count down from eight. All closed doors, every time. Revolving and electric sliding doors don't count, which is a big break in a city like New York.

Only when I'm finished knocking can I open the door and exit the apartment, a sweet-and-sour mix of relief and shame heavy in my bones. I skip down the four flights of stairs—some elevators are okay, but the rickety one in my building makes me feel as if I were in a closed coffin.

Unfortunately, my building is prewar, which means old swinging doors in its lobby. This is my eighth year living on West Eleventh Street, though, and Ivan and the rest of the doormen don't even blink when I do my knocks. They also know there's no point in opening the door for me; if it's closed to begin with, I have to do the knocks. If the door is propped open, which is often the case in the late spring and summertime, I'm off the hook. Those are my favorite months in the city.

Heading south on Waverly Place, I relish that I can slam my boot on every crack on the sidewalk without caring. This wasn't always the case—it took substantial strides in therapy and an upped dose of Anafranil, but I got there. I am no longer Jack Nicholson in *As Good as It Gets*.

Still, I'm feeling a little panicked as I approach Rosemary's. Breathing deeply, I think of Dr. Salam's advice to focus on the good parts of someone that you love, the reasons why you love them. With Andie, it's always easy to remember.

In the fall of seventh grade, after Mom died, I was so sad I couldn't speak, my vocal cords gnarled underneath my collarbone, choked by grief. For weeks after the funeral I hid inside and screwed my eyes shut while the world outside browned and fell and curled in on itself, another death. I stayed in bed and refused to go to school. My mind was a videotape on repeat: My mother's colorless face hours before she stopped breathing and the door of that awful waiting room. And me knocking, knocking, knocking, a never-ending count to and from the number eight: *one two three four five six seven eight; eight seven six five four three two one.* My brother on the chair in the corner listening to his Discman, head bent between his knees.

If I'd been older, maybe it would have hit me differently. But I was twelve, and the only life I knew was one in which the sun rose and set with Mom. I didn't understand my girl-obsessed older brother, or my quiet, reserved father. Mom had been my ally in the family, the one who took me shopping at the mall and rented our favorite movies from Blockbuster and made sure we decorated every inch of the house at Christmastime. She was my best friend, and it didn't feel possible to exist in a world without her.

In the weeks that she'd been gone all I craved was the weight of her warm, soft body, the comforting rise and fall of her chest. My pillow was damp from days and nights of muffled sobs. Even though I should've been back in school by then, my father simply stood in the doorway of my bedroom and, from within his own black cloud of grief, told me that I didn't have to go back until I was ready.

It was Andrea Roussos who finally rang our doorbell one afternoon after I'd missed yet another day of seventh grade. When no one answered, she let herself in and marched straight up the stairs and into my bedroom.

"Skye!" Andie shook me awake, though I wasn't really sleeping. She sat down on the edge of my bed, and I looked up to her clear hazel eyes, the tiny freckles that dusted her Grecian olive skin. "You have to get up. You have to come to school. We'll be motherless together, and we'll be okay. I swear."

"Motherless," I repeated with a shudder. "You're not motherless, Andie."

"I basically am." She glanced away, and the pain in the contours of her face quickly morphed into something resembling resilience. "She may have given me life, but she's not a mother. You've seen her. She doesn't get off the couch. She stays in her bathrobe all day and swallows pills and watches *ER*. That's how it's been for years, and you know it, Skye."

I sat up in bed. I nodded because it was true; nine out of the ten times I saw Mrs. Roussos she was wearing sweats and sitting in front of the TV in the den, ignoring the world around her. Andie and her younger sister had grown up microwaving their own frozen dinners except for the rare nights when Mr. Roussos came home from work early with takeout. Over the years I'd overheard my parents whispering about Eileen Roussos's addiction to painkillers on more than one occasion. *It's getting bad,* my mother would tell my father, her voice hushed.

"I miss her, too, Skye," Andie whispered, her eyes watery. "I know it's not the same, but I loved your mom so much. She was the best mom in the world. You're so lucky you had her. She'll always be yours."

"She loved you, too," I managed, hot tears dripping down my cheeks.

"Come on." Andie pulled my arm. "Get out of this bed and get dressed and let's go for a walk. It's sunny out. We'll walk into town and get sandwiches at the deli. Aren't you hungry?"

I nodded. My stomach was eating itself—I was hungrier than I'd bothered to notice.

Andie wrapped her arms around my neck and hugged me so tight I almost couldn't breathe.

"You're my best friend, Skye Starling."

Best friend.

Andie was my very close friend, certainly. Ever since first grade, Andie, Lexy, Isabel, and I had been an inseparable pack of four.

But my *best friend*—that had always been Mom. Ever since I was really little, when she'd come tuck me in at night, she'd loop her pinkie through mine and whisper, *Best friends.*

As I got older and more independent, Mom said it was normal if I stopped wanting her to be my best friend for a while, though I would always be hers. But I never did. And more nights than not, she'd still loop my pinkie and whisper, *Best friends,* in my ear, the familiar smell of her face cream comforting me toward sleep.

But that afternoon when Andie marched into my room and got me out of bed, I felt it—the unalterable truth that Mom was gone and not coming back. In that moment, something in my friendship with Andie intensified, pulling the two of us from our foursome toward a connection more profound. And though we never told Lexy and Isabel, they knew. Everyone knew.

Andie's empathy had been my saving grace, and the thing that allowed me to begin to heal. I confided in her about what else had been going on since Mom died, the other thing that had me glued to my bed in sheer terror—the doors. The closed doors that would no longer open without my special knock: *one two three four five six seven eight; eight seven six five four three two one.* One count up to eight, one count down from eight.

"I don't know why it's happening," I'd said to Andie. "All I know is that eight—"

"Was your mom's lucky number."

"I haven't told anyone but you."

"It's okay." Andie had mime-zipped her lips. "We'll figure it out together."

Together.

Andie is already seated when I brush through the door into Rosemary's. The aesthetic of this place always soothes me—I take in the high, wood-beamed ceilings and enormous glass windows, and a calmness settles behind my sternum.

I bypass the hostess and head toward Andie. Even though we're not exactly Thelma and Louise these days, the corners of my lips flip instinctively at the sight of my best friend. The girl in front of me has come a long way since preteen Andie, but she still has the same squinty smile and hazel eyes and narrow frame that magically survived puberty—a body I've simultaneously admired and envied. Clothes look amazing on her, the way they do on women with barely any chest. She wears an army-green jumper that screams Brooklyn thrift store, and her long chestnut hair is loose around her face. In a cropped white turtleneck and light eye makeup, she looks annoyingly good. *Hot.* Andie has always been hot.

The smell of her perfume intensifies as I move toward our table—the white floral and tuberose scents of her signature Fracas—and her familiar grin broadens. But then she sees it. I know because the expression in her eyes hardens, her smile quickly drops. I don't know when Andie and I started instinctively checking ring fingers, only that we did.

I slide into my seat.

"Jesus fucking Christ." Andie is staring at me as if I have a black eye, her lips parted.

"What's wrong?" I cock my head, the grin breaking through my teeth.

Andie grabs my left hand. "Jesus fucking Christ."

I exhale. "What do you think?"

Andie's jaw drops lower as she clutches my fingers. "When did this happen, Skye?"

"Sunday."

"Oh my God."

"What do you *think*, Andie?"

"I mean . . ." She draws her gaze from me to the ring. Then back up to me, her eyes bugging out of her head. "I mean, I think it's *insane*. You met Burke in *September*."

I crane my neck to look for the waitress. I wasn't *not* expecting this, but I need a drink to deal with it.

"It's not that insane, Andie. People fall in love and get engaged. Sometimes it happens quickly."

"No. No, no. *Quickly* is a year and a half. This is five months."

"Six months." I know I sound defensive.

"Six months, whatever. You can't know someone in six months. You can't make a decision to spend the rest of your *life* with someone you've known for six months. It's not safe." Andie runs her fingers through the ends of her hair, searching for split ends the way she does when she's getting worked up.

"*Safe?* Don't be ridiculous, Andie."

"You've never even met his family, Skye. You can't know someone if you haven't met their family."

"He doesn't *have* family, Andie. We've been over this."

"He has those relatives in Phoenix!"

"Right, and he's not that close with them. But I know he's planning on inviting them to the wedding, if that makes you feel better."

"I think it's too fast." Andie quits ripping apart her hair and interlaces her hands across the table.

We're saved by the waitress, a waify girl with a strawberry-blond ponytail and lots of dark eyeliner.

"Two negronis, please," I tell her. That's our dinner drink. Aperol spritzes at brunch and happy hour.

"You got it." The waitress nods without a smile, and I watch her gaze skitter down toward my left ring finger. Or maybe I imagine it. Maybe she was just checking our waters. Still, I clench and unclench my fist, gazing lovingly at the rock. I don't care if I'm acting like the girls I used to resent; I deserve this. I feel Andie staring at me, alarmed.

"Look, Andie." I meet her eyes and keep my voice firm, ready with my rehearsed speech. "You don't have to be so judgmental. We're adults, and I'm supposed to be your best friend, and I'm finally happy. You can think it's crazy that Burke and I are moving this fast—I know, objectively, it does seem fast. But I hope you can find a way to be happy for me and respect my choice, because it's not one I've made lightly."

Andie's picking her split ends again, and I can feel the inside of her brain swirling, ruminating.

"Okay," she says finally. "I'm happy for you, Skye, I really am. I just want to make sure you're *really* certain about this. Because people rush into these things and . . . I just want you to be careful. It's a huge commitment. It's the rest of your life."

The waitress drops our cocktails and I lunge for mine.

"I know it is." I swallow.

"And just because Burke is the first guy, who, you know . . ."

"Who what, Andie?"

"Who . . . who's stuck around. You know what I mean."

Our gazes lock, and sometimes I loathe the flip side of having a friend who knows everything about you.

"I get that you're worried there might not be others. But I promise you, Burke is not the only—"

"So, you think I'm settling?" I feel heat creeping up my chest, toward my neck. "For *Burke*?" Anger seizes me. "Are you seriously unable to admit that the guy I'm with is a total catch? Is that *so* impossible for you? 'Cause if you stopped searching for every possible flaw in him, you'd realize that he's smart and handsome and *mature*, Andie. Burke is a fucking grown-up." I watch my words land with Andie, hoping the last part stings. I want her to know that I think Spencer—with his custom necktie business and worn-out Timberlands—is the opposite of a grown-up.

"I don't want to do this." Andie averts her eyes. "Not here."

"You think I do?"

"I didn't say Burke wasn't a catch, Skye," she says coolly.

"Then what's the problem?" I drum my fingers on the polished wood table, and I wish so badly that I didn't care what Andie thought. "You think he's too old for me?"

Andie sighs. "I mean, maybe. Then again, we're getting old, aren't we?" One corner of her mouth curls.

"Pushing thirty."

Andie and I were born two weeks apart in July. We used to have joint birthday parties every summer.

"I can't believe that." Andie twists the stem of her glass. "Then again, age is just a number. And our generation isn't in a rush. It's not like it was for our parents, where everyone was married with kids by twenty-five."

"True."

"Look, I'm sorry, S." Andie exhales, and her face looks genuinely pained. "I'm sorry I'm not being one hundred percent receptive to this. I'm just . . . it's a lot to process. But I want to hear about the engagement. Tell me exactly how it happened."

I let the story spill from me, grateful to finally be telling Andie every detail of the day that's left me floating on a cloud. I let myself gush, and it feels so incredibly good to be happy like this, to be *normal* like this, to talk to my oldest friend about the man who wants to spend the rest of his life with me. I can't help but intermittently glance down at my ring, checking to make sure it's still there, that this isn't all a dream.

Andie sees me, and I know she knows what I'm feeling, in the perceptive way she can, because she reaches over and squeezes my hand.

"You deserve this," she whispers.

The waitress reappears and asks if we're ready to order.

Andie orders the healthiest salad on the menu, and I opt for the carbonara and another negroni. Fuck it. I have someone who loves me completely.

"I guess I'll do another one, too." Andie gestures to her empty glass and shrugs guiltily, as if having two drinks on a Tuesday is criminal.

Andie didn't used to be such a teetotaler. Before she became obsessed with yoga and quit her job in PR to become a registered dietitian, she used to get wasted on cheap vodka and eat cheeseburgers and stay out till dawn. And even though she's swapped bagels for hemp-seed smoothies, even though she's almost religious about her daily consumption of celery juice, her body doesn't look all that different from how it did before. Andie was always a stick.

"So, have you told Lexy or Iz?" She leans back in her chair and slumps her thin shoulders. Now that she has a drink in her she's not quite so wound up.

"Not yet. Just my family knows. And now you. But I'll call Lex and Iz this week."

The waitress places our food on the table—I love that the service at Rosemary's is so speedy. My plate of oily pasta towers over Andie's little salad, and sometimes I hate going to meals with the new Andie.

"So"—I pick up my fork—"I wanted to talk to you about the wedding."

"What about it?" Andie reaches for her water.

"Well, first of all it's September twenty-first. So save the date."

Andie spits water back into her glass. "*This* September?"

"Yes."

"Skye, that's—that's in six months. It's too—"

"It's not too fast, Andie." I'm annoyed now. "People have these insanely long engagements nowadays, and it's too much pressure. I can't even imagine what that would do to my OCD. Plus, look at my parents. They got engaged in April, they were married in September."

"That was a *completely* different time. I *know* if your mom were here, she'd be telling you the same—"

"Don't play that card." I shake my head, and Andie is silent. "Look, Burke and I have talked about it. We want a September wedding—that's when my parents got married, and you know I've always wanted that—and we don't want to wait a year and a half. That's how we feel."

Andie shoves a forkful of kale into her mouth and chews indignantly. Only a watery sip is left in her second drink, and I can tell by the slight sway of her shoulders that she's tipsy. It's now or never.

"Andie."

She jerks her head up and swallows. "Yeah?"

"Look, I need you." It's the truth. "I need you to be my maid of honor."

Andie's gaze widens, and she puts down her fork. "Oh, Skye." I watch her eyes fill with tears. "Are you sure that's a good idea?"

"Maybe not, but you know it has to be you."

"I know, but, Skye—what if we fight? What if we

don't agree on anything and it all goes wrong? Maybe you should ask Lex or Iz. Or Kendall."

"God, no. Lexy would try to turn my wedding into an actual music festival, and Iz . . . Iz is just not good with planning. And I love Kendall, but . . . it has to be you. You're my person."

This is something Andie and I started saying to each other back in the prime of *Grey's Anatomy,* copying best friends Meredith and Cristina on the show. But neither of us have said it in at least a year, and a tear slides down Andie's cheek.

"Of course, Skye." I watch her remember that there is no other answer, that this is who we are to each other, for better or for worse. "Of course I'll be your maid of honor."

Suddenly my phone buzzes on the table, interrupting our moment. I glance at it, expecting a text from Burke, but it's an email, and the address on the screen makes my stomach drop: maxlapointe1@gmail.com.

Max LaPointe.

I haven't seen that name on my phone in over a year. There's a chill at the base of my spine, and I shield the screen from Andie as I open the email. The words freeze my blood.

A little birdie tells me you're engaged. That poor, poor guy.

Chapter Five

Burke Michaels's Diary

SEPTEMBER 13, 2018

Dear Dr. K,

Last night I took Skye Starling (the girl I met in Montauk) for ramen at Ippudo, this hot spot in the East Village. Years ago, when the neighborhood was seedier, Heather and I lived here and ramen was one of our favorite meals out, because it was cheap and filling.

Ippudo is an ideal date spot, according to Todd, because even though it won't break the bank, it's still considered a legitimate culinary experience, and it's casual enough to take the pressure off. And let's be real—I'm not in the financial position to be taking women out on dates to Michelin-starred restaurants.

The extent to which Todd cheated on his ex-wife is unclear, but he obviously did. He seems to have all the answers I'm looking for, and he doesn't judge. All he said to me when I mentioned I'd gotten this girl's phone number in Montauk was *Your wife is stupid hot, man, but I get it.* Then he gave me the ramen suggestion.

Yes, Heather is hot, especially for her age. Maybe even stupid hot if you're a spectator. But after two and half decades of marriage, that stuff doesn't matter as much as you think it will when you're younger.

I don't know, Dr. K. All I'm saying is whatever I've been doing feels *right,* and things haven't felt right in so long.

Anyway, last Wednesday evening I caught the express train from New Haven to Grand Central. I told Heather it was an informational interview with an ex-colleague and was relieved when she didn't ask any questions.

I got to the restaurant at seven-thirty a little tired, but I jolted awake when Skye entered. I'd sort of forgotten what she looked like. I mean, I knew she was gorgeous, but what I remembered most was a feeling, a vibration in her presence that put me at ease.

But as she strolled toward me, I remembered—Skye Starling has one of those faces that stops wars. Or starts them. What is it that they say? A face that launched a thousand ships, that's it. In a word, she's stunning. Smooth skin, high cheekbones as round as apples, and giant, light brown eyes that brightened when she saw me.

Right off the bat Skye ordered a beer. When I told the waiter I'd stick with water, disappointment crossed her face, and I knew I had to tell her.

"You're going to think I'm a big weirdo, but I lied to you in Montauk. I don't drink. There was no vodka in those greyhounds."

She looked at me curiously. "Why did you lie?"

"In truth, I panicked. I'm not used to . . . walking up to girls I'm interested in. I didn't want to sound sober and lame. Even though that's what I am." I let myself smile.

"I don't care if you're sober, Burke." Skye looked at me intently. "But no more lying. Deal?"

"Deal." Oh, well.

Our food arrived and I loved watching her eat, slurping ramen greedily and washing each bite down with a sip of Sapporo, her face flushed pink from the steam. So many women—my wife included—are afraid of food. Since having kids, Heather has wrestled against her body—racing the treadmill and sprinting up hills to keep herself whittled down to nothing.

Skye told me about her work as a book editor, which fascinated me because I've always loved to read. When I was growing up, English was my favorite subject. Sometimes I think I should've pursued a more creative field, but Heather convinced me I was good with numbers. She thought I'd get rich working in finance, but that was forever ago, and we were wrong about so much.

I went into investment banking with high hopes, guns blazing. I put in the work. I got into the analyst program at Credit Suisse and was a year and a half in when I fucked it up. And do you know what happens when you fuck it up on the I-banker track? Nothing good. To say I was lucky to get my data-entry job at PK Adamson, one of New Haven's shittiest wealth management firms, would be an understatement. A job that—let me remind you—I no longer have.

When Skye turned the conversation toward *my* professional life, I told her I worked for myself as an independent financial consultant. When Skye asked where I lived, I heard myself say Crown Heights, which surprised me, because I don't think I've ever set foot in

Crown Heights. But she nodded and said she didn't venture to Brooklyn much, and I felt myself relax. Of course a girl like Skye Starling doesn't venture to Brooklyn.

I waited for Skye outside the restaurant while she used the bathroom, the ramen heavy in my stomach. A light rain was falling, and when Skye appeared, I watched her open up a red umbrella, smiling as she offered me shelter. This look of hope was in her eyes and I should've felt guilty, for having a wife and kids and being on a date with this nice pretty girl to whom I'd just promised not to lie.

She asked me if I wanted to go back to her apartment "for a coffee" and I said that I did, because *God* I did—I wanted it more than I wanted a clean conscience. You're a guy, Dr. K—you understand what I mean.

Skye said that she sort of liked walking in the rain, so we walked across town, and I don't remember exactly what we talked about, only that we laughed. I laughed more that night with Skye than I'd laughed in years, Dr. K. With Garrett and Hope no longer in the house, and Maggie spending most of her time out with friends—I guess that's what you do in high school—Heather and I pitter-patter around our empty home like strangers, and there isn't a lot of laughter.

I expected a closet-size studio or a bunch of roommates, but Skye's apartment in the heart of the West Village is a true one-bedroom and at least fifteen hundred square feet. Unless she works personally for Stephen King, more than a book editor's salary is paying her rent.

I sank down into a couch as soft as butter, watching Skye shake off her trench coat and grab two espresso mugs from the bar. Her apartment is immaculate and tasteful and screams of money—everything from the art on the walls to the thick beige drapes hanging from the three enormous double-hung windows speckled with rain and glowing from the streetlamps below. Skye is too groomed to be a personal escort or something that would make her money remotely unethical; from the grandfather clock in the corner and the Nantucket Yacht Club tumblers, I've decided to bet on *trust fund*.

Absorbing more of the lavish details of her apartment, I realized that Skye Starling is exactly the kind of woman Heather has always envied—the kind of woman that Heather wanted me to help her become. But I failed. God, did I fail.

Skye slid beside me on the couch, her blond hair fanning the cushions, and pressed a warm mug of espresso into my hands. "Don't judge me, but I'm having a real nightcap." She tilted her mug to reveal two fingers of amber liquid inside.

"I'm not one to judge, Skye." I inhaled the spicy sweetness of her perfume and wondered, not for the first time, if she had a thing for older guys or if the creases around my eyes were not actually as deep as I perceived them to be. After all, she still hadn't asked my age.

I watched her take a sip of bourbon, the way her pink lip pressed against the mug's rim. I couldn't fathom how a girl like Skye could possibly be single. The thought had been sticking in my mind all evening, and I accidentally spoke it out loud.

"Good question." She grinned. "Why are *you* single?"

"Touché." I grinned back, then whipped up a story about an ex named Amanda, a woman I lived with for six years and almost married before I found out she was cheating on me with her coworker.

Skye's face fell, and when she told me she was sorry, she looked genuinely sorry, and that's a rare thing, Dr. K, when somebody you hardly know cares that you've been hurt. I could tell she wanted me to elaborate on Amanda, and that was the last thing I wanted to do, so I kissed her, there on her beautiful couch in her beautiful West Village apartment. And I may be pushing fifty, but I know the right way to kiss a woman. After that there was no more talking.

Chapter Six

Heather

NOVEMBER 1989

I started to get the feeling that Libby Fontaine's money grew on trees. I knew nothing about art, and I wasn't particularly fond of the several pieces of Peter's I'd seen in the house, but I knew he had to be doing something right based on the steady stream of twenty-dollar bills in Libby's silver Chanel wallet, which my friend Kyla says retails at around five hundred dollars. Kyla used to shoplift.

Libby was paying me fifteen dollars for every hour I spent "babysitting," which included the time we spent sipping tea and chatting at the kitchen table while the kids slept. That was more than double what anyone else I knew was getting paid for part-time work. Sometimes it felt as though Libby was trying to give her money away, which baffled me.

I could tell that she craved company; whether it was mine specifically I didn't know. But every night when she and Peter would come home from dinner in Platts-burgh or wherever they'd been, Peter would head out back to his barn studio and Libby would look at me with pleading eyes and ask me to stay for a mug of Earl Grey.

And I always did. Even when it was late and Gus had

been at the neighbors' for too long, I couldn't refuse the extra hour or two that Libby would pay me to sit with her. First and foremost, I needed the money, but I was also enthralled by everything about her. Being in her presence put me in a kind of trance.

One night it was past eleven when Libby shuffled through the door, her cheeks rosy pink from the sharp November cold. Her pale blond hair was pulled up into a ponytail, and she was wearing dark eye makeup. She looked so pretty it was almost agonizing.

"The kids get to sleep okay?" She unzipped her smooth leather boots.

I nodded.

"Sorry we're so late."

"That's all right. Is Peter out back?"

"But of course." Libby rolled her eyes. "He's most inspired in the middle of the goddamn night." She formed air quotes around the word *inspired*.

I refrained from mentioning that Peter also seemed to spend most of each *day* closed off painting in the barn.

"Tea?" Libby glanced at me, hopeful, and reached for the kettle.

"I shouldn't." I wanted to stay, but that night Gus had a cold, and I knew I needed to pick him up from the Carsons' and get him in his own bed.

"Wine?" Libby's mouth slid into a small smile, and there were those hopeful eyes again. It was the first time she'd offered me alcohol. I couldn't imagine the kind of wine she and Peter drank, but I knew it'd be better than the jugs Kyla's older sister bought us.

"I could stay for a glass." I nodded. "Thanks."

I watched Libby open a bottle of red with expert hands, twisting the screw into the cork and whisking it out in an easy flash. She wore an ivory silk blouse that billowed around her bony chest, and tight black pants that made her legs look like chopsticks. I had begun to envy every single piece of clothing she owned.

She poured two glasses and slid one across the counter toward me. Libby held her stem and, closing her eyes, lowered her perfect nose to the rim. She inhaled, and her face flooded with something satiated and dense. I drew in the details of the elegant way she sipped, tilting her chin up ever so slightly.

I knew nothing about wine; I'd only ever had it from a plastic cup. I attempted to take as graceful a sip as Libby's, but I pitched the glass too far back and it sloshed all over my throat. Still it ran down smooth, and a warm glow settled in my belly. An even sweetness lingered on my tongue. I could've drunk the whole bottle.

"So." Libby shifted forward. "How's the boyfriend?" She hadn't asked me about Burke since that first day.

"We broke up," I stated, proud.

"Oh?" Libby looked surprised. "Is that good news or bad news?"

"Well, I'm the one who ended it."

"I see."

"So, good news." It was the story I was telling myself, the conviction I used to bury the part of me that was cracked in two without Burke, unhinged and flailing. "He parties too much." The truth.

"If I'm being honest, my initial hunch was that you

were way too good for him." Libby twirled the stem of her wineglass. "I mean, he's good-looking. But my hunches tend to be pretty on point."

I nodded. I understood that Libby could see beyond Burke's tall frame and pretty blue eyes, past his status as the dreamiest guy in the junior class at our high school. She saw the Marlboro Reds and the bad manners; who, in Libby Fontaine's world, would flick a cigarette butt out the window onto somebody's front lawn? Somehow, I knew, not a soul.

To Libby, Burke was a hick. White trash. And by some miracle—perhaps my quick transformation or *perhaps* due to something more profound that only Libby could see—I was not. I was mature enough to employ as a babysitter. I was poised enough to drink tea with. And in the short time I'd come to know Libby, that had begun to mean everything.

"I just think that with someone like Burke . . ." Libby drummed her fingertips across the marble countertop. "Well, one, beware the party boy. And two . . ." She looked up, her cinnamon eyes clear. "I know I haven't actually met him, but I get the sense he isn't nearly as smart as you, Heather. And you should be with someone who's smarter than you."

"Is Peter smarter than you?" It came out sounding like a challenge, and I immediately wished I hadn't asked.

"Yes," Libby said, unfazed. "I mean, we're smart in opposite ways. Peter's very mathematically minded, believe it or not. His art is numerical and precise. And I'm better with language and writing."

"Interesting. Is that what you studied in school?"

Libby nodded. "I was an English major at Barnard. I worked in book publishing for a few years after college, and I thought about applying to grad schools and going back to get my MFA . . . but then I got pregnant."

I made a mental note to look up *MFA* when I got home.

"I still write every now and then. Mostly short stories, and I'm working on a longer novella. But with the little ones . . ." She smiled stiffly. "It's hard to find the time."

"I understand." The wine coursing through my veins tempted the honesty out of me. Before I could stop myself, I was telling her about Gus.

Sweet, four-year-old Gus, with his messy head of golden hair and inquisitive eyes, the same shade of green as mine. Gus was born when I was in sixth grade, two years before my mom was found dead in the front seat of her car. Some lady found her slumped over the steering wheel in the Price Chopper parking lot and called the cops.

I wasn't sad, not really. My mother's death was something I'd anticipated long before it happened, an inevitable occurrence that left me feeling ambivalent as I helped my father clean out her closet the day after she overdosed. Except for a short-lived stint when she was pregnant with Gus, my mother had always done drugs. In elementary school we learned that drugs kill you. My mother had been killing herself for most of my life, and I wasn't surprised when she died.

The worst part of her death was what it did to my

father. I was old enough to understand that unlike my mother, my father was one of the numerous addicts in Langs Valley who was able to stay functional. He worked construction to keep us afloat, and though on plenty of nights I'd hear my parents ripping lines in the living room and cackling with laughter into the wee hours of the morning, my father always dragged himself to work the next day, while my mother slept it off or went to a friend's to continue her bender.

My father was lucky to have a job, he always said so. The employment rate in Langs Valley had plummeted since the big cotton mill closed in the late sixties after too many companies took their businesses overseas. The mill had employed hundreds of workers, my grandpa among them, and when it tanked, people lost everything: jobs, health insurance, hope. The town was never the same after that.

Crack cocaine was a city drug, but it made its way to Langs Valley in the mid-eighties, and once my mother had a taste, that was it. I'd overhear my father lecturing her about its dangers, his anger booming through our tiny house when she stumbled home at night, out of her mind.

My mother didn't last a year chasing the crack high. A month after we buried her, my dad was on it, too. I could tell by the smell of the smoke on his clothes, how his hands trembled the same quivery way my mother's had when she was on crack. The messages on our answering machine asking why he hadn't shown up to work. He went from scrawny to gaunt, cheeks hollow and angular, lips black. He started leaving town for days on end; I pieced together enough to know he'd driven to Albany to buy more drugs, Boston or New York if he was desperate.

I explained to Libby that this was why I had ended up caring for Gus—my mother was dead, and my father would be soon.

She was quiet when I finished speaking. I half expected her to fire me on the spot; no matter how liberal she considered herself to be, women like Libby couldn't have the daughter of crack addicts babysitting their kids.

But Libby slid her hand across the counter, and I nearly flinched when she squeezed my palm.

"Heather, you poor thing." Her eyes were watery and wide. "I'm so terribly sorry." She picked up the bottle of red and refilled my glass, then her own. "I have a few things to say. First, I hope—for your sake, as well as the sake of your employment here—that you aren't doing drugs. Are you?"

"I don't do drugs." I shook my head emphatically. "Most people I know do, but after watching what they did to my parents, I—I can't. Not with Gus."

It was the truth. Even though coke and pills were nearly impossible to avoid at parties, even though I'd watched my friends blow lines and roll their faces off countless times—Burke more often than anyone else—I couldn't bring myself to touch anything besides alcohol.

"I'm so glad to hear that." Libby sipped her wine. "Drugs will ruin your life. And you have *so* much potential, Heather."

I smiled, wondering if she really thought so or if it was her blue-blooded manners speaking.

"Second thing. I want you to bring Gus here when you come and sit for us. I didn't realize you had a little brother who's alone while you're gone."

"That's very nice of you, but the neighbors—"

"End of discussion." Libby held up her palm. "You'll bring him. Please, Heather." Her eyes landed softly on mine.

I nodded. "Okay. Thank you. He'll like that. He and Nate are close in age."

"Nate will love having someone to play with." Libby smiled warmly. "Okay, last thing. I want to talk to you about your future. I'm not trying to parent you too hard here, but it's an important discussion to have, and I get the feeling it's not one you're having with your father."

I shook my head.

"Have you thought about the future, Heather? Are you planning on applying to colleges?"

The future had always been a hazy white space at the edge of my mind. It once held the probability of Burke, and our shared intention of leaving Langs Valley, getting married, and starting a family. I also had the vague objective of more financial stability than I'd experienced growing up, which meant going to college. A state school, most likely, and ideally one that would accept Burke, too. The only thing I knew with sheer certainty was that when and if I did have kids, I'd raise them nothing like the way my parents had raised me.

But the details of my looming future had come into

razor-sharp focus the day I'd met Libby back in October, the moment I'd tasted a life that was the opposite of mine yet close enough to touch. In meeting Libby and seeing her beautiful house and expensive clothes and groomed manners, I'd realized just how small I'd been dreaming. The seed planted itself in my head, the concrete notion that such a life was possible for me, too. And now, what I wanted more than anything—more than Burke, even—was for every door to open for me and stay that way.

This was what had clawed itself around my heart when I called Burke and told him, with finality, that our relationship was over. Kyla said I was an idiot for dumping him. When I told her the truth—that I wanted to focus more on school and getting better grades—she looked at me as if I were speaking another language. Screw it. Kyla could spend her life waiting tables at the diner and buying coke with her tips, but I wouldn't end up like that, and I wouldn't end up married to someone like that. I was going somewhere, and I finally understood that the only way to get there was to work for it—no one was going to hand me anything. I was going to become a woman like Libby—well, an employed version of Libby, at least until I found someone rich to marry. And if I was going to become an employed version of Libby, then I needed a high-paying job, which meant I needed a college degree from a reputable university, which meant I needed better grades and decent SAT scores. It meant I needed help; I needed someone like Libby to take me under her wing.

"You know, it's funny you ask about the future." I

tucked a wisp of my hair behind my ear. "I've recently started thinking about college and have realized how badly I want to go, but I don't know much about the process. None of my friends have plans to apply, so it's not something people are talking about. I mean, I know a few older kids who have gone to SUNY Plattsburgh, but I . . . I really think I can do better than a state school. It's just complicated because I have Gus."

"Oh, honey." Libby's impeccable face softened; I could feel her maternal instinct kicking in. "We'll figure out what to do about Gus."

We'll.

"Right now, the most important thing is that you start focusing on college. How are your grades?"

"Better this year," I told her honestly. "Freshman and sophomore year they weren't great."

"That's okay." Libby waved her hand. "If you have really solid grades junior and senior year, that's the most important thing for college admission boards to see. My mother worked in college counseling at an upper school for years, so I know how it all goes. I still have all my SAT books, though they've probably got new ones by now. Have you thought about when you might take the SATs? And what schools you might be interested in?"

"I really haven't." I shrugged, loving how easy it was to submit to this helplessness. "I honestly don't even know where to start, Libby. I keep trying to make an appointment with the college counselor at school, but he's really backed up. He pretty much only sees seniors."

"Seriously? Is there only one counselor?"

I nodded. Again, the truth was in my favor.

"That's *ridiculous*." Libby scrunched her perfect nose. "But don't worry. Because I'm going to help you, Heather. You'll get into the college of your dreams. I promise."

Chapter Seven

Skye

I stride west on Seventeenth Street toward my psychiatrist's office half a block from Union Square. When I reach the building, I take the stairs up to the third floor—no elevators for me if I can help it—and breeze straight into Dr. Salam's office.

Dr. Salam is a gorgeous Lebanese woman in her early forties, and one of the top psychiatrists in Manhattan. I've been seeing her for five years now, and she knows me inside and out. Our appointments are monthly; we alternate between Skype and in-person sessions.

For much of middle and high school and even college, I was mortified that I had to see a psychiatrist. It didn't help that, until Dr. Salam, I didn't like a single one of the doctors I saw. First there was Dr. Perry, a man my grandfather's age whose breath smelled like rotten milk. After three years of my complaining about him, my dad thought I might be better off seeing a woman, and I switched to Dr. Lipman in high school. But Dr. Lipman was icy and removed and her office was always freezing, and being around her made me miss my mother so much that I refused to go back after six months. Dr. Antonio was just okay—when we spoke,

I could tell he didn't particularly *care*—but he let almost all our monthly sessions take place over the phone, and I put up with him for the remainder of high school. Dr. Antonio retired right before I started my freshman year at Barnard, so I switched to Dr. McCann, an on-campus psychiatrist who was just out of med school and clearly had no experience treating OCD patients.

Over the next several years I weeded through numerous doctors in Manhattan, all of whom continued to prescribe the antidepressant that was managing my disorder, but none who went much deeper than that.

My symptoms still flared. I had a decent number of friends—Andie, Lex, and Isabel had been my ride or dies since elementary school, and I'd made a handful of close friends at Barnard. My instincts had always been good when it came to friendships; even from a young age I was drawn to the girls who lifted me up, and I had little tolerance for those who did not.

My romantic relationships, though, were a disaster. I wasn't naive; when my breasts made an appearance in seventh grade, the year after Mom died, I knew boys were looking at me differently. Though I never said it out loud, I knew I had a prettier face than Andie or Lexy or Isabel. Adults told me I looked exactly like Mom, and Mom was the most beautiful woman I'd ever known.

Colin Buchanan told me I was the prettiest girl in the eighth grade the night he asked me to go to the movies. It happened over an AIM conversation—because that's how relationships evolved in middle school—and we went to see *Zoolander* that weekend. During the commercials we shared a tub of popcorn, and Colin admitted that a few of his friends had been skeptical when he told them he liked me. I didn't ask why—I already knew—but he was kind enough to tell me anyway that a significant portion of the eighth-grade class thought "the thing I did with doors" was weird. My cheeks grew piping hot.

Colin also brought up the time in American History when I'd run from my chair and jumped on top of Mr. Brenner's desk to reach the clock, which read 11:11. I'd kissed the clock eleven times, then touched it eleven times with my left hand, followed by my right, while everyone in the classroom except for Mr. Brenner and Isabel gasped and snickered with laughter. I remembered the humiliating incident with painful clarity; afterward I vowed never again to check the time in a public setting and thankfully had yet to slip up.

Colin had squeezed my hand as the movie theater darkened. "I told my friends I don't care about any of that," he whispered. "Everyone has done some weird stuff in their past."

I tried to let his words console me, but my mind wouldn't rest. *The thing is, it's not my past,* I thought as the opening credits of *Zoolander* played. *It's my present. As far as I know, it's my future. It's me.*

A week later, Colin invited me over to his house to play tennis. I was nervous, but Andie urged me to go. She said that after we played tennis Colin might ask me to be his girlfriend, and I could still have my dad pick me up before dinner.

The Buchanans' house was a newly built mansion on

the water with a pool, a tennis court, and a bowling alley in the basement. A lot of people in Westport were wealthy—my family included—but my mother had always called flashy homes like the Buchanans' *nouveau riche*. It was a sunny Saturday afternoon in October, and Colin and I played two sets of tennis before we were dying of thirst. He suggested we go inside for some Gatorade.

I hesitated, but what choice did I have? If Colin and I were going to be an item, I would have to be able to go inside his house like a normal person. I followed Colin across the expansive green lawn, through the terrace, and into the Buchanans' enormous, newly renovated kitchen. Colin handed me a cold bottle of orange Gatorade and led me into the den, where his older sister Lindsey and a few of her friends were camped out in front of the TV.

"*Happy Gilmore!*" Colin exclaimed, plopping down on the couch next to them. "This movie rocks."

He shut the door behind us, and that's when I realized how stuffy the room felt. A wave of nausea rolled through me. Reluctantly I slid down next to Colin, my stomach spinning with nerves. Lindsey and her friends—I knew they were the "popular" sophomore girls—had barely registered Colin and me, their eyes glued to the screen.

I'd been so thirsty after tennis I'd drunk the whole bottle of Gatorade, and three-quarters of the way through the movie I was squeezing my thighs together to hold it in. Finally *Happy Gilmore* ended, and I prayed the girls would get up to use the bathroom or search for a snack, *anything* so that I wouldn't have to do my door ritual in front of them.

Lindsey flipped the channel. "Ooooh, *Friends*!" she purred, and her friends squealed in approval. They were staying put.

"I actually love *Friends*." Colin turned to me. "Do you watch it, Skye?"

I knew if I didn't make it to a bathroom in the next sixty seconds, I was going to pee myself; I also knew I wouldn't be able to leave the den without knocking on the door in my systematic order: one count up to eight, one count down from eight. The compulsion was too strong an urge; it swelled through my whole being, a fire burning from my fingertips down to my toes.

Colin settled back into the couch, and I couldn't contain myself any longer. I got up off the couch, a sharp piercing in my bladder, and in that moment a second compulsion seized me, another one I couldn't ignore. The voice inside my head told me that if I didn't knock on every wooden item in the room, I would get a bladder infection and die. I wanted to cry—both from discomfort and the inevitable humiliation I was about to bring upon myself—but that didn't extinguish the compulsion that was eating away at my insides.

Obediently I stood up from the couch and ran to the wooden TV stand. I knocked eight times. I felt Colin and Lindsey and her friends all watching me as I moved on to the coffee table and the wood floors and the side table and the stool, and I wished with every fiber in my body that they could understand that it was physically impossible for me to stop. Lastly I knocked on the door in my usual pattern—*one two three four five six seven eight; eight seven six five four three two one*—before flying out of the room and to the nearest bathroom.

It felt so good to let my bladder break that for a minute I didn't care about the mortification that awaited me. I washed my hands, did my knocks on the bathroom door, and stepped into the hall, where Colin stood staring at me, mouth gaping. He told me I could use the phone to call my dad if I was ready to go home, and it was the last time we ever spoke.

That early experience was a precursor of my doomed love life to come. No one wanted to date the crazy girl. But I was pretty, which meant that if I solely wanted to hook up with guys, I could. And I did want that, especially when everyone else started doing it. I wanted to French-kiss; I wanted to feel a guy grow hard in my hand; I wanted to keep up with my friends as they rounded the bases, one by one.

The difference was, my friends were hitting these milestones with their boyfriends. Sophomore year of high school, Andie gave her boyfriend, Tommy, a blow job after they'd been together for over a year and he'd been begging her for months. A few weeks later, I hooked up with a guy I'd just met at a party in Southport and gave him head in the laundry room. I was too drunk to remember his name, but I told the story proudly.

That summer, Andie and Tommy lost their virginities to each other, and I was twitchy with jealousy. Lexy had lost her V-card several months earlier, and Isabel and her boyfriend, Kevin, weren't far behind.

I hated that I was a virgin. That August on Nantucket, my summer friend Becky and I convinced my brother to bring us to a party. I drank vodka cranberries and squeezed my cleavage in front of every remotely attractive guy. I ended up on a dock with an older guy named Kip—a sophomore at Colgate—and I knew the moment he pressed me down against the cedar planks that I would let him screw me. I was too drunk to notice if it hurt, but the next day I had bruises on my back from where the dock had dug into my skin.

This was how it went with me and boys, for high school and college and throughout my twenties. With the exception of Max LaPointe, I refused to let myself get close to anyone. And Max LaPointe turned out to be an astronomical mistake.

Two and a half years after I graduated from college, a friend from Barnard referred me to Dr. Salam. I walked into her office expecting nothing and spent our sixty-minute session bawling my eyes out. Dr. Salam was kind and curious, and I could tell she was genuinely concerned about helping me as I cried for my mother, for my broken future, for the disaster of Max LaPointe, for every agonizing, mortifying compulsion I'd had to endure over the past decade. During our first session Dr. Salam led me back to the beginning, back to the awful, stifling waiting room at St. Vincent's Medical Center and the unfathomable pain in my twelve-year-old heart, straight to the onset of my obsessive-compulsive disorder.

For the first time in ten years of therapy, I truly connected with a doctor, and as I walked home from

Dr. Salam's office that day after our first appointment, my face sticky from crying, I felt buoyant with fresh hope.

This morning, five years after our first session, I sink down into the plush cream love seat across from Dr. Salam's desk and let the smile take over my face.

Dr. Salam's eyes light up and she raises one dark eyebrow. "Let me get a closer look at that rock."

I extend my arm in her direction. A thrill shoots through me when she says it's absolutely stunning, and I don't think I'll ever get sick of this. Lexy said she got so tired of having to show everyone her ring after she got engaged, but I think she was just saying that.

Dr. Salam crosses her lean runner's legs and leans forward in her chair. "So, Skye. What else is going on? What ground do we need to cover today?"

I'm not in the mood to talk about anything OCD related. My symptoms have been relatively under control lately, and having Burke has been a game changer for my confidence. I think about the email from Max LaPointe, about the questions spinning around my head since he made contact. How on earth did he find out I was engaged? And before even *Andie* knew? I consider broaching the subject with Dr. Salam, but it seems irrelevant, and besides, I don't want to focus on Max. He's a snake who likes to ruffle feathers—he has always been.

Instead, I tuck my legs under my knees on the couch and launch into the wedding-related drama of Andie being all judgmental at how fast everything is moving, and for the first time in Dr. Salam's office I feel like a

normal twenty-nine-year-old woman with normal problems having a normal vent session with her therapist.
The thought makes it difficult not to smile, the corners
of my lips twitching as I relish feeling ordinary.

Chapter Eight

Burke Michaels's Diary

OCTOBER 5, 2018

Dear Dr. K,

For the first few weeks this thing with Skye was just supposed to be about sex. I'd been going into the city to see her every few nights, telling Heather that my ex-colleague Oliver from Credit Suisse was committed to helping me find a job and had set up a number of dinners with clients he knew who were hiring. These dinners almost always went late, I explained to my wife, and it was easier if I crashed in Oliver's spare bedroom rather than risk falling asleep on Metro-North, missing my connection, and winding up in Waterbury (yes, this has happened before).

Oliver didn't exist. I made him up for the sole purpose of continuing my affair with Skye, which I promised myself was just physical. After twenty-five years of marriage, sex with Heather had become stale, routine—we did it to convince ourselves that nothing between us was fundamentally wrong. But the heat was gone, the passion extinguished. The sheets cooled.

Fucking Skye reminds me of fucking Heather during the early years, a primal desire so overwhelming that everything on the periphery becomes blunted. When

I'm not in bed with Skye, I'm thinking about being in bed with her, and I swear, Dr. K, I feel like a teenager, so hyperfocused on this pure, animal want. And that's all it was.

Until last night.

Skye and I had dinner plans, and I was about to leave for the train station when Heather nagged me again about making *sure* I'd be home on the first train the next morning so that she could go to work and I could meet the water-heater guy. She then mentioned that the Visa was maxed out, and could I please take care of paying the balance. Twenty minutes later, I got on the train and used the Metro-North app on my phone to buy an off-peak ticket to Grand Central, and my MasterCard was declined. The only other card I had on me was the Visa, so I tried that, but sure enough, that was declined, too. Naturally I didn't have cash on me, so I spent the rest of the train ride hiding in and out of the foul-smelling bathroom dodging the conductor, while angry passengers pounded on the door. I can't live like this, Dr. K.

I debated staying on the same train and riding it right back out to New Haven because you can't go on a dinner date with a girl with nothing but two maxed-out credit cards in your wallet. But I'd been looking forward to seeing Skye all day, roused by the thought of running my hands all over her smooth, naked body, and the idea of spending another two hours in the train bathroom avoiding the conductor made me want to splay my worthless self across the tracks. So I headed to the restaurant.

Skye had made us a reservation at Le Bernardin, which had four dollar signs on Yelp. I got to the restaurant just after seven and Skye was already there, drinking a glass of red wine at the bar. She wore a silky black top and smelled delicious, like spicy vanilla.

I kissed her cheek and gave my prepared spiel: I was an idiot and had forgotten my wallet in Brooklyn. Could we bag the reservation and order Chinese from Skye's couch?

Skye looked at me with those bright brown eyes and cocked her perfect blond head. "Burke, have you ever eaten at Le Bernardin?"

I shook my head.

"Well, you're in for a treat. And it's on me tonight. No big deal."

No big deal, I thought five minutes later when we'd been seated and I listened to Skye order another $60 glass of wine from the sommelier. Then she told him we'd both do the chef's tasting for dinner, and I caught the price on the menu before the waiter whisked it away—$225.

My curiosity was piqued. As far as I knew, young women in book publishing typically didn't budget for $500 weeknight dinners at four-star New York restaurants. Fifteen minutes later, during one of the many courses, I said as much.

"I'm sorry." Her hand flew to her mouth. "I shouldn't have ordered for you like you're a child. I've just been here so many—" She paused. "This is my dad's favorite restaurant in the city. The chef's tasting menu is expensive, but it's *unreal.*"

I sipped my hot water with lemon—just call me Gwyneth fucking Paltrow—and eyed Skye quizzically. "Well, I feel terrible that I don't have my wallet."

Skye put down her fork. "I should probably be up front about something."

I'm not sure if she was trying to impress me or if she simply wanted to acknowledge the elephant in the room, but Skye didn't beat around the bush. She explained that her mother's grandfather had started a pharmaceutical company called F&C Pharmaceuticals, which was acquired by Johnson & Johnson in 1951.

"My family owns a substantial stake in J and J," Skye clarified. "It was technically my mom's stake, but she died when I was twelve. So, yeah, I'm that trust-fund kid. Which I sometimes hate because I never did anything to earn it and that's a weird feeling. But if there's one thing I don't have a problem dropping money on, it's amazing food." She pointed to the plate between us. "You have to try one of these oysters. They're like pure cream."

I watched as she used the tiny silver spoon to scoop horseradish onto a meaty little oyster, then slurped the whole thing back.

Now, I didn't get specific numbers, Dr. K, but in the men's bathroom of Le Bernardin a quick Google search of *F&C Pharmaceuticals* + Johnson & Johnson led to the discovery that the fortune is substantial. Skye's grandfather appeared in an article on CNBC titled "197 Billionaires 'Too Poor' to Make *Forbes* List of 400 Richest Americans." The article claimed his net worth to be $1.2 billion from "inherited pharmaceuticals."

Holy fucking fuck, Dr. K. I've never been one to believe in the workings of fate, but it's just too strange that in the midst of the direst financial crisis of my life I meet someone like Skye—the trust-fund baby of a $1.2 billion fortune.

I spent the rest of our dinner in an odd, dreamy sort of haze. How many times had I considered the insanely rich before? How many times in the past six months had I thought to myself, *Jeff Bezos has $160 billion; if he could just give me a quick million, all my financial troubles would be solved forever, and he wouldn't even notice.*

This thought is irrational, and one I probably share with every other middle-class American asshole. But last night at Le Bernardin sitting across from Skye Starling—the girl I'd spent the past two weeks wining and dining and screwing—I asked myself a similar question. And perhaps it was the physical proximity to such exorbitant wealth, but somehow, this time, the question seemed entirely rational. The outcome felt attainable.

No, I wasn't going to directly ask her for a million dollars, Dr. K; I'm not a complete fool. But the wheels were beginning to turn. By the time the waiter deposited our final course of burnt-orange crémeux with clementine sorbet, I knew how I would pose the question I couldn't shake from my mind.

"Thank you for being honest with me about your . . . situation," I started.

"Of course." Skye blinked, her eyelashes long and impossibly thick. "I figured I would tell you. We're starting to spend more time together, and it's . . . obviously a part of who I am."

I nodded. "Trust funds can be tricky. I have some clients who've really gotten the short end of the stick in that situation. From a wealth management perspective, I mean. But it sounds like your father didn't get tied up in any trust-fund laws." I paused, sorbet dripping from my spoon. "Sorry, I'm babbling. I don't mean to pry."

But Skye nodded. "No, you're right, I've heard it can be a total nightmare." She swallowed. "But, yeah, luckily the trusts weren't tied up legally or anything. My grandfather made sure of all that before he passed away."

I exhaled a breath I hadn't realized I'd been holding, the plan gathering speed in my mind.

"So, what did you think of your first Le Bernardin experience?" Skye asked as she handed the waiter her black AmEx without looking at the bill.

"That was the best meal of my life," I said, though in truth I'd been too distracted to fully appreciate each of the decadent courses. "You're going to have to roll me back to your apartment."

I don't know much about dating, Dr. K, having married my first and only girlfriend. But I do know that, millionaire or not, a girl doesn't treat a guy to a chef's tasting dinner at Le Bernardin if she's not into him. That's just not the way the world works.

Back at Skye's I used the bathroom and studied my reflection in the mirror above the sink. And it was strange, Dr. K, but for the first time since I met Skye,

I could see what she saw. Staring at myself, tall and clean-shaven in a blue blazer, I could understand what would draw a woman of her caliber to a man like me. I recalled the time, not a year earlier, when I'd overheard one of Maggie's friends say I looked like a dark-haired David Beckham. She and some girls had been watching a movie in the den, and I'd listened to Maggie make puking noises in response while the other girls giggled. Still, that *had* happened. To young women I was handsome. David Beckham handsome. And though I've aged, with my full head of black hair—only a handful of grays if you dig—I could pass for late thirties.

What I saw in Skye's bathroom mirror was a catch, Dr. K. I've been married a long time; I'd forgotten the way I appealed to women before Heather, the way they'd always bypassed Scott and Andy and my other buddies and flocked straight to me. But I'd only ever wanted Heather—spunky, stunning Heather with her twinkly green eyes and ambitious resolve, different from the other conventionally attractive girls whose sly smiles told me I could have them. The man in the mirror was a catch, but he was also Heather Michaels's husband.

I was never a cheater, Dr. K. I'm *not* a cheater—that's what I'm trying to explain. For the past two weeks Skye Starling has been my midlife crisis, but last night, drifting off beside her, I suddenly missed Heather so badly I couldn't sleep. I missed the life we'd spent thirty years building together. I loathed the ocean of lies I'd put between us, and all the other ways I'd let her down. It was more like remembering than realizing. I think love is like that sometimes, Dr. K. It's like finally finding the trail again when you've been lost.

Yes, I've knocked fate in the past, but lying next to Skye, I came to understand that our affair has happened for a reason. That the plan forming in my head during dinner at Le Bernardin has legs. The irony is this: Skye, with her soft skin and hopeful eyes and pharmaceutical fortune, may just be the ticket back to my wife.

Chapter Nine

Heather

JANUARY 1990

Burke had been sending me love letters.

After his initial period of anger when I broke things off in October, he turned into a sad, sulking puppy who was willing to take the blame for everything wrong with our relationship. He wrote in one of his letters:

> I know this is all my fault, Bones. I see that now. I need to be more driven and better at planning for the future, like you are. I need to lay off the drugs, and I'm not just saying that. I promise you, Heather Price, if you give me another chance, I'll prove I can be the man you need me to be. We'll apply to college together, we'll get the hell out of Langs Valley just like we always planned. I love you more than anything in this world and imagining a future without you is devestating. Your breaking my heart. Please give me a call.

Poor Burke. I wasn't surprised he missed me; Burke could have any girl in Langs Valley, but I was the only one who was going to get him out of our dumpy little town and he knew it. With anyone else, his future would be a bleak blur of dead-end jobs and drugs and raising kids in the same shitty way our parents raised us.

Ever since we first got together freshman year—that frigid night in December when he offered to give me a ride home from the hockey game—Burke had been mine. He'd put the heat on full blast and pointed all the vents in my direction, and when we pulled into my driveway, he leaned across the center console and brushed my cheek with the back of his hand.

"You're perfect, Heather," he'd whispered before he kissed me. He tasted sweet and minty, and our lips fit together like puzzle pieces, and that had been that. Something easy and good in my life, for a change.

Of course, I missed Burke. I missed his adorable dimples. I missed collapsing into his strong arms at the end of a long day, the way he made me feel tethered to something real. Aside from Gus, Burke was the only home I'd ever known, and I could never say that we didn't love each other.

But he couldn't spell *devastating,* and when I showed Libby the letter, she rolled her eyes.

"Another one?" She took the paper from my hands, scanning the words. "If he can't use the proper form of *you're* in a sentence, he's not the guy for you.

"I'm serious, Heather," Libby continued, watching me think. "I have no doubt Burke is a decent guy, but you need someone a million times smarter than he is, someone on your level. You're *going* places. And Burke . . . Burke is an addict. He's only going to bring you down."

It was the first time I'd heard anyone say it out loud, but I knew instantly that Libby's words were the truth. Burke was an addict.

"I know, Lib." I sighed, wiping coffee grinds from the kitchen counter into the sink. "Believe me, I know."

I smiled at the sight of Nate and Gus crouched on the floor, intensely focused on Nate's vast collection of toy trucks. It had been nice bringing Gus with me to Libby's. The boys played together well, and I felt far less guilty now that I didn't have to leave my brother at the Carsons' for so many hours. My father, whom I crossed paths with less and less, hadn't said a word to me about Gus's whereabouts. When I asked Gus about Dad, he shrugged his little shoulders. "Haven't seen Daddy. Where'd Daddy go?"

The boys loved when I read to them, and Libby and Peter had shelves and shelves of children's books that I'd never seen at the local library. Gus's favorite was *The Snowy Day* by Ezra Jack Keats, a book about a boy who explores his neighborhood in New York City the day after a big snowstorm. Gus was enamored of the pictures of the snowy city setting—so different from the rural life he knew—and he'd flip through the pages for hours, long after Nate had grown bored of our reading session. Eventually Libby told Gus he could keep *The Snowy Day,* and his eyes lit up in delight.

Libby adored Gus, but Peter wasn't around enough to give him much notice. I'd become wildly curious about Libby and Peter's marriage, especially with Libby's constant advice about choosing a partner carefully. Peter spent almost all hours of the day working out back in his artist's studio in the barn. Whenever he did come through the house for lunch or a snack, dried paint smudging his jeans, he'd wrap his arms around Libby lovingly and cover the kids with kisses. But he left his studio so rarely that I couldn't help but wonder if their marriage wasn't as perfect as Libby wanted it to seem.

I wondered if they had issues regarding money. As Libby and I had gotten closer, she'd revealed enough for me to confirm that Peter's art wasn't the reason for their family's deep pockets, but the source itself was never specified.

The night I aced my first SAT practice test—thanks to Libby and her SAT prep books—we celebrated with some of her favorite red wine. We were having one of our long, easy chats and had already polished off a full bottle when she mindlessly mentioned not wanting to travel with her parents and the kids to Vail over Presidents' Day weekend.

She immediately placed a hand to her mouth. "I'm sorry. You must think I'm an insensitive, privileged fool, being so cavalier about a trip like that. I do realize I'm . . . lucky."

I paused before responding, "To be honest, I don't even know where Vail is."

Libby hesitated, shifting uncomfortably. "It's a ski resort in Colorado. I'm sorry, Heather. I must sound like an entitled brat."

Though I lived in the mountains, I'd never been

skiing and didn't know a thing about it, but flying to a ski resort in Colorado sounded nothing short of glamorous. Nevertheless, I shook my head.

"I don't think you're insensitive, Lib." I touched my nose to the rim of the glass and inhaled the earthy, oaked scent of the wine. "You're definitely not an entitled brat. You're generous and you've been so kind to me. You're probably the closest friend I've got these days."

It was true. Burke was out of my life, and with all the extra time I'd been spending on homework and SAT prep and babysitting at Libby's, I hardly hung out with my girlfriends at all. Kyla was pissed; she told me she was sick of my Pollyanna act and didn't know who I was anymore and had stopped bothering to invite me to parties.

I knew I was being a bad friend, but I was determined to keep my eye on the prize. More than anything else, I knew I had to get out of Langs Valley. Once Peter was finished with his Adirondack Mountains study, likely in May or June, Libby would move back to the wealthy coastal town where she was born and raised. That, too, was where I imagined myself one day: an affluent suburb of New York City where people drink wine spritzers and play golf, where someone else mows your lawn and there isn't a trace of crack cocaine for miles.

I didn't want a career so much as I wanted a vessel toward that life, the life Libby led in which she didn't have to think about work or money, where the carefree possibilities of each day made her fingertips tingle. Getting into a good college was my ticket to meeting a wealthy man, or a man who would be wealthy, and that was what I needed. Gold diggers aren't vacuous; they work hard for the life they get. I'd begun to understand that Peter painted all day because Peter *could* paint all day.

I could smell it on my hands at night, the lingering scent of the blissful freedom money allowed. It worked its way into my bloodstream. It overpowered every choice I made, and I knew, the way I knew the rhythm of my own breath, that now that I had a tangible goal to set my sights on, I could get to where I wanted to go. Burke couldn't. Kyla couldn't. But I could, and I would. At the end of senior year, just eighteen months down the line, I was going to take Gus and get us far, far away from our sad, doomed little town. Nothing was going to stop me.

I couldn't have seen what was coming. It was impossible to know then what lurked in the shadows of the unfurling future. Five months later, everything changed.

Chapter Ten

Skye

APRIL 2019

It's been a month to the day since Burke popped the question, and I want to surprise him with his favorite breakfast—blueberry pancakes. Part of the surprise will also be that I've gotten up before him—I'm not a morning person, and Burke loves to give me grief over my never being out of bed first. My alarm sounds at six-thirty—an Adele song that I now can't stand—and I fight the urge to press the snooze button. Dragging my limbs out from under the warm covers is almost painful, but Burke has an early meeting, and I want to do this for him. I imagine the look on his face when I present him with pancakes in bed, and it propels me forward. I grab my coziest robe and pitter-patter into the kitchen to start cooking.

Ever since we got engaged, it's the simple moments that floor me. As I mix the Bisquick, I gaze lovingly at my ring. I don't care about the diamond, not really. I care about what the diamond *means*. I think of Burke just a few feet away in the other room, still slumbering in our bed, and that he's picked me—that he waited all these years for a woman like me—feels like a miracle.

The first time Burke slept over I was crazy nervous.

I wasn't in the habit of letting guys stay over until I'd set my *boundaries*—something I'd been working on with Dr. Salam. Setting my boundaries meant getting to know a guy through dating, and forming a trustworthy bond before letting him stay over at my apartment. This was therapist lingo for *Don't fuck on the first date*.

I didn't particularly enjoy sleeping with a guy and never talking to him again, but that was the clear alternative to the inevitable hurt and excruciating shame that came from trying to start a real relationship. It made me feel as if I had some control and power in my interactions with men, and it gave me a vague sense of social validation—I had something to contribute when I found myself in a circle of girls talking about sex, and casually referencing a "one-night stand" always made me sound braver and hotter than I actually felt.

The problem was, nothing had changed in the many years since Colin Buchanan. On more than one occasion I'd opened up about my OCD (both voluntarily and involuntarily) to men I'd developed feelings for, with the belief that these feelings were mutual and strong enough to withstand the truth. But it didn't work that way, even with Max LaPointe.

Dr. Salam highlighted my problem: sex. She said that when a woman sleeps with a man, her body produces something called oxytocin, and oxytocin often causes a feeling of attachment. In the past, the men I'd attempted to have relationships with were men I'd been sleeping with, and this was why the failed relationships resulted in emotional injury. But if I didn't sleep with anyone until I'd set my *boundaries*—aka, give potential lovers the heads-up that they were dealing with a disordered person—then emotional injury was much less likely. Because if the man rejected me anyway, at least no oxytocin was involved. This was Dr. Salam's reasoning.

But I pushed her voice aside the night I let Burke Michaels sleep over after our very first date. Well, perhaps it was our second date, if you count Montauk.

It came down to pure physics: my body was simply unable to say no. Burke's warm, dimpled smile filled me with a lulling ease at the same time it made my insides dip and twirl with lust. He was tall, dark, and handsome, the kind of all-American guy I used to imagine myself with when I was a little girl daydreaming of her prince. And I loved that he was older—he was mature and direct and had a thoughtfulness to him that guys my age just seemed to lack.

After our first dinner, at Ippudo, I said I was going to the bathroom and that I'd meet him outside. I didn't actually have to use the bathroom, but I needed to exit alone. I needed to perform my door routine in the presence of baffled strangers and not of the man whose presence turned my legs to rubber. *One two three four five six seven eight; eight seven six five four three two one.* It doesn't seem like that big of a deal, but seeing it—witnessing the sheer oddity of someone needing to knock on a door in a specific pattern before walking through it—is a different story.

I wasn't ready for the night—for the buzzing electricity between Burke and me—to end. I could claim that my intentions were to send him home after a shot of espresso at my place, but if I'm being honest, I knew I wanted him for the whole night. I watched him sink back into my couch, and I loved the content expression on his face, as if there was nowhere else in the world he'd rather be. I loved his worn jean jacket, frayed at the collar, the way it reminded me of something authentic and good. He sipped his coffee slowly, as if he had all the time in the world, and when the mug was empty, he placed it down and kissed me expertly, a fizz running up the length of my spine. Something was clicking between us—even from that dizzying first kiss, it was a kind of synchronized connection I'd never felt before. As we moved toward the bedroom, I briefly wondered how old he was—he was certainly older than any other man I'd been with—but I quickly decided I didn't care.

After it was over, he crashed into sleep, one arm splayed across my torso, and anxiety crept its way into the pit of my stomach as I came back down to earth. My heart thumped loudly in my chest and I tried not to think of what would happen in the morning, or what I'd tell Dr. Salam.

I didn't sleep a wink. It was still dark hours later when Burke's phone beeped noisily and I felt him stir beside me.

"Sorry, my alarm." He leaned over the bed to turn it off. He kissed the back of my neck and my bare shoulder and worked his way around to my lips. "I should've mentioned it last night, but I have an early call with this crazy client. He's in London, so my five-thirty is his ten-thirty. Bastard."

I liked the sound of Burke's morning voice, all low and gravelly.

"Go back to sleep." He touched my nose. "You're really something, Skye."

I watched him climb out of bed and search for his clothes, relief drenching my bones. He was leaving. He wasn't going to linger or suggest we go get breakfast. I wouldn't be forced to show him the side of me I was desperate to keep hidden, at least for a little while longer. The looming pain was so inevitable I could almost feel it, like a clamp pressing my chest. Dr. Salam had been right; I shouldn't sleep with men before setting my boundaries.

"You look so peaceful," Burke whispered as he leaned down to kiss me again. Little did he know. "I'd love to see you again soon, Skye."

"I'd like that, too," I murmured.

Then he was gone.

We texted over the next few days, and Burke mentioned that his client in London was becoming increasingly demanding and had requested a daily Skype call every morning at five-thirty for the next several weeks. That's why, after our next date the following week, I knew it was safe to let Burke sleep over again. And the date after that, and the date after that, and the date after that. It was our morning routine: Burke's alarm went off before dawn and he left my apartment in the dark while I was still heavy with sleep. It was the first time I'd been able to sleep through the night with a guy since Max LaPointe.

After five sleepovers, Burke called me one Friday and

suggested we meet up that evening and finally spend a "regular" morning together on Saturday. The night before we'd gone to eat at Le Bernardin, and Burke had, as usual, slipped out of my apartment at dawn for his client call. My gut twisted with nerves at his proposition, but I knew it was time to tell him the truth.

I braced myself for the worst as I headed to Greenwich Village to meet him that evening. It was the first week of October, and the city was just beginning to evoke that true nip of fall, summer like sand escaping through my fingers. I've never liked the start of autumn; most New Yorkers savor the drop in humidity and the crisp air, but it's the time of year Mom died, so to me, fall is just death. Dying trees, dying light. Everything ending.

I felt particularly low as I walked into the Marlton Hotel and saw Burke sitting at a table near the front windows. He looked so handsome with his jet-black hair combed neat, shirtsleeves rolled halfway up his strong forearms, red tie loose around his collar. More than anything else I wanted this man to be mine, but I knew that he wouldn't be. Not after the shadow I was about to cast over his perception of the girl he'd been seeing. If he was anything like the others, he'd stick around for one or two more dates, then run for the hills.

Burke stood to kiss my cheek, and we both sat. I ordered a negroni from the cocktail waitress. I waited for it to arrive, took a huge sip, then told him everything.

I was diagnosed with obsessive-compulsive disorder when I was twelve, three months after my mother died of liver cancer. It took Dr. Perry two whole months to make the diagnosis, which revealed itself through my symptoms of touching certain things in a specified way. If I was in a room and the door was closed, I had to touch the door a specific number of times in a specified order before I could open it. It didn't matter if someone else opened the door first and held it for me—I still *had* to do my thing to exit the building or room. The same went for clocks; if I looked at the clock at 10:10 or 2:22 or 4:44—any time stamp composed of repeating numbers—I had to touch and kiss every clock in the area in a particular way.

Why? Because I *had* to. I couldn't not. When I tried to resist these urges, there'd be a tightening in my chest and lungs, a giant fist squeezing my windpipe, cutting off my air supply. That would morph into a sharp, lucid panic that prickled every inch of my skin. None of it was in my control. When Dr. Perry finally diagnosed me with OCD, he explained that these random, irresistible urges were called compulsions.

I remembered being occasionally anxious and claustrophobic as a kid, but it was nothing like what I'd begun to experience immediately after my mother passed away.

My father was so clouded by his own grief that it took him a couple of weeks to notice the strange way I was touching doors and clocks.

"Skye, why do you keep doing that?" he asked one night when we were leaving the house for dinner at my grandmother's. He'd gone out the back door before me, and I thought he was already waiting in the car when I did my door taps: *one two three four five six seven eight; eight seven six five four three two one.*

I was startled to see him watching me. "I don't know. I can't stop."

My father peered at me through desolate gray eyes. The next day he made me an appointment with Dr. Perry, the psychiatrist he'd started seeing himself after Mom went into hospice.

When he *finally* diagnosed me, Dr. Perry put me on a low dosage of Luvox, an antidepressant used to treat OCD in children.

The Luvox made me feel slightly less anxious, but it didn't stop my compulsions. I was back in school and kids were starting to notice my behavior. I tried to linger at the end of classes so that everyone else left the room before me, but that tactic wasn't always possible. Andie and Iz and Lexy had my back, but that didn't stop other kids from making fun of me, even when Lexy punched Sasha Bateman in the face when she called me a mental patient. Sasha had a black eye, and Lexy got detention for the rest of the year.

Dr. Perry became interested that only *certain* doors required the special knock. When I mentioned that my compulsion *wasn't* triggered by the electronic sliding doors at the mall or doors that were already propped open by an object—such as the gym doors at school—Dr. Perry's bushy gray eyebrows jumped.

"Well, that is certainly interesting," he said, stroking his beard.

But he never dug much deeper than that; never

seemed to want to look too hard for a cause. It's surprising, in retrospect, that none of the many subsequent doctors I saw were all that interested in determining a potential cause. The onset of OCD often occurred during the beginning stages of puberty; I was twelve when my symptoms started. Doctors didn't seem to need more of an explanation than that.

Until Dr. Salam.

That first day in her office, when I mentioned that my OCD began when I was in seventh grade, right after my mother died, I watched Dr. Salam's large chocolate eyes bloom.

"*Right* after your mother died?" Concern was in her voice.

"Yes. As far as I can remember, my symptoms started that day."

Dr. Salam made me walk her back to the very beginning, to that horrible black hole of a day, the worst day of my life. I didn't see the point in going there—I certainly didn't want to—but Dr. Salam said she had to know. Some instinctual part of me trusted her as she explained that recent research had been connecting the development of OCD to childhood trauma, including grief. My eyes watered as I shook the memory loose, my voice wobbly as Dr. Salam nodded, prompting me forward.

Mom had been sick for almost two years, and we'd known the end was coming, and that terrible summer had been one long, agonizing goodbye. When the Twin Towers fell that September, it felt as though the world were literally ending, as though the safe life I'd always taken for granted was going up in a cloud of smoke. In early October the doctors finally said Mom's time had come. She only had a few hours.

Dad had my brother and me get dressed, and I watched the tears slide down his cheeks as we rode to the hospital in silence. He was so broken at that point—we all were. People who told us we were strong simply didn't know what else to say.

In her hospital bed Mom was a sliver of herself, a speck of the beautiful, vibrant woman who'd raised me. Her thick hair was gone, replaced by a blue head scarf that I hated, that I was sure Mom hated, too. Her body was a tiny bundle of bones, her face hard and jagged in the places where it had once been the softest skin I knew. Mom squeezed my hand, her eyes barely open. Dad had warned us that she was going to be really, really out of it. I told her I would always love her more than anyone else in the world, and even though she didn't say anything back, a smile struggled against the edges of her pale lips, and I knew she loved me, too.

Dad said it was best we not be in the room when Mom passed, and he sent my brother and me to the waiting room down the hall. He said it could be thirty minutes, or maybe a few hours, but that he'd come get us when it was over. My brother sat with his head hung between his knees. It was silent except for the distant music coming from his headphones. I hated the room. It was a perfect square, with rows of chairs lining three of the four walls, but we were the only ones there. A small window overlooked the parking lot, and the carpet was a hideous pattern of maroon and gray swirls. On one of the walls hung a framed print of a grassy landscape, as if some picture of a pretty field might make you feel better if your mom was down the hall, dying of cancer, on the precipice of leaving the world and never coming back.

I will never see my mother again. The thought lodged itself in the center of my mind, and it filled me with so much fear and sadness that I couldn't breathe. Panic seized me, tears coating my face as I tried to catch my breath. I glanced over at my brother, my protector, but he was bent so far over that I could only see the back of his blond head. I desperately needed his help, but he was always mad these days, and even though we were going through the same thing and Mom had made us promise to stick together, I was too afraid to touch him.

I closed my eyes and imagined Mom dying—struggling for a breath that wasn't there and then being gone forever. I knew I'd never feel the back of her soft hand against my forehead again. The panic bolted through me, an electrical charge. In the blackness behind my eyes I looked for her because that was where she'd said I could find her.

I remembered when I was eight years old and curled up in my bed, my pillow sticky from crying as my mother stroked my hair. It was a cold weekend in January, and I was in the throes of a meltdown. We'd woken up that morning to sixteen inches of snow, and the kids on the block had decided to have a snowman-building contest, which our next-door neighbor Christopher would judge. After nearly two hours we'd completed our snowmen, and Christopher had deemed mine the winner. This sent a boy from down the street into a rage, and he'd smashed my snowman to pieces, leaving nothing but a pile of snow strewn with sticks and a bright orange carrot.

Mom rubbed my back as I sobbed and told me that the boy was wrong to do what he'd done, and that she was going to help me make a new snowman.

"But first, I want you to do something, Skye. Something that will help you calm down. I want you to breathe, just like this." She helped me sit up in the bed and took my small hands in hers. She had the longest, most elegant fingers.

"Breathe in for one, two, three, four, five, six, seven, eight," Mom had said, demonstrating. "Breathe out for eight, seven, six, five, four, three, two, one. Just like that. Let's do it together."

And we had. *One two three four five six seven eight; eight seven six five four three two one.*

Mom explained that anytime she was feeling upset or angry or out of control, she breathed this way to calm herself back down. She'd do it over and over until she felt relaxed. "And eight is my lucky number, so that's why I count to eight. But if you want, you can count to and from a smaller number. That might make it easier for your breath."

I shook my head. "I want my number to be eight, too."

From that day on, I used Mom's breathing technique whenever I needed it. Whenever I was fighting with one of my friends, whenever I felt that familiar surge of anxiety in anticipation of a test or a class presentation, I breathed. I breathed up to eight and down from eight, again and again, and I would make it through.

And as I waited for my mother to die, that's what I did.

Breathe in for one, two, three, four, five, six, seven, eight; breathe out for eight, seven, six, five, four, three, two, one.

Except this time, something charged me to my feet; drove me to the door of the waiting room. I couldn't just sit there; I had to be with her while she died. My hand gripped the doorknob, but it wouldn't turn. My hand wouldn't move. My head spun, a rushing spiral of black. I couldn't leave her alone; I couldn't watch her die. I was trapped in between. I dropped to my knees and rested my forehead against the wood; the reality that existed on the other side of the door was unbearable.

But the irony in unbearable things is that they actually *are* bearable. They force you to endure what you cannot comprehend enduring. They demand that you sit in unimaginable pain.

I made myself return to my breath. I don't know why I started knocking in the same methodic order I was breathing, but doing so calmed something in my central nervous system. I couldn't stop. *Knock for one, two, three, four, five, six, seven, eight; knock for eight, seven, six, five, four, three, two, one.* As long as I didn't stop knocking, as long as I stayed on my side of the door, my mother wouldn't die. Our lucky number eight was keeping her alive. I knocked until my knuckles were raw, but there wasn't any pain. My brother finally picked his head up and slid his headphones down around his neck, peering at me through blotchy eyes.

"Skye." He said my name only once, but his voice was small and powerless against whatever had overcome me. He closed his eyes and put his headphones back over his ears, grief swallowing him whole.

I kept breathing and knocking.

12345678–87654321.
12345678–87654321.
12345678–87654321.
12345678–87654321.
12345678–87654321.
12345678–87654321.

I think it was hours, but I don't know how much time passed before my arm collapsed along with the rest of me, a crumpled flower on the floor. My father found me there, half-asleep on that ugly carpet, when he told us Mom was gone.

By the time I stopped talking, I'd almost forgotten it was Burke to whom I was explaining all of this, and I was momentarily stunned to find him sitting across from me. His blue eyes rested softly on mine, sorrow flickering in his irises.

I took a sip of my negroni, which I'd hardly touched.

"Anyway," I said, the gin a warm glow against my chest, carrying me to the finish line, "this is who I am and what I've been through. OCD is still, unfortunately, a daily part of my life, and I thought I should tell you before we started spending more time together." My heart pounded behind my rib cage as I thought about how much I liked Burke; how badly I wanted him to stay despite what I'd just told him. But it wasn't going to be enough, and Dr. Salam was right: I should never have slept with him. The damn oxytocin was going to make all of this so much harder. The pit in my stomach burrowed deeper.

But Burke's hand slid across the table and he linked his fingers with mine. "Oh, Skye." His expression softened. "Thank you for telling me. For opening up to me about this. It means—it means a lot."

"So you don't . . ." Hope bubbled toward the surface. "I mean, some people . . . it can be jarring to be around . . . if you're not used to it. The knocking isn't my only compulsion; there are others, too. If you spend the night, and we spend all day together tomorrow . . ."

"You have OCD."

I nodded. "I do."

"And I'm in recovery, sober for twenty-two years."

My head was spinning. We'd still never talked about why Burke was sober.

"Drugs, mainly," he continued, reading my mind. "It was a while ago. I lost both my parents in a plane crash when I was a teenager, which made it worse. Drinking was a catalyst for the harder stuff, so I quit everything. But it's under control now. Has been for a while. I'm grateful for that. But I get it, Skye." His eyes—a shock of blue, but gentle—landed on mine. "Childhood loss leaves its mark. For me, it was addiction; for you, it's an OCD compulsion, but whatever it is—it's a force that swallows you whole. And that feeling of powerlessness—

that you're a puppet and somebody else has got the strings—it never fully leaves you."

I nodded, tears pressing behind my eyes at Burke's precise articulation of my experience, a mirror image of his own pain. A degree of empathy I'd never known.

I squeezed his hand. "I'm so sorry. Thank you for telling me. And I'm so sorry about your parents. Do you . . . want to talk about it?"

"Let's save it for another night." Burke smiled sadly. "I'll tell you about it soon."

I nodded. "If you're at all uncomfortable when I drink around you, I'd like you to tell me. I should've said that earlier."

"I would have told you if I was."

I could feel the thing between us getting bigger, growing more real, filling up like a hot-air balloon.

"And I don't want you to be ashamed of any part of yourself, Skye. I think you're the most incredible woman I've ever met. I know it's only been a few weeks, and this is going to sound crazy, but . . ." He exhaled. "I think I'm falling for you, Skye Starling."

I opened my mouth to speak, but my heart clogged my throat. Tears burned behind my eyes.

That was the day—not even six months ago—that my life changed.

Chapter Eleven

Burke Michaels's Diary

OCTOBER 7, 2018

Dear Dr. K,

Now I know. I couldn't wrap my head around it before, how a gorgeous, smart, *rich* girl like Skye Starling could be so availably single. I know enough from observing Heather's lifelong fixation on women like Skye to know that women like Skye aren't single at twenty-nine-going-on-thirty if they can help it.

Anyway, I finally found out what was up on Friday night. Skye told me everything.

At first, I was a bit surprised at the revelation, after the way she sat me down, looked at me with huge doe eyes, and told me she had something serious to confess. I thought she was going to say she had a boyfriend, or that she'd found out I wasn't actually an independent financial consultant who lived in Brooklyn. Or worse, that she'd discovered I was married.

But instead she told me about her OCD, which to me, at first, didn't seem like that big of a deal. I'd always assumed a lot of people had OCD, including my mother. She left when I was young, but I still remember the methodical way she used to arrange all the food in the fridge and cabinets, with the labels facing forward, and the way the one bathroom in our tiny house always smelled like bleach.

But Skye isn't a neat freak. She's clean, but she's not a stickler about it the way my mother was. Skye's pantry isn't organized, and there's always at least a dirty spoon in the sink.

The kind of OCD Skye's got is different. As she explained to me, there are *obsessions* and then there are *compulsions,* and she suffers from the latter. Her compulsions are—as she's worked out with her psychiatrist in recent years—a result of the obsessive thoughts that began when her mother died eighteen years ago.

You're a therapist, and I'd be curious to know if you had a case like this before. The way her voice got all strangled when she told me. It sounds like she's had a rough time with this, Dr. K. It sounds like it's been quite the hurdle in her love life. It *sounds* as though Skye Starling has routinely fallen for a certain breed of male—the college laxer turned I-banker from a "good" family whose surname (God forbid) doesn't end in a vowel, whose douche factor is simply too high to allow him to view a medical disorder like Skye's as anything other than an unnecessary complication and second-hand embarrassment.

I know this because I know these guys, Dr. K. They're the pricks I worked with at Credit Suisse—the Doug Kemps of the world. They're one-dimensional, selfish fools with pretty-boy faces and a lack of depth that somehow magnetizes girls like Skye who don't know any better. And *why* don't girls like Skye know any better? Is it a fragile, deep-seated insecurity? Is it daddy issues? I don't know, but *today* it's finally working to my advantage.

Here is what I also know in this moment: my last name ends in a consonant and I am a good-looking Anglo-Saxon, and that's a great fucking start. The rest will be easy enough to improvise. I've already admitted to her that I was once a drug addict, but I'm confident that Skye, of all people, understands addiction as a disease. My family situation is less than ideal, and it's probably better not to share that I grew up below the poverty line in Langs Valley, New York, raised by my grandmother while her Alzheimer's steadily advanced. Better to say I'm an only child from—Phoenix?—whose parents both died in a plane crash when I was a teenager. Dramatic, yes, but again, at least my last name ends in a consonant.

I know that I'm starting to sound like a con artist, Dr. K; I know if you could, you would tell me to press pause on all this. But Skye's pharmaceutical fortune, that's not something I can just unlearn. When you're a middle-aged man without a job and you have five thousand dollars in your savings account and you owe half of that to Eastern Connecticut State University for your daughter's first semester of senior year and two of your three credit cards are maxed out and your hot-water heater is broken and said daughter has no top teeth and you meet someone who spends a fifth of the amount in your savings on a single dinner, you just can't *ignore* that kind of information. And if you come up with a legal way to obtain a slice of said person's fortune— kind of like that couple from Michigan who hacked the lottery—then I think you go for it, Dr. K. You realize that you've got nothing much to lose and everything to gain, and you just fucking go for it.

Yesterday morning, Saturday, Skye and I slept in till half past ten; it was the first morning I didn't set my alarm for the crack of dawn in order to rush back home. I knew Heather planned to do an Uber shift anyway, and I told her Oliver had invited me to play golf at his club on Long Island.

After Skye and I had some lazy sex and lounged in bed, both of our stomachs were making grumbling noises, and Skye suggested we go out for brunch. Leaving the apartment that morning was the first time I saw her OCD for myself. I watched her knock on the door sixteen times in her systematic order—two counts of eight—before pushing it open. It was a tad bizarre, sure, but I didn't think it was a big deal, not really, especially not with what I stood to gain from this girl. Her face was pinched in discomfort as she turned to watch me follow, and I felt sorry for her, for having to endure all that shame. Skye probably isn't crazier than anyone else in this madhouse of a world, and she's too crippled by her own insecurity to realize that. But that's my opportunity, Dr. K, not my fault. If I can pull off the plan that's been hatching in my head since Le Bernardin, Heather and I will never have to worry about money again. More than that, we'll finally be able to live the life that should've been ours all along.

So here it is, Dr. K. I'm going to lay it out bare for you, because frankly I need to get it off my chest. And I need to make sure there aren't any holes.

I am going to marry Skye Starling. There's no doubt in my mind that she wants a husband, that she yearns to be loved in a way she never has been before. I can give her that—I can work with these vulnerabilities and be who she needs me to be. I can give her a whirlwind romance and a diamond ring and the promise of a future. We'll date for a few months, and then I'll propose. We'll be married in less than a year. Technically it's bigamy, but Skye will never find out about Heather, and vice versa.

I'm not on any form of social media—not even LinkedIn—so I'm safe in that domain. Nonetheless, I'll be sure to do a thorough sweep of my online presence and make sure Skye or her friends can never find anything about the real Burke Michaels.

As for Heather and the kids, I'll tell them I've been offered a job overseas, somewhere in the Middle East at a company that's paying six times my old salary at PK Adamson. An eighteen-month contract, then I'm back for good. I'll be making more money than I've ever made in my life; Heather can renovate the house while I'm gone. Do whatever she wants to it.

It'll be fast, but if I propose to Skye at the end of the winter and push for a quick engagement, we could be married by August or September. Our marriage will then begin to unravel soon after the wedding. We'll realize it was a mistake and that we rushed into things. I'll show her I'm not the sweet, loving man she thought I was. I won't be unfaithful or abusive—nothing that could come back to bite me in court. We'll be divorced in six months, tops. Skye's father may want me to sign a prenup, yes, but I'll cross that bridge if and when I come to it. Prenups are a bit offensive, after all, and I'll have Skye on my side to defend my honor.

I won't get half—even with the best lawyer, half doesn't seem feasible—but I have confirmation that Skye's money isn't tied up at all, and even 10 percent would be more than enough. Enough to pay off the mortgage and for Hope's teeth and the rest of her tuition (even with our kids taking out student loans in their own names, our family's contribution to their tuitions has not been insignificant). Enough to let Heather quit driving fucking Uber. Enough to move to a nicer part of Connecticut. Enough to give Heather the life I was always supposed to give her. The life she deserves.

It's money Skye doesn't even need, if you think about it. When you have tens of millions of dollars, losing a fraction of that isn't even noticeable.

I've never considered myself to be a bad person, Dr. K. I've done some things I'm not proud of, but at the end of the day, my heart's been in the right place. And I truly feel that my heart is in the right place now. If there's one thing I've realized, it's that life doesn't hand itself to you—unless you're born lucky, you've got to go out and make things happen for yourself. You've got to outsmart the motherfucking system. And if Skye Starling is the one casualty in all this, so be it. Self-exposure comes at a cost, and that's a good lesson to learn. She'll get over it eventually.

Chapter Twelve

Heather

Libby threw Gus a *Sesame Street*–themed birthday party. It was Libby's idea, and Libby's wallet; I'd never had the foresight or funds to do anything more than buy cupcakes from the A&P on Gus's birthday. He'd definitely never had a birthday party.

But Gus was turning five, and Libby insisted on doing something special. I could tell she'd grown increasingly fond of Gus in recent months, often treating him like her second son. Sometimes when we went out for meals or ran errands—Libby, her kids, Gus and me—it felt as though Gus were one of Libby's three children and I was their babysitter. I didn't hate it. It alleviated some of the weight on my shoulders to see Gus coddled in Libby's maternal hands—the way she knew exactly what to do when he had a sore throat, or how she didn't allow the boys more than one hour per week in front of the TV.

Too much television stunts growing brains, she'd tell me, never caving when the boys screamed and whined for more *Sesame Street.* Libby was kind but firm, generous but strong-willed; I thought she was the most perfect mother I'd ever witnessed. Though I was the one raising Gus, though I loved him fiercely and would have done anything to protect him, I was only his sister. I didn't know the small yet vital truths that only mothers can understand, and I was grateful for the impact Libby was having on my little brother. I even let myself imagine that, a little over a year down the road, Libby might offer to take Gus in when I went to college. She and Peter would be back in Connecticut by then, and I couldn't help but dream of Gus and me escaping Langs Valley, once and for all.

My father had been gone since Christmas—just up and left one day "to get a beer" with his buddy Bill— and he still wasn't back when Gus turned five on February 17. I guess Bill was driving that day because Dad left us the car, which was a rare stroke of luck for me.

Gus's birthday fell on a Saturday, and we went over to Libby's after breakfast to help set up for the party. Six inches of fresh snow had fallen overnight, a blanket of white coating the fields around our house like a layer of fresh whipped cream. A paper bag hung from the front doorknob, sheltered underneath the stoop. The bag had the letter *G* written on the front.

"I think it's a present for you, bud," I told Gus, handing it to him in the Chevy on the way to Libby's.

Gus squealed, and through the rearview mirror I watched him tear open the package.

"Look!" His expression morphed into pure glee as he pulled out a red plastic fire truck.

"Wow, Gussie! Is there a card in the bag?"

"Umm. Yup!" He passed me a folded note. "What's it say?"

My heart dropped into my stomach at the sight of the familiar scribble. *Happy Birthday, Gusser! Can't believe you are 5. Love, Burke.*

"It's from Burke." I stuffed the note in the center console, a strange mix of feelings stirring through me.

"I miss Burke," Gus whined from the backseat. "Where'd he go, Heddah? Why'd he go away like Daddy?"

"I told you this, bud." I tried to smile. "Burke was my boyfriend, but he's not anymore. It was sweet of him to get you that truck, though. We can go see him sometime soon and say thank you. Would you like that?"

"Yes, please." Gus kicked one of his little legs and looked out the window.

A wave of regret tumbled through me. I knew Gus missed having Burke around—the three of us had been a sort of family, oddly enough. Burke's father had been in prison for as long as I could remember, and his mother, a stewardess, chased some guy to California and hadn't been back to Langs Valley in years. Burke used to live with his grandmother, but when her dementia got bad our sophomore year, they put her in a nursing home and sold her house to pay for the cost. After that Burke had more or less moved in with Gus and me, even though he was technically supposed to be living with his aunt Pam in Lyon Mountain.

As the nostalgia bloomed in my chest and I felt a pang of longing for Burke, I quickly shifted my thoughts, the way Libby had taught me to do.

It's easy to think of the good times, she'd explained.

You have to train yourself to remember the bad times. The reasons why you left.

I thought of all the mornings I'd woken up to Burke passed out on the couch, fully clothed, empty beer cans and remnants of white powder dusting the coffee table while Gus sat cross-legged in front of cartoons. Worst was the time Gus showed me what he'd found in Burke's truck, uncurling his little fingers to reveal a skinny glass crack pipe, the bowl stained with dark residue. Tears pricked my eyes as I pried it out of Gus's hand, because that's when I knew Burke had been lying to me.

And why should I have been surprised? I knew better than anyone else that crack was coming through Langs Valley. And I knew Burke—I knew the dark, cavernous void that existed in his heart, the void he would keep trying, uselessly, to fill. I knew because the same one persisted inside my own aortic chambers—the void that comes from lack of parental love. My advantage was that I understood it could never be filled, that the best way to conquer it was to comprehend it. Burke never believed me when I tried to explain that drugs and alcohol would kill him before they fixed him, and you can't move through life with someone unable to grasp that.

I didn't know where the fiery resolve in me had come from, but I was grateful for it. And after meeting Libby, I was even more determined to resist the life into which I'd been born. To resist the easy, chemistry-fueled relationship with the first and only boy I'd ever loved, the person who cared for me more than any other living soul ever had. Because like all of his friends, like his parents and my parents, Burke was an addict. I couldn't allow another addict to play any part in rearing Gus or, God forbid, children of my own. I'd witnessed first-hand the relentless force with which drugs ripped families apart, but I was lucky to be able to see the world in black and white.

I remembered when my mother first told me she was pregnant with Gus. It was summer—August maybe—and she sat me down out back and told me I was going to be a big sister. I was ecstatic; I'd been begging for a younger brother or sister for years and had grown resigned that it wasn't likely to happen.

My mom explained that she was going to get herself cleaned up so she could take better care of me and the new baby when he or she came. She said she was turning over a new leaf, and I could tell that she meant it. When my mom lied, her voice wobbled, but that day her voice was clear and strong.

She did get clean. She stopped taking drives with her creepy friend Shelly. She started eating three meals a day, and the fullness came back into her pretty face. One weekend I helped her paint the baby's room a pale cornflower blue because she was certain it was a boy. My dad was clean then, too, and every night the three of us would cook dinner together and eat it in front of *Jeopardy!* and *Wheel of Fortune*. Afterward I'd do the dishes while Mom lay on the couch and Dad rubbed her feet. Mom said she felt lucky to have such a wonderful family.

When Gus was born in February, a new kind of love

bloomed inside my heart. I loved holding him and staring at his perfect, tiny features—I couldn't believe he was my very own brother.

But Mom was different after Gus was born. She stayed in bed most of the day, and she barely smiled. She breastfed him for about six weeks before she started drinking again and switched him to formula. When I reminded her that she'd committed to staying clean, she looked at me with lost blue eyes and smiled absently.

"I know you'll understand someday, darlin'. It's all just a little too much."

I held a vague awareness of "good parenting," enough to know that my own parents did not fall into that category. I knew what a stable home looked like from TV shows like *Leave It to Beaver,* and—though they were few and far between—I knew a couple girls from school whose mothers packed them carefully curated lunches every day and could afford to take them shopping at the mall in Plattsburgh. I was shrewd enough to know that kind of parenting didn't have to be rare, that Langs Valley was at one end of a wide spectrum. I'd developed a broad enough scope to understand that I hadn't been born "lucky."

We pulled into Libby's driveway, and Gus shrieked with delight when he saw the Big Bird balloon tied to the mailbox. I helped him out of the car and we walked inside, crunching through the fresh snow in our boots. Libby had outdone herself. Balloons were all over the kitchen and living room, along with streamers and *Sesame Street*–themed party hats. A huge cake from a fancy bakery in Plattsburgh was covered in blue icing to look like Cookie Monster, with five cherry-red candles. The best part was the real-life Elmo sitting with the kids in the living room, and my eyes welled up as I watched Gus run over and wrap his arms around the giant red Muppet. I had never seen Gus look so excited.

"Lib!" I threw my arms around her neck. "This is too much. Where in the world did you find Elmo?"

"It's Peter!" she whispered. "He found the costume in Plattsburgh. Isn't it hilarious?"

I watched the kids swarming Elmo from all directions and couldn't help but laugh at the thought of Peter—quiet, mysterious Peter—underneath the red furry suit. Maybe I'd been wrong about him. Maybe he was a better guy than I'd given him credit for.

A few were playmates of Gus's from the neighborhood, but most were pals of Nate's from his private preschool in Plattsburgh. I didn't mind; I liked seeing Gus interact with other boys his age.

"I've never seen him so happy, Libby. Thank you."

"It's the least I can do, Heath." Libby smiled, diamond studs glinting subtly from either ear. "You know how much I love that little guy. And how much I love his big sister." In jeans and a white button-down shirt she radiated classy, easy beauty, her perfect baby girl propped on one hip, and I was overwhelmed by the feeling that so often struck me in her presence. It had become more of a mission than a feeling; with a heightened sense of urgency each passing day, I wanted to be exactly like Libby Fontaine.

Chapter Thirteen

Skye

APRIL 2019

I wake up to another email from Max LaPointe.

Fiancé is an older man, huh? Hope he knows what he's getting himself into, Starling.

My stomach seesaws—Max must have seen my Instagram. The one I recently posted of Burke and me, the selfie from the morning we got engaged. But how? Max and I unfollowed each other on social media years ago. Possibly Max hates me almost as much as I hate him. Instinctively I reach across the bed for Burke, before I remember he's already gone.

Burke leaves for work around eight. Like me, he's a freelancer who works from home. Unlike me, it's not for mental-health reasons, but nonetheless, we can't get anything done when we're both trying to focus in the apartment, so he's been going to a WeWork in Chelsea.

I reread Max's email. I hate the entitled way he's called me *Starling*—his old, flirtatious name for me. I put my phone down and make myself a cup of coffee before sitting down at my desk. I'm about halfway through the first round of edits for my author Jan Jenkins's new book, the next in her hit YA series about same-sex romances in middle school. Jan and I have been working together for almost five years, since before she was published. When she found me, she was disheveled and discouraged—newly divorced with two kids in college and a completed manuscript about a seventh-grade girl named Louise struggling with her sexuality. Unable to land an agent, Jan had decided to self-publish, and with my editorial guidance, her first book in the *Loving Louise* series made the *USA Today* bestseller list. After that she got multiple offers from major imprints, but in the interest of loyalty and maximizing profit margins, she opted to stick with self-publishing, and me. Now that Jan is on a book-a-year schedule, she keeps me busy, but I typically have a handful of smaller projects I'm working on at any given time. Still, Jan is unquestionably my biggest success story—having her as my author is what's propelled and sustained my freelance career. And it's work that would've made my mother, a book-publishing veteran, proud.

I'm just about to dive back into Jan's manuscript when the thought hits me, irrational but unstoppable. *Unless I touch every wooden object in the room right now, Burke is going to leave me.*

Dr. Salam has taught me not to resist my compulsions the way I used to, and instead to "let them pass through."

I sigh, place my coffee down, and then I'm off. *There's too much wood in this apartment,* I think for the billionth time as I knock on the black-walnut desk and mahogany side tables and footstool and each of the wide-plank floorboards. *Wall-to-wall carpet is a nightmare, but I can't live like this.*

I can't live like this. How many times have I thought this? I think of my first day in Dr. Salam's office, and the tiny seed of hope she planted in the midst of my fraught, panicked mind.

"Your compulsions exist because they serve a purpose for you, Skye." Her voice was deliberate and clear. "They help you feel a sense of control in a world that is wildly uncontrollable. But I trust that, someday, they'll no longer serve that purpose, and when that happens, you'll cease to feel them at all."

Someday, but not today.

I'm just finishing my knocks when my phone starts vibrating. *Dad Cell.*

"Hey, Dad." I wouldn't say my father and I are *close,* but I never screen his calls.

"Hey, sweetheart. You sound like you're out of breath. How's it going?"

"Fine," I lie, plopping back down into my swivel desk chair. "Just doing some work."

"Still working on the new book from Jan Jenkins?"

"Yup."

"When does that come out again?"

"We're aiming for November, and she's already working on the next one."

"Oh, wow. That's great, honey. Your mom is beaming down on you. Well, I don't mean to interrupt, but I wanted to let you know that we're all set for Brant Point Grill for the rehearsal dinner on the twentieth."

"Huh?" I swallow a sip of coffee, now lukewarm. "How did *that* happen? I thought they were booked until 2020?"

"Pops gave them a call." Ah. So my grandfather threw money at the problem.

"Look, that's sweet of Pops, but I told you Burke and I are more than fine with another venue—something more low-key—especially since it's such a quick turn-around. We could even do it at the house."

"Your grandmother feels strongly that the location for the rehearsal dinner should be different from the wedding venue."

"Of course she does." I sigh. My grandmother can barely remember Burke's name, but when it comes to the planning of her granddaughter's wedding, she's more lucid than she's been in years.

"Just go with it, Skye. You know it's not worth going against Gammy in these situations."

"I just feel bad. Clearly another wedding had reserved Brant Point that night, a couple who probably planned their wedding two years ago. I hate how Pops pays people off like he's the Nantucket Mafia. I know he's coming from a 'place of love' or whatever, but it makes me feel like a brat. And it's not important, anyway. I don't understand why he and Gammy have to hijack the wedding planning."

"Skye." My father exhales, and I picture him pinching his sinuses. "Just give them this. Please."

My dad is a man of few words, but I know what he means. *Your grandparents lost their daughter. Just let them spend as much money as they want giving their granddaughter the wedding their daughter would've given her.*

I sigh, defeated, picking at the cuticle of my thumb.

"Another option is pushing the wedding back until next summer," my dad continues. "That gives you—and your grandparents—more time to lock down venues. And . . ."

"And what, Dad?"

Telepathically, I dare him to say it: *And more time to get to know Burke before you commit to spending the rest of your life with him.*

"Nothing, Skye," he says quietly.

"Dad, you know Burke and I just want to get married. That's what matters to us. We don't want to wait another eighteen months—neither of us is interested in having a long, stressful engagement. Just—just tell Pops and Gammy that Brant Point sounds great. I'll call and thank them."

"Okay." I can tell my father has more on his mind, but whatever it is isn't for me to know. He's never been good at being emotionally open—that was always Mom's forte. She used to say that getting my dad to talk about his emotions was like prying open a cold clam.

After I hang up with my dad, I edit another three chapters of the new *Loving Louise* before falling into the black hole of online wedding-dress shopping. I cut myself some slack—I'm ahead of schedule on edits for Jan's book, and I need to find a dress. According to Lexy, most bridal stores have at least a six-month turn-around time for dresses, and I'm already going to have to rush-order whatever I end up choosing.

But I have no idea what I want. I think about my

friends. Lexy is definitely the most fashionable. Andie's look is too anorexic Brooklyn hipster for me these days, and Isabel's has always been too J.McLaughlin.

I go to Lexy's Instagram profile and scroll down to find pictures of her wedding from the previous summer. I don't have to scroll far; @lexyblanehill has posted a wedding photo for every month she's been married.

Still not over it. Happy eight months, my love, reads her caption from a post on March 23.

A month before that: *Seven months with the love of my life. I still pinch myself.*

Another month before that: *Six months with @matt hill4. Life is a dream.*

You get the gist.

Lexy's wedding dress is stunning—a strapless Mira Zwillinger sheath with delicate organza flowers that hugs her body in all the right places. I frown. I don't have the arms to pull off strapless.

I check Isabel's profile next. Iz's Instagram etiquette is the opposite of Lexy's, as in she barely uses social media. Her wedding was three summers ago—she was my first close friend to get married—but she posts so rarely that I only have to scroll through a few pictures to find one from her wedding day in 2016. Unlike @lexyblanehill, who updated her Instagram handle to reflect her married name upon exiting the church, @izwaterman has not yet incorporated Maguire, her married name, into her online persona. I'm a tad jealous of Isabel's blasé indifference toward social media; I wish I didn't have the impulse to check Instagram all the livelong day, a habit that makes Burke roll his eyes. At forty-six, Burke's generation missed the roller-coaster ride of coming of age online.

The dress Isabel Waterman wore to become Isabel Waterman Maguire is a poufy collection of tulle and lace that would look ridiculous on my five-foot-eight frame. But on petite Isabel it's perfect; with her sandy-blond hair swept back into a stylish bun, she looks like a confection.

I sigh, hopelessly resorting back to Pinterest, which sucks me in for another hour. Burke is still at WeWork by the time I need to leave for dinner with my brides-maids, which Lexy has organized at Charlie Bird.

The four of them are there when I arrive—Andie, Lexy, Isabel, and then Kendall, my closest friend from college. My sister-in-law, Brooke, is also in the bridal party, but she and my brother live in San Francisco. They met junior year at Berkeley and have been together ever since. Brooke grew up in Marin County, and her whole family lives in Northern California. They don't come back East much anymore.

Iz and Kendall are deep in conversation at the table while Lexy tries to coerce Andie into taking a selfie, no doubt for her Instagram stories. I watch Andie feign annoyance, but I know she secretly loves to pose, the way she pouts her pink lips to further sharpen her cheek-bones.

"*Eeeeee!*" Isabel squeals, and stands when she sees me. "The bride is here!"

"Hi, ladies!" I make my way around the table to give each of them a hug.

Andie looks vaguely uncomfortable; it's the first time

we four childhood friends have all been together since my engagement, and I can tell it bothers her that she's the only one of us without a ring. Kendall isn't married or engaged either, but she isn't in our group of four, so it's different.

Someone has ordered a bottle of champagne, and once it arrives at the table, we get down to business.

"The first thing I think we should discuss is the hashtag," Lexy says, flipping her dark hair, which she's recently cut to her shoulders. "Do you have one, S?"

I can feel Andie rolling her eyes.

"Umm—"

"Because I was thinking #burkeisskyehigh. Clever, right?"

"Sure."

"Great. Now for your bachelorette, we're a little crunched on time since there are only five months till the wedding, but I think that's still enough to plan something cool. I was thinking the Azores. Maybe Tulum." Lexy looks at me. Her eyelashes are almost comically long—she's religious about her biweekly extensions—but she pulls it off.

"Lex, I don't know." I take a sip of champagne. "I was maybe thinking of forgoing the whole bachelorette thing."

"What!" Lexy looks incredulous. "You can't do that. The bachelorette is the *best*. Every bride needs one."

For hers, Lexy took twenty girls to a rental house on Harbour Island in the Bahamas, where she also chartered a full-service catamaran. In total the three-day weekend cost over two thousand dollars a head, and

even though the money wasn't an issue for me personally, I knew several others—particularly Andie—were
hit hard by the price tag.

"A Nantucket wedding in September is already an
expensive ask." I make a point not to look at Andie. "I
really don't want everyone spending too much, especially on short notice."

Lexy sighs. "Skye, fine, we can discuss this later.
Next on the agenda is the *band*. Do you have one?"

"Hey, Mussolini," Isabel interjects. Because Lexy's
Italian, Mussolini is what we call her when she's being
particularly overbearing. "You do realize as a bridesmaid your job is *not* to coordinate Skye's entire wedding? Besides, *Andie* is the maid of honor and *she's*
supposed to plan the bachelorette."

"I'm just trying to be *helpful,* Isabel." Lexy scowls.
"Do you know how far in advance people reserve the
band these days? Her wedding is only five months
aw—"

"Guys!" I raise both hands. "Stop. I have a wedding
planner and we're in the process of booking the band.
And, Lex, you're right that the timeline is tight. I get it."

"I think it's romantic," Isabel hums. "Like the olden
days when couples fell in love and got married quickly
because the man was going off to war."

"Right, but there is no war at the moment," Andie
murmurs, her voice thick with sarcasm.

"That's not entirely true," Kendall points out, and
everyone turns toward her in surprise. A global history PhD candidate at Columbia, Kendall is by far the
most intellectual of my five bridesmaids, and I watch

the others nod in silence as Kendall explains that the United States is currently involved in wars in Afghanistan, Pakistan, Somalia, Syria, Libya, and Yemen.

The waitress comes by, and Lexy orders another bottle of champagne. I watch Kendall twist a lock of strawberry-blond hair around her pointer finger and worry that she thinks my oldest friends are super-basic. I shoot her an appreciative grin. I've always valued her sharp intellect—the two of us can talk about politics and books together to a degree that I can't with my other friends. At the same time, I worry that my friends from home think Kendall is a pretentious know-it-all. I worry that Andie probably wishes she were anywhere else but here, celebrating an engagement she doesn't support. Maybe I should've made Lexy maid of honor. At least she clearly *cares.* Also, maybe I worry about my friendship dynamics too much.

I slip my phone out of my bag underneath the table and text Burke: *Bridesmaid drama [[rolling-eye emoji]].*

He texts back a minute later: *Haha. Isn't that inevitable? Don't worry, whatever the drama is I'm sure they're all coming from places of love.* Then: *And remember, all that matters is you and me.*

My heart swells with love for Burke, for his ability to always know exactly what to say to make me feel better.

When I look up, my four best friends in the world are staring at me.

"What on your phone could *possibly* make you smile

that big?" Isabel teases. "Can't go one dinner without texting your husband?"

"Fiancé," Andie corrects, and I make the mistake of meeting her gaze. She doesn't finish the thought out loud, but I can hear the rest inside her head, behind the hardness in her eyes:

He's not your husband yet.

Chapter Fourteen

Burke Michaels's Diary

DECEMBER 20, 2018

Dear Dr. K,

Merry Christmas, doc. I know it's been a minute since my last entry—sorry about that. But I've been busy. I'm jolly as an elf this year, and I'll tell you why. That plan of mine? It's *working*.

Skye Starling is sweet and beautiful and not a hard girl to pretend to love. She's more or less perfect, actually, aside from her peculiar OCD compulsions.

As planned, two months ago I told Heather that with Oliver's help I'd gotten a tempting job offer in Dubai. I explained it was an eighteen-month contract for a position that, after a two-month training period, would pay six times what I could ever expect to make in the United States, given my unfortunate record.

I'd known Heather would be floored by the prospect of us living on different continents, but I wasn't surprised when her eyes filled with tears and she told me to take the job. She agreed it was the right financial decision for our family, and that some space might not be the worst thing for our marriage. I promised to come back every few months to see her and the kids.

So off I went to Dubai—aka Crown Heights, Brooklyn. I found a decent sublet near Prospect Park for just $750 a month. It was the cheapest place I could find that was not an actual dump; I figured if Skye ever decided she wanted to see my place in Brooklyn, I couldn't be found living in squalor. My roommate is a guy named Ethan in his mid-thirties who does Big Law in midtown and is almost never home.

But I only have ten more days in Crown Heights, Dr. K, because the plan is right on schedule. On January 3, the day after Skye and I get back from spending New Year's with her family in Palm Beach, I move into Skye's spacious one-bedroom in the West Village. It wasn't hard to convince her; in fact, no convincing was needed. Earlier this month, I simply suggested we move in together. I told her that even though we'd only known each other three months, I'd never been so sure of anything in my life. I told her I was in love with her.

Skye's cinnamon-brown eyes had grown shiny and round, and color flushed her cheeks as she nodded fervently and buried her face in my neck. *I love you, too,* she'd whispered against my chest. I knew she'd fallen as fast as I pretended to.

Skye owns her apartment—it belonged to her grandparents before they gifted it to her—so I won't have to put a penny toward rent. It'll be *ours,* Skye said to me the other day. *Ours for the life we're building together.*

It's not that there's no part of me that feels guilty, Dr. K. I'm not a psychopath. I just know that, in the long run, Skye will be fine. She'll get past this unfortunate chapter. It might take a little while, but she'll eventually meet someone else who'll make her deliriously happy, and they'll have lots of little towheaded babies and all the money they could ever want. In the long run, my payout won't make a dent in Skye's family fortune. Would it be easier if we bypassed all the emotional destruction and I told Skye exactly what I needed and she cut me a check, no strings attached? Of course. But that's not the way the world works, Dr. K.

My point is, Skye will still live happily ever after. But Heather and me? Without this plan, we don't stand a chance. We won't be able to afford Maggie's college tuition when the time comes, and Hopie will spend the rest of her life wearing dental flippers. I'll have to get a job at Target, and we'll be forced to sell the house, and I'll wake up every morning next to a wife who feels nothing but disappointment and lost hope when she looks at me, until one day we're both dead. People always say money doesn't buy happiness, but that's bullshit and you know it, Dr. K. If it didn't, you'd take insurance.

What money *can't* buy is love—that's indisputable. I didn't choose to love Heather, and she'll be the first to tell you that she didn't choose to love me. After we got back together the summer before senior year, I asked her all the time why she gave me a second chance. Our love seemed like a miracle, especially after the agony of being apart. But Heather would never answer. She'd always say that she couldn't explain why she loved me, that it wasn't something she could spell out, that it just *was*.

All I know is that it still just *is*, Dr. K. That I would

do anything to give my wife what she needs to be happy. That my own happiness depends upon hers.

There was a time when Heather and I were building a life together, too. We'd finally clawed our way out of Langs Valley, out from under the crushing weight of the lives into which we'd been born, which promised us nothing. We moved to New York, just as Heather had always dreamed. I knew that if I stuck with her, I'd be all right. I would've followed her anywhere.

We worked hard in New York, earning our future. But then I fucked it all up, Dr. K. I made a mistake. After everything we'd done to beat the odds stacked against us from the start, I made *one* mistake. People like Skye Starling—people who are born with the odds in their favor—they can make as many mistakes as they want and never pay for a single one.

Still, I take responsibility for what happened to my marriage, that's what I'm trying to say. And if there's one thing I've learned, it's that if you can find a way to make things right, you do it. And if screwing over a desperate, privileged girl is the price, so be it.

Chapter Fifteen

Heather

APRIL 1990

A week after Easter, Libby made me a serious offer.

It was a mild April evening, and Libby and I had put the kids to bed and were sitting on her back patio drinking wine. The groundhog hadn't seen its shadow that year, and sure enough, spring had come early after a particularly tumultuous winter.

"I've been thinking about something, Heath." Libby placed her glass down and pulled her knees into her chest. She tucked her chin into the crook between them, which made her look so much younger. "I want to take Gus when you leave for school next year."

"I can't ask you to do that," I replied automatically.

"I don't mean *take* him, like, permanently take him. But I want to give him a home while you're away so you can fully immerse yourself in school. He can come live with us in Connecticut. We're in one of the top school districts in the state, and he'll just be starting first grade. And in full transparency, we have more than the means to support him. There's a good deal of money on my father's side of the family—the Fontaine side—which I've inherited. I don't mean to sound tacky, I just want to assure you it wouldn't be a burden on us financially, or in any way, for that matter. And you'd still see him all the time, we'd make sure of it. I've thought this through, Heather. And you didn't ask. I offered."

"Oh, Libby." I watched the smile blooming on her pearly, moonlit face. Finally, the mystery of the family's seemingly limitless wealth had been revealed to me. I momentarily let myself imagine how incredible, how liberating, it would be if some huge amount of money out there had my name on it, that I could claim by simply being born who I was. "I don't know what to say."

"Just say yes, Heather. You know Gus is like a son to me. And we can't let him stay here with your fath—" Libby paused. "You know what I mean."

"No way am I leaving him here with my dad." I nodded. "I figured . . . I guess I figured I would take him with me. But if you're—"

"I'm sure, Heather."

"Peter, too?"

"Peter, too." She grinned. "And I know it's not for over another year, but I figured—with college on your mind in a real way these days—it was probably something you'd been worrying about. Or something you'd start worrying about soon. So I wanted to put it out there."

"I mean, on one hand I can't imagine living day to day without Gus." I sipped my wine. "For the last five years, he's basically been my child."

"I know." Libby nodded. "And he always will be, in a way. You raised him."

"But I also know that I could never turn down your offer to give him the life he deserves."

"And the life *you* deserve, Heather."

"And then, after I graduate—"

"You'll get a great job, Gus will be . . . let me think . . . ten. And he can go back to living with you, if that's what you want. We can figure it out when the time comes. I guess we'll have to see what's on the horizon with your career."

A colder breeze swirled through the porch, and I rubbed my arms over my thin cotton shirt. "Oh, Lib. I'll never be able to thank you enough for the way you've changed my life. And Gus's life."

"Don't thank me, Heather. I've seen your potential, and it's our job as human beings to bring it out in each other. Do you know how much I admire your ambition? Too many women these days are cavalier about their careers—they just count on the fact that they'll meet a husband who will make all the money."

"Mm." I wondered briefly if she could read my mind, if she knew I had the exact same ambition.

"Though my grandmother did always say, 'It's just as easy to marry a rich man as a poor man.' " Libby chuckled. "And then I went and fell in love with a starving artist."

"Well, it was different for you. You knew you'd never have to worry about money."

"I suppose you're right. Peter could've done anything with that math mind of his. He's really brilliant. He could've made a killing in finance—that's where all the money is. But, in his *soul,* all he ever wanted was to make his art. He never cared about the money piece. I think that's why I fell for him. Most men I knew—the men in my family included—were so driven by money, by the status the 'right' job provided. I'd never seen passion like Peter's.

"Not that it's a bad thing to be money driven," Libby added quickly. "It can be quite the opposite. But Peter was just so *different* than anyone I'd ever known. He told me I was his muse. His whole way of being enticed me."

"Honest question for you, Lib." The wine struck a warm confidence through my bones. I felt sure that I could say almost anything without offending her. She was rich and beautiful and educated and articulate, but she was also silly and humble and as open as the ocean. "Playing devil's advocate here, but do you think your financial . . . situation . . . allowed Peter the freedom to continue to be the passionate man you loved?"

Libby pressed her lips together in thought, gazing out over the dark meadow that stretched beyond the backyard. She plucked the bottle of wine from the side table and poured what was left into our glasses.

"To be honest, I don't know," she replied finally. "My family money has certainly allowed him to keep being an artist. If we'd needed money and Peter had been forced to take a higher-paying job, I don't believe our love would have changed. I believe he would have done so willfully, and I believe he would've remained passionate at heart. But the truth is, Heather, you never really know. You hope for the best, but when you commit to a marriage, it's always a risk. You can never truly predict what's going to happen when you take two people and tie them together and blindly throw them out into the great big world." Libby looked at me, the whites of her eyes shiny in the near darkness. "For example, passion means one thing when you're twenty-two and in the honeymoon phase, and another when you're thirty and married with babies."

"What do you mean?" I asked, deeply curious.

"I still love Peter's passion." She sighed. "But I didn't know it would be like this."

"Like what?"

Libby stretched her skinny arms toward the sky. "Oh, that being Peter's wife would mean learning to be okay with the fact that my husband spends fifteen hours a day, six, sometimes seven days a week closed off in his studio, making sure every tiny detail of every single one of his pieces is entirely perfect. That the passion I fell in love with has become a quality I sometimes have to work not to resent."

"I guess I always assumed he was extra busy because of the project here in Langs Valley."

"He is, but there's always some project, and it's *always* this important. Peter had been feeling uninspired in Connecticut and felt like my parents were around too much since we'd had kids, so I promised him a year up north after our second was born. He grew up visiting an aunt who lived in Saranac and had always wanted to come back to the Adirondacks and do a mountain study. But his schedule is just insane. The ironic thing is, I constantly find myself thinking about the fact that it doesn't have to be this way, that he could work twenty-five hours a week and spend so much more time with the kids and me."

"Can't you say anything to him about it?"

"I have." Libby shrugged. "But whenever I do, I can see it just makes him so . . . *sad*. Because this is who he is, through and through. He's an artist, not a part-time artist. And I knew that when I married him. I don't know, I get so confused. He is a good father—he spends time with the kids every day. It's mostly *me* I wish he'd make more time for. Especially because sub-consciously I know that if he worked less, it wouldn't make a speck of difference." Libby rubbed her thumb against her first and middle fingers. "Don't get me wrong—he does fine for himself, much better than a lot of artists in his field. But with the amount in my trust, it's just completely insignificant." Libby glanced down into her empty glass. "Gosh, I've had too much wine and now I'm sounding like a total brat. I'm so sorry, Heather, you must think I'm a—"

"Lib, stop," I interjected, fueled by the alcohol again. "You're allowed to vent to me—we're friends. I'm not lying when I say you've become one of the best friends I have." I omitted the full truth, which was that Libby had become my *only* friend. Kyla and the other girls didn't talk to me anymore, and I couldn't blame them. I was the one who'd cut them out in the first place, right after I'd ditched Burke. The only way I knew how to move forward with my plan was alone.

"Heather." Libby reached for my hand and squeezed my palm. "You have no idea how lonely I'd be here with-out you. You are my *dear* friend, and that's not just the wine talking. I feel very lucky that we met."

"I feel lucky too, Lib." A soft feeling—happiness, perhaps—washed through me.

In retrospect sometimes it's barely believable, the extent to which things changed. The twisted irony of it all. Not two months later I'd learn that meeting Libby Fontaine was the unluckiest occurrence of my life. But by then, it would be too late.

Chapter Sixteen

Skye

Lexy convinces me to have a "low-key" bachelorette party in the Hamptons. I made my friends promise that if I agreed to do a bachelorette, there'd be no fuss around my thirtieth birthday in July. Lexy has arranged for us to stay in her dad's house in Amagansett; Lexy's parents are divorced and her father spends almost all of his time with his second wife at their place in Charleston.

The last weekend in June, eight of us board the Jitney from midtown on Friday afternoon and head east. In addition to my bridesmaids I've also invited Kate, Sophia, and Taylor, my three other closest friends from Barnard, all hallmates from freshman year. Brooke was supposed to fly east for the weekend, but she called to tell me she's eight weeks pregnant and having awful morning sickness. I'm not allowed to share the news yet, but my toes have been tingling ever since I found out she and my brother are having a baby. I'm going to be an aunt.

Lexy's father's house is a shingle-style mansion just past the town of Amagansett, half a mile from the beach. It's offensively large and well maintained for being used so rarely, even in the prime summer months. Mr. Blane doesn't rent it out, partly so that Lexy and her younger sister, Bridget, can use the house as they please, but mostly because he doesn't need to.

Being defined by her family's money doesn't *bother* Lexy the way it bothers me. For better or worse, Lex doesn't have a problem with not actually having a career. Her "job" is essentially the Instagram presence she's created with her hunky kiteboarder husband as they travel the world on her father's dime in pursuit of new content to grow their following.

We could be the next Helen Owen and Zack Kalter, I've heard Lexy muse on more than one occasion. The claim is outrageous on so many levels that it's not even worth the attempt to pull Lexy back down to earth. She's a dreamer and a dilettante through and through, but she's also the most fiercely loyal person I know. In addition to punching Sasha Bateman in middle school, when Lexy overheard Hilary Mandeville telling people I belonged in a mental hospital, Lexy whacked her in the shins during field-hockey practice and got suspended from the team for the rest of the season. When the shit with Max LaPointe went down, Lexy publicly shamed him to her tens of thousands of Instagram followers. I didn't ask her to, but this is the quintessential Lexy Blane Hill reaction when anyone wrongs one of her friends.

Still, Andie is the only one I can roll my eyes with at Lexy's constant over-the-topness; Isabel is too non-confrontational, and my college friends don't know Lexy well enough to remotely understand why she's posing in front of her pool in a yellow Kiini one-piece five minutes after we get to the Amagansett house.

"Friday evening is one of the best times to post," Lexy explains as she cocks one hip and purses her lips in front of Isabel, who is dutifully snapping iPhone pictures from Lexy's chosen angle.

After she takes twenty minutes to filter, caption, and upload, Lex shows each of us to our bedrooms. Andie and I are sharing, as well as Lex and Iz, and the others get their own rooms, which I'm happy about. I want everyone to be as comfortable as possible.

Everyone agrees that the house is insane and thanks Lexy profusely for hosting.

"Are you kidding?" Lexy waves her hand. "I would do anything for this girl." She circles her arms around my waist and squeezes.

I can sense Andie's annoyance at Lexy as Andie stomps off to the kitchen to start cooking. Iz and I join her while Lexy gives Kendall, Kate, Sophia, and Taylor a tour of the rest of the house.

We've decided to have a low-key dinner tonight and make Saturday our big night out on the town. On the menu is spaghetti and meatballs—simple, but one of my favorite meals—and kale Caesar salad. It's a warm summer night, and we eat outside on the terrace overlooking the Blanes' pristine turquoise swimming pool.

The dinner conversation is heavily based around engagements and marriage and babies in a way it would never have been two years earlier. Kate is four months pregnant and says that giving up wine has by far been the hardest part. Isabel has recently started taking prenatal vitamins, and Lexy says she and Matt will likely start trying to get pregnant within the next six months. I try to catch Andie's eye across the table—Andie and I have only been half joking when we've agreed that a large part of the reason Lexy wants a baby is so she can post about it on Instagram—but Andie is gazing down into her barely touched plate of pasta. I realize then that out of the eight of us, only Andie and Kendall aren't married or engaged. Sophia got married in May and is doling out loads of wedding advice, and Taylor got engaged shortly after I did.

Kendall is too self-assured and career driven to worry about her unmarried status, but I know Andie well enough to be able to tell that she doesn't want to be grouped off as one of the only two single girls in the group.

Not that Andie is single—she isn't. Andie has been with Spencer forever, but without a diamond on her left ring finger she's on the outside of something that the rest of us aren't. And I can tell she doesn't like it one bit. As I watch her mix another tequila soda, I can almost feel the way she desperately misses her Williamsburg yogi friends, the ones who frequent Brooklyn Steel and are years away from investing in fertility vitamins.

I feel it in the bed we share that night, too, the disconnect in the silence between us as we itch for sleep. I can read the thoughts blazing through her mind beside me: *I have been with Spencer for eight years. Skye has been with Burke for nine months. None of this makes any fucking sense.*

The next day Andie wakes up in a cheerier mood. After breakfast she leads us in a group yoga session out by the pool. Post-Savasana, poor Taylor is tasked with snapping shots of Lexy doing Warrior II in her Bandier workout garb, a matching bra and leggings set in a blinding shade of magenta. Once a winning photo has been chosen and posted, we pack a cooler and head to the beach.

It's a beautiful Saturday—one of those flawless summer days when the sun is whole and drenching, not a speck of cloud in the robin's-egg-blue sky. Andie has given me a white one-shoulder Marysia bikini for the occasion; I know it was an expensive gift for her, so I wear it even though I hate being in a bikini around Andie and Lexy and Sophia, my thinnest friends. It's not that I dislike my body—I run and work out enough to stay fit. It's just that I know I'll never look the way some girls do—the way my own waif of a mother did—no matter how many miles I log at the gym. Genetics were kind enough to give me Mom's face, but I unfortunately inherited my grandmother's broad shoulders and curves.

We spend a few blissful hours at the beach, sunbathing and drinking Whispering Angel while Lexy continues to document it all. The Marysia bikini bottoms are digging into my hips, and I swallow annoyance toward Andie for getting me a size small when she knows I wear a medium.

When everyone is sunned out, we go back to the house to shower and play the special surprise game that Andie has planned. Lexy opens more Whispering Angel—she bought a whole case.

I'm not surprised that Andie's surprise game turns out to be Bachelorette Jeopardy. We played the game at both Isabel's and Lexy's bachelorettes, and it's hilarious. But more than that, Bachelorette Jeopardy is the perfect opportunity for Andie to publicly show just how little Burke and I truly know about each other. This part makes my stomach sink. This part—if I'm being honest—is the reason I was hesitant to have a bachelorette in the first place.

Andie has set up a poster board with SKYE'S BACH JEOPARDY in block lettering across the top, and on the second row underneath, five categories each heading their own column: BY THE NUMBERS, BABY BURKE, BURKE'S QUIRKS, BEDROOM BOUND, SKYE'S WORLD.

Andie stands up front by the board to explain the rules. She's showered and changed into a pale yellow maxi dress, her towel-dried hair twisted into a topknot, and she's wearing makeup. Her body is skinny and tan in the places I'm fleshy and sunburned, and any lingering guilt I feel for her relationship status evaporates. Perched on the couch in a red jumpsuit, Lexy is filming everything.

"Okay!" Andie claps her hands together and looks at Isabel. "Izzy, you start."

"Hmm." Isabel twirls a lock of sand-colored hair around her pointer finger. "Bedroom Bound for three hundred!"

"Iz!" Lexy whoops. "Someone's mind is in the gutter."

"I've been overserved!" Isabel lifts her glass and rosé sloshes over the rim and onto the floor.

"Shhh," Andie says. "Bedroom Bound for three hundred, here we go. The question is, 'What is Skye's favorite sex position?'" Andie gestures toward me. "Skye, you're up."

I exhale, grateful that the first question is something simple. "Girl on top."

Everyone hoots and hollers melodramatically.

Andie opens a folder on her laptop that says *SS BACH* and clicks on the file that reads *Bedroom 300*. She positions the computer so everyone can see, then she hits play. Burke's familiar face appears on the screen; he's sitting on the couch in Andie and Spencer's apartment, and a warmth spreads behind my collarbone at the thought of his secretly making the trip to Williamsburg to do this. He wears a blue button-down shirt that matches his eyes, and the hint of a laugh plays at the corners of his mouth. My Goose. He's so adorable I have to fight the urge to get up and kiss Andie's laptop screen.

"What is Skye's favorite sex position?" I hear Andie ask Burke.

He breaks into a full laugh, dimples appearing on either cheek. "Getting personal, are we, Andie?" He scratches his chin. "Skye likes being on top."

Everyone screams and claps. As relief dissolves through me, I swear I see Andie's expression harden.

"Next!" she calls. "Sophia."

Soph eyes the board, weighing her options. Half-Filipino, Sophia tans even more quickly than Andie, and a day in the sun has left her skin a rich shade of cider brown.

"Burke's Quirks for two hundred." Soph winks in my direction.

"Burke's Quirks for two hundred," Andie repeats, looking at me. "'What would Skye say is Burke's most annoying habit?'"

I rack my brain, trying to imagine how Burke answered the question. He knows I hate it when he leaves his wet towels lying on the furniture. I can't think of anything else.

"When he leaves his wet towels lying on the furniture?" I say it as if it's a question.

"*That's* the most annoying thing he does!" Kate exclaims. "God, you're lucky."

"All right, and here's Burke's answer." Andie opens the corresponding file and hits play.

On the screen, I watch Burke's face morph into a dazed expression. "Uhh . . ." His voice trails. "It bugs her when I forget to use the squeegee thing after I shower."

"No dice," Andie announces, victorious. "Kendall, you're next."

Kendall chooses By the Numbers for 300.

"'How old was Burke when he lost his virginity?'"

I guess sixteen. Burke's answer is fourteen.

Taylor chooses the next question: Baby Burke for 200.

"'When he was little, what did Burke want to be when he grew up?'" Andie asks.

I don't have a clue. I chug the rest of my rosé and guess astronaut. Burke's answer is policeman.

Kate chooses Burke's Quirks for 500.

"'What is Burke allergic to, if anything?'"

I say sunflower seeds; Burke answers latex.

"I guess you two never use condoms!" Taylor cackles.

I roll my eyes. We don't—we never have—but still, he's never told me he's allergic to latex. And I could've sworn he was allergic to sunflower seeds. Why did I think that?

I can feel the shift in Andie's energy; she's luxuriating in that I appear to know nothing about my fiancé. My heart is in my lap by the time Lexy chooses Skye's World for 100.

"Skye's World for one hundred," Andie chirps. "'What is Skye's favorite song?'"

"'River of Dreams,'" I mutter. I just want the game to be over. "Billy Joel."

Andie clicks on the matching file and Burke's voice fills the room: "'River of Dreams' by Billy Joel."

The group cheers, and I feel momentarily revived until the next question, Baby Burke for 400.

"'How much did Burke weigh when he was born?'"

"That's a hard one," Isabel says kindly, and I know she knows that I have no idea.

"Seven pounds, ten ounces?" I guess. "Something like that."

"Ten pounds, four ounces," Burke answers when Andie clicks play. "I was a *giant* baby. My poor mom."

I sink back into the couch, my stomach pooling with a feeling that resembles dread. Had Burke told me he'd been such a big baby? Had I simply forgotten?

The questions keep coming. What is Burke's least

favorite vegetable? I say broccoli; the answer is aspara-
gus. What kind of dog did Burke have growing up? I
guess golden retriever; the answer is none—a trick question. What is Burke's favorite TV show? I guess *The
Wire*; he answers *The Sopranos*.

The secondhand embarrassment in the room is palpable by the time we reach the last question.

"I'll read this one." Andie clears her throat. "Bedroom Bound for five hundred. 'What is Burke's biggest
sexual fantasy?'"

"*Yee*-haw!" Lexy jumps on the couch and mime-
throws a lasso while she humps the air. I can tell she's
wasted.

The other girls are looking at me, waiting. I sip more
Whispering Angel, grateful to whoever keeps topping
off my wine.

I have no idea what Burke's biggest sexual fantasy
is. We have what I would consider to be a good sex life—
fulfilling, fun, adventurous enough—but we've never
discussed our sexual fantasies. Somewhere underneath
the five thousand glasses of rosé I've consumed since
noon, I'm humiliated, but in this moment I'm suddenly
clouded with anger.

"I don't know." I glare at Andie. I hate her for making me feel this way, for taking pleasure in it. For ruin-
ing this perfect day with a stupid game that she used
to make her point: that Burke and I hardly know anything about each other because you can't actually *know*
someone in nine months, not enough to commit to marrying the person.

"Guess, then." Andie folds her bony arms across her chest, her hazel eyes piercing.

By now most of the others have lost interest in Bachelorette Jeopardy. Lexy is busy connecting her phone to the Bluetooth speakers, and Kendall, Soph, and Taylor are in the kitchen making margaritas. Only Isabel and Kate are still watching Andie and me.

"Do you know *Spencer*'s sexual fantasy?" I ask Andie. It comes out like an accusation, but I don't care.

"As a matter of fact, I do," Andie retorts sharply, and I wish I'd never asked. I suddenly realize that I'm acting exactly the way she wants me to.

"Fine," I say. "I'll guess Burke's answer. Threesome." I know it's wrong.

Andie hits play on the video. "Oh, boy." Burke laughs. "I guess I'd have to say getting tied to the bed."

"Ooooh!" Kate exclaims. "Now you know what to do on the honeymoon, babe."

I'm thrilled the game is over, but I can't help but notice the triumphant way Andie folds up the poster board and gathers the Jeopardy cards. It's something imperceptible to everyone but me.

Lexy has finally figured out the Bluetooth, and "River of Dreams" blares through the speakers. "Cheers to our sweet baby Skye!" Lexy whips out a small plastic baggie of white powder. "Any takers?"

"You know, for someone who wants to become a mother in the near future, you sure aren't showing very maternal instincts." Andie whisks the baggie from Lexy.

"Shut up, *Andrea*. This is my last hurrah. I might as well live it up while I still can."

"Amen." Kate cracks open a fresh seltzer and stifles a yawn. I've nearly forgotten that she's completely sober.

"I'm joking, Lex." Andie throws her arm over Lexy's shoulder. "Cut me a little one."

"That's the spirit. Who else?"

"I shouldn't." I never do coke anymore—none of us really do, except for Lexy—but I'm drained from all the sun and wine, and the offer is tempting. "Just a small one."

"Iz?"

Isabel purses her lips. "A *baby* line. But don't tell my husband."

Lexy rolls her eyes and cuts seven lines on the glass coffee table—none for Kate, obviously. When Kendall declines, Lexy and Andie split the seventh. I'd forgotten how Lexy brings out the party-girl side of Andie.

We Uber to Sotta Sopra, an Italian restaurant in town, to find that my dad has already prepaid for our dinner.

"That is so *sweet*," everyone sings in agreement.

After dinner we go next door to the Talkhouse, where a cover band is playing hits from the eighties. The Talkhouse always reminds me of being younger, of sneaking in here with Lexy before we were even legal because she knew the bouncers. And it reminds me of my earlier twenties, of the Max LaPointe years. Of being pressed against him near the back bar after too many vodka sodas, his hands running over the back of my jeans.

The band is fun; it's one I've seen before, and they play all the best eighties songs such as "Take On Me" and "Total Eclipse of the Heart." But something about being at the Talkhouse makes me feel old and nostalgic in a way that's unsettling. I take out my phone to text Burke, but I already have a message from him.

Miss you Goose. Don't have too much fun tonight!

I miss YOU. We're at the Talkhouse and there's music and it's fun . . . but I also just want to be home with you.

Tomorrow. Can't wait. I love you.

Love you more Goose.

I feel giddy with affection, wondering for the millionth time how I ever got through life without Burke. Warm, kind, dependable Burke, whom I love with every fiber in my body.

As I slip my phone back into my purse, it vibrates again, and I smile at the thought that Burke has more to say.

But it isn't Burke—it's an email from Max. A wave of anxiety slams my chest. I don't want to read it, but I can't not.

Hope you're staying out of trouble on the bach, psycho bride. How about a drink when you're back? You and me, for old times' sake. Your treat—God knows you owe me.

My insides roil with nerves and I shove my phone into my bag. I know I don't actually have a reason to be scared—Max still follows Lexy and Isabel on Instagram; of course that's how he knows it's my bachelorette weekend. It's not like he's stalking me.

Still, his message makes me feel shaky and sick, and I decide to go home in the first Uber around midnight, before Andie. She, Lexy, Taylor, and Soph have decided to stay out later, and I don't know what time it is when Andie slides into bed beside me. I wake to the smell of perfume, her trademark Fracas. She drapes her arm across my middle.

"I love you, Skye." Her breath is velvety against the back of my neck. "You're my person."

When I don't say anything back, Andie keeps talking. "Don't worry about that stupid game today. I just thought you'd want to play it because everyone else always does, but it's dumb."

I say nothing. I want her to think I'm asleep, but I know she knows I'm awake.

"And I don't know if you noticed, but every single question about you . . . Burke got all of those right. He really knows you. He loves you."

"Yeah," I whisper, realizing for the first time all night that what she's saying is true—*Burke* did answer the questions about me correctly. "I love him, too."

"I know." Andie nudges in closer, her forehead against my shoulder blade, and how is it that she comes back to me when she feels like it, apologizing without an apology in a way that immediately reminds me of how I love her more deeply than I will ever love another friend?

As we drift toward sleep, the tension between us evaporates, a block of ice melting, and it's as though it were never there.

Chapter Seventeen

Burke Michaels's Diary

FEBRUARY 7, 2019

Dear Dr. K,

Sorry it's been so long. It's hard to find the time and space to write, now that I'm living with Skye.

But let me tell you—things are gearing up. Next month I'm going to ask Skye to marry me.

There are just two hurdles, one of which I tackled just a couple of hours earlier at drinks with Skye's father.

Mr. Starling is an interesting man. I think he likes me well enough, but it's hard to tell. He's quiet. Skye says he got even quieter after her mother died in 2001, and he retired shortly after. I guess you can afford to stop working when your wife leaves you millions of dollars. Now he's remarried; I've only met the new wife a couple of times, but Skye isn't her biggest fan. I guess no one can ever replace your mom.

A few days ago, I sent Mr. Starling an email asking if we could set up time to meet for a drink. I know that, in families like theirs, it's protocol to ask the girl's father for his daughter's hand in marriage. Of course, I never asked Heather's father's permission to marry her, but that was a very different situation since at the time

Ernie Price was off on yet another bender, his exact whereabouts unknown.

Mr. Starling asked me to meet him at the New York Yacht Club, a few blocks from Grand Central. The place was sprawling and filled with stiff preppies, so I had to squint my eyes to find him in the mix. I spotted him at the bar. He wore a navy cashmere sweater and was hunched over a glass of Scotch, reading something on his phone. Disheveled but good-looking, he is a cross between a rigid New England WASP and a Black Sabbath groupie. He ran a hand through his tousled graying hair and looked up when he saw me.

"Have a seat, Burke." His voice was thin but gentle. "I ordered you a club soda. What can I do for you?"

This guy is not one for small talk, Dr. K, so I cut to the chase. I told him I was in love with Skye and wished to ask his permission for her hand in marriage. I said that even though it hadn't been long, I had no doubt that she was the girl of my dreams. I played the age card. I reminded him that I was forty-six—God, I feel like a creep sometimes, being forty-six in this scenario—and that I'd spent enough time on this planet to know what I wanted when I found it.

Mr. Starling peered at me through hooded eyes the color of rain, his jawline strong and square. For a moment, Dr. K, I swear I thought he was onto me. He's the kind of man who seems like he can sniff out a lie from a mile away, like a hound tracing blood. I was suddenly nervous.

"I think you're a good man, Burke," he said after a few moments. "Skye is an extraordinary young woman.

Complex, but extraordinary. I'm glad you see that." He smiled absently.

I nodded. "I do."

"If Skye decides she wants to marry you, I trust her judgment. You have my blessing, if that's what you came here for."

And that was pretty much it, Dr. K. He drained the rest of his Scotch while I attempted casual conversation, but I could tell he didn't want to linger or stick around for another. When I took out my one working credit card and offered to pay the bill, he looked at me like I'd spoken in a foreign tongue.

"They don't accept credit cards here, Burke. This is a private club. Our drinks will go on my tab."

It struck me, then, the irony that when you get rich enough, you don't even have to use money.

I left the New York Yacht Club somewhat disappointed. I'd hoped Mr. Starling might say something about a family ring—namely Skye's mother's ring, which I could only imagine he'd want his only daughter to have—but it hadn't been mentioned. And given his detached demeanor, I wasn't about to ask.

The truth is, Dr. K—as I'm sure you can believe—I can't afford an engagement ring. Therein lies hurdle number two.

But I have a new plan. It involves the ring I got for Heather, years ago.

The engagement ring I gave Heather is simple but beautiful, and I've always been proud of it. I didn't buy it until after we were married; we didn't have any money until I started at Credit Suisse, my first job out of college. I knew a ring was important to Heather, so I started putting aside a small portion of each paycheck. When I finally had what I thought was enough, I ventured to the Diamond District in midtown one day during my lunch break.

My grandmother had taught me my bargaining skills. *Never seem too interested,* Grams said. *Always act like you know what you're talking about, even if you don't.*

That afternoon I bought a vintage three-stone ring: a round-cut diamond in the middle framed by two sapphires on a platinum band. It cost me five thousand dollars, which felt like a good deal. The ring isn't anything *too* fancy—all three stones are just under two carats combined—but it's beautiful and unique, and I knew Heather would love it.

And she did. She cried when I surprised her with it that night, and she hasn't taken it off since. Even when she's so angry with me I swear she could rip my head off, she still wears that ring.

Anyway, back to my plan. It began to take shape in my head earlier this evening as I strolled back to the West Village from the New York Yacht Club in midtown. I needed the long walk to have a good hard think.

The key word here, Dr. K, is *moissanite.* In case you're not aware, moissanite is a rare mineral made of silicon carbide, and it's the best fake diamond in the business. The naked eye can't tell moissanite from a real diamond. Same deal with synthetic sapphires. But there *are* ways to note the difference, and something tells me that Skye and her crowd would be the first to figure it out.

Heather, on the other hand—bless her heart—probably doesn't even know moissanite exists. It would never even *occur* to her to suspect that I'd gone through the trouble of swapping her ring with a less valuable replica. A quick internet search reveals that plenty of custom-synthetic-jewelry designers are out there. All I have to do is send them a photograph of Heather's ring.

When I got home a couple of hours ago, Skye was already passed out, the clothes she'd worn to her work dinner sprawled messily beside the bed. Makeup coated her eyes, which told me she hadn't had the energy to wash her face. Skye had been tired lately, plus she tends to drink too much at these bimonthly dinners with the author whose book she's editing. She drinks too much in general, in my opinion. But in cases like tonight's, it works to my advantage, because the girl was out cold. So I opened up my laptop and decided to get right down to business. I can't exactly be wasting time, Dr. K. There's simply too much at stake.

I grabbed my phone and crafted a text to Maggie. I reminded my youngest daughter that I'd be coming home from Dubai in two weeks for a visit and asked if she could do me a favor regarding a surprise I was planning for Mom. I asked Maggie to stealthily take a good clear picture of Mom's engagement ring and send it to me. I told her it had to do with a belated Valentine's Day present I was bringing home.

Next, I researched custom jewelers. It's amazing, Dr. K; you can get *anything* on the World Wide Web. I'm pushing fifty and the internet continues to amaze me. From the looks of it, I'll be able to buy a moissanite and synthetic-sapphire ring identical to the one I gave Heather for just six hundred dollars. When I'm back in New Haven, I'll find a way to swap Heather's ring for the replica. Then I'll take the real ring back to the city and propose to Skye.

Now, I don't expect anyone to be *blown away* by the ring I give Skye. It's a modest piece of jewelry where the Starlings come from, I'm sure, but it's not my fault Mr. Starling didn't offer up his dead wife's rock. Besides, Skye isn't half as materialistic as you might imagine— I've even heard her say that true WASP style is understated and classic. The real significance of the ring is what it *means*. Skye is going to be over the moon when I propose. And that's all I need for this plan to work.

Sometimes I can't believe this is my life, Dr. K. All this scheming makes me bone weary, and I miss Heather something fierce. But you of all people know that love and risk go hand in hand, that marriage will push you to take leaps and bounds you never could've fathomed. You said so yourself in that interview on *The Huffington Post*. You emailed Heather and me the link to the article after our first session. I still have it bookmarked.

Chapter Eighteen

Heather

Libby and Peter were going to a wedding in Bermuda over Memorial Day weekend. Originally, I was going to stay home and look after the kids, but the week before Libby had a change of heart and asked Gus and me to come along.

"It'll be *fun,*" she said. "It's been such a mucky, rainy spring. We could all use a long weekend away from Langs Valley."

I didn't bother reminding her that I hadn't had so much as a night away from Langs Valley in years, not since my mom was still alive and we drove down to Philadelphia for her father's funeral. I also didn't tell Libby that I'd never been on an airplane, but I think she assumed as much when she showed Gus and me how to properly buckle our seat belts. Nate passed out almost instantly; I had the feeling this was far from his first time flying. But Gus's round eyes were a mix of fascination and fear throughout the whole flight, and I squeezed his chubby little hand.

"You're going to love Bermuda, Gussie," Libby said from across the aisle. "Some of the beaches have *pink* sand! And there are tons of fish to see in the water."

"Fishies!" Gus squealed. His eyes bloomed, the same green color as my own.

"Gus can't swim," I whispered to Libby.

"Ah." Libby nodded. "Well, this will be the perfect opportunity for him to take some lessons."

I left out that I couldn't swim, either. Never having been on an airplane was one thing, but I was genuinely embarrassed that I'd never learned to swim. Lakes and ponds were all around Langs Valley.

Bermuda was the most spectacular place I'd ever laid eyes on, I decided the minute we stepped out of the airport into the balmy sunshine. Tall palm trees lined the roads, their trunks reaching up into the sky and spilling open with lush green fronds. Gus stared up at them, speechless, his little mouth gaping in awe.

Libby and Peter's friends, the soon-to-be McCabes, were getting married at the Coral Beach Club, a private club where we also were staying because Libby's parents were members.

Every person at the Coral Beach Club was gorgeous and immaculately dressed, and I knew I stuck out like a sore thumb. My jean cutoffs and grubby tank were proof that I didn't belong here, and I knew that anyone who looked at the six of us would instantly pin me as the help.

Even in her clothes from the plane—white shorts and a red-and-white-striped shirt—Libby fit into the Coral Beach Club seamlessly. Everything about it was clean and tasteful and screamed old money, and I'd never felt further from Langs Valley. If getting to know Libby had been dipping my toes into a new way of life, both my feet were now submerged.

We were directed upstairs to our two-bedroom suite, which was decorated in bright colors and boasted a breathtaking view of the ocean, which was shiny like a coat of wet paint. Peter didn't even seem to register where we were and immediately went to take a shower. Gus kept grabbing my arm and pointing toward the ocean. It was the first time he'd ever seen it.

The first time (and one of the only times) I saw the ocean, I was six. My mom took me down to the Jersey Shore to visit her sister, my aunt Mel. I don't remember much about the visit except being wholly stunned by the vast, limitless sea, and the feeling of sand squishing between my toes. I built sandcastles on the beach with Mel's kids, my cousins, whose names I can't remember because I haven't seen them since. The day we left, I remember Mel handing my mom a folded piece of paper—in retrospect it must've been a check—and telling her to be careful with it because Mel wasn't going to give her any more. That was the last time I saw Aunt Mel, too, though my mom used to talk about her a lot.

Libby said she was going to lie down and asked if I'd give the kids their baths before we all went downstairs for dinner. I was sort of annoyed at Libby for not telling me how fancy the club was—I hadn't packed anything nice, except for my one dress skirt that had gotten too short for me.

"You can borrow a dress if you need, Heath," Libby

said, reading my mind. "I totally forgot to tell you to bring a dress or two, and I bet we're the same size."

"That would be great, thanks." I realized then that Libby probably hadn't forgotten to tell me; she likely *knew* I didn't own anything remotely dressy enough for the Coral Beach Club, and she didn't want me spending my hard-earned money buying new clothes for the trip.

I felt glamorous heading down to dinner in a wrap dress of Libby's, silky and flamingo pink. As we followed the hostess through the dining room toward our table on the patio, I could feel the eyes of several men lingering on me. An irrepressible smile crept up my lips.

Dinner that evening was the most delicious meal of my life. On Libby's recommendation I ordered the softshell crabs and practically licked my plate clean. The boys were content with their chicken fingers, and the baby babbled happily on Libby's lap. At the end of the meal there was no bill; Libby merely told the waitress her parents' account number, and that was that. I'd only seen that before in movies, and I was struck by the irony: when you get rich enough, you don't even have to use money.

After dinner Libby and Peter headed to the welcome party for the bride and groom's guests, and I took the kids upstairs to get ready for bed.

The next day was sunny and even warmer, and we headed to the pool after breakfast. Libby was adamant about hiring a swim instructor to give Gus a lesson.

"The older he gets, the harder it's going to be for him to learn," she explained.

"Right." I nodded. A few of Libby's most glamorous-looking friends were sitting with us on nearby chaises; no way was I confessing the truth about my own inability to swim in front of them.

Libby took Gus to see about a lesson, and one of the friends turned to me, a deeply tanned woman wearing cherry-red lipstick.

"You are the prettiest thing!" she exclaimed. "I have a little sister about your age. She's starting college in the fall."

"Good for her," I said, caught off guard.

"So are you a friend of Lib's?"

"Oh, no. I'm her babysitter. I mean, I sit for her kids."

"*Got* it. That is so great. I used to babysit all the time when I was your age."

"You did?"

"Oh, absolutely. It's the best way to make extra cash." Red Lips smiled at me, one side of her painted mouth curling, and for the first time since I'd arrived at the Coral Beach Club, I considered that perhaps not everyone here had been born into families with CBC memberships. Perhaps more than I'd realized had fought their way in, had bared their teeth and made unthinkable sacrifices to be a part of this world. Suddenly, I felt less alone.

Libby reappeared a few minutes later holding a tangerine drink that resembled the rum punches she and Peter had had at dinner the night before, and that morning with brunch. I watched the way she clutched the glass with her slender fingers, the white rock of diamond that sparkled there. In a cream-colored bikini and jade-green sarong, she looked like a supermodel.

"So, Gus is starting his lesson now, and it ends at three. You can pick him up right over there." Libby pointed across the pool. She teetered slightly, and I wondered how many more rum punches she'd consumed since brunch. "It's all paid for, of course, including another hour lesson tomorrow morning at nine. Peter's already back in the room with the baby, and I've *got* to go shower and change for tonight." Libby giggled to herself, wobbling again. "Sorry, I—these things will *getcha*." She pointed to her glass. "Anyway, you're good with the drill for later? Room service for dinner, and dessert for Nate *only* if he eats his whole meal."

"Sounds good, Lib, I've got it covered. Thanks for doing this for Gus."

"Of course! And like I said, he's done with the lesson at three, so it would be great if you could splash around with the boys for a bit before dinner. You can see what kind of progress Gus made today. And if for some reason baby girl's not asleep by the time we head out, I'll bring her down to the pool in her chair."

My chest tightened as Libby turned to leave, and I knew I had to tell her. Of course I did. How had I ever thought it would be possible to spend a whole weekend in Bermuda with Libby and *not* tell her?

"Wait, Lib." My voice was small. "I have to—I have to tell you something."

She paused, pushing her sunglasses on top of her head. Something in her eyes—the way they wouldn't quite land on me—told me she was tipsier than I'd realized.

"I can't swim." As soon as the words escaped me, I

felt lighter. "I never learned. I'm sorry I didn't tell you before. I was—embarrassed."

"Oh, Heather." Libby reached out and squeezed my shoulder, her lips spreading into a sympathetic smile. "That's okay. Nothing to be embarrassed about, and please, don't apologize. You've been such a rock star this weekend. I'm so glad we decided to bring the kids, and you and Gussie. Isn't this place a dream?"

I nodded, grateful to Libby for changing the subject. "It's unbelievable. The most beautiful place I've ever been." I glanced beyond the pool, out toward the boundless ocean.

"You've got a *lot* more eye-opening trips ahead of you, Heather Price." Libby drained the rest of her cocktail and placed it on the patio table beside us. "I have no doubt about that."

Chapter Nineteen

Skye

SEPTEMBER 2019

I can't believe the wedding weekend is here. After six months of anticipating and planning everything in excruciating detail—from the guest list to the website to the paper stock for the invitation suite to the menus to the table assignments—it's strange to think that in a few days, it will all be over. Burke and I will be married. I've been waiting for this weekend my entire life; for the longest time it felt as if it would never come, yet somehow it's arrived too quickly.

I've always disliked the end of summer—the days leading up to the anniversary of Mom's death—but this year it's a relief to have made it to September. The slog of wedding planning is behind me; Jan's new book has gone to print and is slated for publication the last week of November. I'm partway through my first-round edits of her *next* book, but those aren't due until October when we get back from our honeymoon, and I can finish them on the plane. I purposely didn't take on any new clients in advance of the wedding, so that's all I have going on workwise. I'm feeling good. I'm feeling ready to get married.

The weather in Nantucket in September is chancy,

but it's where and when my parents tied the knot, so I'm willing to take the risk. Following in Mom's footsteps whenever possible is the one thing that makes me feel close to her even though she's gone. It's the reason I applied early decision to Barnard. It's why I've chosen a career in book publishing. It's the reason I refuse to give up Gammy's West Village apartment—the one my mother lived in after she graduated from college—even though I would kill to move somewhere with revolving doors in the lobby. I like to press my nose against the glass of the double-hung windows and look down onto West Eleventh Street after a productive day of editing and imagine Mom doing the same.

Burke says that even if it rains on our wedding day, it'll be fine, because rain means good luck. I don't believe that—I think that's something people say because there's nothing else remotely positive *to* say—but still, I appreciate my fiancé's optimism. It's one of the qualities I love most in him because I lack that innate cheeriness in myself. It's something I've always had to work for, but it comes so easily to Burke.

According to AccuWeather, though—which I've been checking every twenty minutes since we landed on the island this morning—the forecast for Saturday is far from rain. The app shows seventy-five and a big fat sun—no clouds—and if that's not good luck, then I don't know what is.

Everything is on schedule. Burke and I arrived this morning along with my dad, Nancy, Nancy's sons, my brother and Brooke, who's almost five months pregnant and has the cutest bump. We're all staying at Gammy and Pops's, where the wedding reception will take place.

The house is beyond incredible, I will say that. It's nearly forty acres of lush grasslands, wetlands, and woods, with views of Polpis Harbor and the ocean at almost every turn. There's a guest cottage, gatehouse, boathouse, and two moorings. Pops bought the estate back in the fifties, right after he sold F&C Pharmaceuticals, and no one can argue with him when he says it's the best investment he ever made. Just as he predicted, Nantucket real estate skyrocketed.

I can tell it makes my father sad to be here, and I hate that. I know that for him every corner of the island is filled with memories of Mom, and he's kept his distance since she died. He's certainly never been here with Nancy, and for a moment I'm racked with guilt imagining his pain. But I can't imagine getting married anywhere else in the world.

"I'm so excited to marry you," Burke says. The two of us are sitting on the balcony outside the bedroom that Gammy and Pops have designated as mine since I was little. Burke pours me more wine from the bottle on the table between us and gazes out at the expansive ocean. It's after dinner, and we told everyone we were exhausted and wanted to turn in early. In reality we just need some time alone before the chaos begins on Thursday.

"God, me, too." I pull my knees in toward my chest. "It's hard to believe that a year ago we were going on our first date."

"Hey, it's been more than a year. Our first date was September twelfth, and today's the eighteenth."

I grin. "At least one of us has a good memory."

"I couldn't forget if I tried, Goose." Burke looks at me, and I hold his gaze. I always do this with him—stare into his eyes as though I'm searching for something, as though the space beyond his irises contains the answers to every fear or uncertainty I've ever had. Mostly, looking into Burke's eyes just feels like home. They are my haven of blue, and they have been since we met.

When we lock each other's gaze like this, it almost always leads to sex. Burke pulls me into the bedroom and peels off my clothes. I love the moment before anything happens, when we're just naked together, the hum of electricity on our skin. Something feels so pure—almost holy—about being naked with someone you love, the person that you know you'll spend the rest of your life with.

I inhale the smell of Burke's warm skin, the familiar mix of soap and pine. He pins me down against the bed and then I feel him inside me, full and all-encompassing in a way that makes me lose my breath.

Afterward we lay tangled together in the sheets, limbs interlaced as we listen to the sound of crashing waves in the distance. Tomorrow is going to be a busy day, with the bridal party arriving and the clambake Gammy and Pops have planned on the beach. Then Friday is the rehearsal dinner and welcome party, and Burke and I are sleeping separately that night, per tradition. I wonder out loud if this is the last time we'll have sex as an unmarried couple.

"I don't think so," he says.

"You don't?" I prop up on one elbow and study the

details of his handsome face, the face I've grown to love with every ounce of my body. My *husband*. I truly cannot believe that in just three days, Burke will be my husband.

"No, I really don't." Burke's grin broadens until his dimples appear, then he rolls back on top of me, burying his face into my neck.

"Round two?" I laugh. "I don't believe it, old man." When Burke and I first started dating, we used to have sex twice in a row all the time, but that dwindled down after a month or so, and now we only do it a couple times a week. Burke will sometimes attribute his lower sex drive to his "advanced age," which makes me crack up. Burke is the youngest forty-seven-year-old I've ever met.

"You better believe it, lady," Burke growls below my ear. "Because this old man loves you more than anything in the world."

He presses his body against mine, and I clutch his warm back as a breeze rolls in through the open doors of the balcony, the salt air landing softly on our skin, the whole of our marriage on the horizon.

Twenty minutes later Burke is asleep beside me, and I check my phone for the first time in hours. I have more notifications than usual—twenty-two messages from the group text with my bridesmaids and several emails—but one name jumps out at me, a sock in the gut. It's him. Again.

My fingers tremble as I open the three new emails from maxlapointe1@gmail.com.

5:51 P.M.: *You never got back to me about that drink.*

8:02 P.M.: *It's rude to ignore someone, Starling. There are consequences for that kind of behavior.*

10:36 P.M.: *I'm not joking, Starling. Consequences.*

I stare at the words on the screen, my heart beating fast, and the fear inside me is suddenly swallowed by a force of sheer anger. I won't let Max take this from me—not my wedding weekend. He's already taken too much, and I refuse to give him this. I power off my phone and shove it in the back of a dresser drawer, underneath a stack of old T-shirts.

I lie down on the bed and close my eyes, listening to Burke's breathing beside me, deep and steady, willing the sound to calm me. But my mind won't rest. I don't know if it's Max or wedding nerves or just my paranoid brain, but I'm suddenly overcome by the feeling that something has to give, that my life as it stands can't possibly go on being this close to perfect. I sense the compulsion on the horizon before it's there, and as I make my way around the room doing my knocks on the various wooden objects—bed frame, nightstands, bookshelf, baseboards—I wish so bad my mother were here that I can barely stand it. When I'm finished knocking on all the wood, I slide into bed beside Burke and check the digital clock on the nightstand, which reads 11:11. I sigh, defeated again. I press my lips to the clock and kiss the time stamp on the screen eleven times, then touch it eleven times with my right hand, then my left. I grab Burke's phone from the bedside table and am about to do the same thing to his screen when the time ticks to 11:12. Air escapes my lungs; the knot loosens in the pit of my stomach. I'm safe, for now.

Chapter Twenty

Burke Michaels's Diary

APRIL 7, 2019

Dear Dr. K,

I've had a productive couple of days. If you can believe it, I'm currently in Langs Valley. I haven't set foot here since I left in '91, and now, twenty-eight years later, I'm back.

If you're wondering what the hell I'm doing in this dumpy, drug-ridden town—yep, still dumpy and drug ridden as ever—that's a fair question, and I'll get to it. But first let me backtrack.

I'm engaged, Doc. I popped the question a couple of weeks ago, and it went as seamlessly as a man could hope.

Thanks to FoolzJewelz on Etsy (five-star rating, 897 glowing reviews), I ordered a stunning moissanite and synthetic-sapphire replica of Heather's engagement ring for $625, tax and rush shipping included. All thanks to Maggie, who replied to my text with a close-up photo of the ring and a wink-face emoji.

After the proposal and subsequent celebratory brunch I planned with Skye's father and stepmom, Skye and I wasted no time on beginning wedding planning. Lucky for me, Skye is fully on board with a fall ceremony. It turns out her parents were married in September, and that's the time of year she's always envisioned for her own nuptials. It's a tight turnaround, yes, but we both agree that waiting until the *following* September feels unbearably long.

When Skye found out that September 21 was a Saturday, that sealed the deal.

"'Do you remember . . . the twenty-first night of September?'" she'd started singing, squeezing her fist into a pretend microphone. "It's *perfect,* Burke. That can be our wedding song."

It is rather perfect, Dr. K, because I do like that song.

Skye wants to have the wedding on Nantucket at her grandparents' estate, the same place her parents got hitched in the eighties. I still haven't been to Nantucket, but Skye says we can go next weekend to check it out—her grandparents have a private plane they take to and from Nantucket and Westport that she can use at her disposal. This is the kind of girl I'm marrying, Dr. K. A girl with a *private fucking jet.* I'm telling you, she's not going to miss a few million if I pull this off.

That's still a big *if,* Dr. K. Plenty of issues are still at hand. Like this: The other day Skye started jotting down her list of bridesmaids, and it hit me like a sock punch in the stomach—I will have to have groomsmen. I will have to have *guests.*

It's not that Skye is under the impression that I'm friendless; I've coerced my old roommate Ethan into grabbing drinks with us a couple of times, though I'm sure Ethan wonders why I've bothered to stay in touch. Skye and I have also gotten dinner with Todd. Todd's own infidelity means that he knows how to help a guy out. But I haven't told Todd about my master plan, and doing so is out of the question. He may be sleazy at heart, but he still has a reputation and a job to uphold, not to mention alimony payments. He isn't looking to make himself an accessory to a felony.

Skye believes me when I tell her I don't talk to my relatives in Phoenix as much as I used to. She believes me when I tell her that many of my close friends have left New York. She agrees that it's natural to lose touch with people as you get older. She believes me when I say that *she's* my best friend, that ever since we met, my other friendships have taken a backseat. She believes me because she feels the same. Most of the time it's just the two of us "getting drunk off each other," and that's the way we like it.

But this doesn't solve the issue of my groomsmen, Dr. K. I'll ask Skye's brother, yes, but that's standard protocol and doesn't exactly help my situation. Because unless you're a serial killer, you have friends—a handful of people who give your life meaning, whom you call up on their birthdays and think of when that song comes on the radio and ask to be in your wedding when you get married. The real Burke Michaels has plenty of friends, Dr. K. He's got Todd and the guys from PK Adamson. He's got Pat Larson and the other dads who coached youth soccer. He's got Fred Pike, Maggie's best friend's father, whom he used to hit balls with on the driving range most Saturdays.

But the other Burke Michaels does not have friends, and right now, I am him.

I hate this whole big two-hundred-person Nantucket wedding thing. If I had it my way, we'd lock it down at city hall in a single afternoon, then grab cheeseburgers, like Heather and I did all those years ago. But when I mentioned this idea to Skye—excluding the Heather part, obviously—she looked so horrified that I quickly pretended I was joking.

So I spent a few days mulling over my options, and that's precisely how I wound up in this crappy motel room in Langs Valley. I'm not religious, Dr. K, but Grams was a crazy Catholic, and I remembered this passage from the Bible she had taped to the window above the kitchen sink: *Remember the rock from which you were hewn*—Isaiah 51.

I lived with my grandma, you know? My dad was in jail and my mom was gone out West and I lived in that house as a kid, and I read that passage every day when I was rinsing the dishes or whatever, and it's always stuck with me. And now I know why.

I'd forgotten Langs Valley, Dr. K. It was easy to forget because no part of me wanted to remember, and Heather and I were always on the same page about that. But the thing is—and this was my lightbulb moment—to *remember the rock from which you were hewn* is to use your past to set yourself free.

I told Skye I was heading up north for a reunion weekend in the Adirondacks with some of my old buddies, guys I wanted to ask to be my groomsmen. The irony is, it wasn't exactly a lie.

When I arrived in Langs Valley yesterday afternoon, I wasted no time looking up my old buddy Andy

Raymond. Andy and I were co-captains of the varsity football team back in the day, before he developed a particularly bad crack habit and got replaced. I wasn't surprised to find that he still lives in Langs Valley—too many people get stuck here—and once I got his address, I knocked right on his front door. I know enough about drugs to know what an addict looks like when I see one, and let me tell you, Dr. K, Andy fit the bill. So did his wife—a woman named Shelly from Albany with flaming-red hair and giant pupils.

Andy was shocked to see me, but he remembered who I was as though it were just yesterday we were leading group sprints around the track. For him, it might well have been yesterday. For me, that was another lifetime.

I clapped Andy on the back and got straight to the point, spelling it out plainly. I told him what I needed and what I was offering. He said he knew four or five other local guys around our age who were desperate for some cash, one being my old pal Scott Lynch. I had Andy round them up.

It felt a bit sad, how little it shocked me to see that Langs Valley had been swallowed up by the ever-worsening opioid crisis. This poor town never stood a chance.

But here's the good thing about opioid addicts: compared to crackheads, they can almost pass for normal. I'd spent enough time high on rocks to know that it turns you into a twitchy, volatile creature if you're not careful. On the contrary, opioid addicts often look like your average Jack and Jill, and they tend to be quite functional. Sure, they might seem a bit smiley and numbed out, but so do lots of people at weddings. As far as drug addicts go, this is a relatively clean and presentable bunch.

I knew right away that Andy, Scott, and their friends would work just fine. They'll need to spruce themselves up a bit and commit to being on their A games for the wedding weekend, but my options are limited, and you've got to work with what you have, Dr. K.

So, in addition to Skye's brother, there you have my groomsmen: Andy and Scott, my "childhood friends from growing up in Phoenix"; Dave and Brandon, my "closest buddies from NYU"; Wally, my "only male cousin." They've each promised to bring their wives and act presentable and thoroughly believable in their roles for the weekend of September 21. Wally, who Andy assures me is the most articulate of the bunch, will serve as the best man, toast and all.

This arrangement comes at a cost. In addition to providing accommodations for all five men and their dates, I've promised them each $1,500 to see this thing through ($1,700 for Wally). They get half the money up front, and the rest after the wedding.

Andy was really into the whole thing and impressed with my plan in general; he said he genuinely understood the logic behind it, and that he would do anything to save his marriage with Shelly. It was nice to talk to someone about it, Dr. K, especially a guy like Andy from my side of the tracks, someone who knows where

I'm coming from. Andy even offered to secure a couple of "older guests" to play my aunt and uncle from Phoenix. For a small fee, with a cut for himself. Life isn't cheap, Dr. K. But you know that. It's why you charge such a whopping hourly rate.

But I'm looking at this as an investment. Paying off the groomsmen and a couple of wedding guests is going to be chump change in relation to the final payout. And in the meantime, I just have to keep my eye on the prize.

That's another issue I'm bumping up against. The millions of dollars I stand to make when all of this is said and done. I've spent so much time thinking through every elaborate piece of this plan; I don't know how I missed something so vital.

Here's what happened. When I was home in New Haven earlier last month, visiting my family for the first time since I left in October, Heather asked me why I hadn't been transferring payments to our Chase account from my new bank account in Dubai. *My new bank account in Dubai*—it took me a couple of moments to understand what she could even be referring to. I swear, Dr. K, in my new life as a domestic criminal, there's a hell of a lot to keep track of. Thank God for this fucking diary.

So, right. My fake bank account in Dubai where I'm receiving a salary from my fake job in the United Arab Emirates. *That* bank account.

I promised Heather I would get right on transferring the money as soon as I got back to Dubai, and she said that I'd better because the balance in our Chase account was getting low.

Now, this is the part I hadn't adequately formulated. In keeping my eye so firmly rooted on the prize, I'd forgotten that the prize would not actually be available until several months after my marriage to Skye in September. Possibly longer than that, because we all know legal shit takes forever. And in the meantime, I'd promised my wife steady payments from my new and improved salary.

I don't know what I was *thinking,* promising Heather those payments so far in advance. I'd nearly forgotten about it until yesterday, when I got back to my motel room after being at Andy Raymond's and saw a text message from Heather that froze my blood.

Where the HELL is the money you said you'd transfer? It's been over a month and nothing is coming in. Our refrigerator broke and I had to pay the guy to fix it and there's currently $71 in our Chase account.

I'm telling you, Doc, I can't catch a break. I barely slept last night, but somewhere between three and four in the morning I came to what I believe will be a solid solution.

Now that Skye and I are engaged, we have every reason to open a joint checking account. Couples do it all the time; presenting the idea certainly wouldn't be cause for suspicion. I've already been honest with Skye that I haven't had the greatest year financially. So, what I'll do is, I'll tell her I'm still waiting on several payments to come in from clients, but that in the meantime

I'm short on change to cover the cost of the groomsmen's custom tuxes along with some other wedding-related expenses. I'll explain that that's what made me think of proposing a joint bank account, which we'll probably want soon anyway.

I'll call Skye on my drive back to New York later today and present the idea. She's too crazy for me to question it.

APRIL 10, 2019

Dear Dr. K,

Ta-da! This morning, Skye and I officially opened a joint account at Bank of America.

I knew she'd be fully on board, and she is, so long as I promise to update the new direct-deposit information on our Con Ed, Spectrum, and National Grid accounts. Skye *hates* dealing with bills and bank accounts and numbers in general, which is perfect, because now she won't have to. I completed most of the paperwork while Skye scrolled through Instagram, oblivious. Once everything was finalized and I saw the numbers—the amount of money in *my* own checking account—I nearly collapsed in front of the teller.

After we left the bank, Skye headed home and I made my way to the "WeWork" I supposedly work from, actually a coffee shop on the Upper West Side called JoJo's with Wi-Fi and free refills. I don't always come to JoJo's—sometimes I opt for a different cafe. Sometimes I go to a museum or to the movies or take the subway to Brooklyn and walk until it's time to head

home to Skye. But today I sit in JoJo's thinking about
the numbers in my bank account and how *I* made that
happen, and it's really something, Dr. K. I think about
how I'm going to proceed from here.

Now, I can't exactly transfer money to Heather's
account from mine and Skye's; I doubt Skye would
notice, but still, it's too risky to keep a paper trail. So
I'll opt for another route. If I space out my withdrawals, if I take out just $1,750 every week, that means I
can manually deposit $3,500 into Heather's Chase ac-
count twice a month. That's more than double what I
was bringing in at PK Adamson, and it'll be plenty to
tide Heather over until the real money hits.

Even if at some point Skye *does* notice the withdrawals, I can say it's wedding related. I can say it's money
I used to buy her a wedding present, and that I'd paid
in cash to ensure a surprise. But trust me, she's not going to notice. With the magnitude of our account balance and all the wildly extravagant transactions being
made in advance of the wedding and honeymoon, Skye
would have to be looking for something to notice an extra seven grand a month.

Off to the bank now. Wish me luck.

APRIL 12, 2019

Dear Dr. K,

In the words of Beyoncé, I'm feeling myself.

I was just at Chase, where I successfully deposited
the first biweekly payment of $3,500 for Heather. I im-
mediately texted her to let her know that after a few

hiccups with my UAE bank, the money had finally gone through and that there would be lots more where it came from. When she replied a few moments later with a single heart emoji, my own heart skipped a beat.

After all she's been through, Heather deserves this, Dr. K. She's the love of my life and the mother of my children, and something about providing for my family makes me feel almost whole again, makes me know the insanity of the past seven months is well worth it. Life hasn't been fair to our family, so why should we be fair to life? That's how I see it. You can argue that this outlook fuels the problem, that the most important thing in this world is having integrity, but I'll tell you something, Dr. K—I'm doing what I'm doing *with* integrity, with my heart behind my every step.

Chapter Twenty-One

Heather

JUNE 1990

Peter was wrapping up his project, and he and Libby and the kids were slated to leave Langs Valley at the end of June. For me, their departure was a ticking time bomb, and I wanted nothing more than to zip Gus and me inside one of Libby's oversize suitcases. The prospect of getting through senior year in Langs Valley without Burke *or* Libby was a daunting nightmare. But as Libby reminded me, a year is short in the scheme of things; all I had to do was keep my head down, continue to ace my classes, and nail my college applications. After that, the world would be my oyster.

My second-semester grades had come in even better than first semester's. A's in physics, pre-calculus, and U.S. history and A-minuses in English and Spanish. To top it off, I'd gotten into three APs for the first semester of senior year. Freshman and sophomore years I'd never gotten anything above a B. It's amazing what you can accomplish when you stop partying and lose all your friends.

In addition to my near-perfect grades, I'd also gotten my first round of SAT scores back and had scored in the ninetieth percentile. I'd triple-checked the envelope to make sure the results had been sent to the correct person. Libby said my score was so good that I didn't even need to take the test again, unless I wanted to aim even higher.

I was overjoyed and slightly shocked, but I knew I deserved every bit of what I was getting. Aside from babysitting duties and hanging out with Libby, I'd done nothing but study for the past seven months. I'd spent countless Saturday nights poring over my SAT prep book while Burke and Kyla and all my other ex-friends smoked crack and took Ecstasy and rolled their brains out. I was going to go to college, and they weren't.

One evening after leaving Libby's, I dropped Gus at the Carsons' and drove to the A&P to pick up some groceries. It was past eight o'clock when I got to the grocery store, the light still long and soft. June was always my favorite time of year, partly because of the longer days and late sunsets, but also because my birthday fell on the seventeenth. I don't know why I liked my birthday so much—my parents never gave me presents as a kid, and I don't remember ever having a party. I guess I'd always loved that there was this one day—of all the calendar days in the whole year—that was just for me.

As I wrangled a shopping cart free from the stack, Burke walked out of the A&P. He nearly stumbled right into me, and we made eye contact that lasted a beat too long for either of us to pretend we hadn't seen the other.

It was easy enough for us to avoid each other at school. We didn't have any classes together, and whenever I did see him, he was always surrounded by his pack of buddies. A few times I caught him staring at me across the cafeteria or during an assembly, but he never approached me, not after my radio silence in response to the heartfelt letters he'd sent in January.

I kept my hands on the handle of the shopping cart—a buffer between us—and studied Burke, the way he stood tall with his weight on one foot, plastic grocery bag slung under his elbow. He wore broken-in jeans and a worn Boston Red Sox T-shirt that I'd yanked over his head too many times to count. For a moment I forgot that we hadn't spoken in almost six months and I nearly blurted out the news about my SAT scores. Burke had been more than my boyfriend—he'd been my best friend, my go-to confidant.

But then I remembered that everything was different now, and I held my tongue. Burke shifted his weight to the other leg and gave me that adorably awkward grin where he blew air into his cheeks—the grin that meant he was uncomfortable. The part of me that just wanted to grab his face and kiss him was quickly bubbling to the surface.

"Hi," I said finally.

"Hey, Bones. You look great." His voice sounded soft and the same, and it was so good to hear it that I knew I was going to cry.

"So do you, Burke." He did look great. He always looked great, except when he was high out of his mind, which I had to remind myself was an awful lot. But sober, Burke made my knees weak. He had that lean, strong build I knew every inch of, those shocking blue eyes, and that thick head of glossy black hair. He looked as handsome as ever, and I couldn't imagine how many girls had raced to jump into his bed since we broke up. My stomach curdled at the thought.

"How are things?" he asked.

"Things are okay. I—I'm sorry we haven't talked." I felt my voice crack and knew I had to get out of there before the tears broke loose. "Let's try to catch up sometime this summer?"

"I'd love that. Have you been—"

"I'm sorry but I've got to get these groceries, Burke," I blurted. "It's late and I haven't made Gus's dinner yet."

"Don't worry about it." His smile was sad, but those telltale dimples still formed on either cheek. "Hey, tell the Gus man I said hi, will ya? Tell him I miss him."

"I'll tell him." I bit my bottom lip, tightening my grip on the handle of the cart and heading toward the store's entrance.

"Hey, Bones," he called behind me, and I couldn't stand how much I loved that he still called me that. I forced myself to turn. "If I don't see ya beforehand, I hope you have a really happy birthday."

I managed a strained smile before turning back around and pushing my cart through the sliding doors of the A&P, the tears already dripping down my face.

Chapter Twenty-Two

Skye

OCTOBER 2019

Our wedding was a dream. From the idyllic weather to the flowers to the stunning sailcloth tent erected on my grandparents' property overlooking the ocean, the physical details couldn't have been more perfect. I felt more beautiful than I had all my life, and it wasn't because I was so busy and stressed leading up to the wedding that I forgot to eat and finally lost five stubborn pounds. And it wasn't because I was wearing a satin Carolina Herrera dress or because the makeup lady made every blemish on my face disappear while simultaneously brightening and sharpening each of my features. It was because during the momentum of the weekend I stopped being afraid of the happiness pulsating from every inch of me, and instead I let it envelop me, let it fill me up to the brim. Moments before the ceremony Andie fastened my mother's sapphire bracelet around my wrist—my somethings borrowed and blue—and I knew then that Mom was with me, I felt her in the marrow of my bones. I remembered how she used to say that beauty radiates from within, and for the first time I finally understood that it hadn't worked out with Max

LaPointe or anyone else because it was meant to work out with Burke.

"You deserve all this, Skye," Andie had whispered as she fastened the clasp of the bracelet. And I'd felt it, the relief of knowing how right she was.

The honeymoon was magical, too. October 2 marked the eighteenth anniversary of my mom's death, but for the first time—being in another country with my new husband, my partner forever—the day came and went without the crushing sadness I've come to expect. We flew home last night, and now even though I *should* be doing edits for Jan—I was too exhausted to work on the plane—I can't stop looking through our wedding pictures. Andie started a shared album and invited my family and friends to contribute, and the photographer just sent a few teaser shots by email this morning. There we are at the altar, the moment we became Mr. and Mrs. Burke Michaels; there we are running out of the church, ginormous smiles plastered on both our faces as white rose petals rain over our heads. There are too many perfect shots, and I can't wait for Burke to see them. There are some nice family photos, too. My favorite is the one without Nancy, Aidan, and Harry—the one that's just my brother, Brooke, my dad, Burke, and me. The one where Mom should've been standing beside us.

There's Andie giving her toast, looking stunning in her maid-of-honor dress—a blush Rachel Zoe column— her long hair loose around her shoulders. I smile remembering Andie's toast, which was heartfelt and touching and, in the best possible way, not at all what I expected.

I keep flipping through the photos. There's my brother looking handsome in his groomsman suit, the ranunculus boutonniere pinned to his left lapel. There's Burke's cousin Wally, the overserved best man, slurring his toast—the one hiccup of the night. Then there's Burke's friend Andy—insert sigh of relief—after he took over for Wally and ended up giving a phenomenal toast on the spot. There's Burke and me during our unforgettable first dance to "September." There's a beautiful shot of my father and me during our dance to "She's Got a Way," which I chose because it was my parents' wedding song. Mom got our family crazy about Billy Joel. In the picture the skirt of my dress is a billowy cloud of satin, and my dad's arm is hooked under the small of my back as he dips me, his smile wide, even though I know tears were in his eyes. I can nearly hear the words, the perfect way the band played the song my parents used to dance to in the kitchen when I was little.

> She's got a light around her
> And everywhere she goes
> A million dreams of love surround her

I'm still trying to choose the best photos for Instagram—Lexy is astounded that I haven't posted yet—when my phone buzzes. Andie.

"Hi!" I press the button for speakerphone so I can continue my photo browsing while we talk.

"Hey, Skye." Andie's voice is flat, and I can tell right away that something is wrong. "Get home safe?"

"Yeah. We got back late last night. What's wrong?"

"What do you mean?"

"Something in your voice is weird. What's going on?"

Andie exhales audibly, and I know I'm right. "What are you doing right now? Is Burke home?"

"He's out running some errands. What's going on, Andie? Tell me."

"I really need to talk to you." Her voice has a grave edge that makes my stomach sink. "But it needs to be in person. Can you come over here?"

"Right now? What is it, Andie?"

"I can't talk about this on the phone. I'm serious."

"You're really freaking me out." I close my laptop. My fingers are trembling.

"I'm sorry, Skye, but this is something I need to talk to you about in person, and it needs to be now. Catch a cab and get over here."

"Andie, wait. I'm panicked. Please just tell me—did—did someone die?"

"No," she says flatly. "No one died."

I feel some relief, but not enough. "All right. I'm on my way."

I wish I were one of those cool New Yorkers who likes venturing to Brooklyn, but I just don't. Bridges make me nervous, and it takes a unique circumstance to drag me over one. This is one of those circumstances.

My palms are damp as the cabdriver swerves through the Sunday traffic, making me nauseated. I barely even register when we're on the bridge; my thoughts and emotions are frozen, on standby until Andie tells me what the fuck is going on. I close my eyes and breathe in through my nose: *one, two, three, four, five, six, seven, eight*. Then out for *eight, seven, six, five, four, three, two, one*. Just as Mom taught me when I was little. The simple breathing technique that turned out to be the stamp for my self-destruction.

After what seems like hours, the taxi finally slows to a stop in front of Andie's building on North Ninth Street in Williamsburg. I throw the cabbie two twenties and sprint toward Andie's door. Andie and Spencer live on the fifth floor of a walk-up, and when she buzzes me in, I fly up the stairs so fast that I'm coated in sweat and gulping for air by the time I ring the doorbell.

Andie is wearing sweatpants and one of Spencer's T-shirts. Her long hair is combed straight, and the color is drained from her face.

"I sent Spence out. It's just me."

"This better be good, Andrea, because I'm having an actual panic attack. Tell me what the hell is going on."

Andie leads me into the tiny living room. She sits down on the couch and opens up her laptop.

"Sit." She gestures to the space beside her. "And I'll tell you everything."

I sit.

Andie tells.

She explains how earlier this morning she received an email from Burke that she was clearly not supposed to receive. It was obviously intended for someone else and sent to her by accident. She shows me the email.

From: burke.michaels@gmail.com
To: andier@me.com
Date: Oct 6, 2019, 8:02 AM
Subject: (no subject)

Andy,

Got your text, sorry I'm just getting back to you now. Skye and I have been on our honeymoon and just got back last night, so I haven't had much time to myself the past couple of weeks.

First of all, thank you so much for all of your help with the wedding. I honestly don't know what I would have done without you (especially stepping in for Wally during his toast—that was one for the books). I'm glad we've been able to reconnect, and I hope all continues to be well (or as well as it can be) in Langs Valley. I don't mean to be a preacher, but I meant what I said at the wedding—try to stay off the Oxy, and if you can't, get some help. I've been where you are, and I can tell you that the drugs aren't worth it. I know the treatment programs are costly—if you ever need help with money, don't hesitate to ask.

I've given some thought on how to best answer your question about my situation with Skye, seeing as it's something you may want to consider down the line. It's a lot to explain. This might sound a little wacko, but I've been writing about it in a journal I keep on my computer. Heather and I were seeing a couples therapist for a while who suggested we write our feelings down in a diary or journal or whatever, and I ended up writing him all these letters—my therapist, that is—right around the time I met Skye, when things with Heather were crappy. I've never shown them to anyone and frankly I never planned to, but I don't really know how to begin answering your question, and I think the letters (attached) will tell you everything you want to know.

Give my best to Shelly, and don't be a stranger.

Thanks again for everything, I'll always be grateful.

Burke

By the time I've finished reading the email, my heart has stopped. My blood is frozen.

"I'm getting you some water." Andie stands.

"Andie. Wait."

My brain feels like an expanding balloon, the pressure building with no room to give.

"Who the fuck is Heather?" My throat is dry, like sandpaper. "What the fuck is this, Andie? What are these letters Burke is talking about? Have you read them?"

"Skye." Andie sits again. "All I know so far is that Burke meant to send this email to his friend Andy, the guy who was in your wedding. And he must've confused our email addresses, or mine popped up automatically when he started typing in *Andy* and he just didn't check. . . ."

My head is a cyclone. I'm suddenly convinced that none of this is real, that Andie's disdain for Burke has caused her to push the limits too far.

"Andie," I start, my voice shaking. "Did you make this shit up because you want me to break up with Burke? Did you create this *bullshit* just because you fucking *despise* my husband and have since the day I met him?"

"What?" Andie shrieks, her hazel eyes growing watery and wide. "Are you kidding? Do you think I'm some kind of sociopath? I would *never* fucking do that, Skye!"

I'm crying, too, now because I know she would never do that; I said what I did in a blind fit of terror, and the worst part is that there's more.

The letters.

The *situation* with Skye.

"I know," I choke, and Andie is beside me, pulling me close. "I'm sorry. Andie, you have to tell me. Did you read the letters?"

"I was just going to read one," she says, her voice small. "But after I started reading, I couldn't stop, Skye. I'm sorry. But I think it's better that I read them first because, oh, Skye—they're terrible. It's terrible. I don't want you to read them. I know you're going to, but I think—I think maybe I should just tell you first. So you know what to expect. And then you don't have to read them if you don't want to."

The dread is violent, all-encompassing; my insides twist viciously, my skin prickles with heat.

"How—how many letters are there?"

"Eleven. But some of them are pretty long."

My phone vibrates in my pocket and I pull it out. Burke. Two missed calls. I throw the phone across the room with all my might. I can't see where it lands, but I hope the screen shatters into a million pieces.

My mind reaches toward every possible terrible scenario the letters could reveal. From what I've already read, it sounds as if Burke was in a relationship with this Heather person. But I've never heard him mention anyone named Heather. In our brief discussions about past relationships, Burke has only ever mentioned his longtime girlfriend from college and then his ex, Amanda, the one he almost married before she cheated on him. Maybe his college girlfriend was named Heather? But, no, that wouldn't make sense, because in his email he said that he met *me* right around the time things were crappy with Heather. Who the fuck is Heather?

Everything inside my head is a hurricane, and I don't know if I have the strength or stamina to read through each of the letters in the attachment, to wait in excruciating fear for the picture to fill itself.

"I need to see the letters, Andie." I don't recognize the sound of my voice. "I need—I need to read them for myself."

Andie squeezes my hand. "All right. But I'm going to stay right here with you while you read them, okay?"

I nod. I take the laptop from Andie and double-click the attachment to Burke's email, something titled "BM Diary." A Microsoft Word document floods the screen.

I start reading.

September 8, 2018

Dear Dr. K,

Her hair is yellow and thick, nothing like my wife's. Isn't that awful, that when I first notice an attractive woman, I instantly compare her to my wife? I used to think I was a good person, the kind of man who wouldn't be struck dumb by the tumble of blond hair down a creamy, anonymous back.

It takes me nearly an hour and a half to read all eleven of Burke's entries, but I don't stop until I get to the very last word of the very last one, from September 22, 2019, the day after our wedding.

Then I scream.

Chapter Twenty-Three

Burke Michaels's Diary

SEPTEMBER 22, 2019

Dear Dr. K,

I am a married man. Twice over, actually, but let's keep that between you and me. Where I come from, bigamy is frowned upon.

Of course, it won't actually be bigamy for long. After the honeymoon and several weeks of wedded bliss, I'll start winding things down. Details on my exact method TBA, but if all goes well, I'll be divorced by Christmas.

The wedding went smoothly enough, and the potential issue of a prenup took care of itself. Lucky for me, Skye's father has some baggage around the whole prenup thing—apparently, he was forced to sign one when he married Skye's mother, a requirement that left him eternally humiliated. Perfect.

Our big day was not without a few hiccups, I will admit. My "best man," Wally, got shit-faced during cocktail hour and was speaking gibberish during his toast. Scott had to escort Wally off the stage area while Andy took over the microphone, and I have to hand it to them for saving the day, because Mr. Starling's face had turned as red as the beets on our farm-to-table salads.

With zero preparation, Andy gave an impromptu toast about what a great guy I was that knocked everyone's socks off—even *I* was impressed with myself.

Nantucket is a stunning place, Dr. K; all quaint shingled houses and rolling green fields and soft ocean air. If you've never been, I highly recommend visiting. I'd like to go back with Heather and the kids someday, rent a house on the water.

Skye was a radiant bride, as I knew she would be. But I won't lie; it hasn't been easy seeing her so happy all weekend and knowing it's all a sham. It's an uncomfortable feeling, Dr. K. But I played my part, and when I had to, I closed my eyes and thought of Heather, and how Heather never got to have a wedding day like this, and how Skye would have the chance again. I thought of something I read the other day that said we're all responsible for our own choices. Skye chose me, and that isn't my fault. Skye missed the red flags—they were there, Dr. K—and that isn't my fault, either. At the end of the day Skye isn't a victim; she's a girl who didn't have her eyes open, who chose emotion over pragmatism. Survival of the fittest is a legitimate thing.

#burkeisskyehigh, that's what the kids are saying, and I know enough to know what a wedding hashtag is, thank you very much. And I *am* sky-high, quite literally. Tomorrow my bride and I are off to Italy for two weeks, and I'd be lying if I said I wasn't excited. I've never been out of the country, if you can believe that. When we were first married, Heather and I had big plans to travel and see the world—she was dying to go to Paris—but it never happened. Instead she got pregnant with Garrett, and then I went and fucked everything up.

It warms my heart to know that Heather and I will still have our chance, that one day soon I'll be able to give her Paris and beyond. She's content with the payments coming in. She even says she's proud of me. She tells me that she misses me and loves me, and that she's ready for me to come home.

It's funny, Dr. K; when I think about the person I was just over a year ago—that lost, broken man slipping off his wedding ring and slinking into Gurney's looking for something I couldn't define—it all makes sense to me now. I was driven there for a reason. I had to veer off the beaten path to find what I was looking for, and it was more than just momentary respite. Subconsciously, I knew this. Meeting Skye Starling that sunny Saturday in Montauk was my destiny, my answer, my way back to the love I'd lost with Heather, my way back home. And, God, I'm ready to go home.

But first stop, *Italia*. Tomorrow we fly to Florence, where we'll spend a few days seeing the museums and the famous Duomo and the Arno River; then we rent a car and spend the rest of the week driving through the vineyards of Tuscany. The next stop is Rome to see the Colosseum and the Vatican, and then finally down to Naples and the Amalfi Coast, where we'll cap off the trip on the island of Capri.

Most of the honeymoon was paid for using Skye's and my joint account, and some of it was covered by Mr. Starling. I guess it doesn't matter who pays for what in a family where there's more money than you know what to do with. Aside from the Wally incident, Mr. Starling seemed happy with me throughout the wedding weekend. I was unsure at first, but I've concluded that he likes me. He may not be blown away by my credentials, but I know he sees how happy I make Skye, and at the end of the day, that's what counts. *Sei d'accordo?*

Skye and I have been taking a Rosetta Stone course online to practice our Italian. Hers is decent—she studied abroad in Rome her junior fall of college—and mine is what she likes to call "a work in progress." Touché. I never did have a knack for foreign languages.

I guess I'd better get packing, then. It's not every day you jet off on a two-week vacation to Italy, first-class, all expenses paid. Skye says there are orange trees in Capri, and the best pizza in the world in Naples, and wine that runs down your throat like velvet in Tuscany. Tonight I'll dream of it all, and tomorrow I'll wake up in my dream.

Chapter Twenty-Four

Heather

JUNE 1990

The day I turned seventeen—my golden birthday—
Libby suggested we pack a picnic and drive to Chazy
Lake. This windy but beautiful day, the piercing blue
sky was cloudless and bright.

Even Peter decided to take the day off and come
along, and the six of us crammed into the Caravan and
headed east toward the lake.

We set up our picnic on a small beach where the boys
could wade. Gus was cranky when I told him he had to
wear floaties in the water.

"Nate isn't wearing floaties!" Gus pouted and kicked
at the sand.

"Gus, come here." I pulled him onto my lap. "Nate
knows how to swim. You're still learning how to swim,
remember?"

"I learned how to swim in Ba-*muda,* Heddah!" He
punched his little fist against my shoulder.

"You took a couple of lessons in Bermuda, that's
right, bud." I rubbed his back. "And you can practice
some more today, and you'll be swimming on your own
in no time. But for now, I want you wearing those floaties. No buts about it."

Gus scrunched his nose and ran over toward Nate, who was digging a hole in the sand. Libby propped the baby up on the picnic blanket in front of a pile of toys. Peter had his camera out and was squatted down on the shore, snapping photographs of the mountains peeking up behind the cobalt-blue lake.

Libby opened the cooler and removed a wheel of Brie cheese along with some crackers and a bottle of champagne. A gust of wind blew strands of pale hair in front of her face.

"So blustery today! How about a glass for the birthday girl?"

"Aw, Lib!" I smiled. "You know, your kids are luckier than they realize. You are the coolest mom ever."

Libby rolled her eyes. "We'll see. I'll probably become a complete warden about their drinking. Tell me the truth—am I totally out of line letting you drink a little with me?"

"Are you kidding? Most of the kids I grew up with were getting drunk when they were twelve. Parents in Langs Valley are hardly around, and if they are, they're not paying attention."

"Yes, but that's not exactly the behavior I want to aspire to." Libby's eyes softened. "My mother was *so* strict about alcohol—when I was your age she found a six-pack of beer under my bed and grounded me for a month. I hated the way she was. So I always told myself I'd be cool about letting my kids have a glass of wine or two, as long as they did it with me, under my roof. We'll see if it actually happens."

I watched her pour champagne into two paper cups.

She wore white shorts and a red bikini top, her long flaxen hair falling loose past her svelte shoulders. Her stomach was pale and perfectly flat, even after two babies.

"So I'm your guinea pig?"

"Something like that." Libby grinned, her brown eyes sparkling. "Though you're more like a little sister to me than a daughter."

"True. If I was your daughter, you would've been . . ."

"*Thirteen* when you were born. Not even possible. I didn't get my period till I was fourteen. Late bloomer. . . . *Careful,* guys! The water's rough today. Not too far out." Libby stood on her knees and squinted toward the lake, where the boys were splashing around in the shallow water. Whitecaps were visible in the distance. "And you listen to your sister and keep those floaties on, Gussie!"

"Cheers, Lib." I tapped my paper cup against her own. The champagne was fizzy and cold down my throat.

"Cheers, beautiful birthday girl. May all your dreams come true. Hey, Pete! How about a glass of bubbly, love?"

Peter stood and walked over to the blanket. He placed one hand on the back of Libby's head. "I'm actually going to take a little stroll, if you girls don't mind. I want to get some different shots of the lake."

"Of course. Have a nice stroll. Heather and I will hold down the fort."

Peter leaned down to kiss his wife, and the image of Burke outside the A&P rushed into my mind.

Libby refilled our cups and we sat basking in the sunshine, chatting into the afternoon while the boys continued to wade. The lake was beautiful, and not as crowded as I remembered it from years past. The sun sat high in the sky, warming us despite the wind and casting a shimmery glow over the velvety-blue water. At one end of the beach a couple of rowboats were tied to a floating dock, their hulls bobbing in the waves. At the other end was a water trampoline with blue-and-yellow-striped sides, about thirty meters out from shore.

"Oooh, Mom!" Nate exclaimed. "I wanna go jump on that trampoline! Can I?"

"Not now, sweetie," Libby told her son. "You can't swim there by yourself. When Daddy gets back from his walk, he can take you."

All of a sudden, the baby let out a sharp cry. Libby and I whipped our heads around as her eyes filled with tears, a couple of yellow jackets circling her tiny body. Her face grew red and scrunched, her little mouth gaped open, and I heard the wails in my head before they escaped her lungs.

"Oh, my baby girl!" Libby snatched her daughter up and hurried her away from the yellow jackets. "Shoot, Heather. I think she got stung." Libby pointed to the baby's upper arm, a small crimson dot surrounded by a circle of puffy white skin, as she continued to scream. "I don't know if I've ever heard her cry like this, Heather! She's never gotten stung before. What if she's allergic?" Libby's voice was panicked, hollow with fear.

"I—I don't know. It looks like a normal beesting to me. Wouldn't it look different if she was allergic?"

"I have no idea! I've just never heard her scream like this. I don't know what to do. Shit! Where's Peter? Can you find Peter?"

I resisted the urge to tell Libby that I *had* heard her daughter scream like this—I knew Libby had, too. But I understood the way she was as a mother—nothing like my own had been—and that my attempts to calm her down would be futile. The most productive thing I could do would be to look for her husband.

"I'll go find Peter." I scrambled to stand.

"Thank you. Hurry!" Libby called behind me.

I ran to the end of the beach, shouting Peter's name, the wind deafening the pitch of my voice. He was no-where to be seen. I clambered back up toward the grass and continued along the shoreline. How long had Peter been gone? How far could he have gotten? Burke had once told me that Chazy Lake's circumference was eleven miles—his knowledge of random facts like that was one of the things I'd loved about him.

But eleven miles—that was a significant distance. And I didn't even know which direction Peter had headed. I continued on for another five minutes, shuffling through the tall grass around the lake's edge as I called for Peter.

An older couple sitting in fold-up chairs noticed me.

"Everything okay, honey?" the man asked.

"I'm looking for someone." I paused, catching my breath. "He's my—my friend's husband, he's thirty . . . something. Six feet or so, light brown hair. He would've had a camera around his neck. Have you seen him?"

The couple shook their heads. "Sorry." The woman's

voice was slow and raspy. "We haven't seen anyone out here today. It's so darn peaceful. Good luck."

I was suddenly racked with a sick, wrenching feeling in my gut that something horrible had happened or was on the verge of happening. An overwhelming sense of doom clobbered my chest.

I thanked the couple and turned back the way I'd come, my legs heedlessly breaking into a sprint. Perhaps Libby's instinct had been right; maybe the baby *was* having an allergic reaction to the beesting, and locating Peter within eleven miles of shoreline suddenly seemed impossible. If the baby was allergic, we needed to get to a hospital and we needed to get to one fast.

My heart thrashed against my rib cage as I ran back toward our beach. I finally spotted our blue picnic blanket, and my blood froze when I saw the baby sitting there alone. I heard Libby's scream first—a violent, barbaric noise—and when my eyes found her, she was in the lake, about five meters out, Nate's arms around her neck as they swam toward the shore.

"Heather!" Libby yelled, the panic in her voice guttural. *"GUS!"* She flung her arm out of the lake, pointing toward the water trampoline. My heart dropped to my stomach. I scanned my eyes for Gus in his yellow floaties, two pops of color against the deep blue, but they were nowhere. Then suddenly I saw them, six feet from where I stood, discarded on the beach.

"GUS!" Libby screamed again, her arm thrashing out toward the water behind her.

Immediately I felt as if I were being choked, as though someone were squeezing my neck with all his or her might, cutting off my air supply. Adrenaline surged through me and I ripped off my shorts and T-shirt, sprinting into the water, a primal force taking over.

"GUS!" I wailed; the noise that came out of me was bloodcurdling, something from an animal.

Suddenly I saw his little fingers scraping at the surface of the water, halfway out toward the water trampoline, where the waves were choppy and the wind was blowing offshore. I was screaming, tears blurring my vision. I glanced over at Libby, who was closer to the beach. Nate was still clutching her, but now, just a couple of meters from the beach, they could both stand.

"Libby!" I called, but she didn't answer. "Libby, *HELP!*"

I waded out farther, until everything but my head was submerged. I couldn't swim. If I tried to save Gus, we would both drown. But I would try anyway—I was running out of time, and Libby was distracted. I sprang forward and dunked into the lake, thrashing my arms in front of me underwater. Terror seized me; I couldn't breathe. I gasped for air, choking on water as I fought my way back toward a place where I could stand. Finally, miraculously, my feet touched the bottom, and I gulped air hungrily into my lungs. I used the grip of my toes against the sand to pull myself back toward the shore.

Once I could fully stand, I ran out of the lake, my chest heaving as I fought to catch my breath. I couldn't swim. I would die in that water before I ever reached Gus.

"LIBBY!" I howled, clambering toward her as she wrapped Nate in a towel. He was crying, but he'd made it safely out of the water. The baby had started wailing again.

"LIBBY!" My voice was shrill and shaking with hysteria. "Please! *Gus!* I can't swim! You know I can't swim!"

Just as Libby turned toward me, her eyes pooling with fresh panic, I heard Peter's voice from the other end of the beach. "Libby! Heather! What the hell is going on?"

"Please!" I ran toward him, pointing at the water where I'd last seen Gus. "Gus is out there!"

In a flash Peter was in the lake, his strong arms pulling him toward the place where I'd pointed. I crouched into a ball and waited, tears streaming down my cheeks in torrents. I didn't know if it was thirty minutes or thirty seconds later when Peter appeared at the surface, one of his arms hooked around Gus's still body.

Moments later they were back onshore, and I rushed to my brother's side, tears spilling out of my eyes and onto his limp little chest. I was still shrieking as I watched Peter perform CPR, over and over. But Gus wasn't breathing.

"We need to get him to a hospital." Peter's voice was hoarse.

I barely remember leaving the beach or the drive to the hospital in Malone, thirty miles west of Chazy Lake. The rational part of me knew Gus was already dead, that a hospital could do nothing, but I must've been clinging to a measly shred of hope because when the doctors pronounced him dead on arrival, I went mad.

Libby tried to console me, but I pushed her away. I screamed into my hands until my throat was raw.

I couldn't look at Libby. I hated her. I hated her for leaving Gus to die while she saved her son, who already knew how to swim. I tried not to listen as Libby explained through muffled sobs her version of what had happened, but I couldn't block out the sound of her voice.

While she had been tending to the baby and I'd been off looking for Peter, the boys had wandered farther down the shore. Libby had been in a hysterical frenzy over the beesting, convinced that the baby was experiencing an allergic reaction, and hadn't noticed the boys wade deeper into the lake from the other end of the beach. She hadn't seen Gus remove his floaties. A few minutes later she heard the boys screaming, and when she looked up, she saw them out in the water, nearly halfway toward the trampoline, their small arms flailing. The waves were stronger than she'd realized and must've caused them to drift. Libby immediately stripped down to her bathing suit, left her daughter on the blanket, and plowed into the water toward the boys.

I listened to Libby explain to the doctors that though her son could swim at a base level, he'd never been in such deep water, and she'd found him completely panicked. Both boys were crying. At first, Libby tried to swim with one under each arm, but she couldn't make any headway carrying two forty-pound

five-year-olds in such wind, and they were both growing more and more hysterical.

I knew Libby well enough to know how she would
justify the next part, and I didn't need to hear it. I didn't
need to hear Libby defend her subconscious decision to
save her own son's life first. My blood boiled at what
she omitted in her spiel to the doctors—that Nate, unlike Gus, was a capable swimmer. Despite being panicked, Nate could've gotten back to shore on his own. But
with a mother such as Libby—overbearing, egocentric,
high-handed, despicable *Libby*—Gus's life never stood a
chance against Nate's.

Libby said her plan was to get her son safely to shore
and then go back for Gus, but that when she saw me
reappear, she was still in the water and knew I could
get to Gus sooner. She explained to the doctors that
she was preoccupied with Nate and hadn't known I
couldn't swim.

"You knew," I whispered through tears. "I told you."

"What? *No,* of course I didn't. I would have remembered something like that." She reached for me and I
flinched.

"In Bermuda," I growled, anger creeping up through
the grief. "I told you in Bermuda. You were drunk."

Libby emitted an indiscernible sound. Her hand rose
to cover her mouth, and she said nothing.

One of the doctors asked who Gus's legal guardian
was, and I held up a limp hand. He peered at me, un-
convinced, and asked for my age.

"Seventeen. I turned seventeen today. Today's my

birthday." I heard Libby choke back a sob, and I prayed it would suffocate her.

The doctor replied that seventeen wasn't old enough to be someone's legal guardian. "Is there anyone else we can call? Parents?"

"My mom's dead. My father is on the road."

"Where on the road? How can we get in touch with him?"

"You can't." I shrugged. "I don't know where he is. Haven't seen him since December."

"I'm sorry." The doctor sighed. He didn't sound sorry. "What about relatives? Grandparents? Aunts or uncles?"

My head was dense with fog and pain, but I tried to think about whom I could call. My dad had run away from his parents when he was eighteen. They were somewhere in Canada, and I'd never met them. I didn't know their names. My mom's parents were both dead. Her sister was down in New Jersey, my aunt Mel, but I hadn't seen her since the time we visited when I was six. I didn't know her phone number, and even if I had, calling her would've been like calling a stranger.

"There's no one," I told the doctor.

"Let us help," Libby begged, her voice squeaky. "Please, Heather."

I shook my head. "You need to go. Please just get out of here."

"Heather—"

"I want you to leave. *Now*." I stared into her caramel eyes, red around the rims and sticky from crying. No part of me cared if I was hurting her. The only thing I knew was that if it hadn't been for Libby's selfishness— for her frantic preoccupation with a measly beesting, for her special treatment of her son over my brother, for her being too drunk and forgetful to remember my pivotal disclosure—Gus would still be alive.

"Heather, please—"

"Leave!" I screamed. I wanted to spit in her face, and I would've if multiple doctors and nurses hadn't been staring at us. Nate started crying.

"Libby, come on." Peter took hold of his wife's elbow, his face colorless. "I'm so sorry, Heather." It was barely a whisper. I watched him lead his family out of the stale, stuffy hospital where Gus lay dead.

My brother was dead. Never again would he open his curious green eyes or let out one of his high-pitched little Gus giggles or nuzzle his golden curls into my neck. My heart was frozen, my body numb. Uncontrollable tears dripped down my face and onto my lap.

A nurse approached me. "Is there really no one you want to call, honey?"

I wiped my cheeks and blinked, and there, in the well of my deepest, most unthinkable pain, was the only answer. "There is, actually." I nodded. "There is one person."

I called Burke. And he came running.

Part

TWO

———

Chapter Twenty-Five

Heather

Dear Dr. K,

I've determined that it should be *my* turn to do your little diary exercise, because the only way this couples therapy is going to help is if we both put in the work. Isn't that what you said?

Besides, I could really use the journalistic release. The cathartic part is getting it all out, and then I'll trash this document. For prime security, maybe I'll even toss my laptop into the ocean, like the old lady does with the heart diamond at the end of *Titanic*. Gone forever.

First off let me just say, I don't regret my actions. This wasn't the original plan, but it had to be done. Soon enough you'll understand that, too.

Now, before you start pointing fingers, I deserve to tell you my side of the story. My side of the *true* story, that is. Let me start at the beginning. Well, one beginning. When I look back on my forty-five (almost forty-six!) years of life, I subconsciously divide it into two sections: before Gus died and after Gus died. After Gus died was a second beginning, and the more significant genesis in Burke's and my story.

It was June 1990 in Langs Valley. Burke and I never

officially established that we were back together, but we didn't need to. The day Gus died and Burke showed up to the hospital, I was in the midst of a long, dangerous fall, and I let him catch me. There was simply no other way I could have gone on.

The rest of that awful summer was a pit of darkness. I don't remember much about the days that followed Gus's death. I couldn't fathom making any arrangements, so Burke stepped in. Burke called the funeral home and chose the tiny teak coffin. Burke found a burial plot near our house, next to the meadow where Gus loved to chase crickets and butterflies. Burke organized the small service at the Episcopal church in town, and Burke gave the eulogy. I was too numb to speak, and my father wasn't there. No one had been able to track him down since Gus's death, and for all I knew he was dead, too.

The only thing I remember being adamant about was that Libby and Peter not attend the funeral. Libby called endlessly, and when I wouldn't answer the phone, she showed up at the house. Per my directions, Burke told her to get lost. Well, I'm sure he said some polite version of that. Burke has always had annoyingly good manners—Grams raised him well in that arena.

Bottom line, I couldn't see Libby. I knew she cared, but I also knew that what she wanted, above all, was my absolution. She wanted to hear me say that it was a terrible accident, but I couldn't do it. I wouldn't give her the satisfaction of agreeing that Gus's death was blameless, because it wasn't. We both knew that if Libby hadn't been drunk that day in Bermuda, she would've remembered me telling her I'd never learned to swim. We both knew that if it weren't for her carelessness— her *selfishness*—Gus would still be breathing.

When Burke wasn't there to ward off Libby, I locked the door and stayed in bed, ignoring the sunshine and intermittent knocking. She left notes and baked goods and fruit baskets on the front stoop. I threw her letters away without reading them and left the food for Burke.

One night at the end of June, Burke sat down at the edge of the bed, a crumpled letter in hand. I recognized the handwriting on the envelope—it was one of Libby's I'd tossed in the trash. The narrow slit at the top told me Burke had opened it.

"What are you doing?" I sat up in bed. "Throw that out. I don't want to see it."

"You want to see this one, Bones." Burke's voice was soft, but serious.

"No, I don't. Why'd you open it? Have you been opening her letters?"

Burke sighed, his blue eyes landing on mine. "I— don't be mad, Bones. I wanted to check and make sure . . . I sort of expected there might be something like this." He handed me the envelope.

I knew what it was, then, because subconsciously I'd been expecting it, too. It was part of the reason I hadn't opened a single one of Libby's letters. I knew the sight of it would make me sick.

When I didn't remove the contents of the envelope, Burke did it for me, and there it was, a big fat check, alongside a small white card with the initials *LRF* in a pink monogram at the top. My stomach churned.

H,

Perhaps it will give you some relief to know that we leave Langs Valley tomorrow. There is nothing I can do to make this right, not now, not ever. I know that. But please take this. You deserve it, and it comes from a place of nothing but love.

Libby

Burke watched me carefully. I stared at the check, a block at the base of my gut.

"It's a shit ton of money, Bones," he said finally.

I nodded because it was. It was a comical amount of money. It was the kind of money that flips your world on its head overnight, like winning the jackpot. The check was made out to me, Heather Price, for $500,000.

But it was Gus's life. Some things you just know in your soul, things you do because there's no other choice, because to do otherwise would be to go against your life force, to poison the marrow of your bones.

Burke winced as I ripped up the check. I walked to the bathroom and threw the pieces into the toilet. I pressed down on the handle and watched them swirl, the little green specks of Gus's blood money, then disappear.

I walked back into the bedroom and found Burke's gaze, daring him to say something, to object. But he nodded silently—just once—and something in his eyes looked a whole lot like pride.

The rest of the summer was a blur, a vacuum of grief. My heart was shattered, and along with it the world. The hopeful, carefree days preceding the accident felt far away, almost as if they'd never existed at all. I spent the long, light-filled days of July and August underneath the covers with the shades drawn, Gus's absence a searing hole in my life. Burke was working part-time at the Mobil station, but whenever he wasn't, he'd come home to be with me. Sometimes he'd crawl into the bed and hold me; other times he'd sit in the chair by the nightstand and read comics. In that unspoken way that Burke had always known what I needed, he knew just to stay near me.

The week before Labor Day, a few days before Burke's birthday, he finally got me to put on some real clothes and get out of the house. We walked into town to get burgers at the diner. I'd lost so much weight that my clothes hung from me like a potato sack, my jean shorts sliding off my hips.

At that time of year the edges of the leaves start to brown and curl, and the end of summer feels tangible in a way that permeates the air with a sense of looming desolation. I had always found these final, transitional weeks of the season to be tough, but this summer, from within my interminable ocean of grief, I barely noticed the shift.

Burke sat across from me at the diner and watched to make sure I ate everything on my plate. My burger tasted like nothing—soggy, chewed-up mulch that I struggled to swallow. The vanilla milkshake Burke insisted I order was thick, flavorless air. I sobbed silently into my plate, tears melting into my greasy meal at the memory of how much Gus loved the diner's cheeseburgers. I thought of his little bites revealing the tiniest teeth marks in the bun, of how long it always took him to finish eating and how impatient the waitress used to get when the diner was crowded.

Across from me, Burke slid out of his seat and into my side of the booth. He covered my hands with both of his and squeezed.

"Bones, I know you're sad. I am, too. But we need to talk about some things. Some important things."

I watched Burke's mouth move as he continued to speak. He was as handsome as ever, but the contours of his face had changed. Sorrow was there, an edge of gloom in his smile that I didn't recognize. I'd been so absorbed in my own grief that I'd barely noticed his, and I saw then that losing Gus had changed Burke, too. But it was more than that; I suddenly realized that I hadn't seen him with a drink in his hand since we'd been back together, since the day I'd called him from the hospital.

I listened as Burke lectured me on the importance of keeping up my new and improved grades, sounding oddly like Libby. He said he wanted us both to go to college.

"I've been an idiot, Bones." He sighed. "Everything you said last year was true. I was fucked-up. I was drunk and high all the time, and you were right, I did bring you down. You were smart to let me go."

"Oh, Burke—"

"No. Hear me out. I'm so proud of what you accomplished last year, Bones, and beyond that I'm inspired. I still think you're the most amazing girl I've ever known—I always have—and all I want is to build a life with you. But I want it to be the life *you* want and deserve. I want to get the fuck out of Langs Valley, together. And I know you're in pieces right now, I know that, Bones. But we're about to start our senior year, and you can't let what's happened ruin the future you've worked so hard for. *I* won't let it happen. I swear to God, Heather, I won't."

Burke's blue eyes grew brighter as he spoke, and I felt the faintest spark catch and sizzle behind my sternum. For the first time since Gus died, I could see a wedge of clear ground at my feet. I thought of something my mother used to tell me when I was little and having a bad day. She called it a gratitude practice, and she said that whenever I was feeling crummy, all I had to do was think of one thing that I was grateful for, and that doing so would instantly lift my spirits. It had worked. Ironically, my mother was often the reason behind a bad day, but I employed her gratitude practice regardless. When she was coming down from drugs and in one of her foul moods, I thought about how fun it was to play tetherball at recess, and how much I loved having Kyla as a best friend, and focusing on those things made me feel lighter. When my mother would disappear for days on end after Gus was born and I'd feel sick with anger and frustration, I'd think about how grateful I was that Gus existed, that I got to have him as my sibling.

That day at the diner, as Burke held my hand and helped me see a clear inch on the dark path ahead, I fought my way toward some semblance of gratitude. Burke was a good person, and he loved me, and I had never fallen out of love with him, not really. I'd let

Libby convince me that Burke was bad news, that loving him came at the cost of my own self-destruction. But Libby had been wrong, and I'd been too enamored of her effortless sophistication and glamorous lifestyle to see that she knew nothing about love at all. The love Burke and I shared ran miles deeper than anything she had with Peter—invisible Peter, the ghost who'd led Libby to the middle of nowhere on his agenda, who'd left her to steep in her loneliness.

Burke and I were stronger together than Libby and Peter could ever dream to be, and a wave of anger rolled through me at the thought that Libby had nearly driven us apart.

I pressed my face against Burke's shoulder, my tears staining the cotton of his shirt. "I can't do it alone, Burke," I whispered. "College, I mean. Senior year. Applications. The future. Getting out of Langs Valley. All of it. You're so right about everything you said. But I can't do it alone."

"You won't have to do it alone, Bones." Burke smoothed the back of my head, following the tumble of hair down my spine. "We're in it together. I'll be right beside you, every step of the way."

"Where will we go?" I lifted my head and fixed my gaze to his—clear and blue.

"Anywhere you want."

"But what if we can't get into the same school? No offense, but—"

"I know your grades are better than mine, smarty-pants." Burke grinned, his dimples deepening. "We'll make sure we end up in the same city. In a big city, there'll be lots of options for colleges. And I'm going to stay sober and seriously start applying myself. I'm not just saying that, Bones. I don't want to end up like my dad. I want us to have a real shot at the life we both deserve. We're going to end up in the same place and we're going to make this work. You and me. Okay?"

"Okay." I pressed close to him again, inhaling his familiar scent, woodsmoke and pine. My sweet, strong, loyal Burke. "New York City," I said, imagining the way Gus's green eyes lit up when I'd read *The Snowy Day*. "Let's go to New York."

With those five words I had a dream again. I cradled New York in the palm of my hand; pushed its image to the front of my thoughts. The problem, Dr. K, was that I couldn't forget about Libby Fontaine. No matter how hard I tried, I couldn't shake her loose from the mad, obsessive corners of my mind.

Chapter Twenty-Six

Skye

The room spins. I wrestle for air.

One two three four five six seven eight; eight seven six five four three two one.

One two three four five six seven eight; eight seven six five four three two one.

One two three four five six seven eight; eight seven six five four three two one.

I am back in the hospital waiting room and my mother is dying. Time is running out, but I can keep breathing for both of us. I can be the person she was.

When you die, do you inhale your last breath, or is it an exhale? I wish I could have been there to see for myself. But I was trapped. I am still trapped. I will always be trapped.

I knock on the inside of Andie's bedroom door until my knuckles are raw. I flop onto the bed and stare at the ceiling. When Andie gets back from work—she had clients she couldn't reschedule—she curls up beside me.

The world is upside down.

It's been twenty-four hours since I learned that Burke Michaels, my husband, is an impostor who never loved me, who married me so that he could divorce me and take my money back to his real wife and kids. It's so preposterous that a small part of me threatens to explode with laughter, but the destroyed part of me is so much bigger, and far too debilitating.

What I wouldn't give to go back twenty-four hours in time, to unknow all that has unraveled my world overnight. To the time when Burke and I were in love, newlyweds just back from our honeymoon—the length of our beautiful, promising marriage stretched ahead of us.

Save for a lone crack down the middle of the screen, my phone didn't break when I hurled it across Andie's living room. Burke continued to call. He called so many times that Andie blocked his number on my phone.

I feel untethered from reality, my consciousness a whirl of so many emotions that they all cancel each other out, leaving me static and numb. It isn't possible to wrap my head around the reality that our entire relationship—every last speck of it—was a lie.

How is it possible? My brain replays a hundred different conversations at once. Hours and hours of discussion of the future—of our future. The sound of Burke's voice is audible inside my mind.

I can't describe it to you, Goose, the relief of knowing that I'll have you in my life forever.

Maybe in a couple years we'll get out of the city. We'll build a house without any doors inside, just archways, somewhere on a great piece of land where we can see the stars at night.

And the most searing memory of all, from just a week before our wedding, Burke's lips pressed against my ear in the shower, hot water dribbling down our backs.

How many kids do you want, Goose? However many you want, I'll give them all to you.

"I called Jan on my way home."

I've forgotten Andie's beside me. I flip over onto my side so that we're facing each other. "You called Jan?" My voice is small.

"Well, I remembered you have that big round of edits due to her this week—the ones you were scrambling to finish on the plane, for her *new* new book. Right? Anyway, I told her you were having a family emergency and would be out of commission for a few days."

"Oh. Thanks."

"And I canceled dinner with my mom."

"You shouldn't cancel, Andie. She just got back from rehab."

"For, like, the fifth time this year. Besides, you're way more important."

I sigh, too miserable to be fully grateful for Andie's selflessness. Her mother hasn't been doing well, and despite their complex relationship, I know Andie's been looking forward to seeing her for weeks.

"You should really go to dinner," I squeak.

"I'm not going. And you need to eat something, Skye. What can I make you? Or I'll order takeout? Anything you want."

"I'm just not hungry."

"I know, but it's been twenty-four hours. You have to eat."

"No, I don't. It won't kill me."

"Skye." Andie sighs. "What do you want to do? Do you want to call your dad?"

So far, Andie and I have told no one about the email that unraveled my entire life in moments. A fucked-up part of me wishes Burke hadn't been such a dumbass and could just have sent the email to the *correct* Andy. Whoever said ignorance is bliss hit the nail on the head.

"Skye?" She's inches from my face, but Andie's voice sounds far away. An echo. "What do you think about calling your dad?"

A fresh wave of horror washes through me. "I can't tell my dad." Fresh tears burn behind my eyes. I've cried so much in the past twenty-four hours that I'm afraid to look in the mirror. "Not yet."

Andie says nothing, and I know she understands. How can I tell my father, who just shelled out a quarter of a million dollars on his daughter's dream wedding, that the entire thing was a sham? I let this happen. I vouched for Burke to my family. I married a con man.

For some reason our wedding registry pops into my head. I think about the wasted hours I spent on its curation, the level of thought I put into the selection of items such as cheese knives and bath rugs. The extent to which I contemplated place settings. Tory Burch spongeware or Juliska Berry & Thread? A decision that consumed me for weeks, that kept me up at night. Irrelevant now.

"I'm so fucking sad, Andie." The tears spill over. "And so angry."

"I know."

"And I *miss* him. How fucked-up is that?"

"It's not fucked-up. Cut yourself a break, okay? This just happened. Your entire world is shattered. What *he* did is fucked-up. I mean, *fucked-up* doesn't even begin to do it justice. It's criminal. He could go to prison."

"I know," I say, though I hadn't thought about it that way.

"It's bigamy. And actually, when your dad finds out about this, he'll make *sure* Burke goes to prison."

A seam splits through my heart at the sound of his name. Burke. My husband. My husband cannot go to prison. My insides twist at the thought.

"I'm sorry." Andie sighs. "Maybe you're not ready to think about that."

I shrug. "In some moments I am . . . but then it switches over so quickly to . . . just . . . brokenness."

Andie blinks. A few moments of silence pass.

"Your heart *is* broken, Skye," she says eventually. "Even though the circumstances are outrageous, it doesn't negate the heartbreak. God, I'm so sorry. I so wanted you to be happy." A tear slips down the hollow of Andie's cheek.

"You never trusted him." I lock her gaze. "You said it was too fast, and I should have listened to you."

"Fuck what I said. You loved him, and you listened to your heart. Who's to say I wouldn't have done the same?"

I shake my head. "You wouldn't have, Andie. You're too smart for that. And too strong."

"That's not true. I—" She pauses. "I'm a wimp for not telling you, but Spencer told me six months ago that he might never want to get married." She looks back at me. "It's why I was being a bitch to you at your bachelorette, if I'm honest. I just kept thinking, 'I've done this whole routine for so many of my friends, and now I'll never have it myself.' But still, here I am, staying in a relationship with no future."

"Oh, Andie." I swallow. "You should have told me."

"I know."

"Spence is probably just nervous. You guys will get married. Of course you will."

She shrugs. "This isn't about me. I just wanted to tell you because I should have told you a while ago, but I was . . . embarrassed, I guess."

"You had no reason to be embarrassed. I'm mortified. I don't know where to go from here."

"I told you, we're going to figure it out. And in the meantime, you're staying here with me."

"That's nice of you, but I can't evict Spencer."

"Screw Spencer." Andie props up on one elbow and reaches for her phone on the nightstand. "I just realized that we need to call your bank and have Burke blocked from the joint account. We also need to cancel any credit cards he has access to."

I nod slowly. "Right."

"I'll call. What's the bank?"

"Bank of America Private Bank."

"Do you know the account number offhand?"

I shake my head. "I can go on the app and check."

I sit up in bed, leaning back against the pillows. I take out my own phone as though I'm on autopilot and log in to the Bank of America app. As it loads I realize how rarely I check the account. The balance is always so much more than I need, and since Burke and I moved in together, he's taken care of paying off the credit cards.

But my heart goes still when the recent transactions appear on the screen. I blink, rereading the top line. It's possible I'm hallucinating.

"Andie." It comes out as a whisper, a choke. I tilt the screen in her direction, my hands trembling as I point to the latest transaction on the account:

Oct. 3, 2019: External transfer—$2,000,000

"What the . . ." I watch Andie's eyes bloom with fury, the black of her pupils filling her irises. My head feels heavy, a balloon of sand.

Burke has stolen two million dollars from me. He transferred it right out of the account, right under my nose. How is that even possible?

The world tips. I'm suddenly angry. Starkly, insanely angry.

"We need to call the police." Andie's voice is thin.

"No," I say, flooded with conviction. "I need to talk to Burke first. I need to look *my husband* in the eye and tell him that I know what he did."

Andie chews her bottom lip. "I don't think that's a good idea, Skye."

"I don't care." I'm so livid I'm trembling.

"Fine." She swallows. "But you're not staying there.

Tell him to pack his shit and be out of your apartment by the morning. And then you come right back here."

"Okay."

"Tell me you swear."

I'm suddenly overcome with déjà vu; Andie's commanding tone is the same as it was that day in seventh grade shortly after Mom died, the afternoon she marched into my room and told me to get out of bed.

"I swear," I tell her. "I'll come right back."

I grab my bag and jacket from the living room couch and head toward the door. I want to scream at the compulsion that stops me in my tracks on the way out of the apartment. *There's a chance you'll wake up from this nightmare, Skye, but only if you knock on wood.*

I do my knocks in a blur of misery, knowing it won't change a thing but, as always, unable to resist the urge boiling over inside me. I get to every wooden object in Andie's living room, then finally the door, to leave the apartment. I rush down the stairs and out of Andie's building toward the open air, where there's nothing left to knock. Outside is where I'm usually free; today, everywhere is a prison. The sky is bright and piercing blue, and maybe my mind is up there somewhere, tangled in the atmosphere with the rest of the unknown.

I hail a cab to take me back to the West Village. The ride is too short and I don't have enough time to think about what I'm going to say. All I can feel is an unthinkable rage leaching into my bones as I pay the cabbie on West Eleventh Street, imagining Burke in the apartment. A stranger to me now.

I get out of the taxi and go upstairs.

Chapter Twenty-Seven

Burke

Skye is gone.

It's been over twenty-four hours and I'm in a full-blown panic. I haven't seen her since ten o'clock yesterday morning when I stepped out to run some errands. She was still sleeping when I left the apartment—we got back from our honeymoon in Italy late Saturday night, and I knew she was exhausted. Unlike me, Skye can never sleep on airplanes. So I left her a note, and off I went.

I did run errands—I was out of shaving cream—but I also needed to walk. Walking is when I do my best thinking, and so much has been on my mind.

When I got back to the apartment around noon, Skye wasn't there. I figured she'd gone for a jog or out to get breakfast, but when she didn't come back by two and I couldn't get her on the phone, I started to worry. Now it's one in the afternoon on Monday and she still isn't here, and I'm completely losing my mind. I mean, she's my *wife*. I've called and texted her countless times, but nothing. I've texted her friends; Lexy, Isabel, and Kendall all responded that they hadn't heard from her. But

Andie hasn't responded, and she didn't pick up when I called, either.

This gives me a strange sense of hope that Skye and Andie are together. That, at least, Skye is okay, and perhaps, for some bizarre reason, neither of them have their phones. It's the only reason I haven't called Mr. Starling—it doesn't exactly look great to call your new bride's father two weeks after the wedding asking if he's seen her—but if I don't hear from Skye in the next few hours, I will.

Her laptop is sitting on her desk and I stab at the keys—there's no password—as the machine comes to life. The screen is open to iCloud Photos, to the shared album that Andie started after the wedding. Skye was a perfect bride—beautiful and collected—and I'm pondering which ones to have printed as a surprise for her, when I hear the sound of keys jangling in the lock. I jump to my feet, drenched with a wave of relief.

"Where have you been?" I ask as she walks through the door.

But the second I see her eyes—cold and unfamiliar—I know something is wrong.

Skye drops her bag on the floor. She holds out her phone so that the screen faces me.

"What the fuck is this, Burke?"

"What the fuck is what, Goose?" It's such a relief to see her, to know that she's safe. All I want to do is wrap my arms around her, pull her close. My wife. The woman who has, in such a short amount of time, truly become my counterpart.

"Don't you dare call me that," she spits, her gaze icy. "Tell me what the fuck this is."

I take the phone from her grasp, swallowing the lump in my throat. What I'm most afraid of happening cannot be happening. Can it?

Carefully, I look down at the screen. It's open to an email, one from me to an address I don't recognize. I read the first few lines:

From: burke.michaels@gmail.com
To: andier@me.com
Date: Oct 6, 2019, 8:02 AM
Subject: (no subject)

Andy,

Got your text, sorry I'm just getting back to you now. Skye and I have been on our honeymoon and just got back last night, so I haven't had much time to myself the past couple of weeks. . . .

My heart drops into my lap. Instantly, I know I didn't write or send the email. My head spins violently, an intersection of questions crashing together.

I finish reading the message, a chill in the base of my spine. I read it through a second time, the words blurring together.

I blink to make sure I'm not dreaming.

Skye is watching me, her chocolate eyes panicked and wide—a window into the confusion and fury and sheer horror blowing through her mind.

I can hardly breathe. I force a few choppy inhales, willing myself to think rationally. What I know, and what whoever is trying to frame me knows, is that the message was meant to be sent to Andy Raymond, my old friend from Langs Valley who I paid to be in the wedding. Whoever impersonated me has crafted it to look like an accident on my part, like I made the mistake of sending the email to Skye's best friend, Andie Roussos, instead of my friend Andy Raymond.

"Burke." Skye's voice is shriller than I've ever heard it, and I suddenly remember that she's still staring at me, waiting. "What the *fuck* is this?"

I open my mouth to speak but nothing comes out. How is this happening? *What* is happening? My mind is racing too fast; I can't keep up with the thoughts diving in and out. Did Andy Raymond do this? Or was it one of the other "groomsmen" I hired from Langs Valley? Does someone want money? Does someone have an old beef with me? Is this payback for some idiotic crime I committed when I was obliterated out of my mind in high school?

Then I remember the attachment "I" referenced near the end of the email.

I think the letters (attached) will tell you everything you want to know.

I look down at Skye's phone, still in my hand. My fingers quiver as I open the file, titled "BM Diary." A Word document fills the screen.

September 8, 2018

Dear Dr. K,

Her hair is yellow and thick, nothing like my wife's. Isn't that awful, that when I first notice an attractive woman, I instantly compare her to my wife? I used to think I was a good person, the kind of man who wouldn't be struck dumb by the tumble of blond hair down a creamy, anonymous back.

No. It can't be.

I scroll through the document, skimming over the digital diary while Skye watches me. It goes on and on; the entries are letters, pages and pages of them, all written from my perspective. But I didn't write them. I didn't write a single word.

"I—I didn't write this, Skye," I say finally. I step toward her and she backs away, her jaw clenched. "There's some stuff I need to explain, but I swear I didn't write any of this. Not the email or the diary. I swear to you on my life."

"You fucking liar," she hisses. "I've caught you red-handed and you're still lying? Grow a pair, Burke. Own up to what you've done. Own up to the *two million* dollars you stole from me."

"What?" My heart storms inside my chest. "Skye, I didn't steal two million dollars from you. I *swear.*"

"And why should I believe a fucking word you say?" She's crying now, thick tears running down the apples of her cheeks. Her skin is mottled and red, but she's still the most beautiful woman I've ever seen. All I want to do is hold her.

"Answer this simple question, Burke." She wipes her face with her sleeve. "Is it true you have another wife, and children?"

I say nothing. Pressure swells behind my eyes.

Fresh tears spill down her cheeks. "You piece of shit." Her voice is a cracked whisper.

"I'm so sorry, Skye." The words feel stuck in my throat. "But I promise I didn't write that email or those diary entries. For—for what it's worth."

Skye shifts in her stance. She rubs the creases of her eyes. "I'm leaving. When I come back here at six tomorrow, I want you out."

"Skye, please don't—"

But she's already doing her knocks on the door, and I feel equally helpless and devastated as I watch her, a slave to her disease even now. And then she's gone.

My chest feels hollow and tight, as though the wind has been knocked out of me. I am numb as I sink down on the couch and open my laptop. I log into my email. Sure enough, in the sent-items folder is an outgoing message "I" sent to Andie yesterday morning.

I scroll to the bottom of the email and click the attachment. The Word doc floods the screen and I force myself to read it thoroughly, all the way through.

Each letter or diary entry is addressed to Dr. K.

Dr. K.

Why does this sound so familiar?

Dr. K. Dr. K is Dr. Kendrick, our old couples therapist.

A memory of Dr. Kendrick takes shape in my mind.

A balding man with a Roman nose in his fifties or sixties, third-floor office near the train station. Blue leather couch, a coffee table strewn with old issues of *Psychology Today*. We only saw him for a couple months; he didn't take insurance, but Heather had heard he was one of the best therapists in New Haven and insisted we go. She said couples therapy would be her birthday present to me that year, as if that somehow made it more appealing. I hadn't even realized our marriage was in such a bind, but in retrospect we weren't doing well. In the end the therapy was too expensive, and given that money was the source of our problems, we stopped going.

I remember Dr. Kendrick's advice during one particular appointment, the low, clear sound of his voice: *As an assignment, I'd like you each to write in your own journals. Write whatever comes to mind—it can be about each other, or what you're feeling in general, or anything at all. If it feels more natural, you can write the journal entries as letters to someone—to each other, or even to me. Of course, I'll never see them. No one will. These are purely for you, an exercise to get to know yourselves better, as individuals independent of your relationship.*

Heather and I had laughed about it in the car on the way home, about the "assignment" and how dumb we were for paying three hundred dollars an hour to have someone tell us to write in a journal, and that no wonder we had money problems. We'd howled over it; it was the first time we'd laughed together—*really* laughed—in months. I didn't tell her a week later when

I bought a navy Moleskine at the pharmacy, fueled by Dr. Kendrick's advice. I didn't tell her that I started writing in it, that the words rushed out of me like tap water, ready at the turn of a knob.

It's so ironic it might be funny if it weren't utterly horrifying, the sight of my impersonation on the laptop screen, at the open "BM Diary" document in front of me. I read through the whole thing and by the end I feel warped, as though I'm not in my body but floating far up above. There's a long skinny hallway and a door I can't unlock, a door that's laughing, pointing, and I've been here before, many times, powerless and trapped in my own mind. It's what addiction does to you. It's what Skye's OCD does to her. It's the battle we both endure, and I've never met someone who gets it the way she does, who sees me as lucidly, as compassionately, as she does. Or did. If I lose her, which I will, I'll never forgive myself. This I know.

I blink my way back into my body, willing myself to comprehend what I've just read. Awareness of the impending damage oozes its way into my consciousness, a pooling sickness in my gut with implications far worse than what I can fully grasp—for losing and destroying Skye, for the fate of Garrett, Hopie, and Mags, for the inevitability of the legal repercussions that lie ahead. Most wrenching of all is the realization that none of this has anything to do with Andy Raymond or the guys from Langs Valley.

I realize what I already know. What I've known since the very first page of the document. I know who wrote these letters.

Chapter Twenty-Eight

Heather

Dear Dr. K,

In July 1991, Burke and I moved to New York.

Oh, *New York*. There's really no place like it, Dr. K, which you obviously know because you live there now. I'm sure you and the wife take full advantage of your backyard—museums, Saturdays in Central Park, Michelin-star dinners, Broadway shows. I've seen your Cartier watch—God knows you have the resources.

When Burke and I first arrived in New York, it felt like a miracle. It was by far the happiest I'd been in the horrible year since Libby Fontaine let my little brother drown in Chazy Lake. Senior year I tried to keep up my grades as best I could, but my being so depressed made it hard. For much of the year I felt depleted, as if the drive and stamina I'd had before had died in the lake with Gus. Despite Burke's efforts to help me out of the muck, my fall semester average still dropped from a 3.9 to a 3.0.

I didn't retake my SATs—my scores from the previous spring were strong enough—but with my new GPA the college counselor said it was going to be nearly impossible to get any kind of scholarship to Barnard, which had been my first choice. Burke encouraged me to apply anyway, but the application was complicated and daunting, and besides, Barnard was Libby's alma mater. I realized I wanted nothing to do with it.

Sticking to our plan, Burke and I applied to schools exclusively in New York City. I got a partial scholarship to NYU and a full ride to Fordham University, so even though NYU was much higher ranked, I enrolled at Fordham. Burke's transcript was a nightmare; the only redeeming quality was that his GPA showed a steady improvement from a 1.7 freshman year to a 3.0 senior year. I helped him write a personal essay on visiting his father in prison as a child, and he received a partial scholarship to CUNY Medgar Evers College.

Burke had stepped up senior year—he'd stayed off booze and drugs—and I was proud of him by the time we arrived in Manhattan. More than that, I believed in him. I knew he was smarter than anyone in Langs Valley had ever given him credit for, and it filled my heart with pride to know that he had started to believe it, too.

We lifted each other up, Dr. K. That's what love does, and we loved each other fiercely. We were more than the other young couples drifting hand in hand around the city—much more. Burke and I were each other's family.

We found a cheap studio apartment in the East Village, nearly equidistant from Fordham in the Bronx and Medgar Evers in Brooklyn. I know the East Village is trendy nowadays, but back then the area was seedy. Still, it was all we could afford off campus with our housing stipend, and Burke and I had made a firm commitment to live together in spite of our commutes. Plus, being from Langs Valley, we'd seen our fair share of shit, and we were scrappier than average eighteen-year-olds. The apartment was three hundred square feet with a single window overlooking an alley, but we made it home. We found a cheap mattress and some dishes at a tag sale, and a paint-chipped dresser on the sidewalk marked FREE. We tacked my favorite photograph of Gus to the wall above the dresser—the one where he's sitting in the meadow next to our old house with his little knees tucked into his chest, blowing on a dandelion.

That first summer in New York was *hot*—a kind of heat we'd never experienced living in the mountains. We couldn't afford an air-conditioning unit, but we got a fan that we blasted on full speed while we slept.

We weren't always comfortable, but we were happy. For the first time since Gus died, I felt as if the weight on my shoulders had lightened, and I stood a little taller when I walked. They say you can't run away from your problems, that your problems will chase you wherever you go, but if my problems followed me to New York, I think the city swallowed them right up. Its utter size and magnitude were more than I could comprehend; walking the streets or riding the subway uptown, I was floored by the sheer number of human beings that filled every inch of space. And everyone had problems. People were sick and homeless and fighting and crying—it was impossible to feel isolated by your own issues in a city that so publicly cursed the world. I loved it.

Burke got a job at the movie theater near Union Square, and I started waitressing at a Greek restaurant near our apartment. We both enjoyed going to work because of the air-conditioning. Some nights the restaurant manager let me bring home leftovers, which Burke and I would eat on our bed with the fan on full blast while we dreamed about the future.

We were going to keep studying hard and get perfect grades. Burke would get into business school at Columbia, and after graduation I would get a good job to tide us over while Burke finished his MBA. I didn't have a specific career in mind yet, but I'd declared a major in economics and a minor in English, figuring this combination would open a variety of doors. After Burke finished grad school, we'd get married and have a beautiful wedding somewhere classy, like the Botanical Gardens or the Waldorf, paid for with Burke's signing bonus from whatever top investment bank swept him up.

Once we had plenty of money saved, we'd have a baby—of this I was certain. I *wanted* children, from a deep place inside me. I wanted to hold them and protect them and give them the world. We'd move to a big white house in Connecticut; not in Libby's town, but somewhere like it. Burke would be making bucketloads by then; we'd have so much money we'd never need to worry about anything. We'd be able to give our children everything they needed and more. All we had to do was stick with the plan, and with each other.

The one piece of the plan I didn't share with Burke was that I still wasn't all that interested in having a career, as he assumed I was. I aimed to work for a couple of years, certainly—perhaps in advertising or PR—but mostly I wanted to not *need* to work. I yearned for financial freedom, and days that belonged to me; I'd spend them raising our babies and decorating the house and planning vacations and reading glossy magazines in the bathtub with a glass of good wine. *This* was the true goal, to live the way Libby did. To be the kind of mother she was to her children.

But I couldn't exactly admit to Burke that my real aspiration was to luxuriate in the wealth he provided—not yet. It would happen naturally down the line, but in the meantime, I needed to keep Burke focused. For him to succeed he had to believe that we were in the trenches together; he had to continue to find inspiration in our shared plan.

So we'd fall asleep like that, whispering dreams in the dark heat. We'd wake up in the mornings, our limbs tangled and sticky with sweat, but grateful to be where we were. We'd made it out of Langs Valley, and we were never going back. For the time being, that was enough.

Chapter Twenty-Nine

Skye

Andie and I get to my building at a quarter past six. I feel like I've been gone for months, even though it's barely been twenty-four hours since I was here confronting Burke. I give Andie my keys and she goes up to the apartment first, to make sure he's not there. I wait in the cab on West Eleventh, the meter still running. Outside a light rain has begun to fall, streaking the windows.

"Just another minute or two," I say to the driver.

I told Andie I'd go up to the apartment with her—even though I'd told Burke to be out by six, half of me desperately hoped he'd still be there, that he'd pull me into his strong arms and I'd breathe in his sharp, woody scent and be momentarily pacified. But Andie read the look on my face and told me to wait.

My phone vibrates in my lap, a text confirming the coast is clear. I head into the building and wave at Ivan behind the front desk, as though it were just another day.

Andie is waiting upstairs. The apartment feels different immediately; a sense of deflation is in the air; an empty space is to the right of the bathroom sink where Burke kept his toiletries. The framed photograph of us from the day we got engaged is missing from its usual place on the mahogany side table. I know Andie wanted a few moments alone here to remove any lingering traces of him.

My heart rattles with emptiness. Just two mornings ago I'd woken up here as Burke's wife, and now he's gone. I am alone again.

Alone.

The feeling swallows me whole and I crumple onto the floor, fresh tears spilling from my eyes. Andie catches me in her pin-thin arms, which are freakishly strong, and pulls me onto the couch. She lets me cry. I cry as the light dies outside. When it's nearly dark, Andie gets up to turn on some lamps.

"I'm going to order us some dinner. How does Thai sound? That place on Bleecker with the amazing spring rolls that aren't too greasy?"

Andie's voice sounds far away. *How does Thai sound?*

I'm reminded of a night right after Mom died. My dad was ordering pizza and asked what toppings I wanted. I had the feeling he was speaking to someone else. What did I want on my pizza? How could I consider the toppings I wanted on my pizza when my mother was dead? Her body was in a refrigerator waiting to be burned to ash, and I was supposed to choose pepperoni or mushroom. I wanted to laugh in my father's face at the same time I wanted to scream at him for not knowing my pizza order—peppers and onions, always. For years it had been the same. But I realized only Mom knew that kind of small thing, that Dad had never known because he'd never needed to, and he'd never been interested enough to learn. I also realized that even though I still had my father and brother, in many ways I was now on my own.

The sensation is similar now; the appeal of spring rolls is laughable because the day before yesterday I had a husband and today my husband doesn't exist.

"Skye," Andie pleads, "You need to eat."

"I can't eat right now. I need to talk to Dr. Salam."

Andie orders Thai anyway, and I type out a text to Dr. Salam telling her I need to talk. I know she's left the office for the day, but she's usually responsive via text. She replies several minutes later.

Emergency?

Yes, I text back. *Please.*

She responds that she'll be home in twenty minutes and can do a Skype call then.

"I'm Skyping with Dr. Salam in my room," I tell Andie, who is foraging in the fridge.

"Good." She digs out carrots and hummus. "That will be good. I'm starving. Food is on its way. I'll save you some. I really think you should eat, Skye."

"I'll try in a bit."

"And I'm gonna call the locksmith now, too. I almost forgot we need to do that."

"Right." *Right. We need to call the locksmith to come change the locks to my apartment so that my husband of two weeks can't get back in, lest he attempt to steal any more of my property for his (other) wife and his three children, none of whom I knew existed two days ago.*

"Here's my credit card." I place it on the kitchen counter. "If the locksmith comes while I'm still on the phone."

When Dr. Salam's familiar face appears on my laptop screen twenty minutes later, I break down again.

Something about the smoothness of her skin—the color of a coffee milkshake—always puts me at deep ease. Dr. Salam has no lines on her face except two creases running parallel between her brows that sharpen when she's concerned. I think about her clearing space in her evening schedule—a dinner she planned to cook for her husband, or emails she needed to answer—to make time for me. Dr. Salam is there for me the way Andie is, the way I'd thought Burke was, the way only a few precious people in life end up being. My heart trembles.

"Talk to me, Skye." Dr. Salam's voice is clear. "Tell me what happened."

I crack open. I'm a flash flood tearing down a wall, a roaring river of rage and desolation and terror. Dr. Salam absorbs my pain like a sponge. I watch as she glances sideways and wrings it out, ridding herself of any lingering subjectivity so that she can return to the session even-keeled and ready to help. She is good at what she does. Unlike Andie, Dr. Salam isn't allowed to scream and object on my behalf; she is my therapist, not my friend.

But today a horrified expression lingers in Dr. Salam's dark eyes. I've never seen her look so affected—not even when I told her the truth about Max LaPointe.

"I'm so sorry, Skye," she says when she finally

speaks. "That is some of the more abominable behavior I've heard of. And I've heard a lot."

I say nothing.

"I want you to remember that none of this has anything to do with you. Burke was going to do what he was going to do, and it was never about you. It's about him. He could have done this to anyone. I'm so sorry you got put in this unlucky position. It really isn't fair."

"I can't help but know it's me, though. A stronger, smarter person wouldn't have let this happen to her. In retrospect I barely knew him when we got engaged. There were"—I exhale—"there were red flags. But I made the choice to trust him because I so badly wanted to believe that what we had was real."

"Being vulnerable isn't a weakness, Skye. On the contrary, it's bravery. 'Vulnerability is the birthplace of connection and the path to the feeling of worthiness.' Brené Brown said that."

A hot tear rolls down my cheek. "I don't know what to do."

Dr. Salam sighs. "We're going to take it one step at a time. First step is to eat some dinner. Andie is right that you need to put food in your stomach. Then try to get some sleep, and come to the office tomorrow morning. My first appointment isn't until nine-thirty. Why don't you come at eight?"

"I will." I nod, my voice squeaky. "Thank you."

I click the laptop shut. There's a roiling in my gut, and I'm suddenly ravenous. I head toward the bedroom door to go make myself a plate of Thai, and that's when I notice the yellow Post-it note on the nightstand, tucked under the lamp. I instantly recognize Burke's familiar scribble.

I'm so sorry, Skye. I wish I could explain, but I can't. I love you.—B

Burke's words burn the space behind my sternum, blistering my cracked-open heart. My head fogs with confusion and fresh anger and shameful hope. I read the note again, tracing my fingers over the ink, lost in my mind.

"Skye!" Andie calls from the other room. "Are you off the phone?"

I love you.

He loves me. After everything that happened, why would he say that if he didn't mean it?

My hands quiver as I slide the Post-it underneath a stack of books on the nightstand. I know that if Andie finds it, she'll rip it to shreds, and I can't let that happen. It's all I have left of my husband.

Chapter Thirty

Burke

OCTOBER 2019—*ONE DAY WITHOUT SKYE*

I don't wait until the morning to leave West Eleventh Street. The idea of sleeping in the bed without Skye is too depressing, and besides, she wants me out.

It doesn't take me long to pack up the few items in the apartment that are mine—clothes, toiletries, computer, a few books. Mostly everything was Skye's to begin with, and the place hardly looks any different by the time I zip my duffel.

A stack of Post-it notes sits on Skye's desk, and I peel one from the top. I want to leave her with a few words—I can't not leave her with *something*. I try not to think about the ramifications of what's happening as I leave the apartment.

I take the subway to Grand Central, where I catch the train to New Haven. It's surprisingly full, and I wonder why anyone else might be journeying from Manhattan to New Haven on Monday afternoon. A lot of crazy people are in this world, but I wonder if anyone is carrying as outrageous a secret as I am.

I check my texts with the frequency of a teenage girl, and for the first time I understand why Maggie is constantly glued to her phone. But Skye doesn't text or call. No one does.

I imagine Skye arriving home and finding my note. I imagine her lighting it on fire.

The weather has turned, and it's raining by the time my train rolls into the station around a quarter of six. I can't bear the thought of asking Heather for a pickup; instead I spring for a cab with the little cash I have left. Rain smacks and streaks the windows of the taxi as it heads to the east side of town, toward the white-shingled split-level where I raised my children.

It's a complicated feeling, being back here. So much has changed inside me since I left. Nothing changed for twenty-five years, and now everything is different because I am. I wonder if this is how Garrett and Hope and Maggie feel when they come home after months of being away at school or in their new adult lives, after all that time evolving and being shaped by the complexities of the world. It's a strange, sad thing, after all that, to come back home and see the physical sameness of it. The steady constant of the place you left.

I didn't have that with Langs Valley. When Heather and I moved to New York, neither of us looked back.

On the front stoop I pause, listening to the rain drum against the roof of the portico. I shift from one foot to the other. I imagine Skye back on West Eleventh Street. I picture her sitting on one end of the couch with her knees tucked. I imagine the apple smell of her hair. I miss her so badly I feel split open with a kind of homesickness, and maybe this is what I do, maybe this is what I have always done. I make my home in the women that I love and remain lost inside my own self.

Dusk is descending and lights pop on from within, the first-story windows glowing yellow. I don't ring the doorbell. I locate the spare key underneath the garden-gnome statue to the right of the stoop—the usual hiding place—and let myself in. I let the door slam.

She rushes from the kitchen, her eyes glassy and wide. Heather's giant green eyes always used to stun me, but in the past few years they've started to appear buggy, too big for her face. I used to feel guilty for having that thought.

"You scared me!" She catches her breath, and fear is in her face. Several long seconds pass before her lips spread into a smile that sends a chill down my spine. "Welcome home, Husband."

Chapter Thirty-One

Heather

Dear Dr. K,

The fall of my junior year at Fordham, I got sick. Really, wrenchingly sick. At first I thought it was a bad bout of the flu, but when I was still puking multiple times a day after three weeks passed, Burke insisted I see a doctor.

I'd never liked going to doctors. Something about the stuffy, chemical smell of hospitals and medical buildings always made me feel nauseated, and it had gotten worse since Gus died.

I asked Burke to come with me, but he was swamped prepping for a test, and I was too proud of him that fall to make a fuss. He'd recently started classes at NYU; in his first two years at CUNY Medgar Evers he'd received perfect grades, and with a 4.0 GPA and glowing references from his professors, he'd been accepted to NYU as a transfer student.

It was a crisp Saturday morning in October when I headed to the doctor's office in the Bronx, just a short walk from the campus library where I'd been tackling some work. I felt faint with nausea, but my Cultural

Theory midterm paper was due the following week, and I'd barely made a dent in the outline.

A cheerful man with a salt-and-pepper beard introduced himself as Dr. Wayne. He asked me a number of questions, checked my vitals and blood pressure, and poked around in my ears and mouth with his instruments. He said everything looked fine, that it was probably just a prolonged stomach bug, but that a nurse would take some blood tests to be sure. I'd always loathed needles, but looked the other way and let the nurse prick my pointer finger. She said the doctor would be back in several minutes.

I was starting to get antsy; I'd made only pathetic progress on my paper, and I'd failed the pop quiz the week before because I'd felt too ill to do the reading. It was too early in the semester to be sure that my grades were dropping, but I'd never failed a quiz before.

Nearly twenty minutes later Dr. Wayne reappeared with the nurse at his side. They both wore smiles that stretched their faces like cartoon characters.

"You don't have a stomach bug." Dr. Wayne beamed.

"That's good, I guess." I tried to smile back, but suddenly wanted to hurl again.

"You're ten weeks pregnant."

That must've been enough to send me over the edge because the bile came rushing up my throat and I vomited all over the floor, partly on Dr. Wayne's patent-leather loafers.

Like most sexually active college-aged women, I subconsciously knew that despite my daily birth control pills—pills that made my period almost nonexistent—I was not fully immune to pregnancy. During that stage in my life I'd always assumed that on the off chance Burke and I ever did get pregnant by accident, I'd get it taken care of. I'd never had an abortion, but they hadn't been uncommon in Langs Valley. I'd taken Kyla to Planned Parenthood twice in high school, held her hand while the doctor did his thing.

So that day in Dr. Wayne's office, after I apologized for puking on his shoes, I opened my mouth to explain that I'd need an abortion. But instead of the words, tears filled my eyes and the back of my throat felt full, and I couldn't speak. I knew then that I was going to have the baby.

I'd expected it to be a choice, but it wasn't. Perhaps losing Gus had instilled in me the fragility and preciousness of life, or maybe it was the knowledge that inside me was a cluster of cells that was a mix of Burke and me, the product of our love. Our *baby*. I couldn't simply turn my back on this miracle, not even if I'd wanted to.

That night I waited up for Burke. He crawled into bed beside me, and I sat straight up and told him the news. Burke cried—underneath his masculine exterior he'd always been a sensitive soul—and agreed that we had to keep it. He pressed his face against my stomach and whispered a promise to our baby that he would be the best dad in the world.

I continued to have awful morning sickness for another month. By the second trimester my nausea had mostly subsided, but I was utterly exhausted. I knew my grades were slipping, but for the first time in years I didn't care. After all, I was *pregnant*. Besides, Burke was getting straight A's at NYU. Since the news of the pregnancy he'd been working even harder in school and had already lined up a summer internship at Credit Suisse. If he did well there, he'd likely be offered a place in their two-year analyst program after graduation. With the baby coming, Burke and I decided it would be ideal for him to work for a couple of years before applying to business school. Analyst salaries at banks such as Credit Suisse started in the low six figures; if Burke could get that kind of position, we'd be more than fine financially.

As I grew visibly pregnant, I noticed the way my classmates and professors looked at me, and I learned to ignore their judgmental stares. To them I was a tragedy, a poster child for what not to do—another dumb girl who'd gone and ruined her future by getting knocked up. But I didn't care; I saw the future that Burke's work ethic promised us, and I began to let myself relish in the feeling of being taken care of for the first time in my life.

I wasn't concerned with what the students at Fordham thought of me. Since I spent most of my free time holed up in the library or at home with Burke, I hadn't bothered to make many friends, but the few girls I had gotten to know began to distance themselves, which came as no surprise. A college campus isn't exactly an ideal setting for a pregnant woman, and I was no longer invited to the bar for cold pints after a tough exam.

Burke sat me down one day in late March, when

I was seven months pregnant. He'd been circling me like a hawk for days, and I could tell something was up. On this Sunday afternoon we were eating noodles at our favorite cheap ramen joint in the Village.

"I think we should get married," Burke said after I demanded he spit out whatever was bothering him. He nodded in the wake of his confession, as though agreeing with himself.

I sometimes forgot that Burke's grandmother had raised him Catholic, that lodged into the pit of him was a hearty dose of unsettled Catholic guilt.

"Look, Bones." He took my hand across the table. "We're going to be a real family. And it makes the most sense for tax purposes and health insurance and stuff. I've looked into it. And we're planning on getting married one day anyway. Why wait?"

I knew he was right. While I didn't love the idea of such a visible shotgun wedding, I suspected the city hall clerks had seen it all.

We got married that Friday, with a friend of Burke's from NYU as our witness. The whole thing took less than two minutes, and just like that we were husband and wife. Even though Burke and I had been together for nearly seven years—our brief high school hiatus not included—the knowledge that we were officially Mr. and Mrs. Burke Michaels made me giddy.

We didn't have any money for rings back then, so we used a black Sharpie to draw them on each other's finger. Our Sharpie rings lasted for a few weeks until they faded in the shower, but the bond between us was stronger than ever.

Our son was born on a warm, drizzly afternoon in May of 1994. He was tiny and purple with a full head of black hair, just like his dad's. I was still drugged up from the epidural when I tried to name him Gus Jr., but thankfully Burke interjected that he didn't think it was right to give our baby a name that would always make us a little bit sad. We agreed that his name should start with a *G*, though, in honor of his late uncle. A few hours later, after the drugs had worn off, Burke suggested the name Garrett.

Garrett's arrival flooded my life with a joy so strong it was almost surreal. I was exhausted, yes, but it was a peripheral feeling, one surmounted by the indescribable love and obsession I had for my son. Burke urged me to finish my second-semester finals so I'd receive credit for junior year, but I was too focused on our baby to even think about school.

Burke started his internship at Credit Suisse two weeks after Garrett's birth. His hours were brutal; he was out the door at six every morning and rarely came home before midnight. But I didn't complain; I knew this was what Burke had to do to maximize his chances of getting into Credit Suisse's highly coveted analyst program after he graduated, and besides, I loved being alone with Garrett. I loved the warm, downy scent of him, his miniature fingers and toes, the weight of his soft little body in my hands. For the first time since Gus died, the hole in my heart was beginning to fill.

Chapter Thirty-Two

Skye

I don't tell Andie about the Post-it note Burke left on my nightstand. I don't tell anyone, not even Dr. Salam. Instead I fold it into quarters and shove it in my top dresser drawer, underneath some socks. Still, his words play on repeat in my head.

I'm so sorry, Skye. I wish I could explain, but I can't. I love you.

I'm not a total idiot; I do realize that this is undoubtedly bullshit. The rational part of me understands that Burke wrote this note as a final attempt to fuck with me, because that's what sociopaths do. I've read about it— they get high on that kind of stuff.

I do feel as if I'm going slightly crazy, but Dr. Salam says that's to be expected. I've undergone—or am undergoing—a major trauma, not unlike a death. The Burke I thought I knew is dead. I'm supposed to be kind to myself.

But it's hard to be kind to yourself when you want to rip your hair out for being so stupid. Looking back on the past year, I now see nothing but red flags. How strange it was that Burke never told me more about his job, his work as an "independent financial adviser." He was constantly in front of his laptop "finishing up some emails" or rushing out to his WeWork office on Twenty-ninth Street. The other day, when Andie prompted me to call that particular WeWork location, the receptionist found no record of a Burke Michaels ever using work space there.

How unusual it was that I never met any of his friends, except for a man named Todd, a supposed ex-colleague whom he then didn't even invite to the wedding. I never met Burke's family, either—the so-called relatives in Phoenix—though he sometimes mentioned speaking to them on the phone. "I talked to Aunt Lynn today," he'd casually say. "She can't wait to meet you at the wedding."

When I did meet "Aunt Lynn" at the wedding, she was a sixty-five-year-old drug addict from Burke's hometown in upstate New York—one of the numerous people he'd hired to act as his nearest and dearest.

The one time I pushed him on whether he wanted to add anyone else to our guest list, he gently reminded me that his friends were scattered, that he didn't come from money, and that most of the people in his life couldn't afford the travel to Nantucket or a four-hundred-dollar-per-night bed-and-breakfast on the island. I felt so guilty that I immediately dropped the topic entirely.

And then, Burke spent a *year* in prison. He *admitted* to this—the night he told me he loved me—and I cast his crime off as an innocent mistake. I gave him the benefit of the doubt at every turn, when I should have been running for the hills.

Recalling these red-flag moments makes me sick to

my stomach. I'm not ready to tell my father. I'll never be ready to tell my father. But it's been almost two weeks since I found out about Burke's betrayal, and Andie and Dr. Salam are right—I can't wait any longer.

And so this morning I texted him that I'd be taking the train out to Westport after work. I said I needed to talk to him, and that I needed to do so in person.

From my window seat on Metro-North I gaze out at the bleak rush of trees. It's been a cold fall, and only a few stubborn leaves cling to the branches. I normally detest going over the Park Avenue Bridge, but today I'm too anxious and preoccupied to notice as we cross into the Bronx. I don't know exactly what I'll say to my father, only that it's time to say something. The same goes for my friends. Lexy was tagging me in so many Instagram posts from the wedding that I finally deleted the app so I wouldn't be tempted to look at them. When she texted asking why I hadn't liked any of her photos, I made something up about a social media cleanse.

My father is waiting for me in his old green Tahoe when my train rolls into the station. Even with all his money, he's never wanted to drive anything but an old truck.

His face falls the moment I climb into the passenger seat, and I remember that he hasn't seen me since the wedding. I must look like shit.

"Skye." His voice is barely a whisper.

"Hi, Dad."

"You're . . . You're so . . . thin."

Looking down at my body, my once-snug jeans baggy over my thighs, I realize that I am, indeed, thin.

The irony is too much. I spend six months leading up to the wedding working out like a maniac to lose ten pounds, and I barely shed five. I stuff myself to the brim with carbs and wine on my honeymoon in Italy. I'm unable to eat for a week and a half after finding out my husband is a con artist, and *now* I'm thin. Momentarily I wonder how much weight I've lost, but then I remember that it doesn't matter. Nothing matters anymore.

"Are you okay?" My dad is still looking at me, his gray-blue eyes intense. He hasn't put the car in drive.

"Let's talk at home." I glance ahead.

We ride in silence. I stare out at the familiar scenery as we wind through the roads whose curves I know by heart, a kind of muscle memory. This is still the place I call home, even though I don't come back as often as I should. It's been eighteen years, but when I'm here I can barely stand how much I miss her.

When we reach town, Dad bears left and I feel myself relax. I don't think I could handle coming back at all if he and Nancy still lived in our old house, the big Dutch Colonial in the other direction—overlooking the water—the house where she lived and loved and deteriorated.

The Tahoe crunches over the gravel driveway and slows to a stop in front of a modern-looking taupe bungalow. After he and Nancy got engaged, my dad put our old house on the market and moved in here with Nancy and the twins. I know Mom would've hated everything about the midcentury house, from its oversize windows to the horizontal roof. Sometimes I think my dad was so sad after Mom died that he looked for her utter opposite. Someone to whom he'd never be able to compare her.

"Nancy's at a dinner tonight," my dad says, as if reading my mind. "And I doubt Aidan and Harry are coming home anytime soon."

"Being home on a Friday night as a teenager is a death sentence, if I remember correctly." I'm suddenly overcome with the memory of how Andie, Iz, Lex, and I used to spend our weekends in high school. We'd gather at someone's house—usually Lexy's because she had the best clothes—and get ready for whatever party was happening that night. Something was usually "going on," and if not or we hadn't gotten the invitation, we'd pout for an hour and then end up having the best night anyway. Lexy would steal a bottle of wine from the cellar and sneak it upstairs, and back then a single bottle was enough to get the four of us toasted. We'd laugh so hard there'd be tears streaming down our cheeks, and when our stomach muscles hurt too much to laugh any longer, we'd fall asleep in Lexy's king-size bed. Two of us could have stayed in the guest room, but we never did. We always liked cramming into Lexy's big bed together.

The Blanes got divorced Lexy's freshman year of college and sold the house, and now the memory of spending all those carefree nights there feels like one from another world. But then I think, at least I still have them. At least after all these years I still have Lexy and Andie and Isabel. That's something.

"Can I get you anything?" My father's voice pulls me from the well of my nostalgia. He runs a hand through his light brown hair, flecked with grays but not bad for a man in his sixties. "Tea? Water? Wine?" He shifts his weight to one foot. Something about our interaction feels oddly formal, and I can't remember if it's always been like this. Maybe it has.

The kitchen is all sleek stone countertops and flat-panel cabinets—another look Mom would've hated.

"I'm okay. Thanks," I slide onto one of the raised metal stools in front of the center island.

"You look tired, sweetheart."

"I am tired, Dad."

"Do you—do you want to talk in here?"

My father has never been good at navigating emotional conversations. That was Mom's forte. His emotion goes into his art, and nowhere else.

I shrug. "I think it's as good a place as any."

"Okay." He exhales. "Tell me what's going on, Skye."

I open my mouth to speak and realize I should have thought this through. My throat is so tight it hurts, and I have no idea how to explain any of this to my father. The furrow of his brow—so intense with concern—fills my eyes. Even though he's terrible at expressing it, I know my father cares deeply in his helpless way. My mother was the best at getting him to open up; I suddenly hope Nancy is, too.

"Skye?" he presses, his voice a whisper.

The tears are too heavy behind my eyes as something breaks loose inside me.

I tell him everything. I tell him what's happened since Burke and I got back from Italy—the misdirected email to Andie, the sham of our marriage, the stolen two million dollars—all of it. I can't bring myself to look him in the eye until I'm finished.

I can feel his rage first; I feel it before I drag my gaze up to see an expression on my father's face that I've never witnessed.

"And this—" His voice cracks. "This happened nearly two weeks ago?"

I brace myself for his recriminations, my face hot with shame. "I'm so sorry I didn't tell you. I wanted to, I just—I needed some time. But I canceled all the credit cards, and I took him off the bank account. And I changed the locks. I'm so, so sorry, Da—"

"Stop." He holds up a hand, and I see that his fingers are trembling. He walks around the island and covers me in his arms, squeezing me closer than he has in years. "You have nothing to be sorry for, Skye. *Nothing.* This is—this is *my* fault. I'm your father. I knew there was something off about that man. I sensed it. I just—I guess I just—I wanted you to be happy. And you'd been so, *so* happy. Oh, Skye. This is not your fault. I'm so terribly sorry."

Tears stream loose down my face, so many the world blurs. A hardness inside me crumbles, and I realize how badly I've needed to hear these words.

"I don't know what to do, Dad." My voice is muffled in the soft flannel of his shirt.

"Don't worry, sweetheart." He smooths the back of my hair, and I can't remember the last time we were this physically close. "I'll take care of everything. Everything is going to be okay. I promise."

"But what does that mean?" I pull away, wiping

my cheeks. "What's going to happen? Will Burke go to prison?"

"If I have anything to do with it, he'll go to prison for a *long* time." My father's voice stiffens, color flushing to his face. "What he's done is illegal on so many levels, Skye. I'm going to call Davis tomorrow morning. He'll probably need you to come in and . . . provide some information. When you're ready."

I nod. Davis is our family lawyer. He's got the bearing of an old New England WASP and the ruthlessness of a mafioso.

"There's probably something else you should tell Davis," I say. "When you talk to him."

"What is it?"

"Burke—Burke went to prison. When he was twenty-four. It was for something white-collar. He said he was the fall guy for something that happened at work, but he spent a year behind bars. He told me some of the details, but now I—I don't know what's true. I'm so sorry I didn't tell you, Dad."

"*What?*" Anger flushes my father's face, but his expression quickly softens. "Oh, Skye. It's okay. I don't— I'll fill Davis in on everything. I'll have him look into it. I wish you'd told me, but I—I understand your instinct. To protect someone you . . . love."

I say nothing.

"And I need you to forward me the bank account statements. And the email. The one Andie got from Burke with the diary attached." My father begins pacing the kitchen. "Skye." He pauses. "Is there *anything* else you've found—aside from this digital journal—

that incriminates Burke? Not that we need more, but it can't hurt. Maybe a social media profile? Photos of his—God—his *fucking* family?" My father's eyes are hard, two bolts of anger that soften when they land on mine. The color of the ocean when it rains. "I'm sorry, sweetheart. I know this is—"

"I did find something." Nerves prickle my insides. "Burke—he doesn't have social media. Not even a LinkedIn. He always said he had no interest in using Facebook or Instagram, and I just assumed it was true, the way you're not on it either. But after what happened, Andie and I went on Facebook and searched for his wife. Her name is Heather, according to the journal entries. So we searched for Heather Michaels. There are tons of women named Heather Michaels, but we narrowed down the search by location, to New Haven, since that's apparently where they live. And we found her, Dad." I swallow hard. I pull out my phone and go to my recent photos, where I've stored a screenshot of Heather Michaels's Facebook profile. Her picture is of a family—a petite blond woman in a fitted sweater who must be Heather, three college-aged kids, one of whom is Burke's doppelgänger, and Burke. The five of them are standing together at what appears to be his son's college graduation, their smiles wide and bright. I can't bear to see the photo again—I've looked at it too many times to count since Andie found it—so I hand the phone to my father and stare at the intricacies of the pristine countertop, the tiny speckles of marble buried in the stone.

My father says nothing. At least a full minute passes.

When I finally glance up at him, his face is white as a sheet, and I notice the phone is slipping in his fingers.

"Dad?"

"I know her." He speaks slowly, placing the phone down carefully, as though it were a ticking bomb.

"You do?" I stare at him, shock seizing my chest. "Heather Michaels?"

He nods weakly, finally dropping his gaze to meet my own. "She used to babysit for you and Nate. Heather. Heather Price."

Chapter Thirty-Three

Burke

OCTOBER 2019—*TWO DAYS WITHOUT SKYE*

Heather claims to be rushing out the door to work. She says the most profitable time for Uber drivers is the night. I don't believe her—she always used to say early mornings were busiest—but I let her go, for now. I need a moment alone in my house.

When she's gone, I march straight upstairs to the office where Heather keeps her laptop. I flip it open and turn up the brightener—she always turns the screen light all the way down before she closes it—and type in her password, which I know is her initials followed by the numbers for the kids' birthdays. But *Incorrect password* flashes on the screen. I try two more times without success—she changed it. She hasn't changed her computer password in at least a decade, and *now* she changes it.

Frustration drowns me and I drop to my hands and knees, scurrying through the papers on the floor and in the desk drawers. It's mostly recent bills and forms from Maggie's school, and I'm hit with a sinister wave of dejection at the reminder that I haven't lived in this house in nearly a year. I haven't taken Maggie on a single college visit or seen Garrett's new apartment in Somerville.

I keep digging through the desk. I don't know exactly what I'm looking for, but there has to be something that will give me answers. I reach into the very back of the bottom drawer, and beyond the edge my hand touches an object—a book of some sort—that feels instantly familiar in its supple leather exterior and frayed edges. I yank it out from where it's lodged behind the desk, my heart dropping into my lap when I see what it is—my navy blue Moleskine, the one I've been missing since the winter.

And then I remember, that weekend I was here in February. It had been a bad day, too cold to go outside, and Heather was on my case about money and moving forward with the Big Plan. I knew I'd fallen in love with Skye—there was no turning that ship around—but it was a feeling that crushed me as much as it buoyed me. I'd quarantined myself in the office to let my thoughts spill out into the Moleskine while Heather made chili downstairs. When Heather and Maggie barged in, telling me the meal was ready, I shoved the Moleskine behind the desk before Heather could catch a glimpse of it.

After weeks of searching—mostly through Skye's apartment—I'd concluded that I must've left it on the subway or that it had fallen out of my briefcase on the street. But how had I not realized? *This* is where my Moleskine has been all this time, shoved between the back of the desk and the wall in New Haven.

I can't remember exactly what I wrote at the time, only that my entries were often lengthy and sprawling and emotional.

I open the Moleskine, its leather spine creaking softly. The first entry I've written is from nearly seventeen months earlier, before I met Skye.

May 24, 2018

I know Heather and I aren't in a good place, but I don't know if I can go through with the Big Plan. I blame myself for where we've ended up—well, I also blame fucking Herb Wooley, but that's beside the point. If I go through with this, I could get in big trouble. Again.

It's my fault that Heather's dreams got crushed. I accepted that a while back. I failed her, and I've done my best to make peace with it. Sometimes I do the whole what-if thing and wonder what would've happened if I'd let Heather go years ago, before we were married, back when I had the chance to let her truly be free of me. I was an addict then, and even though I vowed to get sober, I was always only one slipup away from destroying the future she banked on. I knew that then, and I know it now. She may have done so willingly, but I let her board a train that was heading straight for a brick wall.

But the thing about life is, you can't know how you'll feel about something in retrospect when it's happening in the moment. I remember exactly how I felt about Heather Price back then, and I know I wouldn't have done anything differently. She was my Bones. I couldn't have fathomed loving anyone more. When a girl you love that much chooses you, you choose her back. You just do.

It was so much more than her looks. Heather has always been a knockout, but the real kicker was, she had this drive in her that mesmerized me. Everyone else our age in Langs Valley was complacent; indifferent to the future that awaited them. It wasn't that they wouldn't have wanted what Heather did; they simply weren't aware of the possibilities that stretched beyond our shitty little town. But somehow Heather knew what else existed, and she'd had that dreamy sheen in her emerald eyes since we were kids. And when a girl like Heather Price plants a seed in your mind and in your heart that life could be so, so much bigger, when she grabs your arm and wants to take you with her, you go. God, you go.

Here's another what-if that always gets me— what would've happened if Heather hadn't started babysitting for Libby Fontaine and Peter Starling the fall of our junior year. Heather already had it in her, of course, but Libby was the one who gave her that extra push, that inexplicable drive to become someone else. Libby made Heather greedy, I think. I wonder if it weren't for Libby, would Heather have settled for less? Would what I offered have been enough?

But it's complicated, see, because if Libby hadn't entered the picture, Gus wouldn't have died. And if Gus hadn't died, Heather and I wouldn't have been sealed together by her pain. I truly can't make sense of any of it. Sometimes I push my mind to a place where I admit that maybe, from a purely objective standpoint, Heather and I shouldn't have gotten married. We were young, too young. But my mind won't push any further than that because then I think of the kids, and considering a life without Garrett and Hope and Maggie in it makes the least sense of all.

It's crazy the loops and circles that time takes. Here we are thirty years later, and even though Libby is dead, she's somehow back in the picture.

Anyway, the Big Plan. The world has played dirty with me—with us—so perhaps it's my turn to play a little dirty with the world. Apparently, the Starlings have so much money they don't know what to do with it. And then there's Gus— we'd finally be getting justice for his life. I don't know. It still feels cruel, the Big Plan, if it's even possible.

To be clear, if our finances weren't in the toilet, I wouldn't be considering any of this. When I got laid off from PK Adamson earlier this spring (I STILL don't understand why Herb fired me, to be honest), we'd just finished renovating the master bathroom. I'd been promising Heather we could renovate it since we moved in—she was desperate for one of those big Jacuzzi tubs and she loathed the preexisting tile—and after my Christmas bonus, a renovation was finally feasible. It would be costly, but it had been a good year at work, and I wanted to make Heather happy. Little did I know I'd lose my job four months later, a $7,000 balance still owed for the new master bath.

Where does all the money go? I ask myself daily. All I've ever wanted is to get to a point in life where money isn't a topic that grips my mind like a pair of forceps around my skull. But it feels impossible, like I'm constantly logging in to Chase to find the outstanding balance on the credit card is twice what I'd expected, the number in my checking account ticking lower and lower until the ACH hits on payday and I can breathe again.

Except now there is no payday—thanks, Herb, thanks, PKA. You're welcome for twenty goddamn years. What there IS now is our mortgage, both our car payments, Hope's Eastern tuition, taxes, the renovation balance, the foreseeable and exorbitant cost of poor Hopie's dental implants, and outstanding bills from couples therapy. Then there's the family vacation to Yellowstone National Park in August that Heather already put on the Visa because she found "cheap" flights to Salt Lake City and Maggie is mortified to be the only one of her friends who's never been on an airplane. The list of expenses goes on. Even when I did have a biweekly salary, there was never enough money in our house. Not even close.

Some time ago, I suggested to Heather that we move someplace where the cost of living is lower, where life is a little simpler. I made the mistake of mentioning Langs Valley, the idea of moving back there or somewhere like it. That didn't go over well. The second I said "Langs Valley," Heather's face reddened, the way it does when a storm is brewing inside her. She looked at me, her expression full of venom, and asked why I would ever think to say a thing like that.

And I get it, I do. Heather and I promised each other a long time ago that we would never go back the way we came from, that we'd always do everything in our power to give our children a real shot in life—the kind of shot we never had. And I vowed to keep that promise, even after we came to terms with the fact that our life wasn't going to play out the way we'd so diligently planned. After what I'd done to unravel us, it was all I could do to attempt to save us.

Chapter Thirty-Four

Heather

Dear Dr. K,

The fall after Garrett was born, I was supposed to go back to Fordham. Technically I still hadn't finished my junior-year credits, but I could catch up and graduate a semester later than planned. Burke and I had saved what little money we had—including his summer-internship compensation from Credit Suisse, which wasn't nothing—for day care.

But I was so attached to Garrett that the idea of going back to school was unthinkable. I couldn't fathom pulling myself together and enduring the stuffy, crowded subway ride to Fordham, all the while imagining my perfect baby boy in someone else's hands. The notion of pulling my attention away from Garrett to finish the term paper I still owed for Economics of Gender made my head spin.

So I didn't go back. Burke had found out at the end of the summer that he'd secured a place in the two-year analyst program at Credit Suisse, contingent on his keeping his GPA close to perfect. The analyst job meant Burke would be receiving an annual salary of a hundred grand, which was more money than either of us could fathom. It would certainly be enough to get us out of our stuffy little studio, and I didn't complain when Burke essentially moved into the NYU library that fall.

As the days grew shorter and the weather turned frigid, any lingering thoughts of returning to college were snapped by the cold. Garrett and I nested together in the apartment, sheltered in our warm bubble. I relished the feel of his chubby cheek against my collarbone, the way his tiny fist wrapped my whole pointer finger. Every moment with him was a miracle.

When January came and I didn't return to Fordham, Burke didn't object. He was too busy and tired to keep fighting me on it. I told him I'd reapply to schools in a couple of years—NYU, maybe—when the timing was right. I knew with incontestable certainty that what mattered most was being the best possible mother to my baby.

Burke started his job at Credit Suisse in May, shortly after Garrett's first birthday. The one downside was his hours; they were worse than they had been during his internship, if that was possible. Still, it was a sweet summer, one I spent reaping the joys of motherhood and busying myself decorating our new apartment in Gramercy. With Burke's analyst salary we'd upgraded to a two-bedroom with a renovated kitchen and huge, east-facing windows that flooded with morning light. The monthly rent was higher than we'd initially budgeted, but I reminded Burke that we weren't paying for day care and that he would only be making more money as his career progressed. That Christmas, Burke got a five-figure bonus, which he used to buy me a long-overdue engagement ring—a brilliant cut diamond framed by two round sapphires.

Burke worried I'd get bored being home alone with Garrett all day, but I relished my life as a stay-at-home mom. I got to know some of the other young mothers in our building and, through them, joined a playgroup that met weekly at one of our apartments. While our babies played we'd drink coffee—sometimes mimosas—laughing and ruminating about our babies' futures and whose daughter was going to end up married to whose son. For the first time since I'd met Libby junior year of high school, I had friends.

When Garrett turned two, I told Burke I wanted to try for a second baby. At first he thought I was joking—he'd been sure I'd want to go back and get my degree before considering more kids. I did want my degree, but that could wait. I explained to Burke how many of the other mothers in Garrett's playgroup were on their second or third babies, and how they'd made me realize the importance of giving children siblings without too great of an age gap. It took several weeks of convincing, but Burke finally agreed that it would be nice for Garrett to have a baby brother or sister.

I got pregnant again almost right away and was well into my first trimester by the end of the summer. My second pregnancy was light-years easier than my first; there was no morning sickness and my energy levels were through the roof. As my belly expanded, I grew more and more invigorated by motherhood; I prepared special arts-and-crafts projects for playgroup and took Garrett on outings to kid-friendly museum exhibits all over the city.

Most days, my life felt close to perfect. There was still the pit in my heart that was Gus, and even though I knew it would never completely go away, having Garrett helped more than I ever could've dreamed. The one thing that had started to weigh on me was how little I got to see my husband. I missed Burke desperately—the piney smell of his skin, the grounding sound of his laugh, the way it felt to rest my head against his chest. And I wanted Garrett to know his father better, too. But Burke was already well into the second and final year of his analyst program. Come June his boss had promised to promote him to associate; he'd get a significant pay bump and hours that were far more bearable. By then the new baby would be born, and Burke would be home in time to help me put the kids down at night. We'd probably need to move into a bigger apartment, but that wouldn't be an issue with Burke's new salary.

Sometimes I had to pinch myself. Here I was, Heather Price Michaels, twenty-three years old and living in a gorgeous apartment in New York City, married to the investment banker of my dreams with an adorable toddler and baby number two on the way. I had a two-carat diamond-and-sapphire ring on my finger and access to a comfortable bank account and an ever-improving wardrobe that was—thanks to Manhattan's plentiful consignment shops—almost enviable. Things were working out just as I'd planned. Life in Langs Valley was a forgotten bad dream, and I couldn't imagine being happier.

That's the thing about being on top, though—the higher you get, the harder the fall.

Chapter Thirty-Five

Skye

My dad is handling everything with Davis as he builds a case, while I try to wrap my head around the unthinkable connection between my old babysitter and my husband. Her husband.

My dad says that aside from the initial statement I made about Burke's deception, I only have to be as involved in the legal process as I want, assuming this doesn't go to trial. In the meantime, he wants me to focus on allowing my life to go back to normal, though I'm not sure that's possible.

For starters, I can't stop wearing my ring. My wedding band I had no problem burying in an old jewelry box, but the engagement ring—that's another story. I've gotten used to how it feels on my finger, the sheer weight of it on my left hand. I like the way it makes me stand a little taller as I stroll through the West Village, passing crowded bars of twenty-somethings who've succumbed to day drinking with the hope of finding their soul mate in a tequila-induced blur. *You've already found yours,* the diamond on my ring finger reminds me with a sparkly wink.

The only time I do take it off is when I'm going

to meet my friends. Such as today. It's a chilly, gray Saturday—New York fall has reached that point where it loses its appeal—and while I'd like nothing more than to sit in the bath and sulk, I've agreed to attend Isabel's husband's thirtieth birthday party at a bar in Williamsburg.

"I know you don't like Brooklyn," Lexy tells me in the cab. "But this is a new chapter, and I'm telling you—it's *all* about Brooklyn."

"Then why don't you live there?"

"Because *Matt* is too fucking lazy to leave Tribeca." She rolls her eyes. Matt sits next to her wearing AirPods and chatting on the phone, oblivious of our conversation. Being in the cab with the two of them makes me miss Burke more than I can stand.

When we reach the Williamsburg Bridge, I close my eyes and bite the insides of my cheeks. I can feel Lexy watching me.

"Shit, I forgot about your thing with bridges." She takes my hand and squeezes. "Just breathe. Almost there."

Lexy has me wearing one of her Herve Leger dresses, and she's done my makeup, and leaving her building, when I caught a glimpse of myself in the lobby mirror, I was struck by my appearance. When you realize your husband is an impostor who married you for your money and you stop being able to eat and sleep, you lose fifteen pounds and suddenly have the banging body you weren't disciplined enough to achieve before. Lexy has covered my dark circles with some miracle under-eye paste, and now, to the outside world, I'm a vision.

Inside I'm a destruction zone. The minute we step into the bar—a loungy place called Freehold—I want to leave. It's one of those trendy Williamsburg spots with a different DJ in every corner, the result of which is a piercing mash of beats that stabs my eardrums.

"Drink!" Lexy leads us to the bar, where Isabel and Andie are already gathered with their significant others. We all greet one another and tell Will happy birthday, and I wish the ground would open right up and swallow me under. Seven of us are in the circle: Isabel and Will, Lexy and Matt, Andie and Spencer, and me. I've never felt so acutely alone in my life. Andie squeezes my hand.

Lexy orders us jalapeño margaritas.

"I know you don't feel ready," Lexy says, pressing the icy glass into my palm. "But Matt has a superhot friend here, and he's a total sweetheart. A good guy. I could introduce you?"

My stomach sinks. I rub the bare space around my ring finger and feel my throat tighten. The audible reminder that I'm back on the market makes me want to rip my skin off.

"C'mon, S," Lexy pleads. "You look *smokin'* tonight."

I swallow the full feeling in my throat. "Let me get this drink in me first."

"That's the spirit!" Lexy throws her arm around my neck and nods toward the corner of the room. "He's over there, if you want a little preview. Light blue button-down."

I follow her gaze, which leads to a sea of attractive men in a uniform of oxfords and jeans. Two years earlier I might've downed my jalapeño marg and made my way in their direction, keeping my eyes peeled for wedding-band-less hands.

But now nothing is appealing about these potentially single men, and with each sip of alcohol I'm only surer that my heart is somewhere else, and that even though it's in a place it shouldn't be, there's no untangling it from where it is, at least not tonight.

Besides, there's something I no longer like about the type of guys that are here, Will Maguire's finance pals with their dry-cleaned shirts and clipped haircuts and playful, insatiable eyes. Perhaps it's because they are boys, and I married a man.

Then a finger taps my shoulder, and the world is too small and weird, and something primal in me hitches—an urge to run—but I turn around anyway. Of course it's him. Neat, sand-colored hair, cold brown eyes, bow-shaped mouth. A blade slices my chest. The syllables of his name are a slow drag in my head. *Max. La. Pointe.*

My mom used to say that resentment is a wasted emotion, that holding on to anger is like swallowing poison and hoping the other person will die. Maybe she was right. Still, I hate Max LaPointe so much I feel sick. The sight of him—which used to flood me with affection and intoxicating lust—now fuels a nauseating fire in the pit of my stomach.

"Starling." He grins wickedly, his eyes moving up and down the length of me, and I feel my knees quiver. The sight of his gold wedding band sears the invisible circle around my own naked ring finger. "I thought I might have the displeasure of running into you here." His devious gaze locks mine. One corner of his mouth curls, but it's not a smile.

That I didn't even consider the possibility of running into Max at Will Maguire's birthday party feels like a small victory. The last time I'd physically seen him was at Iz and Will's housewarming party a year and a half earlier, before he was married. He'd recently gotten engaged, and *she* was there—Anastasia what's her face—linking her model-skinny arm in his as they weaved through the party like conjoined twins. Seeing him that night—seeing them together—had floored me. A confusing, wrenching envy had stayed with me for too long after, which didn't fully evaporate until months later when I met Burke.

"Heard you got married, Starling." Max looks at me, and his eyes are the color of espresso, almost black. "What a goddamn miracle for you."

Suddenly, from the depths of my mind, I remember his emails. For a brief, psychotic moment I want to laugh; I've been so preoccupied, so debilitated by my pain over Burke, that I completely forgot about Max's emails—the snide, incessant, almost threatening messages he started sending me after Burke and I got engaged.

I recall the most recent ones, the three he sent in a row, just days before the wedding:

You never got back to me about that drink.

It's rude to ignore someone, Starling. There are consequences for that kind of behavior.

I'm not joking, Starling. Consequences.

"You need to stop emailing me, Max." I'm surprised at the level of anger in my voice. "Whatever you're trying to do, it's not working."

Anastasia—now Max's wife—whips her head around. Her eyes narrow. "What emails?" she spits.

Max cocks his head ever so slightly. "I don't know what you're talking about, Starling."

"I don't have time for this, Max. Just fucking grow up and stop playing your little games."

He smirks and wraps his arm around Anastasia. "No offense, Starling, but I have better things to do these days than dick around sending *you* emails."

How pointless it was to confront Max, to give his sadistic mind the satisfaction of knowing he's gotten to me. I suddenly feel so ill I'm strangely lucid, as though I'm dreaming. I feel myself float up out of my body, and then I'm hovering above, watching myself huddled with Max and Anastasia. There is no jealousy, only a sharp, poignant sadness. For her, mostly, for having ended up married to a man like him. The feeling spreads across my chest, constricting, and the truth pulls me back into myself, so that I'm standing back on the ground with a sense of accountability I've never known before. Or maybe I'm just drunk. I didn't eat dinner. I place my empty glass down on the bar and trace my gaze from Anastasia's to Max's, then back to hers.

"Your husband is a rapist," I say bluntly, because

every woman deserves to know whom she sleeps next to at night.

I've admitted these words to so few people that they sound foreign coming out of me. Anastasia's face twists oddly; it takes me a moment to realize that underneath her Botox, it's a scowl.

I lock my eyes to Max's once more—they are small and dark and bitter—before turning around.

"Psycho bitch," I hear him mutter as I walk away.

I feel free, and drunk from one cocktail, and too horrible to stay at the bar for another second. I leave without saying goodbye to my friends. I hail a cab, and only once its wheels are spinning do I let the tears break loose—silent, hot streams that drip down my neck and sternum.

I met Max LaPointe in the city when I was twenty-two, the fall after I graduated from Barnard. He was one of Will Maguire's good friends from Duke, had cousins my family knew from Westport, and was one of those guys who seemed to know everyone, and who seemed to be everywhere.

"Starling," he'd said the first time we'd met, locking his eyes to mine. "That's a fucking great last name."

After a monthlong flirtation we finally made out during a drunken night at Acme, after which I Irish-exited and left him stumbling around the dance floor. He called me a dozen times that night, but I was too scared to answer. I *liked* Max; he was the first guy in years whom I felt comfortable around.

But it was dangerous territory for me, to act on my feelings for someone. Doing so meant he'd inevitably

learn about my OCD—there was no way to hide it—
and that always, always ended badly.

Andie came over the next morning and gave me a
pep talk. She told me that if I really liked Max, I had
to be willing to take a risk and be honest with him. She
said if he was freaked out by my compulsions, then he
wasn't someone I wanted to be with, anyway.

I called Max that afternoon. I apologized for ditching him at Acme and asked him to meet me for a drink
at the Village Tavern. He showed up in jeans and a Duke
T-shirt, his dirty-blond hair adorably tousled, and a feeling of tenderness washed through me. If nothing else,
Max and I had become friends, and I genuinely believed
that he was a good guy. I took a generous sip of my
vodka soda and told him everything.

Max listened carefully, twirling his beer glass around
in his hands. When I finished, he was quiet for a while,
then cleared his throat.

"So, you're telling me you have OCD and that it
makes you touch doors in a certain pattern every time
you leave a room?"

I nodded, heat creeping up the sides of my neck.

"That's it?" A hint of a smile crossed Max's face.
"That's what you're giving me a heads-up about? Everyone in this city has something wrong with them, Starling. Besides, I already knew you had OCD."

"You did?" I was surprised. "How did you know?"

"Will mentioned it, I think." Max shrugged, then
reached across the table and placed his hand over mine.
"You don't have to worry about it. I think you're gorgeous, and cool. I'm into you."

I was touched by Max's words, and speechless. It was the first time in my life I'd had an honest conversation about my OCD with a guy I liked. After the incident with Colin Buchanan in eighth grade, I'd retreated into myself, and the shell shock had lasted through high school. I was still void of self-esteem by the time I started at Barnard, and the college environment didn't help my insecurity. I hooked up with a few Columbia guys who got weird when they witnessed my OCD knocks firsthand. One asked me if I was a medium who was talking to dead people. Another time, I was standing in line for the bathroom at a party and overheard the guy in front of me ask his friend, *What was the name of that blond girl Derek used to bang? She's hot but, like, has those psycho mental problems.*

Me. It was me. I was the girl with those psycho mental problems Derek used to bang. On the verge of bawling, I'd fled the bathroom line to go find Kendall.

Kendall had always attributed my unsuccessful love life to my not yet having met the right person.

But Max—perhaps Max was the right person. *Finally* I'd met someone who could see past my disorder, someone who shrugged it off so that it stopped defining me in my own mind. Max was charming, and smart, and being around him I felt beautiful, and confident.

That night, after another round of drinks at the Village Tavern, Max and I interlaced our fingers and walked back to my apartment, electricity humming between us. After we had sex, he stayed the night, the first time I'd let a guy sleep over since junior year.

Max stayed over every night that week, and the week

after that. My bed was our little cocoon, our paradisia-cal shelter from the world. Max said our bodies fit to-gether perfectly, and I agreed. We'd curl into each other after sex and talk for hours, our conversations stretch-ing time. When I had to do my knocks, Max watched me quietly, never with a smirk or a laugh. Sometimes he'd kiss my cheek and tell me that my quirks were adorable.

After two weeks with Max, I called Andie and told her I'd fallen in love.

"You know how people always say you should marry your best friend," I sang into the phone. "Well, Max is my best friend."

"I thought *I* was your best friend."

"You know what I mean, And. Like, what Spence is to you. I really think Max could be that person to me."

As if on cue, that night Max didn't call. He didn't respond to my texts, either. I tossed and turned in bed, sleepless, checking my phone every twenty seconds and wondering if Max had died.

The next morning he texted me apologizing, ex-plaining that he'd had a crazy night at the office and would be traveling for business over the next few days. He said he'd call when he got back, which implied he wouldn't be reaching out while he was away.

A whole week went by and I didn't hear from Max. I finally mustered the courage to text him: *Back yet?*

His reply came twenty-four hours later: *Back tomor-row!*

But tomorrow came and went and he didn't call or text, and I lay in bed paralyzed with confusion and anxious misery. My friends concluded that Max LaPointe was a royal douchebag and that I was better off without him. Isabel said she'd heard through the grapevine that he had a small penis; I couldn't bring myself to tell them that I thought his penis was perfect.

A few more weeks of radio silence passed. Two weeks before Christmas, when I'd given up all hope of ever seeing the name *Max LaPointe* on the screen of my phone again, he texted me.

Starling! How are you? I'm so sorry I've been MIA, it's no excuse but I've been drowning in work and grad school apps. Things are settling, though, and I'd love to take you out to dinner. I remember you were telling me about that place Rolf's with all the Xmas decorations? Can we go there? I miss you.

Max's text filled every inch of my body with the sweetest relief. I hadn't been crazy to think that our connection was special. Max worked in finance; he'd told me numerous times how demanding and unpredictable his job could be. And he missed me, just as I missed him. *God,* did I miss him.

That week Max and I went to Rolf's. We drank mulled wine and ate schnitzel and I laughed like I hadn't since our last night together at the end of October. Max apologized for being such a poor communicator, and the pain I'd experienced during our time apart instantly felt melodramatic and far away. After dinner we took a cab up to Rockefeller Center, and in front of the great, shimmering tree, Max kissed me in a way that made me believe in the magic of Christmastime in New York.

But after New Year's, Max went MIA again. A few

weeks after that, he left me a heartfelt voice mail. In March he disappeared. In April he came back. And so continued our chemical, agitating on-and-off cycle for the next two years. If I'd been stronger, or smarter, if I hadn't been quite so in love with him, I'd have nipped our cyclical "relationship" in the bud. But I was vulnerable and Max was good at his game; each time he lured me back in, he always promised a little bit more. It got worse when he started business school at NYU Stern the following fall.

When school stops being so insane, I think this could really be something, Starling.

I'm so bad at relationships, but you make me want to be better.

I enjoyed dropping Max's name to people who asked about my love life. Max was ambitious and cool, the kind of guy everyone seemed to have heard of, and I was proud to be involved with him, whatever it was. When friends and mutual friends inquired about our status, it only affirmed my claim over him. I listened to songs such as "Hot N Cold" by Katy Perry and "With or Without You" by U2 on the treadmill and sprinted faster, imagining us. Just because our dynamic was complicated, it didn't mean what we had wasn't real. On the contrary, true love was supposed to be tumultuous—it meant there was passion. Max and I were Carrie and Big, Ross and Rachel. Our happy ending had to be earned.

But on the days when I got honest with myself— usually miserable, hungover mornings after a night of sending one too many drunken texts—I knew that what little he gave me wasn't enough, not even close. And the longer our charade continued, the worse my emotional distress over the situation grew.

The summer I turned twenty-four, Max and his friends got a share house in Montauk. Max and I had been on the outs for most of the summer—I'd heard from Isabel that he'd started sleeping with some girl in the Hamptons—and I was a wreck. I'd promised my friends that I was done with Max, for good this time, but one weekday morning in late July a dozen white roses were delivered to my apartment, a card attached to the bouquet.

Happy belated, Skye Starling. I'm a fool. You're prettier than all the white roses in the world. Please come out to Montauk this weekend so we can make things right.

In retrospect it was just another empty gesture from Max, but in that moment it was everything I needed to hear. My friends forbade me to go, but I was adamant. I'd been in a pit of gloom all summer, and I *needed* this weekend.

When she realized she couldn't stop me, Andie insisted on coming, too. Spencer got pissed at her for ditching him last minute, but Isabel and Will weren't going out to the share house that weekend, and Andie refused to leave me unsupervised with Max.

When we arrived in Montauk on Friday evening, Max said he was exhausted and not up for going out. Naturally I stayed in with him. I asked about the girl he'd supposedly been seeing, and he promised it was nothing—a "drunken, casual thing" that was over. We had make-up sex for hours, while everyone else danced the night away at Memory Motel.

The next day was sunny and hot, and we all packed a picnic and headed to the beach. Andie and I read paperbacks on our towels while Max and his friends played spikeball. He looked obnoxiously good, his sandy hair longer and lighter than usual, his skin golden brown from so many weekends in the sun. He seemed to be cracking open a new beer every ten minutes, and by the end of the day I could tell he was hammered. Max had barely spoken to me at the beach, and I was feeling shittier by the second. I couldn't keep doing this to myself—I *couldn't*. Back at the share house I decided to tell Andie that she'd been right, to beg her to take a Jitney back to the city with me that evening, but she was deeply invested in a group game of bocce ball outside. I'd always envied Andie's ability to make friends wherever she went.

I decided to take a shower and was heading toward the bathroom when I heard Max's voice call my name from upstairs.

"Starling! Where's my beautiful Starling?"

My heart bloomed and quickly shrank; around Max, it was never sure how to feel. Nonetheless, I followed the voice into the bedroom upstairs, which was dark.

When Max saw me, he placed his hands under my arms and scooped me up, kissing my neck and chest. He threw me onto the bed and began wedging my legs apart with his knees. The smell of booze was thick and sour on his breath.

"Cut it out, Max." I pushed him off me. "We need to talk."

Then I heard the door slam shut, the room suddenly falling pitch-black. The lock clicked. Something uncanny wobbled through the air and my breath hitched—Max and I weren't alone.

"We need to talk, Max, you're in *big* trouble." A male voice mocked my girlie twang, followed by the sound of collective snickering.

"Chase, shut your trap," I heard Max's voice, and as my eyes adjusted to the darkness, I saw him looking at me, his pupils unfocused, inches away from my face. "Show some respect for this beautiful girl. Look what she can do."

"Show us already, LaPointe," called a third male voice that I recognized—Max's friend Wiley's.

"Okay, okay. Hang on." Max pinned his hands to my shoulders and leaned down to kiss me, pressing me into the bed.

"What the fuck, Max?" I whispered. "Stop it."

He smiled, releasing his grip and standing. "Sorry about that, Starling. My friends are drunk losers. You can go now." He flipped the switch on the wall, and the room was bathed in light.

I stood, smoothing my beach cover-up. I glared at Max as I headed for the door, stopping in my tracks as the familiar, immobilizing sensation seized me.

I knew then, and the fear was like a worm slinking through my insides. I knew why all three of them were staring at me. I knew why Max had called me into the room.

"Go on," Chase prompted, waving me toward the door. "You can go now."

"Max," I said slowly. I tried to meet his gaze, but he was staring at Chase.

"C'mon, Starling, you heard Chase," Max said. "You can leave now."

I stood, frozen.

"*Skye.*" Max pushed me back onto the bed again. This time I struggled against him, but he held me down. He slid one of his hands underneath my cover-up, jamming his fingers around my bathing suit and inside me.

"Max!" I screamed, kicking him off. Chase and Wiley sneered behind him.

"Whoa, Starling, I said you could go." Max stood again, stepping to the side to let me by. I was only a few feet from the door. I stepped closer, placing my hand on the knob. The current of my blood quickened, anxiety seizing me, tears pricking the corners of my eyes. Turning the knob was not possible. We all knew I was trapped.

"Fine, you psycho," I croaked, unable to look at Max. "If this is what you want, you're sick."

I lifted my fist in front of the door and began to knock. I felt three pairs of eyes glued to me. I heard the snickering, but I forced myself to keep going. I thought of my mother. Lucky eight. The breath. *One two three four five six seven eight; eight seven six five four—*

An arm grabbed my middle so forcefully I cried out.

"Shhhh," Chase whispered, throwing me down on the bed. When I continued to scream, Wiley clamped his hand over my mouth.

"LaPointe says that if your knocking thing gets interrupted, you have to start all over again," Chase continued. "Is that right?" He smiled vindictively, tracing his fingertips up the length of my thigh toward my bathing suit. My scream muffled into Wiley's hand as Chase pressed his fingers inside me, just as Max had done moments before.

"Okay, okay, all done." Chase stood. "Now you can go."

Wiley removed his hand from my mouth. I was trembling, too afraid to make a sound.

"You can go now," Chase repeated, nodding toward the door.

"What do you want from me?" I whispered, my eyes brimming with fresh tears.

Max took a long pull of whiskey, then handed the bottle to Wiley. "We just want you to go, Starling. It's time for you to leave." Max's eyes looked plastic.

When I first got diagnosed with OCD, my father used to worry that if I ever got stuck in a fire, my compulsion would prevent me from escaping. I'd told him not to be concerned, that self-preservation would most certainly override my OCD in a life-or-death scenario. But in that moment, in that shitty share-house bedroom with Max and his cohorts, I knew my father had been right to worry. Here I was getting sexually assaulted, powerless against my own deluded mind. Max and his friends could rape me—even kill me—and I'd remain helpless.

The boys watched me do my knocks again; this time Wiley grabbed me before I could finish counting down from eight. They pinned me against the bed, Chase covering my mouth with one hand as Wiley stuck his fingers inside me. Out of the corner of my eye I saw Max take another swig of whiskey, watching us.

Finally they were off me, and Max handed Chase the bottle, which was nearly empty.

"We're sorry, Starling, we really are," Max slurred. "I told them what a special girl you were, and they didn't believe me. I told them you had the tightest pussy in the world, and they didn't believe that, either. I had to let them see for themselves." Max shrugged and stumbled out of the room, Chase and Wiley cackling in his wake.

I can count on one hand the number of people who know what happened that evening. I'd told Andie, sobbing uncontrollably in an Uber on the way back to the city later that night. I told Dr. Salam when I started seeing her several months later. Lexy, Isabel, and Kendall know abbreviated versions of what happened, but I never told them the full story. I was simply too humiliated.

Afterward, Andie couldn't let it go. I don't blame her, I suppose, as she'd seen my pain firsthand, the way the trauma consumed me in the weeks and months that followed. Andie was the one who called NYU and reported the incident that fall. The administration investigated, and two other girls from Stern came forward with official complaints of Max's sexual aggression. He was expelled from Stern in January, four months before he was slated to graduate. The details were never made public, but Max knew what Andie and I had done. I knew he despised me, possibly as much as I despised him.

Five years later, when I hadn't spoken about the incident to anyone in longer than I could remember, I told Burke. The thing that I shared with no one else, I shared with him. Something soft and safe was in his eyes, something that told me he'd take my darkest secret and bear some of its weight. And he did. And after that, my load was a little lighter.

And my load is still lighter, I think to myself as the taxi pulls to a stop on West Eleventh. I pay the cabbie and head up to my apartment.

I have two missed calls from Andie and one from Lexy, so I text our group chat and apologize for Irish-exiting. I tell them I just needed to go home.

I nestle underneath my covers still thinking about Burke, about the words *I love you* on the Post-it note I can't shake from my mind. I think about how even though Burke and I are no more, even though what we had was nothing, my load is still lighter because of him. And that is something.

My phone vibrates on the bedside table. A new email from maxlapointe1@gmail.com. A cold shiver runs through me.

A word to the wise, Starling—don't forget what I said about consequences.

For the first time since he contacted me last spring, I let myself think long and hard about what Max LaPointe might actually want from me.

Chapter Thirty-Six

Burke

I am on the floor of our home office, the scratchy fibers of the wall-to-wall carpet digging into my ankles. A dull pain numbs my knees, but I can't get up. I can't stop reading the old entries of my Moleskine, barely able to wrap my mind around how much has changed in just a little over a year.

June 2, 2018

I have to say, there's something about writing in a journal that helps. When our couples therapist recommended it a few months ago, I privately cast it off as something I would never do. But since getting fired (well, "let go") from PKA, and with all this internal debate about moving forward with the Big Plan, my head feels like it's on the verge of detonating, and letting my thoughts bleed on a blank page seems to provide at least some relief. At least it did last time. So here we go again.

To be clear, we're no longer seeing said therapist. He charged three hundred dollars per hour-long session, none of which was covered by insurance, so after losing my job I quickly called and canceled our upcoming appointment. We are not going to reschedule.

Heather is pissy about this—she loved couples therapy and claims it was saving our marriage. Which is weird, because she has always been patently against therapy; thinks it's woo-woo shit for weak people. Besides, I know Heather, and I know she thinks that MONEY is the thing that will save our marriage. She isn't wrong.

I wish that weren't true. I wish I were the kind of man who believes that love trumps all, that the power of love will hold us together even in the darkest days. But I'm not, at least not anymore. I've witnessed enough in my forty-five years on this planet to know that unfortunately love isn't enough, not even close.

What I do still believe in these days is family—it's something Heather and I both believed in from the start, and I'm proud of us for that. Neither of us grew up with real families of our own—it's part of the reason we became each other's.

I hardly knew my father; my parents were high school sweethearts who divorced when I was still in diapers, and my dad ended up in prison a couple years after that. My mom ran off to California with some guy when I was eight and never came back, so my grandma—my dad's mom—raised me. Grams was the closest thing I ever had to a parent, even as her Alzheimer's grew worse and worse. She died the year I started college in New York. She didn't have much memory left by that point, but I like to think she knew I'd left Langs Valley. It would've made her happy to know I'd gotten out of there.

So Heather and I chose our own family—we chose each other. And after Garrett was born, we promised to keep choosing each other, and our son, and any future children we brought into the world. We knew all too well what a broken home looked like, and Heather said she'd die before she raised her kids in one. She was committed to giving Garrett, Hope, and Maggie everything her own childhood had lacked—stable, loving parents in a solid marriage was at the top of the list. Education was a close second.

Even when it felt impossible, I'd always admired Heather's approach to raising our children. Our marriage became my religion. It's where I've laid myself bare—whole and splintered. My unconditional love for the kids has never been a choice, but my union with Heather is—it has always been. The key is to keep choosing it, to stick with it like a kind of blind faith. And when you have a deep enough faith in something, it becomes a miracle. That's what Heather taught me. That's what she's given me.

That's why I've decided to do it. I have the summer to find employment—three months to land a decent job, one that pays more than what I was making at PKA. And if I'm still unemployed come September, then I'm going to move forward with the Big Plan. I'm going to do it for my family.

Wish me luck, journal, universe, cosmos, whatever it is that you are. I'll need it. It's not the first time in two decades I'll be applying for new jobs—PKA never paid well, and I tried hard to go elsewhere. I didn't stay at the company for twenty years out of loyalty or because I loved what I did. I stayed because I was lucky to be there in the first place. When you get yourself into a mess like I did in '97, no one will hire you.

Chapter Thirty-Seven

Heather

Dear Dr. K,

I know what you think. I saw the way you looked at my husband when we came in for counseling. You think he's the good guy and I'm the villain. But you need to know the truth about him—as his therapist, you *deserve* to know the truth. So let me tell you what really happened.

One freezing cold morning in January, when I was sixth months pregnant with Hope, I was woken by pounding on the front door.

Burke has always slept like a rock and he didn't even stir. It was barely six A.M. as I waddled toward the foyer, bleary-eyed but anxious. I opened the door slowly. Two men in blue jackets stood with their arms crossed. They announced themselves as FBI and told me they'd come to arrest my husband.

Panic seized every inch of me as I watched them storm into my home, helpless as they marched into our bedroom and roused Burke from half sleep.

"What the fuck is going on?" I yelled as Burke dressed, the agents watching from the doorway.

"Your husband has been arrested for insider trading,

ma'am," one of the FBI men said. "He'll get a call later today. We suggest waiting by the phone."

"This has to be a mistake," I said desperately, grabbing Burke's arm. From his bedroom, Garrett started wailing.

"Just stay by the phone, Heather." Burke's eyes landed on mine. I'd never seen him look so terrified. "I love you and Garrett more than anything."

The day stretched on forever while I sat on the couch, panicked, waiting for the phone to ring. Garrett was fussy—I knew he needed a walk in his stroller—but I refused to leave the apartment. Finally, at a quarter past four, Burke called. The sound of his familiar voice instantly settled me, like a glass of warm milk. He said to come down to the courthouse and sign him out. As long as I'd be a suretor on his bond, he could come home.

"For now," he added, and I felt the panic inside me spread.

I stuffed Garrett into his down suit and winter hat and barreled down to the lobby. I waited impatiently while the doorman called us a cab. It was rush hour and took nearly forty minutes to get to the downtown address Burke had given me.

At the courthouse I was directed to sign several forms, which I did without thinking, my signature a quick, illegible line.

Burke looked paler than I'd ever seen as the guards led him out of the holding cell, dark circles ringing his eyes. As soon as they'd uncuffed him, he kissed me, and for the first time in six years I smelled alcohol on him, its pungent, lingering scent. I hadn't noticed it the night before, but he'd gotten home late from the office, after I was already asleep.

Burke took Garrett from my arms, cradling his son close. Tears stained Burke's cheeks and beaded the ends of his thick, dark lashes, and I realized I hadn't seen my husband cry like this since Gus died.

I made every effort to stay even-keeled on the way back to the apartment—I didn't want to discuss any of this in front of Garrett. Orange light glowed through the taxi windows as we sped uptown, the sun a neon sliver between the buildings to the west. Burke leaned his head against my shoulder. The stink of the booze on him made me want to scream. How had I not noticed it this morning?

At home, I put Garrett in his crib, praying he'd fall asleep. Burke headed straight to our room and climbed into bed, but I yanked the covers back.

"What the fuck, Burke?" I yelled. "Is that really alcohol on your breath? Since when the fuck have you been drinking? And why the hell did two FBI agents come to our apartment this morning? Why did I just bail you out of *jail*?"

He looked truly terrible as he sat up straighter, rubbing his nose and propping himself against the pillows. His normally clean-shaven face was coated in a layer of dark stubble.

"Oh, Bones." Fresh tears gathered in his eyes. "I'm so sorry."

"Just tell me what's going on, Burke." I forced my tone to soften. "Tell me this is some kind of misunderstanding."

"I—it's not, Bones." Burke's voice was gravelly.

"*What?* How?"

Burke sighed, and I listened to him explain how it had started a couple of months ago, during the height of the merger he'd been working on all fall.

"At first it was just a line or two at the office. Everyone does it."

"Everyone does *cocaine* at the *office*?"

"A lot of people do, Heather. You don't understand. You have no idea what it's like. We're all drowning in work and exhausted and . . . I watched the other analysts and associates do it for months. I couldn't pull such late hours and I was falling behind—"

"So you turned to drugs?" I scowled. "*Back* to fucking drugs? After all these years? Jesus Christ."

"I made a mistake." Burke bowed his head, rubbing his eyes again. He reminded me of Garrett when he did that. "I fucked up. And then—soon after that I—I started drinking. I was out with a colleague one night—Doug Kemp, I'm sure you've heard me mention him before. He's in Global Markets but sits on my floor, and he always makes an effort to say hi to me, even though most of these guys all know each other from their college lacrosse teams and don't give a shit about trying to be buddies with me. Anyway, I'd had a particularly awful day. Just tense and long and horrible. Doug saw me heading for the vending machine around dinnertime and suggested we grab a burger. It felt so nice to just hang out with a guy who gets it, you know? Then Doug ordered a Scotch, and I had all this coke in my system and I just—I just couldn't not order one, too.

That's the best way I can explain it. I just couldn't not order one."

"Because you're an addict, Burke." I dropped to my knees on the floor, feeling cold and numb. "That's why you committed to getting clean in the first place."

"I know." Burke nodded solemnly. "I'm an addict."

I exhaled. "So then what happened? What does this have to do with you getting arrested for insider trading?"

I listened to Burke explain that a couple of nights later—a night he told me he was working late—he and Doug went out drinking again, and Doug presented him with an idea. Doug had a close friend, Julian Martell, looking to invest a substantial amount of money in the market. Apparently, Julian's last remaining grandparent had died, and Julian was looking to grow his inheritance (what *is* it with these trust-fund babies?), and Doug was thinking of giving him a heads-up about the impending merger. It was illegal, tipping someone off, but Doug said if done correctly, sharing the information would be simple and the returns astronomical.

But Doug couldn't do it alone. Doug and Julian had gone to UVA together—they were in the same fraternity for Christ's sake—the connection would've been obvious to anyone who noticed Julian's gains from the potential investment. That's where Burke came in. Burke—a stranger to Julian—would provide Julian with the information he needed to profit. Doug, Burke, and Julian would then split the return—Doug promised at least half a million in total—and no one would know a thing. And if anyone ever did look into Doug, there'd be nothing to find. The plan was bulletproof.

Well, the plan was bulletproof to my idiotic husband, who'd begun numbing himself with Johnnie Walker and coke after six and a half years of sobriety. And nothing is what it seems when you're on a two-month-long bender and putting the fate of your job in the hands of a guy named Doug Kemp, a sleazy opportunist who sees that you're vulnerable and doesn't think twice about using you as a human shield.

The SEC noticed Julian's gargantuan stock purchases. They informed the FBI, who linked Julian to his lifelong friend and college-fraternity brother Doug Kemp of Credit Suisse. And the FBI didn't stop at Doug; they plowed deeper into the system and discovered Julian's multiple phone calls with Doug's colleague Burke Michaels, only twenty-four hours before the order was placed.

For the life of me I couldn't fathom why Burke had done it, why he had risked the job he'd worked so hard to get for an amount of money that could've been his annual salary a few years down the line.

"I was shit-faced last night, Bones," he said finally, his face crumpling. "Some guys and I went out for a nightcap after work. I've been shit-faced for two months, if I'm being honest. That's why I did this. That's why I let this happen. I'm so fucking sorry."

How had I not known? How had I—his *wife*—never traced the Scotch on his breath until that day? And then I remembered a couple strange nights. Nights when something in Burke was off. A sour smell to his shirts in the wash. But it would've been unthinkable, Burke off the wagon again. Perhaps we only see what we want to see.

"Burke." I sat down next to him on the edge of the bed, smoothed his forehead. "This happened. You made a mistake. But if you do it again, you'll make me wish I'd never married you."

"I'm gonna get clean again, Bones. I promise."

"I know you will. I believe in you. I have always believed in you."

"But the arrest, the FBI—"

"Take a deep breath," I told him, though my own mind was spinning. "It'll all be okay. You'll have to pay a fine, I'm sure, but try to have some perspective. It's not like you killed someone. If Credit Suisse fires you, you'll get a job at a different bank."

"*If* Credit Suisse fires me?" Burke met my gaze, his blue eyes watery and lost. "You don't get it, do you, Heather? I'm already history to Credit Suisse, and a fine is the least of my concerns. This thing is going to court. Insider trading is a federal crime. If they find me guilty, not only will I get prison time, but I'll never work in finance again."

I heard the words come out of his mouth, but they wouldn't land. They remained in the air, floating in the space between us like weightless dust particles.

Garrett began to howl from his crib, and I turned from Burke, not saying another word. A surge of equal parts panic and fury filled every cell in my body. Burke had understood these consequences, and he'd done what he did anyway. He'd made a conscious decision to blow coke with Doug and drink himself into oblivion. High or not, it had been Burke's *choice* to put the future of our family—our *growing* family—on the line.

The next day an HR person from Credit Suisse came by the apartment with the contents of Burke's desk, along with an official letter of termination.

The plea hearing was a month later. Burke pleaded guilty, as was the plan, and was sentenced to fourteen months at the Metropolitan Correctional Center.

Doug Kemp, who'd claimed the extent of his involvement was merely introducing Burke to Julian Martell at a party several months earlier, wasn't even charged. Neither the FBI nor Credit Suisse pushed a deeper investigation; Doug's father's golf partner served on the bank's board of directors.

For a man like Doug, a man like Burke—a nobody from bumfuck nowhere who fought tooth and nail to get a spot in the Credit Suisse analyst program—was the perfect casualty in his failed scheme. Burke had no important connections or worthy background of note, nobody in his family had ever worked in finance, and he had no friends in common with Doug or anyone else in Doug's circle. The phone records said it all, but even if Burke did try to accuse Doug of lying, no one at the company would believe him.

In a follow-up letter to Burke's official termination, the CEO of Credit Suisse wrote that he did not envision Burke moving forward with a successful career in banking—this was corporate talk letting him know he'd been blacklisted.

Burke was at the Metropolitan Correctional Center, a

month into his prison sentence, when our daughter was born on a rainy morning in April. If the baby turned out to be a girl, Burke had wanted to call her Margaret, after his grandmother. But he wasn't there, so I named her something more fitting, something I needed in that moment. I named her Hope.

Chapter Thirty-Eight

Skye

A week before Thanksgiving, my dad says I need to go with him to talk to Davis. I take the subway up to Bryant Park and head toward Davis's office on Sixth Avenue. The cold air bites my face, and I duck my head to break the wind chill. The midtown streets are already packed with tourists who've flocked from all over the world for a taste of the holiday season in New York. I'd always loved the holidays, especially Christmas, up until several years ago when being single this time of year started to feel like a cruel punishment.

But last year, with Burke, Christmas had been a dream. We'd done some last-minute shopping together the day before Christmas Eve, and I remember the feel of his protective arm around me as we navigated the swarm of Fifth Avenue. We weren't yet engaged, but I remember being sure that I'd never spend the holidays alone again. I'd finally found my person.

Sometimes I wish I were the kind of woman who could be happy on her own. I was, for a while. At one time I relished my independence, I excelled because of it. After I started seeing Dr. Salam and she helped me screw my head on straight about Max LaPointe and everything else, for a good long stretch I didn't want to prioritize anyone but myself. I threw my energy into work, discovering Jan and the *Loving Louise* books, all of which became *USA Today* bestsellers. I trained for a marathon, read six novels a month, prioritized my friendships, and taught myself how to cook. And for the first time in a long time, I was happy.

Not until I fell in love with Burke did I realize the difference between contentment and joy. I had found a way to be content, as a single woman. But I didn't feel true joy until I met Burke.

Davis's office is on the twenty-first floor, so I suck it up and take the elevator. I'm running late, and my dad is already there. Davis raises his eyebrows when I walk in—that's as much of a smile as you'll get out of him—and interlaces his meaty fingers across his desk. He's around my dad's age but grayer, with broad shoulders stretching the span of his suit.

I slide into the vacant seat next to my father, who squeezes my arm and gives me a tight smile.

My phone buzzes on my lap. A text from Jan:

S—I need those edits ASAP. You said you'd have them last week, and if we want the next Louise to launch in July (which I DO!) we need to stay on track. I know you're going through some serious stuff right now (though I don't know what, let me know if I can help . . .). Feeling a bit in the dark here and we're a month behind schedule and I'm starting to freak. Also, launch party is Friday, tell me I'll see you there???

Fuck. Not only have I completely neglected the edits for Jan's next book, I've entirely forgotten that the *current* book—the one I worked on tirelessly all spring and summer—launches this week. How is that possible?

"Skye." Davis looks at me and blinks. "Water? Coffee? What can I have Trina get you?"

"I'm fine, thanks." I shuffle out of my coat, wanting to get this over with so I can get home and work.

"Okay," Davis nods, "I appreciate you being here. I understand not wanting to be overly involved in the details of the lawsuit against your ex-husband."

"Husband," I blurt with instant regret. Heat flushes to my face. "I mean—we're still technically married."

Davis nods again.

"Unfortunately," I add pathetically. My father stares at his lap.

"Yes." Davis clears his throat. "Well, we're hoping to have that sorted out soon. You'll absolutely qualify for an annulment. Since Burke was already married, your marriage is illegal."

Your marriage is illegal. The permanent knife in my gut finds another way to twist.

"The state will prosecute for grand larceny," Davis continues. "They won't really do anything about the bigamy, unfortunately, but we can address that in the civil suit. Regardless, bigamous marriages are void, and grounds for an annulment. An annulment is ideal, of course."

I want to scream. *IS IT? PLEASE TELL ME WHEN AN ANNULMENT IS EVER IDEAL.*

"As opposed to divorce," Davis adds. "It's much faster and cleaner. There's no division of assets. It'll simply be as though your marriage never existed." He smiles, as though this were good news.

The knife twists deeper still.

"Skye." My father turns to look at me, shifting uncomfortably. "The reason Davis wanted you here is because . . . well . . . you know we need to push this thing further. Beyond the annulment, that is. Burke has committed serious, serious crimes." My father glances toward Davis, silently begging him to take over.

"Yes," Davis grunts, rearranging some papers in front of his bulky chest. "The bastard stole two million, right from under your nose. I won't lie—at first, I was worried the state wouldn't be able to get him for grand larceny, since the money was stolen from a joint account to which Burke was entrusted by you as his spouse. But fortunately, since we know Burke intends to plead guilty, we're golden." Davis grins slyly. "Getting him for grand larceny will be a *huge* win for us, Skye."

"Wait." My heart picks up speed. "Burke has already pleaded guilty?"

"He intends to, according to his lawyer." Davis looks at me blankly. "It's not completely surprising. With the email he sent your friend and the attachment of the electronic letters to the therapist—all of which he admits are factual—the evidence shows that this was all premeditated. It's stacked against him. We also have the bank records, proof of his ATM withdrawals, the payments he was sending to his—er—first wife. Not to mention the generous transfer he made to his now-dead neighbor, right before you removed him from the joint account. Sneaky son of a bitch."

I say nothing, picking at the cuticle of my thumb.

"The reason I wanted to speak to you in person, Skye, is to ask if there is any other hard evidence—*anything* you can think of—that we can add to strengthen our case." Davis drums his round fingertips across the desk. "The state prosecutor—a guy named Frank Bruno—tells me that with what we have now, and given the defendant's criminal history, Burke is looking at five years and a substantial fine. In addition to returning what he stole."

"Five years in *prison*?" I stare at Davis.

"That's right," he replies enthusiastically. "Potentially *more,* Skye, and that's why I wanted to see you. If you can think of anything else to contribute to the case against Burke Michaels, the time is now."

I imagine Burke spending five years in prison and my throat feels tight. I will myself not to cry in front of Davis. I have to find a way to be stronger, to be *glad* that the sociopath who ruined my life faces five years in jail.

"Skye?" Davis prompts. "Anything?"

"Sorry. Um, nothing that comes to mind," I answer carefully. "But I—let me give it some more thought over the weekend. If I think of anything, I'll call you first thing Monday."

Davis nods slowly, his gaze unflinching. Then he claps his hands together and the pressure in the room dissolves. He and my father make small talk as they politely leave the office before me so I can do my knocks on Davis's door in psychotic privacy.

My dad turns to me in the elevator. "Lunch?"

I shake my head. "I can't. I'm so behind on work."

"Okay." He looks at the floor as we step into the lobby, and I swallow a pang of guilt. "I want to tell you something, Skye." He picks his head up.

"What is it?"

"I—I should've told you this a few weeks ago, when I first realized that Burke's wife is Heather, your old babysitter."

"Okay." Nerves prick my insides.

"I haven't mentioned any of this to Davis because I wanted to talk to you about it first." My father pauses, his jaw clenched. "Your mother became very close to Heather during the year she babysat for you and Nate."

My head spins. "Mom was close to Burke's wife? How old was she?"

"Heather was in high school at the time. Sixteen or seventeen, maybe. But it was the year we were living in upstate New York—I was there for a study on the Adirondacks—and the house we rented was in this small, kind-of-run-down town called Langs Valley—where Burke grew up, too, although I only pieced that together recently. I was really immersed in the project and not around as much as I should've been. Your mom was lonely, I think."

I press my tongue against the back of my teeth, a dark, sinister feeling wobbling through me. "So, what are you saying? You think all this is somehow . . . tied to what happened with Burke and me?"

"I wouldn't be surprised. See, your mom and Heather had a falling-out."

"What happened?" The sound of heels clicking on marble surrounds us as people enter and exit the bustling lobby. I see now why my father wanted to get lunch.

"Heather had a little brother. Gus." My dad swallows. "Gus . . . died. In a drowning accident, when he was five. Long story short, Heather blamed your mom for his death."

"What? That's awful. I mean, awful that he drowned. Why did she blame Mom?"

"To be honest, Skye, I never fully understood it. I wasn't there right when it happened. It was summer and we were picnicking at a lake, and I'd gone for a walk to take some photographs. You got stung by a bee—you were just a baby—and Mom was scared that you were having an allergic reaction. So she sent Heather to go find me. And then I guess she was still preoccupied with you and didn't notice Nate and Gus drifting out farther into the lake. It was windy that day. And they were only five—Nate wasn't a strong swimmer and Gus couldn't really swim at all. Your mom didn't see the boys until she heard them screaming, and of course she tried to save them. But I guess she couldn't swim with them both at once, and she could only save Nate." My father pauses, hesitant, as if the rest is even more difficult to say. "When I got back to the beach, Gus was still in the water, and Heather was back by then, standing on the shore screaming. Turns out she didn't know how to swim, either. So I jumped in and swam Gus to shore, but it was too late." My dad closes his eyes and shakes his head softly. "It was horrible, Skye. After that, Heather refused to speak to us. We tried, but she was adamant. We even tried to give her some money, to help with things—she grew up with nothing, as far as I could tell—but she refused it. We left Langs Valley that summer, and we never heard from Heather again."

My mind is reeling, grasping to make sense of what my father has just described.

"So you're saying that Heather blamed Mom for saving her own son before Gus?"

"More or less." My father's voice is thin. "But like I said, there are pieces missing for me. Your mom hated talking about it—whenever I tried to broach the subject, she'd just shut down or start crying. The whole thing really haunted her, that much I know. I always got the sense that she harbored a great deal of guilt because of it. That in some way she felt responsible. In truth, it put a real strain on our marriage, in the year that followed. I should've pressed her to talk about it more, maybe see a therapist. But I didn't. I just wanted us to move on."

I swallow the lump that's formed in my throat. "And you're telling me this because you think . . . you think Burke going after my money was all some sort of plan to get back at Mom?"

"Look, Skye." My father sighs. "I don't know what I think. I just want you to have all the facts. You deserve that. Burke already pled guilty. He's admitted that what he wrote in the letters to his therapist is true, and he said that Heather wasn't aware or involved. But what I can't quite accept is that this is all a coincidence. Burke randomly meets a girl in Montauk and, upon learning she has a trust fund, decides to go after her money? And that *same* girl just happens to be the daughter of the woman his wife blames for her brother's death? It's a little too convenient."

My head is a tornado. "So you think Burke is lying?"

"I don't know, Skye. I think . . ."

"Just tell me, Dad. Please. Tell me what you think."

"I think he's lying, Skye, yes." His eyes clip to mine. "I think he lied to protect Heather, so that they don't both go to jail. But I think they were in on this plan together, and that it isn't random that he met you at all."

"But—but then how do you explain the letters? They don't mention anything about Heather's brother drowning and her wanting to get back at Mom."

"That's the part I can't figure out." My father pinches his sinuses.

"I don't understand, Dad. Why haven't you told Davis about this? I thought you were telling him everything."

"Because if I tell Davis, he's going to do what any good lawyer would—advise that we press charges against Heather, too. He's going to want to look for evidence. And that would drag this whole thing out—it could take *years,* Skye. And I don't want to do that to you, sweetheart. I want this to be over, for your sake, so you can let go of this nightmare and move on with your life."

The lunch rush seems to have died down, and we're suddenly the only two people in the lobby. It's eerily quiet.

"Skye, it's ultimately up to you. If you want to go after Heather, too, then we will."

"I—I don't . . ." My brain feels like a water balloon, filling, expanding, on the verge of bursting. "I need to process all of this."

"I understand." My father pulls me in close, smoothing the back of my hair. "Take your time. Call me if you have any questions about . . . anything. Or if you just want to talk."

After he leaves for Grand Central, I stay in the lobby for a minute to check my phone. There's another text from Jan—a row of question marks—and a new email from Max, sent twenty minutes ago.

It's seriously not okay to ignore someone, Starling. You'd be wise to remember your manners. Let me know about that drink, or you'll be sorry. Very fucking sorry.

I step out into the blinding cold. A sharp pain is in my stomach, and I'm so confused I can barely walk straight. I stumble into a woman carrying a miniature poodle and she snaps at me to watch where I'm going. I continue forward in a daze, caught between too many versions of the same awful narrative.

There is the story revealed in Burke's letters to his therapist, Dr. K. This is the story in which I'm a mistaken hookup turned marriage-saving opportunity.

There is the story my father has pieced together involving Burke's wife, Heather. This is the story in which I'm an unwitting pawn in a larger revenge plot.

There is the story on the Post-it note Burke left me, a story that feels impossible but is still out there, incomplete. *I'm so sorry, Skye. I wish I could explain, but I can't. I love you.* This is the story in which Burke loves me. It can't be true. But what if it is?

And then there is Max LaPointe. Max, who's still harassing me for some unknown reason, who seems oddly curious about my relationship with Burke. Could *Max* somehow be tied up in all this?

The truth has to be somewhere in these tangled narratives. And I have to find it.

I hail a cab home. I don't let myself think about my not having answered Jan's texts or the degree to which I'm letting her down or that she's probably going to fire me or that at this rate Max might show up at my apartment and slit my throat.

I'm so distracted that I don't even remember to wave hello to Ivan in the lobby of my building. But from within my clouded stupor, I hear him calling my name.

"Skye! What perfect timing. A package just arrived for you." Ivan smiles, holding out a small cushioned mailer—the kind I use to send out galleys for work.

My heart catches in my throat; I instantly recognize the familiar sight of Burke's angular scribble on the package. There's no return address, but the handwriting is Burke's. Positively, undeniably Burke's.

"Thanks, Ivan," I hear myself respond.

I run upstairs. I wait until I'm safely inside my apartment before I tear open the package. Inside is a navy blue Moleskine notebook with a folded piece of paper sticking out from under the front flap. I unfold the paper first. It's a letter—handwritten—from Burke.

Goose,

I've started some version of this letter to you so many times without finishing it because, the truth is, I don't know how to make sense of what's happened in words. In my heart I know and feel the truth, but in my head it's a mess.

First and foremost, I want to tell you that it's been torture not being able to talk to you these past couple of months. It's agonizing not knowing how you've been feeling, and that's part of the reason I haven't been able to reach out. The rational part of me imagines you despise me—as you should—and that you will tear up this letter and throw this notebook in the fire before reading a word of any of it. This part of me believes—and hopes—that you have found the strength to move on, to pick up the pieces of the wreck I made of us and to know in your heart that better things lie ahead—things you deserve. You didn't deserve this. I didn't deserve you.

Then there's a smaller, pathetic part of me that believes perhaps maybe you still love me the way I love you. And confusingly enough, this smaller part of me is just as hopeful as the bigger, rational part. Perhaps it's cruel to tell you that I love you after the destruction and pain I've caused you, but I've decided that I can't not.

The crazy truth is, I wasn't supposed to marry you. That wasn't part of the plan. I was supposed to leave you before the wedding, but I couldn't.

And so, selfishly, I didn't. You deserve to know that I loved you when I married you, and that I still love you. I know that's not enough. Love isn't enough. I never used to understand that expression, but I do now. You can love someone completely, and it still isn't enough to make it work.

It's not your fault, by the way, so don't go thinking that, even for a second. I've racked every corner of my brain trying to figure out how to communicate the choices I've made so that you can begin to understand, but I honestly can't, Skye. All I can say is that I have to put the safety and well-being of my children before anything else in my life. I simply don't know another way.

I'm so unbelievably sorry for deceiving you; I'll live with the shame of it until I die. I know you wish more than anything that you'd never met me—and for your sake, the better part of me wishes that, too. But selfishly, meeting you and falling in love with you has been one of the greatest gifts of my life. When we met, I was in a marriage I thought I could save. Spending time with you only made me realize that my marriage was built on a foundation of tragedy, a cyclical rhythm of brokenness that perpetuated this cavernous void inside me—a marriage that was far beyond repair.

But it was so much more than that, Skye, and that's the thing. It wasn't just that you gave me a new perspective on my relationship. You are the first and only person I've ever met who sees the world the way I do. Who's cracked and marred in the same places I am, but who fights ferociously to be better, to create change from within. You've experienced tremendous grief and made it part of you; you've grown strong from suffering. You will never know how badly I needed to meet you, and how lucky I will always feel that I did. Aside from my children, you are the only person I've ever met who has shown me that painful things don't have to harden you—you're the only one who has made that void inside me feel full. You opened my mind and my heart. You are a bright star, and I am a terrible cliché.

Here in this package is my journal—my *real* journal. I went back and forth in my head so many times, debating whether I should give it to you, because it's only part of the truth. As you'll see when and if you choose to read it, there are pieces I had to omit. But, ultimately, I decided that you deserve to know as much of the truth as I can give you.

I wish there were a way for me to tell you everything. Perhaps one day you'll understand why I can't give you the whole truth now. In the meantime, I hope you can make peace with not having all the answers. I hope you will live a life that is as radiant and beautiful as you are, and I hope you will find a way to believe—if you don't already—that I got what I deserved.

I know that I am not the love of your life, Skye

Starling, but for what it's worth, know that you are mine.

Love,

Burke

My heart hammers behind my ribs, shock pricking my skin. I feel as though I'm on the verge of waking up from a long, insane dream. I reread Burke's words from the second paragraph:

The crazy truth is, I wasn't supposed to marry you. That wasn't part of the plan. I was supposed to leave you before the wedding, but I couldn't. And so, selfishly, I didn't.

Could that be true? An unsettling combination of dread and hope pools in my stomach as I open the Moleskine. The pages are tattered, and some lines have been covered in thick black Sharpie. Entire sections have been ripped right out of the spine.

My head spins as I devour the first two entries, which are from May and June 2018, consecutively. They nearly kill me—they're full of Burke's love for Heather, his devotion to his family. But then a shiver licks my spine when I reach the third entry, dated September 8. The day Burke and I met.

This can't be real, I make sure to remind myself. None of these words are real. Burke is a sociopath.

Nevertheless, I continue reading.

Chapter Thirty-Nine

Burke

OCTOBER 2019—*TWO DAYS WITHOUT SKYE*

I'm two entries into the Moleskine. I hate reliving the details that led me to this excruciating reality, but I can't stop reading my own words.

September 8, 2018

Well, I tried as hard as I could. I can't tell you the number of jobs I applied to this summer—I lost count. Aside from our trip to Yellowstone, that's all I did, all summer long, while Heather upped her hours driving for Uber—our only source of cash flow.

But no one wants to hire an ex-felon who spent a year in prison for insider trading; the only companies who called me for an interview did so because their applications skipped the "felony" question. So then I had to bring it up during the interview—my old mentor Eric from Credit Suisse gave me that advice. Eric was a VP and the only person from the company who agreed to talk to me when I got out of prison, and he said being upfront with the truth would be the most helpful thing I could do for myself during future job interviews. He said any hiring manager would find out during a background check regardless, and that it was better not to look like I was trying to hide anything. Eric had helped me get my job at PKA. I took his advice then, and I took it this summer. But every interview ended the same; after I finished speaking my piece, explaining how I've learned from the mistake I made when I was twenty-four, the interviewer's smile stiffened. The air in the room shifted. "We'll be in touch," they all said. They never were.

My forty-sixth birthday fell over Labor Day weekend, the last Friday in August. I've never been a big birthday guy, but it was something Heather always liked to celebrate. The kids came home for the night and she made burgers on the grill and the coleslaw that I like. Hope and Maggie baked a carrot cake that made the whole house smell warm and sweet like molasses. They covered it in cream-cheese icing and wrote *HAPPY BIRTHDAY DAD* in blue gel frosting. It was something they would've done when they were little, and it squeezed my heart in a way that made me happy and sad at the same time.

Heather gave me a gray sweater from Brooks Brothers that I didn't need, but I knew she'd likely spent hours selecting it and waiting for a sale to buy it, so I told her I loved it. The kids all went in on a sterling-silver picture frame that undoubtedly cost more than they could afford; inside was a photo of the five of us taken in front of Yellowstone Lake earlier that month. Tears pricked the corners of my eyes when I opened the present, and Garrett, Hope, and Maggie's faces flushed with sunny pride, and I felt grateful then, and happier than I had in longer than I could remember. A feeling of peace washed through me, simple and whole—the peace of knowing that nothing else mattered, that fighting to preserve moments like these was worth anything.

The next morning, the first of September, I didn't wait for Heather to come to me. I didn't want to give her that control. I woke early, staring at the contours of my wife's face while she slept, the rise and fall of her small body as she breathed. Lately I love studying her like this, before she's awake. All peaceful and still, I can almost pretend that it's the old Heather I'm watching, the Heather who once was proud of me, whose dreams rested on me. She's in there, somewhere.

But as soon as her grass-green eyes flip open, the old Heather has swirled down the drain, and the battle is on again. This strange, silent war that's invaded the space between us. She opened her mouth to speak, but I beat her to the punch. I told her what she already knew— that I hadn't gotten a job. And that I was ready to move forward another way.

I don't know much about Libby Fontaine's

daughter, only that she's a twenty-nine-year-old book editor in New York. And she's rich. Very rich.

I haven't had a drink in twenty-two years, but I'm telling you, I could use a Scotch right about now. I can acutely imagine the way I'd feel after just one drink, the way the liquor would streak through the current of my blood, bringing a pleasant weight to my limbs.

But I can't do it, and I won't. I made a pact with myself twenty-two years ago, and it's not one that's breakable. So it's down to the pool sans alcohol. One step at a time, and Heather and I stand to make millions of dollars.

I don't like to let myself think about the catch—the trade-off for all that money. The fact that if everything goes according to the Big Plan, we may have to disappear for a while. The very legitimate possibility that Garrett, Hope, and Maggie won't come with us, wherever we go.

Today I have to keep my eyes on the prize. One step at a time. There's no way to mess today up. All I have to do is be a guy flirting with a girl at a pool in Montauk.

In my mind, this is where it gets complicated. I am a forty-six-year-old man. I have noticeable grays in my hair that was once all black, and a "Dad bod" for sure (or so Maggie tells me). A washed-up father of three in the prime of middle age. Skye Starling is twenty-nine and, from what

I've seen, a total knockout. Prettier than her mom, even, and though I only met Libby a few times, she always looked like a model.

But apparently Skye has severe obsessive-compulsive disorder, which means she's vulnerable, and single. This is the perfect time for me to swoop in. Jesus Christ. I hate myself.

Time to go down to the pool now. Here goes nothing.

September 30, 2018

Something is going on, and I can't quite put my finger on it. It's been two weeks since I started seeing Skye, and I'm worried I'm starting to fall for this girl. It's a strange thing to say, since I've only ever "fallen" for one girl in my life, and I'm wishing I had a little bit more dating perspective right about now. Or at least someone to ask.

I have gotten some guidance from Todd. It was originally Heather's idea for me to seek his input, seeing as he has firsthand experience cheating on his wife. I didn't tell him about the Big Plan—of course not. I only confessed that I'd started seeing a girl on the side—a girl I'd met in Montauk—and Todd seemed to understand completely. He even offered to come into the city to meet Skye and me for dinner—an offer which I gladly accepted. It felt strange, certainly, but I was grateful for the opportunity to introduce Skye to one of my genuine friends. For a fleeting moment, it made the whole thing feel like less of a farce.

But Todd doesn't seem to grasp that my feelings for Skye might be legitimately real. He views her as my midlife crisis, an itch that felt too good not to scratch. And maybe he's right. I don't know. All I do know is that I can't stop thinking about Skye.

Something about her face makes me feel like everything is going to be okay. She's got this smile that spreads across her whole face like butter on hot toast, and big brown eyes that warm the space behind my chest, bringing me this sense of ease. I don't know how to explain it. Even though I'm pretending to be someone else when I'm with her, I don't know if I've ever felt more like myself.

When I'm not with her, I'm thinking about when I'll be with her next. It's crazy. Completely crazy. Sometimes I feel like I'm cheating on Heather, and I have to remind myself what this is all for.

Every time I remember what I'm actually doing, I feel sick to my stomach, so I've trained myself not to think about it. For the past couple of weeks I've slipped out of Skye's apartment early (feigning an early start time for my fake job) to head to a coffee shop or my place in Crown Heights and hit the ground running on my search. The way I see it, there's still time. If I can manage to land a decent job in the foreseeable future,

I can drop this whole con-artist act and go back to my life, leaving Skye unscathed.

October 28, 2018
I just reread my last entry—so much has happened since then. For starters, I am indeed in love with Skye Starling.

I probably knew it after our first real date, but the situation was new and overwhelming and bizarre, and in retrospect, I couldn't have recognized it. If I had, I might've found the strength to put my foot down, to go back to Heather and demand we find another way.

But I'm too deep in it now, and when you remember how incredible it is to be in love, there's no turning back. It reminds me of that Billy Joel song—

I'll take my chances
I forgot how nice romance is
I haven't been there for the longest time

Skye is the one who's gotten me back into Billy Joel. His music reminds me of Langs Valley, but not of Heather. It just reminds me of me, I think. And now Skye, too.

What I'm realizing is, I *haven't* been there for the longest time. The more time I spend with Skye, the more I realize that I've fallen out of love with my wife. And it isn't *because* of Skye. I don't think I've been in love with Heather for a while now, and I'm not quite sure what to do with that. I never realized it was possible to be so happy and so sad at the same time.

Skye is nothing like Heather. You can't compare them. There are just . . . these things about Skye that fill me, that make me feel whole.

She's got one of those old vintage turntables, and it's her face when she puts on a record, the way the corners of her mouth poke up toward her ears as "The Stranger" fills the room. It's how her eyelids grow heavy when she's had a couple of negronis, the way it doesn't bother me to watch her get drunk. It's how nice she is to waiters, how thoughtful she is toward her friends, how diligent she is about work, and the way her whole face always seems to be on the verge of a smile. Skye is good at her job, but even though she won't admit it, I can tell that book editing isn't her passion. Not really. And I want her to *find* her passion. I've only known her six weeks and I want that for her. I want it for her even more than I want it for myself.

Skye has this thing she says about the way people laugh. She says a laugh is like a fingerprint, the way each one is unique to every person in the world. Isn't that incredible? I love the way she makes observations like this that are so simple, but profound.

Skye thinks her OCD defines her, but it doesn't. I'm not lying when I tell her that I've mostly stopped noticing her routines, but I don't think she believes me. I don't know how to get her to understand that she's so much more than this stupid disease.

The thing is, Skye *is* vulnerable. Skye's compulsion to knock on doors and wood and clocks in a specific method under certain circumstances is no easy cross to bear. It's interruptive for her life, certainly. It's the reason that she works from home as a freelancer. And it's the reason some pretty horrible things have happened to her, most notably an ex who used Skye's OCD to sexually assault her. When she told me that story, tears visible in the corners of her eyes, I was overcome with the desire to find this asshole and knock his teeth in, especially when she said she'd never pressed charges. She did report the incident to the jerk's grad school, which thankfully resulted in his expulsion, but she didn't want the reasoning made public. She said she'd been so insecure at the time, she hadn't wanted to draw more attention to her OCD. I was practically fuming on Skye's behalf, an anger so strong I couldn't shake it until I saw my own reflection in the bathroom mirror and stopped, frozen with disgust. If this guy was bad, I was worse.

November 17, 2018
Last week I told Skye that I love her.

I hadn't been thinking about it before I said it. We were sitting on her couch, listening to the Beach Boys on vinyl and talking, and I swear I could talk to her forever. I found myself telling her things about my past, straying far from the narrative I'd rehearsed. I told her about my drug and alcohol problems in high school, how I got sober senior year, and then how I relapsed during my second year at Credit Suisse.

I probably should've stopped there, but I didn't, I don't know, it just felt right to tell Skye about the incident with Doug Kemp, how he got off scot-free, my arrest, and the nightmare of a year I spent in prison. Once I started talking, it was like something cracked open inside me, and I couldn't stop. I told her about the corrupt guards at MCC, the prolonged isolation, the filth, how cold it got in my cell at night, the interminable stretches of monotony punctuated by flashes of explosive violence. Things I've never told Heather. I didn't even think about how horrifying it must've all sounded until I stopped rambling and saw the shell-shocked look on Skye's face. Girls like Skye Starling don't date ex-felons. But then her expression softened, and her eyes filled with tears.

"I am so sorry that happened to you," she said. It was a simple response, but one that warmed the space behind my chest. No one had ever said that to me before. Heather was ecstatic when I got out of MCC, but she was equally furious at the financial position I'd put us in by losing my job. She'd certainly never asked for details or exhibited any sympathy toward me. I was starved for connection; I craved open dialogue, some gaping channel of release for my pain. I told Heather I wanted to try Alcoholics Anonymous, but she said AA was for suckers, and that I needed to land on my own two feet like a man. She dealt with my relapse and my year in prison by pretending it had never happened. We never even told the kids.

As liberating as it was to open up to Skye, it also felt strange to reveal the darkest part of my life without telling her the whole truth. Without being able to describe the pain of sitting helplessly behind bars while my daughter came into the world, while my son turned three and became a big brother.

As Skye smoothed the hair from my forehead and planted my face with kisses, I was suddenly overwhelmed with gratitude for her, for whatever insane, appalling circumstances had brought her into my life.

I told her I loved her without a thought. When she pulled me in close and whispered it back, I felt a weight slide off my shoulders.

December 27, 2018

I'm home in New Haven for Christmas, and I feel like I'm cheating on Skye. Not only because I lied to her about my holiday plans—I said I was going to Phoenix to visit relatives—but physically, I feel like I'm cheating on her. I swear, Heather hasn't been all over me like this since before we had kids. The prospect of money has always been an aphrodisiac. I wish there were a way to avoid having sex with her while I'm home, but the last thing I need is to make her suspicious. So I just have to deal with it for a couple more days; on Saturday I'm flying to Palm Beach to spend New Year's with Skye and her family.

Of course, I hate to sound like that, because having Christmas at home with Garrett and Hopie and Mags is everything. Being away from the kids for such long periods feels unbearable at times, and lying to them is chipping away a piece of my soul. It's a bizarre sort of comfort to know that despite the giant mess I've landed myself in, the love I have for my children still trumps everything.

The financial problems in our household are worse than I realized. Heather pulled me aside on Christmas Day, after we'd opened presents and the kids were vegged out on the couch watching *Elf*. She reminded me that I still hadn't written a check for Hope's second-semester tuition, and that we'd just received our third reminder from the dentist requesting the balance be settled for Hope's dental implants, a whopping total of $19,000. For fake teeth. Heather explained that the money she'd been bringing in was only enough to cover groceries, electricity, and internet bills, and half the monthly mortgage payment. I nodded, swallowing the knowledge that the only money I have to my name is five grand in savings, and told Heather I would figure something out.

"Make something happen soon, Burke." Heather folded her skinny arms across her chest. "Or else we're fucked."

We're already fucked, I wanted to respond. But then Mags scrambled off the couch and clasped her hands around my middle. She looked up at me with wide green eyes, her blond hair pulled back—a mini-Heather—and said that having me home from Dubai was the best Christmas present she could've asked for. A swell of love surged through me and I had to blink back tears as I held my youngest daughter close. For the life of me I don't know how I got here.

February 2, 2019

The groundhog saw his shadow this morning; looks like it'll be six more weeks of frigid New York winter. But living with Skye, my heart is warm. Sometimes I imagine that our apartment is our own little cocoon, sealed off from the rest of the world. I like it best that way.

Outside West Eleventh Street, the pressure is building. Nothing has come of my (private) job search, and I'm starting to feel it's a hopeless endeavor. I'm due in New Haven again at the end of February, and Heather says we need real money coming in by then. She says we got a notice from Eastern that if we don't pay Hope's second-semester tuition by the end of April, she won't be able to graduate with the rest of her class in May. And I won't let that happen—I just won't. So I'll do it, I'll email Peter Starling and set up a time to meet him this week so that I can ask for Skye's hand.

Some days I want to jump off the Empire State Building. I wouldn't; I'd never do that to my kids or to Skye. To Skye! Look at me. Here I am, all protective of Skye and her well-being while simultaneously on the path to destroying her life. I can't stand myself.

February 23, 2019
I feel like I'm on the verge of a panic attack, and writing in this journal is my only release. I'm back in New Haven for the weekend, cooped up in the office while everyone is downstairs hanging out—Heather and Maggie are making that chili I love for dinner. I told them I needed to answer some work emails. The kids are so happy to see me and have so many questions about Dubai that it makes me physically ill, and I don't know how I can continue on this way. Even Todd has been reaching out, asking how Dubai is. I hate lying to everybody. I hate it so much.

What I do know is that I have to propose to Skye, and I have to get our joint bank account opened so that I can start transferring some money to Heather. All of this has to happen soon because we are in serious, serious debt. Not to mention if I don't come up with the money,

Hope will have to drop out of college. But I will get the money—I asked Peter for Skye's hand a couple of weeks ago, and he said yes. So now I just need to get the ring from Heather, and then I can propose. I know I'm not actually going to go through with marrying Skye—that's not part of the plan—but it doesn't make this any easier, or any less evil. I just wish there was a way to—

That's where the journal ends, the sentence of the last entry unfinished. That was the moment Heather and Maggie walked into the office and I slid the Moleskine behind the desk, so they wouldn't see.

Sleep isn't possible, that much I know. I go downstairs and wait for Heather in the kitchen, anger building inside me like a wave. I'll wait all night if I have to. An open bottle of Malbec sits on the counter, and it takes every fiber of self-control in my body to keep from chugging the entire thing.

Instead, I find a pad of paper and a pen and I start writing a letter to Skye. I must crumple up a dozen different versions.

I'm in the middle of a new draft when the wheels of Heather's car finally crunch over the driveway. I imagine her turning off the ignition, slumping over the steering wheel for a moment to prepare for our interaction before she comes inside.

It's two A.M., but she knows that I'm wide awake, waiting for her.

Chapter Forty

Heather

Dear Dr. K,

It hit me in waves, as I nursed Hope and waited for Burke to get out of prison, that our life would never again be the same.

He was released in March, a few months early, one year after his sentence. Our lease was up at the end of the month, and no way could we afford to renew. I'd gotten by on our savings while Burke was away, but with our pricey Gramercy rent and two babies to care for, the balance had notably dwindled. I watched tears glaze my husband's eyes when he checked our bank account for the first time since being home.

We moved to a cheap two-bedroom in Astoria. I lied to my friends in our Gramercy building as we packed up the apartment, explaining that we were moving to a house in the suburbs with a backyard and a pool. I couldn't bring myself to admit that we were downsizing to a small walk-up in Queens without a dishwasher.

I felt gutted during our first few days in Astoria, as though someone had died. I missed the shiny marble floors of our old lobby, the cheerful greeting from the doorman, and the sleek, speedy elevator. Garrett's new room doubled as Burke's office, which Burke used to hit the ground running on his job search. He was angry, and devastated, and motivated like I'd never seen him before.

The harsh winter melted into a forgiving spring, but Burke was still jobless. By the time summer rolled around he was becoming more and more discouraged. He'd sought out every position in finance under the sun—he applied to big banks, small banks, hedge funds, insurance agencies, accounting firms, you name it. Search agencies wouldn't work with him once they learned of his background. A felon who'd done time for insider trading was the last person welcome on Wall Street—or anywhere else.

Despite our increasingly thrifty lifestyle, by the end of the summer we were running out of money. Burke took a job busing tables at a Thai restaurant in our neighborhood. They paid minimum wage and ignored that Burke had checked the felony box on his application.

Burke did hustle, I'll give him that. Whenever he wasn't working at the restaurant, he was home at his desk applying for jobs, or out networking. He met with a couple of his old professors from NYU for guidance, and even one ex-colleague from Credit Suisse agreed to give him advice. Burke would come back from these meetings buoyed, a bright splash of hope on his face.

I, on the other hand, was sinking deeper into a pit of misery. I found myself wishing Burke had never gotten into the Credit Suisse analyst program in the first place. I wished he hadn't transferred from CUNY to NYU. I wished he'd never found the drive to keep his transcript perfect. Because now, having had a sweet taste of the life we could've had, I knew I would never be satisfied by anything less.

I didn't consider leaving him, not actually. I could have left, and I might have if it hadn't been for Garrett and Hope. I was still young, and the way men's eyes lingered on me in coffee shops and elevators told me that even after two babies, I was still desirable. I'd accumulated a lavish enough wardrobe over my years in Manhattan to make myself appear as though I'd belonged. These were clothes I refused to sell, and Burke didn't know enough about fashion to suspect that they were valuable. My point is, I could've found another man to love me, a man with the money and upward mobility that Burke had proven to lack.

But I'd meant the promise I'd made to myself, and to Burke, when I first found out I was pregnant with Garrett. We swore that we'd give our children everything our parents had never given us, all of the advantages we'd never had. And first on that list was a mother and a father who loved each other, who stayed together for better or for worse, whose marriage was the rock that weathered all storms. I refused to put my babies through the agony of growing up in a broken family.

Besides, I still loved Burke. Even though part of me hated him for his selfish stupidity, even though sometimes I wanted to wring his neck for the position he'd put us in, I knew I would always be in love with Burke Michaels. I found strength in that. I found power in knowing that our marriage was stronger than Libby and Peter Starling's had been, and that because of this our children were going to be better off than Nate and Skye. To me, that counted for a whole lot.

That winter, nearly a year after Burke had been out of prison, he got a call from his old colleague Eric from Credit Suisse. Eric told Burke that Eric had a cousin who owned a small wealth management firm in New Haven called PK Adamson that was looking for someone to do data entry. Eric had vouched for Burke—unlike most people at the bank, he recognized Doug Kemp for the scheming scum that he was—and PK Adamson agreed to bring Burke in for an interview.

A week later Burke took the train out to New Haven for the interview, and Eric's cousin offered him the job on the spot. The cousin said he was impressed with his background at Credit Suisse, and that he was willing to overlook his criminal history because he owed Eric a solid. The starting salary was $25,000 a year.

I couldn't understand why Burke was so thrilled to accept a position that would be paying him a tiny fraction of what he'd been making before. He reasoned that it was an opportunity to get his foot in the door at a decent wealth management firm, that it could be a stepping-stone on the path toward becoming a financial adviser. He'd likely never make what he would've in investment banking, but he squeezed my hand and told me that perhaps a lucrative career in finance was still in the cards for him after all.

What neither of us admitted was the undeniable truth that this was our only option. Clearly no one else was going to hire Burke, and his gig busing tables at Bangkok Garden wasn't sustainable—we had two young children, and we needed health insurance.

I wasn't sad to pack up and leave Astoria; with two very mobile kids we were quickly outgrowing our nine-hundred-square-foot dump of an apartment. Besides, our downgraded life in New York nagged at me like a chronic ache, our proximity to Manhattan a constant searing reminder of what we no longer were, of the promising future we'd lost.

When I used to imagine moving to the suburbs of Connecticut one day, I certainly hadn't pictured New Haven. Libby used to say that Fairfield County was the only decent place to live in the state.

As far as I knew, she was still there in Westport, luxuriating in her daily schedule of spa appointments and tennis matches and luncheons at the club. Nate and Skye would be thirteen and nine by now. I'd have been lying if I said I didn't still think about the Starling family. It was an unshakable obsession, a private indulgence, and certainly something I never mentioned to Burke.

When Burke was at Credit Suisse, I used to dream of the house in Westport that we'd buy one day—a big white Colonial with blue shutters sited on acres of lush kelly-green grass overlooking the ocean. Eventually I'd run into Libby at the supermarket or the post office; she'd be in her forties by then, her eyes sunken, crow's-feet infesting the skin around them. I'd be golden and glowing, maybe with our third baby on my hip, and Libby would look jealous and tired because she was past her prime and her own children were moody adolescents who avoided her like the plague. If she tried to make small talk, I'd slip in that Burke had had a great year at Credit Suisse and we'd recently bought the big place on the water by the yacht club. Libby's face would harden because she'd know I hadn't needed her after all. She'd finally know that her intuition about Burke had been wrong, that he *had* been the real deal, and that I'd been right to love him, to choose him.

The first week of February, we packed all of our earthly belongings into a U-Haul and headed north for New Haven. As we drove over the Triborough Bridge in the weakening sunlight, I stretched my neck to catch a final glimpse of the city that had been mine for a sweet moment, and the dreams I'd leave behind there, its skyline dipped in muted-orange dusk, an almost unbearable blend of nostalgia and loss and rage tightening its grip around my heart.

Chapter Forty-One

Skye

I stare at the open Moleskine. My heart bangs inside my chest as I reread the last sentence of Burke's final entry.

I know I'm not actually going to go through with marrying Skye—that's not part of the plan—but it doesn't make this any easier, or any less evil. I just wish there was a way to—

I flip the pages of the Moleskine, searching for more. But this last entry is from February 23—that was shortly after Burke asked my father's permission for my hand in marriage. Why isn't there more? Why does the journal stop there?

Nonetheless, it's on the page: confirmation, *if* the journal is authentic, that Burke wasn't supposed to marry me. But that he did so anyway because he loved me.

Or so he says.

A storm pounds inside my head. My phone vibrates on the desk, Jan Jenkins's name flashing on the screen. Wrenching guilt floods me, and I stare at the incoming call. I know I should pick it up, but I can't talk to Jan right now. I just can't.

I don't know what to do other than pull on spandex

and lace up my running sneakers. Then I'm out the door, skipping down the stairs and out onto the street, where a cold snap of wind hits my face. But it feels good, and I head west until I reach the West Side Highway and turn right on the running path. I always feel the most free when I run outside, where no doors or walls or clocks will hold me back. I run fast, the soles of my Asics hitting the pavement, springing me forward through the chilly air. I don't know how far I've gone when I turn around, and I don't realize how cold I am until I get back to my building and see my face in the lobby mirror, my nose bright red, the tips of my ears pink.

"Just looking at you makes me cold!" Ivan calls from behind the front desk.

I smile tightly, too numb to speak.

"Skye . . ." Ivan's expression softens. "Are you okay?"

No is the answer. No, I am not okay. I am so very far from being okay. But how can I even begin to explain my situation to someone like Ivan, who works around the clock to send half his pay back to Ecuador to his mother and father, whom he hasn't seen in six years.

"I'm okay," I tell Ivan. "Thank you for asking."

I walk the three flights up to my apartment and sink down into the couch, my breath still choppy from the cardio and the cold.

I think about what I've just read in Burke's Moleskine. I think about how anyone familiar with the situation—Andie, my father—would say that this "real" journal is merely a continuation of Burke's lies.

Yet I know something in my gut, a hunch I can't

shake. Whatever I've just read in Burke's journal doesn't sound like a lie. It sounds like Burke.

And suddenly I know the truth, and I realize I've known it all along. That Word-document diary that landed in Andie's in-box—that file that turned my world upside down—didn't sound like him at all.

Chapter Forty-Two

Burke

My eyes are slits, peering at Heather through the window as she makes her way toward the house. She opens the door. When she sees me sitting at the kitchen table in the dark, she startles. Good. I hope I scared her.

She flips on the overhead light and says nothing. She wears leggings and an old flannel, and her blond hair is dirty and limp. There are new lines around the corners of her liquid green eyes.

"Why'd you do it, Heather?" I spit, standing from the chair. I'm furious. I'm ready now. "*Fuck,* Heather."

She places her worn leather bag on the kitchen table and removes her phone. She scrolls through, searching for something.

"Because this is *bullshit,* Burke." Her eyes narrow, and she flashes the phone in my direction. "You fucking *married* her? You gold-digging, idiotic piece of shit. You weren't supposed to marry her."

I squint at the screen, at the message Heather has pulled up. It's the text I sent her after the wedding. Skye and I left for Italy the next day—her grandparents' private jet flew us from Nantucket to LaGuardia, where we caught a midmorning flight to Florence—and I'd sent the text as we were leaving the reception, while Skye was off saying goodbye to friends. I was rushed, but I also had nothing left to say to Heather.

My phone has been off all day. I'm sorry, but I couldn't go through with it, and I'm not coming home to you. I married Skye. I love her, and I'm happy. You know it was over for us a long time ago. We'll figure out a way to pay for Maggie's college. I'll always love and support you and the kids. I hope you know that.

"Look, a message *I* actually wrote." I glare at Heather. "And I am not a gold digger."

"So what are you?" Heather scowls. "A man in 'love'?" She uses air quotes around the word.

"Yes." My voice is thin, but strong. "I said it in my text and I'll say it again. I fell in love with someone else. And in return, you fucking framed me. Admit it."

I swear, her lips are on the verge of a smile.

"Tell me why, Heather," I say louder. I'm so angry I'm almost laughing. "You set me up. You made me a pawn in your plan and then you turned on me. You left me out to dry."

"*You* turned on *me,* Burke," she snaps, the vein running across her temple blue and bulging. "*We* had a plan. The Big Plan. And it was working, it was moving along perfectly until you decided to go fucking *rogue.* You went and had some melodramatic midlife crisis and convinced yourself you'd fallen in love, then blew the whole thing up."

"It wasn't a midlife crisis, Heather. I know that's what you want it to be, but it's not."

"Fuck you, Burke. Don't be such a victim. You're

a big boy. If you want to bring me down with you, go right ahead. Love is a battlefield." She draws her shoulders back, a coldness sweeping over her face.

"Goddammit, Heather." My jaw clenches. "You and I both know I'm not bringing you down with me because we have three children, and after all we've overcome, we're not gonna fuck it up so bad that they have to watch their father *and* their mother go to prison for this deranged conspiracy."

"You're so loyal when you want to be." Heather's lips curl into a snarl so that her incisors are bared. "It's one of the things I've always loved about you."

"Tell me why." I step toward her, towering over her small, birdlike frame, and I've almost forgotten how much taller I am than she is. With Skye, our height difference is only a few inches; with Heather it's nearly a foot. I could hit her, I think. I could easily hurt her. But she knows I'd never hit a woman, not ever, and she isn't afraid. "Tell me why you set me up, Heather. I need to know."

"You ruined my life, Burke." She moves backward, lowering herself onto one of the kitchen chairs. She looks tired, as though she hasn't been sleeping. Her voice is calm as her eyes lock onto mine. "I did everything for you, and you ruined my life."

"What the hell did you *do* for me? Besides hang me out to dry for a scheme I never wanted any part of? Oh, *and* steal two million dollars and frame me for it. I almost forgot."

"What did I *do* for you, Burke? Hmm, let's see." Heather's voice drips with sarcasm as she presses her pointer finger against her chin. "I convinced you to get sober senior year of high school so you could actually make something of yourself. I literally kept you on the straight and narrow until you *finally* found a little thing called motivation. I convinced you to transfer to NYU because I knew their finance program would help you land a better job. And then, while I was busy growing and raising *your* babies, you went and blew your entire career. Literally!" She cackles, plugging one of her nostrils and inhaling sharply.

"Screw you, Heather."

"Oh, I'm not done," she hisses, digging her bony elbow into the table. "I made the best out of our life together."

"Aren't you a fucking saint."

"When you proceeded to get fired—*again*—I was the one who made a plan to financially save our family."

"Your plan involved breaking the *law,* Heather."

"Yeah, something you've proven you're more than comfortable with," she spits. "Something that runs in your fucking blood. Apple doesn't fall far from the tree, babe."

She's hurling the most painful things she possibly could at me, and I can tell from the relief on her face and the venom in her voice that she's been thinking them for a long time. For years.

"Fuck you, Heather. I fucking did what you wanted. This *insane* plan. I did it! For *you!*" The back of my throat is raw from screaming, but I can't stop. I want to tear my hair out.

"*You* fell in love with another woman!" Heather

howls. Her face is twisted and red, and when she blinks, tears spill from her eyes. "You fucking fell in love with another woman," she repeats, quietly this time. "There's no worse betrayal than that." Her voice is suddenly so low and hoarse I can barely hear her. "Especially for us. We're the only family each other has, Burke. Remember?"

I close my eyes. I'm back in high school, at a party in Scott Lynch's parents' barn. I'm drunk as shit, and Andy Raymond is cutting us more lines, and out of the corner of my eye I see Heather, golden haired and pretty and all mine, and something inside me clicks. Sexy, intelligent Heather Price is my girlfriend, and she will drive me home from this party when I'm too wasted to stand, and tomorrow I'll wake up with my arms curled around her warm body, and I'm the luckiest guy in the world.

When did I stop being the luckiest guy in the world?

I sink to my knees, defeated. Pain pinches my heart, and I understand now why my parents got divorced. I understand how it is possible to fall out of love with someone with whom the sun once rose and set. People never want to break apart. But when they do, there's no way to stop it.

"This plan was our chance, Burke." Unmasked desperation is in Heather's voice. "This money was our shot to start over. We're supposed to be in the Maldives right now, remember?"

"Running away to the Maldives wouldn't have fixed our problems, Heather. *Money* wouldn't have fixed our problems."

"You don't know that."

"Heather." I steady my voice. "You have to understand. It's not that I just fell in love with another woman. I had already fallen out of love with you when I met Skye. And I think you had fallen out of love with me, too. I think we were both clinging to each other because—because we didn't know where else to turn. But together we're—we're broken. We've been broken for a long time."

"That's bullshit," Heather croaks, shaking her head.

"We have to dig deep. We're not sixteen anymore. We're not twenty-five anymore. And we can't keep going on like this."

"What are you saying, Burke?" Her bottom lip trembles, apprehension pooling in her eyes, and for the first time all night I realize just how scared she is.

"I'm saying . . ." I exhale slowly, resting my gaze on hers. "I'm saying what I already said in my email. We're over, Heather. I want a divorce. And I'm moving out."

The words are an instant ocean between us, and for a moment I don't believe I've actually said them out loud. I feel as though I'm in some sort of dream, tiptoeing the line between conception and delivery.

But then I hear Heather's breath hitch and register the expression morphing her face—something wild, boiling, unhinged. Suddenly she grabs the bottle of Malbec from the counter and hurls it across the room with all her might, sharp shards splitting across the kitchen in dozens of pieces, red wine splattering the white-washed cabinets like blood.

Heather stares at me, her eyes watery and inflamed, her cheeks flushed crimson. "You bet your ass you're moving out, Burke," she hisses. "You're moving to fucking prison, and for longer than you think once the Starlings' lawyer discovers you can't pay back any of the funds you stole."

"What are you—"

"All the 'salary payments' from your fake job that you transferred to me? The two million dollars that disappeared from your joint account? That money's gone, Burke. You'll never find it. And as for your beloved Skye Starling? She'll never forgive you. She and her family will make sure you're locked away for a long, long time."

With one final look of searing contempt, Heather walks upstairs, leaving me on the floor in a pile of shattered glass. I realize I'm still holding my half-finished letter to Skye, clutching it against my chest. The words I've written suddenly feel wrong, incomplete. I think of the Moleskine that's now tucked safely away in my briefcase, those nine entries that are, for better or worse, the only actual account of the truth, from my eyes.

Heather's words echo inside my head, scorching the space behind my heart. *And as for your beloved Skye Starling? She'll never forgive you.*

I'm suddenly desperate to show the Moleskine to Skye. If only there is a way to tell her the truth—the important parts of the truth, at least—I think I could make her understand. After all, Heather doesn't know Skye the way I do. Heather has never been able to forgive, let alone forget. It's why our marriage was over a long time ago, though it took me ages to realize it. It's why I fell in love with Skye.

Heather is nothing—*nothing*—like my wife.

Chapter Forty-Three

Heather

Dear Dr. K,

I missed New York like an old lover—or how I imagined one might miss an old lover, since I'd never been with anyone but Burke. Nonetheless, I swallowed my feelings and did my best to settle into our new life in New Haven. Burke's hours at PK Adamson were more than manageable; he never got to work before nine, and he was always home by five-thirty. Two years into the job he received a small pay bump—nothing drastic, but enough that we could seriously start thinking about buying a house instead of dumping cash down the drain each month on our rental.

We found a reasonably affordable four-bedroom split-level in Amity, a suburban neighborhood about a ten-minute drive from downtown New Haven. It wasn't close to being my dream home except for its being white, and Burke promised we could paint the shutters blue. The kitchen was dated and the windows drafty, but the street was safe, the backyard was a decent size, and the owners accepted our lowball offer of just under a hundred grand. We closed a few days before I found out I was pregnant with Maggie.

The thing about getting pregnant by accident when you're married with two kids is that you can't entertain the idea of not keeping it. It was my own fault. With a seven-year-old and a four-year-old to keep tabs on, it often slipped my mind that I was only twenty-seven and still very much in my fertility prime.

Burke thought it was fate that I'd found out I was pregnant the same week we closed on a house with four bedrooms.

"One for each of them." He'd beamed, placing his palm to my stomach.

"The fourth was supposed to be a guest room," I'd muttered when he was out of hearing distance. Libby had told me how important it was for all houses to have a guest room; it was a piece of her WASPy guidance that had no place in my life now, yet I could never unknow it.

Nonetheless, on a base level I was overjoyed, the same way I'd been overjoyed to discover I was pregnant both times before. A sense of ethereal wonder filled me at the thought that a whole new life was growing inside me—*I* was the source of this brimming center of possibility. Deep down I'd always wanted a third baby. When women could claim themselves a *mother of three,* it had always struck me as some tangible measure of success. Plus, it would mean I'd surpass Libby Fontaine, mother of only two.

I worried about money, but Burke was optimistic that data entry would only be temporary, that his career path at PK Adamson would eventually lead to financial adviser.

With Garrett starting second grade and Hope pre-K, I'd begun looking into university programs with the hope of finishing my degree. But after finding out I was pregnant, applying to schools was once again tabled. It wouldn't make sense for us to stick the baby in expensive day care while I went into debt taking out loans to pay for my education.

I didn't mind my time alone. On days when the kids had camp or school, I relished the hours between nine and three, when I had the house to myself and could curl up on the couch with a snack and binge-watch old movies on Fox Family. Sometimes, when I felt like it, I'd go for a drive. Shortly after moving to Amity, Burke and I had purchased a used Dodge Caravan—it was impossible to exist in the suburbs without a car. He took the bus to and from work, so during the day the Dodge was mine for errands and getting the kids around.

And, unbeknownst to Burke, for long solo drives. My favorite route was down the coast to Fairfield County; without traffic I could get there in forty minutes, a breeze on I-95. I never mentioned it to Burke, but since our move to Connecticut, I'd gotten into the habit of keeping tabs on Libby.

It was easy enough to find her address in the phone book; the Starlings were indeed still in Westport, in a massive white Dutch Colonial on eight acres overlooking Long Island Sound. The property was gated, but I liked to drive by anyway, slowing to a near stop as I peered through the iron bars at the manicured green lawn, imagining what Libby might be doing inside her castle.

I'd strolled through picturesque downtown Westport enough to know that Libby volunteered at the local library; I came across her picture on a flyer by the entrance. *Volunteer of the Month: Libby Fontaine*, the poster read, below it a picture of Libby flashing her broad smile, still maddeningly beautiful in her forties.

But during many of my visits to Westport I found no evidence of Libby at all; I simply enjoyed driving through the winding roads, admiring the magnificent houses and immaculate, rolling golf courses. I watched groomed women in perfect clothes run errands, slinging creamy leather purses over their sculpted shoulders, their hands tied up with shopping bags from Theory and Simon Pearce. Sometimes I sat in my parked car and didn't realize I was crying until I registered a cold wetness on my cheeks. The voice in my head was relentless: *If Burke hadn't fucked up, this is what my life could have been. This is the world I could've given my children.*

One weekday in early October I dropped the kids off at school and drove south toward Westport with the windows down, the last gasp of Indian-summer air like velvet on my skin. I was six months pregnant and could feel the little life kicking inside me—he or she was by far my most active baby yet. It had been a busy summer with the kids, and I hadn't made it down to Westport in a couple of months. As I approached the Starlings' road, a tingly sensation brushed my skin the way it always did when I neared their house. I slowed the Dodge to a stop when I noticed a row of black town cars lining the street around the entrance to their driveway. One of the guys in a driver's seat motioned for me to pass.

I stuck my oversize sunglasses on and rolled down my window. "What's all this?" I asked, aiming for nonchalance.

"Funeral."

My stomach dropped. "That's awful. Who—who died?"

"Are you a friend of the Starlings, ma'am?"

"No, I—I live around the corner," I lied, infusing my voice with an almost British quality that I associated with privilege, and hoping the man wouldn't note my crappy car. "I've met them a few times. I hope everything is all right."

"Mrs. Starling passed away over the weekend."

I felt my blood ice over. For a second—a split second—I hoped I didn't know what he meant. I hoped it was someone else. "Do you mean Libby? Libby Fontaine?" Libby hadn't changed her name when she married Peter, as I knew from the checks she used to write me when she was out of cash. I guess once you have a name like that, an important name, you don't let it go.

He nodded solemnly. "Yes, right. Ms. Fontaine."

"Oh, God." My voice broke. "What—what happened?"

The driver shot me a puzzled look. "She was sick for a couple years, ma'am. Cancer."

My hand flew to my mouth, which felt like clay. "I do remember hearing that," I lied. "I just didn't realize it had gotten that bad."

He nodded solemnly. "Sad news."

"The service is today?"

"Eleven at Christ and Holy Trinity."

"Thank you for the information." I ducked my head and put the Dodge back in drive.

I didn't feel much at all as I headed toward the church, where I sat in the parking lot for a long time. The sky was a cloudless, blazing blue, and birds ran over it in thin threads. It was a horrible day for a funeral.

I waited until eleven on the dot before sneaking into the church. An usher told me all the pews were full, so I stood at the back and listened to the eulogies from Libby's mother, sister, college roommate, and, finally, Peter. All of them spoke of her kindness, her unparalleled generosity and deep maternal love. In the front row were two yellow-haired adolescents, and I watched the backs of their heads as Peter spoke. I knew they were Nate and Skye without having to see their faces; they both boasted the same ribbony pale hair as their mother—the kind of natural butter blond I'd never be able to achieve, no matter how many store-bought shades I tried. I couldn't stop thinking about the implausible sum of money the two Starling children possessed, simply by being born. Their whole lives would be anything they wanted them to be—beautiful clothes, paid tuitions, fancy cars, club memberships, luxurious vacations—they'd never have to earn a speck of it.

The man to my right glanced at me and shook his head dolefully. "Not a dry eye in the house, huh?"

I wanted to laugh in his face; I wanted to scream from the balcony that Libby killed my baby brother, that she wasn't the exemplary, self-sacrificing madonna they'd all placed on an eternal pedestal, but a murderer who deserved her early death. But I said nothing, a slow rage burning through me, and the man handed me a tissue as a salty tear slipped into one corner of my mouth.

Libby had been sick for two years; she'd known she was dying. She'd had ample time to tie up loose ends, to make things right, to say goodbye. Yet she hadn't come for me. How many times had I imagined it in the tiniest, most private crook of my heart? Libby, one day, tracking me down. Her profuse apology, the tears streaming down her face as she admitted she'd never forgiven herself for Gus, never stopped carrying the weight of it after all these years, never stopped wondering if I was doing okay. That secret hope inside me, a desire so vicious it felt inevitable, was extinguished forever now that Libby was dead.

I left the church before the closing prayer, brimming with white-hot fury and another, more complex emotion I didn't recognize, one that left a pit gnawing the base of my stomach. Goose bumps prickled my skin despite the warm weather, and I drove back to Amity in a stupor. Once I reached home, I sat on the front stoop and waited for Garrett's and Hopie's school buses to arrive. I only felt like myself again when my children rushed up the walkway and into my arms.

Chapter Forty-Four

Skye

NOVEMBER 2019

Dr. Salam's thin fingers tremble slightly as she places the navy Moleskine down on the coffee table between us. After twenty-four hours of agonizing over Burke's journal alone, I FedExed it to Dr. Salam and asked her to read it in advance of today's session. If there's one thing I've learned in my eighteen years of therapy, it's the importance of asking for help when you need it.

I haven't spent a second working on Jan's edits, though I finally texted her saying that I needed just a few more days and apologized that I wouldn't be able to make it to the launch party Friday. I didn't give a reason, and she didn't reply. But I don't have room in my brain to think about that right now. All I can think about is Burke's Moleskine and Heather Price and Max's emails and what it all means, and what the hell I'm supposed to do.

The expression in Dr. Salam's wide brown eyes is indiscernible. She says nothing for several long moments, then asks, "You received this journal from Burke in the mail a few days ago? And the letter came with it?"

I nod. "I should've called you right after I read it. I

should've called my dad—I still haven't. I just—I don't know what to do."

Dr. Salam folds her hands over her lap. "I read it." She sits up straighter. "Let me ask you this: What do *you* make of it?" She blinks and points her chin forward, shifting back into shrink mode.

"I believed it, at first," I answer honestly. "But now I can't stop going back and forth in my head. Sometimes I'm almost certain he's telling the truth. It's his handwriting, it sounds like his voice. And the digital diary never sounded right to me, it sounded too cool and sinister and conniving. But then I think, that's absurd, that's obviously the real Burke, and the one in the Moleskine is the fake version that he gave me for our entire relationship. I—I feel like I'm losing my mind."

Dr. Salam crosses her legs.

"My dad has this theory that Burke's wife is involved. God, I haven't even told you this part yet." I tell Dr. Salam about the conversation I had with my father several days ago, after our meeting with Davis. I explain Heather Price's close friendship with my mother, and their intense falling-out after Heather's brother's death.

"Oh, Skye," Dr. Salam says when I've finished. "I'm so sorry. This—this is a lot to take in. And all the missing pages and holes in the journal, it's all very . . . confusing. Has your father presented his theory to the lawyer?"

I shake my head. "No. That's why he brought it up with me, I guess. He thinks if we mention it to Davis, Davis is going to want to go after Heather, too, and it's going to prolong the whole legal process. And my dad doesn't think that will be good for me. He thinks the sooner this is all over, the better. And as things stand now, Davis thinks it's going to be at least a few more months until the plea hearing is even scheduled. And then we're also planning a civil suit, which is separate."

Dr. Salam nods, taking all of this in. "And in terms of investigating Heather's involvement, you don't know what you want?" Her tone makes it more of a statement than a question.

"I—I don't know. Clearly there's something Burke isn't telling me—something he *can't* tell me. But maybe my dad is right, that prolonging all this is a bad idea. And when I last spoke with Davis he said"—my voice cracks—"he said Burke will likely go to prison for five years." There's a fullness behind my eyes and in my throat. "Five *years,* Dr. Salam. And then I read the Moleskine, and this letter, and—it's a *love* letter. And if I'm being honest with myself, I still love Burke. I do. I mean, we got *married* not that long ago. I can't just turn that off."

"Of course you can't." Dr. Salam's voice is warm but pained.

"But he's a sociopath. I know that, rationally. He's a sociopath who plotted to ruin my life. And *God* knows what's missing from those pages of the Moleskine and why. This is probably all just some ploy to make me soft, to fuck with me, to manipulate me into asking Davis to lessen his jail time or something. And I should *want* to put him in jail. But then . . . he's also the man that I love, and imagining him sitting behind bars is just—it's agony, it makes me sick." The tears are falling now, dripping down my cheeks. "Maybe I have been brainwashed, Dr. Salam. I'm just so confused."

Dr. Salam's brow creases and she hands me the box of Kleenex from her desk, as she's done countless times before.

"And then"—I exhale—"then there's something else I haven't told you about. It involves Max."

"Max LaPointe?"

"Yes." I sniffle, rubbing my nose with a tissue. "He's been . . . contacting me. I should've told you about it a while ago but I didn't because I—well, you know I hate rehashing that part of my life." I tell Dr. Salam how Max started emailing me right after Burke and I got engaged. I show her his most recent message from a few days earlier, the day Burke's Moleskine arrived in the mail.

"I don't understand." Dr. Salam shakes her head, her voice thick. "I can't believe Max has been contacting you . . . so aggressively like this."

"It's weird." I nod, hesitating. "It's a little too weird. Maybe I'm crazy, but I have this feeling that Max might be . . . *involved* in this situation somehow. With Burke."

Dr. Salam presses her lips together. "Why would that be?"

"I'm not sure." I let my shoulders drop.

"Well, we know Max has sadistic tendencies, Skye. You don't think his timing is merely a coincidence?"

"I really don't know." I feel helpless, anxiety worming its way into my hands. I stab at the cuticle of my thumbnail with my pointer finger.

"Have you told Davis?" Dr. Salam asks. "About Max?"

"No, but I've been wondering if I should. I mean, the last thing I want to do is tell Davis about Max—about . . . what he did to me. My father and Nancy don't know, I never told them. But there's this feeling I can't shake. If Max is somehow behind any of this, if *he's* the one who's gotten Burke in trouble . . ." I sigh. "I won't let him ruin my life again."

"Oh, Skye." Dr. Salam stares past my shoulder, her gaze glassy and distracted. "I suppose—I suppose maybe you're right to let Davis in on all the facts."

I tear at the cuticle until a strip of skin peels back. The layer underneath is red and raw, pulsing blood. I cringe and look up at Dr. Salam, waiting for a piece of thoughtful advice or guidance, *something* to hold on to, some port in the storm that's unfurling around me.

"I'm so sorry, Skye." She shakes her head ever so slightly. "I wish I could tell you what to do, but I can't. But be gentle towards yourself. The truth will come."

"Will it?"

"It may take time, but yes. It always reveals itself eventually." Dr. Salam stands and smooths her pencil skirt. "I hate to do this, but we're already past the hour and my three o'clock is here." She taps her watch. "We'll pick this up during the next session, okay?"

I nod. My stomach is a hard knot as I stand and poke my arms into my black puffy jacket. "Can I ask you just one more question, Dr. Salam?"

"Anything."

"Do you think it's possible that what Burke wrote

in his letter and in the Moleskine could be true? That he wasn't supposed to marry me, but did anyway? Because he really does love me?" Stale air escapes my lungs—a breath I hadn't realized I'd been holding. I mentally replay Burke's letter. *You deserve to know that I loved you when I married you, and that I still love you. I know that's not enough. Love isn't enough. I never used to understand that expression, but I do now. You can love someone completely, and it still isn't enough to make it work.*

Dr. Salam is silent for several moments, her gaze fixed toward the window past my shoulder.

"Skye," she says finally. "I wish I could answer that, but I can't." She sighs. "Love is a mystery. But I believe you'll find a way to answer that question yourself." She gives me a small smile and squeezes my arm.

"I'm scared." The words come out hushed; I barely realize I've spoken them aloud.

Dr. Salam nods, her chocolate eyes landing on mine. "Being scared is a part of this journey called life. And sometimes fear has something to teach us." She glances at her watch. "Come back and see me as soon as you wish. And call me if you need anything at all."

I nod, biting my bottom lip. Dr. Salam waits patiently while I do my knocks on her office door. I want so badly to stay in the sheltered cocoon of her office, protected from the world. But I can already hear her calling the next patient's name as I leave the room.

Chapter Forty-Five

Burke

I've spent the past six weeks living in Todd's guest room, waiting for what's next.

The night I'd first arrived at Todd's, suitcases in either hand, he sat me down and I came clean about everything. After I'd finished explaining the entire preposterous saga, he paced the apartment for about five minutes without speaking. Then he finally said, "I never could wrap my head around the fact that you'd taken a job in Dubai," and we both burst out laughing. That's the difference between women and men, I suppose— what might constitute a betrayal between women is swept under the rug by men. Or maybe that's just Todd. He's probably the most nonjudgmental person I know.

Todd *was* alarmed. He continues to be alarmed. *I* continue to be alarmed. Some nights, when Todd and I are grilling steaks and he's drinking bourbon, the past year feels like a crazy dream, the kind you're relieved to wake up from.

They officially arrested me a couple of weeks ago. It was nothing like my first arrest—when the FBI stormed my apartment and cuffed me in front of Heather at the crack of dawn—and I'm thankful for that. This time, all I got was a phone call from the NYPD telling me to come in to the station. I did—I wasn't going to fight them. Bail was set for ten thousand dollars, and Todd— bless his soul—dug into his savings and got me out.

I've been indicted for grand larceny and assigned a lawyer by the state, though I don't feel I need one. I already know I'm going to plead guilty. But Todd put his foot down—he says it's essential to have legal counsel regardless of your plea.

Heather has called me several times since the night I moved out, but I can't bring myself to pick up the phone. I know the kids will be home soon for Thanksgiving, and I know we need to tell them something about what's going on, but the idea of even being in the same room as Heather makes my blood boil.

Most nights, lying in Todd's spare bedroom alone in the dark, I miss Skye so much I can't sleep. Some mornings I roll over groggily and reach for her body next to mine, a few seconds passing before reality hits me like a punch in the gut. Skye is not in bed with me. Skye will never again be in bed with me. Skye is gone. I've lost the woman I love, and I'm going to prison. Again.

I've accepted that I'm going to prison. My lawyer, a public defender named Brian Dunne, says my sentence might just be a couple years, but that it could be longer. He'll know more after he speaks with Skye's attorney before the plea hearing. There isn't any way around a prison sentence, and I refuse to plead innocent. I'm not innocent. But when I get out, I'm going to find a way to live a better life. To be the best father I can possibly be for the three incredible humans that are somehow, magically, my children.

Maybe I'll even find love again. Great love, the kind Skye showed me, the kind I never experienced with Heather. What Heather and I had—what I mistook for love all those years—was a naive, dangerous kind of loyalty.

Since I moved out, I've been going to AA meetings five days a week. It was Brian's idea—he said it could make me look more sympathetic at the plea hearing—but it's been both humbling and empowering. I wanted to go to AA all those years ago, after I got out of the Metropolitan Correctional Center, but Heather was turned off by the whole thing, so I never did. Ironically, AA has made me realize the unhealthy degree of power I granted Heather over my choices. Exploiting my guilt became her strongest weapon. She never understood that my addiction ran deeper than using drugs and alcohol; she never accepted my identity as an addict. She wanted that part of my makeup to simply disappear, by sheer force of will. But Skye *did* accept that piece of me. We forged a connection that was built from our mutual affirmation of each other's interior worlds, wounded parts and all. That's why the love I felt for her was so much deeper and more freeing than anything I'd ever had with Heather.

Today I finally mailed the letter I'd been drafting to Skye for weeks. The kindest thing is probably to let her hate me—hating someone is uncomplicated, a relatively easy and quenching use of energy. But—perhaps selfishly—I want her to know that I love her. I want her to carry on with her life knowing that, for what it's worth, our love wasn't a sham. That's why I decided to send her the Moleskine along with my letter.

Part of the Moleskine, anyway. I had to remove the sections implicating Heather, but in a fit of blind hope, I figured sharing some of the truth was better than none.

Now that the package is in transit, I'm less confident. Maybe I'm just an imbecile who thinks the girl whose life I ruined will appreciate receiving my old shredded Moleskine in the mail, missing pages and all.

Thanksgiving comes, and with it a cold front sweeping southern Connecticut. The morning after the holiday, I wake up in my old house for the very last time. I'm on the living room couch, and through the windows I see a white blanket of snow coating the earth. I've always loved waking up to snow, how it makes the world appear so peaceful. Untouched. A clean slate.

But not today.

Your mom and I have decided to take some time apart, I'd explained to Garrett, Hope, and Maggie over pumpkin pie the evening before. *I've been staying with Todd while we figure it out. Please know that we love you three more than anything, and that this is not remotely your fault.*

Heather, stiff as a board next to me, had chortled and veered off script. *Your father seems to have gotten himself into some legal trouble.* The next word was a whisper, under her breath. *Again.*

It had been a terrible night; Garrett was stoic, but the girls were full of tears and confusion and begged me to sleep on the sofa instead of going back to Todd's.

I wake up with a pain in the middle of my back and clean the whole kitchen. I make coffee and wait for the kids to get up so I can say goodbye. As Garrett, Hopie, and Mags stumble downstairs, three caffeine-dependent young adults, I realize they're not kids at all. In a stupor of pride that they're mine, that I created them, I watch them fix their coffees. There's Garrett, with his long, lean build and sleepy eyes, the same blue color as my own. Hope has those little freckles on her nose and her honey-brown curls, the hair she's always battled. I hate that she doesn't know how beautiful she is. And then there's Maggie, my baby, the spitting image of her mother. In certain lights, the resemblance is more than I can handle. It takes me back in time. I am in awe of the three of them, of these perfect creatures that are half of me.

Imagining how they're going to feel when they discover the full truth of what I've done—when they find out I'm going to prison for it—is more than I can stand. It's my whole heart gone. Even if I wanted to tell them the truth, I can't. I can't tell anyone. Heather has me backed into a corner.

I will my mind to a state of blankness when I hug them goodbye. My throat is tight and there's no way to edge out the pain. I tell them I'll call later. I say we'll make a plan to grab dinner or see a movie before the weekend is over. But their sadness is far less discernible after a good night's sleep; the girls' faces are dry, and my children nod ambiguously and watch me leave the house as if they're not sure they know me at all.

I've borrowed Todd's car—a leased Ford Mustang—and on the drive back to his condo I feel so depressed I can barely stand it. I want to stop in for a Scotch at a gritty-looking bar on the way—I can almost taste the chemical bite of the liquor on my tongue, the way it would numb the horror inside me so efficiently, so quickly. But it's a scar, not a scab, and I keep on driving.

Rain begins to fall on the roof of the Mustang, and I do what I always do lately when I find myself craving a drink. I let myself think about Skye's sunny face, about the easy happiness that was waking up next to her on three hundred mornings, those precious moments between sleep and awake before the guilt and panic crept in, that sacred state when all I knew was the safe integrity of loving her.

Chapter Forty-Six

Heather

Dear Dr. K,

Everything changed in 2006, the year Facebook grew in popularity. Looking back, I was probably among the first of Generation X to start using it.

I was working part-time at a boutique in downtown New Haven called the Kitchen Kettle, just to bring in some extra cash. Burke had been bugging me to finish my degree already and get a "real" job, but I'd told him countless times that wasting money on my education when we had three children to think about made zero sense. Besides, I didn't mind my gig at the Kitchen Kettle. The store was usually slow—because who in New Haven shops for high-end kitchenware?—and I often spent my shifts reading glossy magazines behind the counter or listening to the gossip of whichever hyper-emotional high school girl was also working that day.

My sixteen-year-old colleague LeeAnn first introduced me to the world of Facebook. She was utterly consumed with the website, always using the store computer to log in to her account and update her photos and stalk boys she liked. I watched LeeAnn obsessively check the little red notifications that appeared in the upper-right-hand corner of the screen and couldn't believe such a platform existed.

"God, I hope my son isn't on here," I commented one afternoon while LeeAnn was poring through photos of a guy she'd made out with over the weekend.

"Let's look him up and see," LeeAnn replied. "What's his name?"

"Garrett. Garrett Michaels. But he's only thirteen." I watched nervously as she typed his name into the search box, three profiles for *Garrett Michaels* appearing in the results.

"Any of these him?" LeeAnn snapped her gum loudly.

I peered at the square profile photos of the other Garrett Michaelses of the world, relieved when I didn't see my son's face. I shook my head.

"Well, it's only a matter of time," LeeAnn assured me. "Facebook is blowing up. It used to be just college kids, but now everyone's getting on it. Some boys are kinda late to the party. What else is new."

I scratched my chin. "So you can just search anyone's name and see if they have a profile?"

LeeAnn nodded lazily. "Yup."

Half an hour later, while LeeAnn was busy helping a customer near the front of the store, I went to the computer and saw that she was still logged in to Facebook. I moved the cursor up to the search box and typed in the name that had been stuck in my mind for the past thirty minutes.

Skye Starling yielded a single result. I clicked on the profile photo and the image expanded. It was her, without a doubt. Her body type appeared to be different from her mother's—stronger, curvier—but her flaxen hair and angelic face were Libby's. Underneath her picture was a single line: *Lives in Westport, CT.*

"Who's that?" LeeAnn's voice called from behind, making me jump.

"Oh, um, sorry!" I stammered. "It's my friend's daughter. I just started searching for people I knew to see who might be on here. I'm bored." I shrugged.

"She's really pretty. Amazing skin."

I nodded, starting to relax at the realization that, in LeeAnn's eyes, I hadn't done anything all that abnormal. "This is the only photo of her, I guess. You seem to have a lot more on your profile."

"Well, I can't see her photos 'cause I'm not Facebook friends with her," LeeAnn explained knowingly. "If you're not friends with someone, you can usually only see their profile photo and, like, where they live. Not their whole profile. Unless they're public, but that's creepy."

"Oh." I felt my brow crease in confusion.

"*I'm* not friending some rando I don't know. Just make your own Facebook profile and then you can add your friends who have it. Or your friends' kids or whatever."

I nodded, still puzzled by the concept, but determined to find a way to see Skye Starling's full profile.

Navigating Facebook turned out to be much easier than I'd anticipated. That night I stayed up late, long after Burke and the kids had gone to bed, using our clunky Mac to create my account and profile. Only after I was finished did I realize I couldn't just "friend" Skye. She had no idea who I was. And if I sent her a message and tried to make the connection, Peter might find out I'd contacted his daughter, and it could look suspicious.

But then I remembered the way LeeAnn was always squealing when she received a new friend request, and I suddenly realized why Facebook was so appealing to teenage girls—it was a literal metric affirming how popular you were.

"I have *five hundred* Facebook friends, Heather!" LeeAnn had gleefully announced one afternoon, marching into the store with a ginormous smile.

"Five hundred friends?" I'd looked at her in disbelief. "I don't think I know half that many people."

In truth I probably didn't know a hundred people. I didn't have many friends in New Haven. It wasn't that I hadn't had the chance—as a parent of three, it would've been easy enough to become friendly with the mothers of my children's playmates. I simply wasn't interested in getting to know these women, with their bad dye jobs and bargain-shopping addictions and designer-knockoff purses. They only reminded me of all the ways I'd failed in my life, and of everything Libby Fontaine was that I would never be.

So I declined their invitations to join book groups and garden clubs and made peace with my antisocial existence. The one friendship I did sustain was with Mrs. Lucas, our elderly next-door neighbor who lived alone. A lung-cancer survivor, she'd been married three times—most recently to a Yale law professor—and cherished her collection of Hermès scarves; I liked everything about her. I visited Mrs. Lucas once or twice a week; we'd play cards or watch old movies. Sometimes we'd drink wine and she'd tell me stories about her life.

In the shop, LeeAnn had rolled her eyes. "I don't, like, actually *know* all five hundred of my Facebook friends. A lot are acquaintances or whatever."

"You agree to be friends with people you don't know?"

"Just people who I have other friends in common with. I figure that I basically know them by, like, the transitive property. Or something." LeeAnn blew a giant bubble with her gum, the saccharine smell of artificial strawberry filling the air.

I'd stared at her, baffled by her generation and silently praying my own daughters turned out nothing like LeeAnn.

But for better or worse, I knew LeeAnn was an accurate representation of something essential: a teenager's hunger for popularity. The more Facebook friends you had, the cooler you were.

So I created a second Facebook account, a fake profile for a Julia Miller, resident of Norwalk, Connecticut, one town over from Westport. For her profile picture I uploaded a zoomed-out stock photo from Google of a girl jumping into a lake, her features indiscernible. Then I searched Facebook for others living in Norwalk and Westport and sent friend requests to a couple dozen people from the results. I powered off the computer and climbed in bed beside Burke, jittery and sleepless, like a kid on Christmas Eve.

The next morning, the minute Burke and the children were out the door, I rushed to the computer to check Julia Miller's Facebook account. *Eleven* people had accepted my friend requests. A rush of adrenaline surged through me.

By late morning four more users had accepted, and I decided that having fifteen Facebook friends from Fairfield County made my profile legitimate enough. It was time to send a request to Skye. I poured a splash of vodka into my orange juice and mustered the courage to click the gray Add Friend button next to her name.

Afterward I sat staring at the screen, waiting for something to happen. When ten minutes passed with no activity, I remembered that it was the middle of a Thursday and Skye was probably at school. She'd be a senior by now, if my calculations were correct. Or would she be a college freshman? Math never was my strong suit.

I showered and dressed for my shift at the Kitchen Kettle. The afternoon dragged; I was practically twitching with the urge to get home and check Facebook. The owner, an older woman named Deb, was in on Thursdays, so even though the store was dead, I couldn't get away with messing around on the computer. Instead Deb had me doing inventory and refolding dish towels, and by the time eight o'clock rolled around and my shift was over, I felt as if I'd escaped solitary confinement.

Burke had already given the kids dinner by the time I got home, and the four of them were watching football in the den. I logged on to the computer and into

Julia Miller's Facebook account, my hands trembling with anticipation.

I nearly yelped when I saw the notification that Skye Starling had accepted my friend request. Grinning from ear to ear, I joined my family in the den to watch the rest of the game. I've always been good at delayed gratification.

I waited until everyone was asleep before sneaking back downstairs to take a deeper dive into Skye's profile. I didn't want to be interrupted. Scenes from her life unfolded before me, a collection of images and messages on her wall that revealed her existence. For me, a gold mine. I took my time perusing the seven photo albums she'd uploaded, unable to believe how easy it was to explore the inner workings of her world. Within a half hour I knew that Skye loved Billy Joel, and that her three best friends were girls named Lexy, Isabel, and Andie. Her family owned a house in Palm Beach, and her grandparents still had that stunning estate on Nantucket that Libby used to talk about. I learned Skye was a senior at a private school in Westport, and that she'd gotten into Barnard early decision. One of Skye's albums was titled "Lib" and consisted only of pictures of her mom. Dozens of people had liked and commented on every photo. *Twins; love youuuuu; the most beautiful soul inside and out; miss her so much; angel; watching down on you forever, babe.*

I scrolled through the album so many times my eyes started to hurt from staring at the screen. One photo in particular I couldn't stop going back to—a picture of Libby standing on the porch of the Starlings' old house in Langs Valley. In it she held baby Skye, a bundle in her arms, while Nate clutched her leg. To the far right of the frame a toddler sat on the porch; he was faced away from the camera with his little knees tucked, his golden curls illuminated in a ribbon of sunlight. *Gus.* My stomach knotted at the sight of my baby brother, at the crystal-clear memory of that moment. I had taken the picture, and I'd told Gus to shift over so he wouldn't be in the Starlings' family photo.

It was nearly four in the morning when I shut down the computer and tiptoed back upstairs, sliding into bed beside Burke. I dreamed of Libby and Skye and Gus and Langs Valley, the fractured images already slipping away when I woke up hours later in a cold sweat.

I started checking Skye's profile every time I logged on to Facebook, which was often several times a day, and saw her life transpire before me. I watched her high school graduation followed by her lazy postgrad summer on Nantucket. I followed her college years at Barnard, filled with parties and boozy dinners at edgy New York restaurants. I watched her semester abroad in Rome, her luxurious family vacations to places like St. Barths and Cape Town and the Alps and countless weekends in Palm Beach. I saw her graduate from college with a major in English, magna cum laude. I watched as she started a career in book publishing, following in her mother's footsteps. The posts and photos became less frequent after her college years, but the content was enough to keep me in the general loop. Outside of work, Skye's early twenties in New York seemed to be filled with dinner parties and wild weekends at summer share houses in the Hamptons. She didn't see her brother much; he'd gotten married to his longtime girlfriend and they lived in San Francisco. Her best friends were still the same three girls from high school.

What struck me was the perpetual absence of a boyfriend in Skye's life. She continued to be beautiful—her striking, heart-shaped face eerily identical to Libby's—with a high-end, consistently updated wardrobe. I didn't understand the lack of romance in her life.

One suspect did begin to appear in some of her tagged pictures in 2013—a good-looking guy with dirty-blond hair named Max LaPointe. But the photos didn't make it clear if their dynamic was romantic; perhaps it was merely a casual fling, or nothing at all. Her captions had a forced quality to them, as if she was playing at being a cool girl.

Skye didn't post much on Facebook at that point; when she did, it was usually about the Libby Fontaine Foundation, a fund that had been created in Skye's mother's name on the ten-year anniversary of her death. The existence of the foundation made my blood boil, as did the sight of Skye's posts asking her Facebook friends to donate in honor of her "selfless, generous" mom. As if the family needed to be asking for other people's money. As if Libby—a selfish, entitled *murderer*—deserved to have her life honored while Gus's existence had essentially been erased.

I noticed when Max LaPointe liked one of Skye's posts about the foundation and donated to the fund, but I still couldn't figure out if he was her boyfriend.

In the fall of 2017 the truth about Skye's love life was

revealed to me. By then I'd quit working at the store and had started driving for Uber. It was humiliating, my having resorted to such a blue-collar job, but the money was better and I could work longer hours, and with Hope in college and Maggie soon to be, we desperately needed to up our income. Burke seemed to have plateaued at PK Adamson; he hadn't gotten more than a 15 percent raise cumulatively in the past decade. He was still making less than his first-year analyst salary at Credit Suisse, which I hated to think about because it made me so depressed. Even though he'd studied for and aced his CFA exam, PK Adamson had since emphasized that because of his record, they'd never be able to place him on the CFA track. The more I learned about the industry, the less I understood why this came as such a shock to Burke—insider trading was more or less homicide in the financial world. He was lucky to be employed by a wealth management firm at all.

Driving for Uber was certainly nothing to write home about, but I preferred it to the Kitchen Kettle because I could make my own schedule. And I'd never minded driving. One Friday in early October I decided to take the morning off and spend a few lazy hours in bed, drinking coffee and trolling the internet on my laptop. As was second nature by then, I logged on to Julia Miller's Facebook to check Skye's profile.

I wasn't expecting to find much, but my attention snapped to life when I saw a new post from Skye from the previous evening. It was a link to a blog post on the Libby Fontaine Foundation website: "Sixteen Years Without My Mother" by Skye Starling.

I clicked the link, adrenaline shooting through my bloodstream as I began reading. In the post, Skye shared the struggles she'd faced since losing her mother at age twelve. Namely, she wrote about her battle with obsessive-compulsive disorder, with which she'd been diagnosed just after Libby died. Skye revealed how the disease had become a regular obstruction in her career and relationships and added:

This isn't something that's easy for me to disclose. But my mom believed in finding transformation and connection in your most painful experiences. She may be gone, but she'll always be my greatest role model— the woman I will strive to emulate, who's still teaching me lessons every day. This year, the Libby Fontaine Foundation will match all donations and give that amount to the Yale OCD Research Clinic.

When I'd read the post twice, I leaned back into my pillows, thoroughly stunned. There it was—the explanation I'd been seeking for years. Skye wasn't a closeted lesbian. She was *mentally ill.*

White-hot anger struck through my bones. Libby never "found transformation and connection" through "painful experiences." Instead, she hid from them. She hid from what she did to Gus—she took it to her grave. She was a liar and a hypocrite whose daughter was clearly cut from the same cloth of delusion and entitlement—a daughter who was obsessed with her, who wanted to be exactly like her.

The Big Plan must've begun to form in some small, dormant crevice of my mind long before I became aware of it. In retrospect I see that my obsession with the Starlings had to have still lingered after nearly thirty years for a reason. But this Facebook post illuminated my path to closure.

Burke and I had never broken out of the middle class. We were never not behind on bills, mortgage payments, tuition checks. After all these years we still clipped coupons and bought furniture at tag sales and shared a car. I'd been forced to accept that money— *real* money, the kind I'd planned for—was out of the question for us.

Or had I? Is it possible to give up on the things you seek in the deepest, most sacred corner of your heart? Or do they stay in your subconscious, persisting, festering, always subliminally searching for a way out?

All I knew was that when the Big Plan revealed itself to me, I was ready for it. I also understood that for it to succeed, its execution would require elaborate plotting and precision. The hard part would be getting Burke on board. If nothing else, Burke prided himself on being a father and a family man. But that quality was a double-edged sword, and I could use it to my advantage. All I had to do was make him question the well-being of his children and remind him that he was the reason for our family's struggles.

That's why the first step had to be to make our financial position even more dire. Throughout the fall, I complained to Burke that he still hadn't followed through on his long-standing pledge to renovate the master bathroom, which was hideously decorated in dated brown tile. He'd been promising me a Jacuzzi tub and sleek white marble since we bought the house seventeen years earlier. We had the money stored away, I reasoned; we *could* afford it.

"I don't know, Bones." Burke had hesitated. "Remember we got that estimate and it's going to be at least ten grand. That's too much out of our savings."

But I continued to pester him, arguing that the renovation would increase the resale value of the house, which we needed to think about anyway since we were soon becoming empty nesters. He finally conceded.

As a belated birthday gift for Burke, I gifted him a half dozen sessions of couples counseling with good old *you*, Dr. K. The fall issue of *Seasons of New Haven* had named you one of the top marriage and family therapists in the region, *and* you didn't take insurance. Perfect.

When I told Burke about couples therapy, he'd discreetly rolled his eyes, the way he did whenever I gave him a present that wasn't so much a gift as a dent in our bank account. But when I feigned tears and told him I was seriously worried about our marriage, he agreed to go.

I waited until after the holidays to tell Burke about the Big Plan. On a snowy Saturday in January I sat him down and told him about Skye's confessional post on the Libby Fontaine Foundation website, laying out my proposition in detail. I showed Burke pictures of Skye looking her most beautiful and explained that she was dying to meet someone. I told him that the Big Plan wouldn't be anything worse than what the Starlings had already done to us, that Libby had never suffered any consequences, and it was time someone paid for what had happened in Langs Valley. It would mean financial liberation for our family, for the kids; we were owed that, at the least.

I couldn't tell him the other part of the Big Plan's appeal—that Libby had always viewed Burke as trash, a doomed addict who would never amount to anything. The idea of Burke—a so-called Langs Valley washout—enticing Libby's precious daughter made my blood run fast and hot with glee. I could almost taste the satisfaction of watching it all unfold.

Burke said nothing for several long beats, staring at me, his jaw agape—an expression that made him look dumb and disarmingly young.

"You want me to seduce this girl, propose, plan the whole wedding, then rob her of millions before ditching her at the altar? That's insane. Not to mention *illegal,* Heather," he whispered, as if someone were spying on us in the privacy of our own home. "And probably impossible. And even if it's not, it means leaving the country permanently. No way."

"Who cares? We'd be millionaires. We'd be free! And honestly, if we pull this off, I wouldn't be surprised if the Starlings are too mortified to press charges. In which case we wouldn't have to go anywhere at all."

"That's a ridiculous gamble, Heather. And I'm sorry, but if you really felt money could make anything right with the Starlings, you would've taken what they offered you back then."

I'd never regretted my choice to tear up Libby's check. The Big Plan was different. This was justice *I* would claim for Gus; it wasn't a payoff that Libby magnanimously handed down and I submissively accepted, leaving her with a clean conscience and my brother in the ground.

Burke's response didn't surprise me, so I tread lightly after that, bringing up the Big Plan about once a month. He continued to balk at the idea and tell me I was off my rocker, but I was making progress. I'd cut my Uber hours in half—when Burke asked why my income had plummeted, I told him demand for the app was at an all-time low—and made it a habit to remind my husband of the ever-dwindling balance in our savings account. Though I continued to up my spending, I did so discreetly and ensured every purchase could be deemed necessary. There was Maggie's math tutor (she needed a boost in Algebra II), the new hot-water heater, a new washing machine (I lied and told Burke the old one broke), and a family vacation to Yellowstone National Park that I was planning for the summer. Garrett had been dying to go, I'd found reasonable flights to Salt Lake City on Kayak, and I explained to Burke that Maggie was mortified to be the only one of her friends who'd never been on an airplane. (In truth, Maggie was terrified by the prospect of flying; she'd confessed this private phobia to me years earlier.)

Despite my efforts, by the end of the winter progress with the Big Plan continued to stall. Money was tighter than ever, and I'd never seen Burke look so stressed—his gray hairs had doubled since New Year's—but his stance on the Big Plan was firm.

"It's insanity, Heather," he said when I mentioned it the last week of March. His voice was uncharacteristically angry. "We aren't con artists. We're not those kinds of people. End of discussion."

Now, I'm not proud of what happened next, Dr. K. But I was at my wit's end. I'd become so unbearably *tired* of letting Burke call the shots, of living a life steered by his pathetic choices.

That's why I picked up the phone one afternoon and called Herb Wooley, Burke's boss at PK Adamson. Herb had only been at the company for six or seven years— not nearly as long as Burke—but from our first meeting, I could tell he had eyes for me. It was the holiday party, and Herb was there with his wife. She was my age, but dumpy looking, with sausage arms and peach fuzz on her upper lip that she hadn't bothered to wax. I could tell she was one of those middle-aged women who'd let herself go.

Herb obviously hadn't slept with his wife in years, and he didn't try to hide his attraction to me. He came up behind me at the bar and squeezed my ass. "I could just devour you," he whispered in my ear.

Calling Herb Wooley and asking him to meet me for coffee made me physically ill, but it was also my ticket to power. We met downtown one morning in early April. It was warm out, and I wore a pair of white shorts that showed off my legs, and a fitted, low-cut sweater in the shade of green that matched my eyes. I blew my hair out and applied mascara, then perfume. When I walked into the Starbucks, Herb was already there, and he stared at me as if I were a piece of meat, his gaze fixed and hungry.

"Mrs. Michaels," he growled as I slid into the seat

across from his. My blood turned cold as he leaned across the table to peck my cheek. His lips were wet and his breath smelled like onions. "What can I do for you?" he asked coyly.

I kept my eye on the prize and told Herb that I needed his help. I let the story I'd crafted tumble out, explaining that my father had been trying to convince Burke to come work for his company—a contracting business based in Waterbury—but that Burke was resistant out of loyalty to PK Adamson.

"It's the best financial opportunity for us," I told Herb. "Burke would be able to take over the company when my father passes, and I don't know if you know, but Dad's health has been declining—" I let my voice crack. "I'm sorry, I don't want Burke knowing I came to you, I just thought I might see if you . . ." I exhaled a stream of air and folded my hands across the table, shifting them closer to Herb. "Burke feels indebted to PK Adamson after all these years. And I get that, but it's clouding his judgment. This career move would be a chance for us to make better money, to pay off the kids' student loans. And if Burke worked for my father, it'd mean keeping the business in the family, which is what Dad always hoped for, and he—he only has a few years left, at best. I really, really want this. I need this, Herb. Haven't you ever needed something?"

One edge of Herb's mouth curled into a small smile. I forced myself to stare into his beady gray eyes, feigning something I couldn't bear to acknowledge.

"Also"—I pouted my lower lip, ready to lay down my biggest card—"it would be so nice if my husband didn't work for you. The current dynamic makes it hard for us to have a real . . . friendship. You know what I mean?"

That was all it took, Dr. K. The whole experience wasn't pleasant, but it was easy. The following week, Burke was let go from PK Adamson. Herb told him that for financial reasons the company had to make some cuts, that it wasn't anything personal.

Burke was a mess. He didn't move from the couch for several days, though I knew from his bloodshot eyes he hadn't been sleeping. One night I woke to the sound of his crying like a baby in the bathroom. I felt badly, harboring the knowledge that I'd caused my husband this terrible pain, but I also knew that only something this extreme would break him.

One morning in May, when Burke's severance payments had ended and he'd spent a month applying for jobs without any luck, I sat him down. Lightly, delicately, I broached the subject of the Big Plan. I reminded him of our ever-expanding debt, of the nearly maxed-out credit cards, of how Hope would need to drop out of Eastern until she could reapply for increased student loans, and of how, at this rate, the thought of paying four years' college tuition for Maggie was inconceivable. And finally, *finally,* something in Burke gave way. We struck a deal. He agreed to a three-month deadline. He could have the summer to find a job—a job that paid more than what he'd been making at PK Adamson—and if by the end of August he was still unemployed, we would move forward with the Big Plan.

This was the ultimate catalyst for Burke, and he applied for work like a madman. Given his felony, I knew his chances of getting hired by a company in the financial sector were slim, but I got nervous when he started applying for positions in other industries, such as marketing and nonprofits.

One morning in July, when Burke hopped in the shower and left his laptop open on the bed, I double-clicked the file for his 2018 resume and took matters into my own hands. I deleted Credit Suisse from his work experience and changed his college GPA from a 3.9 to a 1.9. He didn't get any interviews for the rest of the summer.

On September 1, I didn't even have to show Burke the balance in our bank account or on our credit card statements. He already knew our finances had never been direr, and that his three months were up. A look of unprecedented fear swept over my husband's face as he conceded.

A few days later I was browsing through Skye's Instagram—thankfully a public account, and the social media platform where she now posted far more frequently than on Facebook—when a recent upload caught my eye. The picture showed Skye and her skinny brunette friend, the two of them arm in arm on a deck overlooking the ocean. They wore expensive-looking sundresses, and each held a bright orange cocktail that matched the sunset behind them.

Skye's caption read, *Missing this view, can't wait to be back this weekend with my soul sista @andieroussos.* The location, marked at the top of the picture, read *Gurney's Montauk Resort & Seawater Spa.*

That afternoon, I called Gurney's and booked Burke

a room for Saturday. I packed him an overnight bag with the preppiest beach attire I could find in his closet and informed him of his first task. When he protested—claiming he had zero clue how to flirt anymore, he'd been out of the game for thirty years—I told him to confide in Todd, to get a few tips from his friend. Everyone knew Todd cheated on his wife.

"Don't tell him *everything*," I added. "Just say that you've met a younger woman but you don't know how to make the first move. That slimeball won't judge you."

Burke nodded reluctantly, his expression resigned.

The Big Plan was on. It was go time.

Chapter Forty-Seven

Skye

DECEMBER 2019

Time creeps by while I wait for the plea hearing, which isn't even scheduled yet. Davis has brought the criminal case against Burke to the state, which will prosecute. In the meantime, his team is focusing on the civil suit. Everything is moving more slowly than I anticipated.

I hardly leave my apartment except to run along the West Side Highway. Andie comes over most evenings when she's finished with work. She brings red wine and a little dinner and sits with me. One night the first week of December, I finally tell her about Burke's letter and the Moleskine, and about Max's emails.

Andie stares at me with her mouth half-open, her bottom lip stained with wine. "Why didn't you tell me before?"

"I don't know," I say truthfully. "I should have. I'm sorry."

She asks me what I'm going to do about work, and I shrug. She tells me that Jan is probably going to fire me.

"I know," I say, without much feeling at all.

I drink the wine as if it were water, so that it's warm in my stomach and a film covers my thoughts, rinsing the lines from Burke's letter that stick stubbornly on repeat inside my head: *I know that I am not the love of your life, Skye Starling, but for what it's worth, know that you are mine.*

On Monday afternoon, the inevitable email from Jan finally lands in my in-box.

Skye—I can't imagine what you're going through right now; I can only assume it's worse than I can possibly guess based on your extreme lack of communication this past month. But my career is on the line, and I can't cut you any more slack. An editor from Putnam was at the launch party last week, and we talked. You and I need to do the same. Thursday 10 am at Stumptown? Please confirm that you'll be there.

I type a one-line response and click Send: *I'll be there. I'm so sorry, Jan.*

I close my laptop and feel a sickness wobble through me, deep down, underneath everything else.

Above are the thoughts that won't leave me alone, a repeating cycle. Burke. The digital journal. The Moleskine. Heather. Heather's brother. My mother. My father. Max.

Max. Thoughts of him slow to a stop in the front of my mind. It's been a while since he's emailed me—a month, at least. I still haven't said anything to Davis about his messages, but I think it's time. I click on the window of my computer that's open to Gmail and type Max's name into the search box. When I do this, I notice something I haven't before. Two email addresses pop up: maxlapointe1@gmail.com and mlapointe88@gmail.com.

I click on the first address, watching as Gmail filters

and loads all emails from maxlapointe1@gmail.com. These are the strange, threatening messages Max sent me starting in April, right after Burke proposed. But nothing from that address dates back further than that.

Then I click the second, mlapointe88@gmail.com, and watch as a new, larger batch of emails fills the screen. The most recent one is from July 2013, over six years ago—an email Max forwarded me containing the address of the share house in Montauk.

I stare at the screen for several minutes, reading through old emails from Max, from the years we spent weaving in and out of each other's lives. Links to songs and YouTube videos we sent each other, our old G-chats, a few lengthy, emotionally charged emails that make me cringe to read. All from the old email address. He must've gotten a new one.

But something isn't sitting right, and without thinking I pick up my phone and call Isabel.

She answers on the second ring. "Oh my God, Skye."

"Hey, Iz. Sorry, I know you're at work."

"No, it's fine. It's so good to hear from you. I've been worried."

"I know. I'm sorry."

"How're you doing? You've been—you've been MIA since Will's birthday. I've tried calling so many times. Andie won't tell us anything."

My head suddenly feels thick, and very heavy. I've almost forgotten that I haven't told Isabel and Lexy what happened, only that Burke and I split after the honeymoon and that I wasn't ready to go into details. I stare out the window behind my desk. Little snowflakes float through the sky.

"I'm so sorry, Iz." I chew my bottom lip, searching for the right words. "Things aren't okay, really. I promise I'll explain everything soon, but I need to ask you a question. It's going to sound really random, but it's important."

"Ask me anything, Skye."

"Did Max LaPointe get a new email address?"

"What? Oh, Skye. You're not—you and Max aren't—oh, God—"

"No, Iz, it's nothing like that. Look, between you and me, I've been receiving some strange emails from Max, but I'm not sure it's actually him. It's not the email address he was using before, and I just needed to check—" I exhale, my thoughts crashing into each other too quickly, like dominoes. "Can you check and see if he uses the email address maxlapointe1@gmail.com?"

Isabel repeats the address, and I picture her at her desk, typing it into Gmail. Several moments pass.

"No. I've never gotten an email from that address."

My stomach feels small and twisted. "Okay. But you do get emails from him lately? From a different address, I mean?"

"Yes. He just sent a mass email last week, an invitation for Will and me to some New Year's party. You know I don't want to go, I can't stand Max—"

"And that was from what email address, Iz?"

"Uhh, let's see." I listen to her fingers clicking the

keyboard. "It's mlapointe88@gmail.com. That's what it's been for years."

"Got it. Thanks, Iz. Look, *please* don't say anything to Will about this, okay?"

She's quiet for a few moments. "I won't. But, Skye, you're scaring me. Lex and I—we've been so worried."

"I'm sorry. I've been a terrible friend. I—I can't get into it now, but I promise I'll call you later this week. Okay? I have to go now."

I tell Isabel I love her and hang up the phone.

I think of Max's face at Will's birthday party in November, the cold, genuinely bewildered look in his eyes when I mentioned his emails.

I don't know what you're talking about, Starling.

The truth is like a gong striking the center of my chest. Max LaPointe didn't send me those emails. Someone else did.

I am suddenly overcome with a deep, hollow loneliness. I want to tell Andie to come over, but she and Spencer have tickets to a concert at Brooklyn Steel, some trendy rock band she's been gushing about for months. I could ask Isabel and Lex, but there's too much backstory to explain. I reach for my phone and text my father.

Okay if I come out to Westport for the night?

He responds right away: *I would love that. Stay as long as you like.*

I rinse the coffeepot out in the sink and wipe toast crumbs from the kitchen counter. All I've eaten today is a piece of sourdough, but my appetite is extinguished. Tidying the apartment gives me some vague sense of control; when everything is clean, I pack a bag and head to Grand Central to make the 6:20 train to Westport.

Outside the sky is the color of cotton, and it's snowing heavily by the time the train rolls into the Westport station. As I lug my bag down the platform and squint to find my father's car in the parking lot, I spot Nancy's white Volvo SUV instead.

"Where's my dad?" I blurt as she rolls down the window.

"He's grabbing takeout." She smiles brightly, a single crease sharpening between her eyebrows. "He said you'd be here for dinner and there's really no food in the house, so we ordered Chinese. Just for the three of us, the boys are out. They always seem to be out these days."

I toss my bag in the back and climb into the passenger seat. Nancy has the heat blasting, and I watch fat snowflakes melt into my wool jacket.

"Some snow we've been having, huh?" There is effort in Nancy's voice.

I nod. "Yeah."

"The schools were closed today because the roads were so bad earlier. I'm sure the city is a mess."

I can't think of anything to say, and we ride the rest of the way home in silence.

The house feels festive and cozy inside, a fire roaring in the fireplace. A big Christmas tree fills one corner of the living room, its branches decorated with white string lights and all of our old ornaments, even the gold-painted macaroni ones Nate and I made when we were little. Garlands with burlap ribbon weave

through the banister of the staircase, and potted poin-
settias are sprinkled throughout the downstairs. My
breath catches at the sight of my mother's porcelain
crèche on the front hall table. It hasn't been displayed
at Christmas since she died; I didn't even know my father had kept it.

"I—did you do all this?" My chest feels full as my
eyes meet Nancy's.

She nods. "I found boxes of these gorgeous ornaments and decorations in the basement. It's our third
Christmas together and your father never mentioned any
of this existed!" She lets out a small laugh. "The poin-
settias are from Home Depot. On Black Friday you can
buy them there for only ninety-nine cents."

"It looks beautiful," I say sincerely, because it does.
Not tacky, not overdone—simple and elegant and festive, just how my mother used to decorate for Christmas. Nancy also has some of my dad's recent paintings
displayed around the house, as Mom always did. He's
technically retired—he used to say Mom was his muse,
and I know he found it hard to continue painting after
she died—but his art is still a part of him.

"I love that crèche." I point to the hallway. "It was
my mother's. But I haven't seen it in years."

Nancy holds my gaze for a moment, then blinks. "Do
you want some wine?"

"Okay." I slide onto one of the kitchen island's stools
and watch as Nancy uncorks a bottle. The red liquid
glugs through the mouth as she pours.

Nancy passes a glass to me, and I take a large sip.
The wine is earthy and smooth down my throat.

"Gamay," Nancy says. "Similar to Pinot Noir."

"It's good."

Nancy looks toward the crèche and exhales. "I can't imagine how much you must miss her."

I stare at the countertop, the wine heating my chest.

"It's gotten easier with time," I say finally. "But Christmas is always hard."

"Always." Nancy gazes into the bowl of her glass. "My mother passed away when I was twenty-seven. Car crash."

"I didn't realize it was a car crash." I look up at her. "That's awful. I'm sorry."

Nancy shakes her head. "Hey. Having her for twenty-seven years beats twelve. You got dealt the harder hand, Skye. But I get what you mean about the Christmas thing. I miss my mom so much this time of year. And around her birthday."

"Yeah, her birthday, too." I take another sip of wine, feel it loosen my limbs. "I mean, being that young when my mom died, I feel like I remember her less and less. But then I see things like the crèche and . . ."

"The memory comes rushing back." Nancy finishes my sentence. "So strongly it's overwhelming."

"Exactly. And then I think about how long it's been, and how much of my life I've lived without her, and I just wish—I just wish more than anything that I could call her, you know? Just to check in and get some advice. Especially during a time like this."

When I see the tears in Nancy's eyes, I have to blink back my own.

"That's what I miss most, too. I'm fifty-one years old,

and I'll never stop missing talking to my mother on the phone." Nancy reaches for the bottle and refills both of our glasses. "I know it's not the same. Not even close. But why don't you try me? Maybe I can give you some advice. Tell me how you're feeling about everything."

I hesitate. I've never had a real heart-to-heart with Nancy before.

"Only if you feel like it," she adds quickly. "I mean, no pressure."

"Okay." I nod and take another sip, feeling suddenly emboldened by the wine, or my stepmother's emotional disclosure, or some combination of both. "Well, there's a big part of all this that I haven't been able to talk about with anyone. Maybe . . . maybe I could tell you."

Nancy's hazel eyes widen gratefully, glassy and red around the rims. "I'm all ears, Skye."

"But you have to promise not to tell anyone what I'm about to say. That's the thing . . . no one can know. Not even my dad. He would want to tell Davis, and Davis can't know."

"You have my word. This stays between us."

I believe her. I take a deep breath, then explain everything. I tell her about Heather Michaels's history with my mom and Heather's brother's death, which Nancy has already heard some of from my father. I tell her about the Moleskine journal and the letter I got in the mail. I even tell her about Max LaPointe and his emails, and how I no longer think they're from him. I let it all tumble off my chest, and it's such a relief to share it with someone other than Dr. Salam and Andie that I barely register how strange it is that that person is Nancy.

"Oh, Skye." Nancy refills my glass for the third time, and I realize that I'm a little drunk. "You know, your dad doesn't talk much about the year they spent in Langs Valley, but from the little he has said, it's clear that your mom carried some serious guilt over what happened to Heather's brother."

"He was saying the same thing to me a few weeks ago." I nod. "I had no idea—when Mom was alive, I mean. I just wish I knew what really happened."

"So does your dad." Nancy sips her wine. "I'm so sorry you're dealing with this. It's impossible to make sense of, isn't it?"

"Yeah." I twist the long stem of the glass with my fingers. "And yet, when it comes to Burke and me, some days I think it's possible that he really does love me. That the things he said in his letter and in the Moleskine are true. That maybe he can't tell me about Heather's involvement because he knows I could use it against him in court, and he doesn't want to bring her down, too, for the sake of their kids. And I know it sounds crazy because, even if Burke does love me, I could never be with someone who willingly deceived me like that. So none of this should even matter. But it just does."

Nancy's face softens, color flushing to the apples of her cheeks, and I realize just how pretty she is. "It's not crazy, sweetheart. It's not crazy at all. What's happened is crazy, but it doesn't make your emotions any less real. I mean, you *love* this man, Skye. Don't you?"

A dull pain presses behind my eyes and forehead. "Of course."

"And if there's a chance he loves you, too . . . well, that's everything."

"Maybe, but it's still not enough. Love isn't enough. I *know* that, deep down, but I need to make myself know it. If that makes sense."

"It does." Nancy nods. She tops off our glasses, draining the rest of the bottle. I listen to the hum of the dishwasher and wish, for the billionth time, that everything were different.

"You know, I'd been divorced for eleven years when I met your father," Nancy says after several moments of silence. "I'd been on so many dates—my friends bugged me incessantly to get back out there, and so I did. I dated for years, and I met so many different types of men, and nothing stuck. I'd basically given up hope that I'd ever find love again. When I met your dad, I didn't want to fall for him. I'd always known I didn't want to be with a widower, not if he had kids. I didn't want to be anyone's stepmom who'd lost their mother. My father got remarried a few years after my mother died, and I hated it. I hated *her.* It just destroyed me and I couldn't accept it. And the last thing I wanted was to be that person to anyone else. So I stopped seeing your dad for a while."

"You did?" I glance at Nancy, surprised. "I didn't know that. But then . . . what happened?"

"I was miserable without him because I'd fallen in love with him." She shrugs. "And I realized that life is tough, and there's so much we can't control, so when you can, you've got to choose love. Even when it's the hardest choice, even when it feels absolutely impossible, you've got to choose it. You've got to *keep* choosing love and fighting for it, over and over, no matter what. There's no other way, really."

Nancy's words seep into my heart, weighing there. A tear slides down my cheek, catching in the crease of my nose.

"Do you think my dad believes that, too?"

"I have no doubt that he does." She smiles softly. "Your father's been through the wringer. He knows all too well that love, regardless of the way it presents itself, is a miracle."

"Thanks, Nancy." Her name suddenly feels different on my tongue. *I'm sorry I've been such a bitch to you,* I want to tell her, but as I fight the words loose, the back door suddenly slams. A moment later my dad appears in the kitchen, a plastic bag in each hand.

"Sorry I'm late, ladies. The snow's really coming down out there and the roads getting out of town were—" My dad pauses when he sees Nancy and me sitting together at the kitchen island, our eyes watery. "Is everything okay?" He places the takeout on the counter.

"Yes." I walk over to my father and have to stand on my tiptoes to wrap my arms around his neck. "Nancy and I were just talking."

My dad blinks, staring at us confusedly. But then a wide smile spreads across his face, lighting up his eyes. "Good. I'm glad to hear that."

The three of us plate the Chinese food and eat in the living room, in front of the fire. After dinner my dad and Nancy nestle on the couch in front of the new episode of *Billions,* but I'm too exhausted and preoccupied to concentrate on TV.

I go upstairs to the bedroom that I always use when I stay here, but that has never felt like my own until tonight. Settling into bed, I let the sound of Nancy's words reverberate in my mind: *Even when it's the hardest choice, even when it feels absolutely impossible, you've got to choose it. You've got to keep choosing love and fighting for it, over and over, no matter what.*

I think about Burke, terror and exhilaration filling me at once. I think about the emails from Max, the messages I now know came from someone else. Burke is one of the only people on earth who knows about Max, who knows what he did to me. Yet even understanding how capable Burke is of deceiving me, of betraying me, I still can't quite believe he was the one to write them.

As I drift toward sleep, I finally know what I need to do. I need to talk to Burke.

Chapter Forty-Eight

Burke

The plea hearing continues to get pushed back. It's currently slated for the end of February, a thick rain cloud looming. All of it has taken so much longer than I expected, and the waiting is agony—I just want to be sentenced, get it over with. AA continues to be an immense help; some days the program feels like the only thing getting me through, the only way to see light at the end of a long, dark tunnel. But when I squint really hard, I do see light, faint as it may be.

One morning in January I wake in a cold sweat, shaken from a recurring nightmare about the Metropolitan Correctional Center. In the dream two guards storm into my cell in the middle of the night. One ties a rope noose from the ceiling and the other holds a heavy iron chain, stroking the metal through his fingers.

"Which way you wanna go, buddy?" the one with the chain says, the other snickering beside him. He points to the noose, then to the chain in his hands. "Take your pick." His smile is wide, a mouth with no teeth.

It's early—still dark out—but I know I won't go back to sleep. I check my phone on the nightstand, which reads 5:02, and my heart jumps when I see that I have a new text message, from *Skye!* Sent at 11:50 the night before. I open it, suddenly wide-awake.

I've been thinking about this for a while, and I keep putting it off, but I need to see you. We need to talk. Alone, no lawyers. Let me know if you can meet tomorrow. 5pm, Grand Central Oyster Bar.

Life springs back into my body. Skye wants to meet tomorrow. Tomorrow is *today.* I text her back immediately, a single line. *Of course. I'll be there. See you at 5.*

That afternoon, like a high school kid prepping for a first date, I spend a ridiculously long time getting ready. I shower and shave meticulously, making sure to clip every errant hair, especially the ones near the back of my neck that I tend to miss. I put on khakis and the blue sweater that Skye always said brought out the color of my eyes.

Todd drives me to the train station. He knows I'm going to the city to meet Skye, but he doesn't ask too many questions, which I appreciate. I wouldn't have been able to answer them anyway. I'm filled with shock and a fickle, irresistible hope that has my stomach in knots.

She's already waiting at a table when I arrive at the Oyster Bar two hours later, looking even more beautiful than I remembered in a cream-colored cardigan and dark jeans, her blond hair loose around her shoulders. Seeing her again, after so many days and weeks and months of not seeing her and wishing disconsolately that I could, feels like a dream. My Goose. But she's thin— too thin, I can tell even through her winter clothes.

I want to hug her, kiss her, inhale the smell of her, but I follow Skye's lead, and there's no embrace. She gestures for me to sit. There's a glass of red wine on the table in front of her, half-empty. Or half-full, depending on how you look at it.

"It's so good to see you," I say weakly. "You look—"

"I can't stay long." She uncrosses her legs. She sips her wine, and I notice the absence of the ring on her left hand. It's probably in a dumpster somewhere, as it should be.

"Of course. I'm just—I'm so happy you reached out. You have no idea."

"I'm not looking to reconcile with you, Burke." Her voice is thin and firm. "Just so you're aware."

"I understand." My chest deflates.

"I don't want to drag this out." Her cinnamon gaze lands on mine. "I wanted to see you so I could ask you one specific question, about something that's just not adding up for me. The rest of it—this living hell you've dragged me through—I can comprehend your motivations, despicable as they were. But your threatening emails pretending to be Max LaPointe? The ones you sent from a fake address? Why? *Why* the fuck would you do that? Look me in the eye and tell me the truth, because I need to know."

I'd played out multiple versions of this conversation in my head—imagining what Skye would say to me when and if we saw each other again—but an accusation involving Skye's ex-flame was about the last scenario I'd been expecting. "What are you talking about?" I feel my brows knit together instinctively. "What emails from Max LaPointe?"

"Don't play dumb with me, Burke." She narrows her eyes, her voice angry. "I never told you about the emails while we were . . . together—whatever the fuck that means anymore—I never told anyone. But you were sending them the entire time? You need to tell me why. I won't ask again."

"Skye." My breath is shallow and choppy as I try to wrap my head around her claim. "I swear on my *life* I did not send you emails pretending to be Max. I mean, the jig is up. I've pleaded guilty to everything else. I'm going to prison. If I'd done this, too, I would admit it. I swear to you."

Skye says nothing for a few moments, her brow furrowed. I can practically see the wheels turning in her gorgeous head.

"What did these emails say, Skye?" I ask gently. I'm afraid to hear her response, but I need to know.

She looks away, a mix of pain and shame all over her face. "They were . . . awful. Taunting. Called me names. Threatened me. I didn't want to tell you about the ones I received when we were engaged because I was finally . . . happy." She chokes out the word. "I couldn't let Max ruin that. But now that I know they weren't from him, I can't stop thinking about who would want to hurt me like that. It felt like a low blow, even for you."

Her words make me cringe—*even for you*—and then just like that, I know. "It wasn't me, Skye. I promise you. But I have an idea who it might've been." I add the last part before I can stop myself.

She nods. "Heather." Skye's voice is so small, so quiet, it's almost a whisper.

The shock seizing me must show on my face.

"I know she babysat for Nate and me when we were little. I know she blamed my mom for the death of her little brother, and that she never forgave her for it."

"How do you know all that?"

"Does it matter?"

A waitress comes by and I order a water. The restaurant is busy and bustling with the sounds and energy of Grand Central on a Friday—the squeak of rubber soles on the floor, the clinking of glasses, the loud echo of a thousand conversations happening at once. Now that Skye knows what led me to her, I feel a strange mix of relief and devastation.

"So Heather is really behind all this." Skye shakes her head, recrosses her legs. "You guys needed money, and this was her idea of payback?"

I can't bring myself to speak.

"And since my mom was already fucking dead, she moved on to the next best target?"

I shake my head. "Heather had this obsession with your mom, Skye, like—she wanted to *be* her, it seemed. She never got over the death of her brother, but I also don't think she got over losing your mom. But you didn't deserve any of this and I'm so insanely sorry. I'll be sorry all my life. I meant what I said in my letter, every word. Every word in the Moleskine is true, too."

"Yeah, you mentioned that."

"And you don't believe me."

"I don't know what I believe." She stares into the

bowl of her glass. "In the last entry of the Moleskine you wrote that you weren't supposed to go through with the wedding. That marrying me wasn't part of the plan."

"Yeah. It wasn't." I sip my water, crunch the ice between my molars. I remember how blue the sky was that day, how anything seemed possible.

"But you did."

"Yeah."

"Why?"

"I—I couldn't not." I shrug, locking Skye's gaze. "I had to marry you. I loved you too much to run away. That's the truth."

Little tears pool in the corners of her eyes, her cheeks flushed pink.

"And I wasn't thinking clearly, I know that," I continue. "I just thought . . . I don't know. I thought we'd get away to Italy and have this magical time, and I'd have some space, the chance to clear my head, and then I'd deal with it all when we got back. But obviously that's not what happened."

"So everything that happened next was Heather, then?" Skye wipes her cheeks, tucks her hair behind her perfect ears. "She set you up? She took the money somewhere, and that's why you can't pay any of it back?"

I sigh, wishing more than anything that I could answer that question directly.

"Skye, I can't—I want to tell you the truth, but like I said in my letter—I have children. And she's their mother. And it's just—it's impossible."

Skye exhales deeply, resting her hands on the table.

"You look thin." I regret the words as soon as they escape my mouth.

"I haven't had much of an appetite lately."

"Yeah. Neither have I. Todd's not much of a cook."

"You've been living with Todd?"

I nod. "Since October. Ever since I left New York."

"So you and . . ." I can see her processing the implications of this, trying and failing to keep the faintest tinge of hope out of her voice.

"Heather and I are over. I filed for divorce."

She nods briskly, her expression indiscernible. "So what have you been doing at Todd's?"

"I've started going to AA meetings, actually, almost daily. The program sort of makes me feel . . . hopeful, weirdly enough. I've been thinking a lot about what I want to do with my life—you know, after my sentence is over—and I keep coming back to addiction counseling. I think I might be pretty good at that. I mean, that's way down the road, but thinking about leaving a positive impact on the world, after all the pain I've inflicted—it helps. As much as anything can help right now. Sorry, I didn't mean . . . I know it's been worse for you."

"Maybe not." Skye smiles tightly. "You're looking a little worse for wear, Michaels."

"Really? I spent an embarrassing amount of time shaving today. And choosing these clothes."

"You look pale." She blinks. "And tired."

"You look beautiful, always."

She says nothing.

"Aside from . . . all this . . . how are things? I saw

Jan's new book made the *Times* bestseller list. That's huge."

Skye glances down at her lap. "Jan fired me."

"Shit. Skye, I didn't know." Regret floods through me. I did this. I ruined Skye's career, the thing she'd worked so hard at for so many years.

"I mean, I was doing a truly terrible job. That's an understatement."

"It's my fault, though. That you were doing a bad job. It's my fault you got fired."

"Yeah, it is." Skye drums her fingertips against the wood surface of the table. "But remember how you used to ask me if editing books was really what I wanted to do?"

"I just wanted to make sure you were living your passion. I wasn't trying to—"

"You were right to question it, Burke. You were the only one who ever did. And editing wasn't my passion, that's what I've realized. I think I always knew that, on some level, but I stuck with it because it was what my mom did. But ever since Jan let me go, I haven't been sad or even upset. I mean, I feel guilty that I let her down, but I also just feel . . . free."

"That's good, then." I smile, relieved at Skye's response, at the small wedge of credit I've been given in the midst of my overwhelming culpability. "So you're not taking on any new authors?"

Skye shakes her head. "I've been thinking a lot about a career change, maybe social work. Kendall was the one who first suggested it actually, and it just sounded . . .

right. So I'm considering that, which would mean going back to school and getting my degree. But finding a career where I can use my own experience to help people, kind of like what you were saying . . . I think that'd be pretty powerful. And fulfilling."

She leans her head to the left, stretching her neck that way she does, and I'm in awe of her, of her grace and brilliance and staggering potential.

"I think you'd be an incredible therapist, Skye."

"Thanks."

"Do you want to order anoth—"

"I have to go, Burke."

I don't want her to leave, I'd do anything to stop her from leaving. But I know that I can't, and I try to focus my mind on the positive, on my gratitude for this moment with her, on the sound of her voice speaking my name.

"Well, *good to see you* is an understatement. And thanks for picking this place. You know—making it easy for me." I gesture toward the train-tracks side of the terminal, though I know she didn't just have my convenience in mind when choosing the Oyster Bar. Skye loves this place because it's open to the rest of Grand Central, uncontained by four walls. She can leave without doing her knocks.

She stands and drops a twenty on the table, a class act till the end, and I stand, too, mirroring her movements. She brushes past me and I inhale the scent of her apple shampoo, and I can't not reach for her hand, gently clasping my own around her fingers. I feel her body tense, then relax, and she lets me pull her in close, lets me wrap my arms around her and rest my palm against the back of her head. Just for a second.

The she breaks loose from my grip and disappears too quickly, camouflaged by the swarming Friday-evening crowds of the terminal that whisk her away.

Chapter Forty-Nine

Heather

Dear Dr. K,

I didn't suspect anything until the day Burke came home for the weekend last February. The winter had been long and relentless, the Northeast still a gray tundra with no sign of spring in sight. The house was almost always empty; Garrett lived and worked in Boston, Hope was away at school, and even though Maggie still lived at home, she was *constantly* out with her friends. With no children or husband around, I was starting to go out of my mind with boredom.

I'd started visiting Mrs. Lucas more that year, sometimes three times a week, but that was the entirety of my social life. Some days I'd go into full Suzy Homemaker mode and clean every inch of the house and bake cookies to send to Garrett and Hope. Occasionally, on days I decided to take off from Uber, I'd stay in sweats and binge-watch Netflix in bed with a pint of Halo Top. It wasn't like I was going to let myself go on Ben & Jerry's just because my husband was fucking another woman.

More crushing than my boredom was the desperate way I missed Burke. I wanted him back in the house, craved his warm body next to mine under the sheets at night. I couldn't believe it had only been five months since he moved out and hated that it would be even longer until he could come back home. But every time I was hit with the familiar ache of longing, I made myself think of the Big Plan and the astronomical way it was going to change our lives, and I'd remember that it would all be worth it.

Things were on track, as far as I could tell. Facebook was old news, but Skye's regularly updated Instagram showed that things between her and my husband were progressing quite nicely. There they were at a Christmas party; there was a cute little selfie of the happy couple in Palm Beach. I'd grown used to the diminished frequency of Burke's phone calls; now that he and Skye were living together, I knew he had less time to himself. Once, during one of our rare calls, I asked him how it was being with a girl like her.

"A girl like her? What does that mean?"

"You know. A girl you might find in an asylum," I poked, digging for dirt.

"She isn't crazy, Heather." His voice had an edge.

On Valentine's Day I waited patiently for my phone to ring or for a bouquet of roses to be delivered to the door, but by midnight it was clear that no romantic gesture would be made.

That's the funny thing about red flags, I suppose—not seeing them never feels like a choice.

The second to last Friday in February, the day Burke was scheduled to arrive home for the weekend, I woke up like a kid on Christmas morning. I could tell the minute he walked through the door that something was different. It was in his eyes, the way they passed over my face without lingering, even for a moment. He looked at me, but he didn't *see* me. Claws dug into the pit of my stomach. Then I realized he hadn't even asked for a pickup from the train station—he'd opted for a cab. The claws dug deeper.

"Where are the kids?" was the first thing out of Burke's mouth after our stiff embrace.

"They should be here in an hour or so." Something starkly wrong hung in the air between us; I searched his eyes for an answer, but what I saw in the blazing blue was impenetrable.

"Garrett, too?"

"He might be later since he had to work today, and traffic from Boston could be bad."

"Got it." Burke nodded toward the stairs. "I'm gonna grab a shower."

I waited a couple of minutes to go up to the bedroom, where I heard the shower running in the master bath. But I also heard Burke's voice—it sounded as if he was on the phone.

I tiptoed toward the bathroom and pressed my ear against the closed door.

". . . I love you, too. . . . Yup, I'm about to hop in the shower, but the water is taking forever to warm up. I can't wait to be home from this dumb work trip. . . . Yeah. I know. God, I love you. I miss you so much, Goose, you have no idea . . ."

I felt a punch in my stomach, solid and quick, as if the wind had been knocked out of me. Carefully, I crept away from the bathroom door, my body numb with shock.

But this is all an act, one half of me justified. *This is the Big Plan. Burke is acting, and he's supposed to be leading Skye on, and he's doing a damn good job. You should be proud of him.*

But the other half of me—my gut—said otherwise. I'd spent thirty years with Burke, and I knew him, almost better than I knew myself. The different octaves of his voice and their respective meanings were deeply ingrained in me; Burke was a charmer, and I could tell when he was turning it on, spewing bullshit, and when he was being genuine. This was the latter.

Burke loved Skye. He missed her. His nickname for her was *Goose*. How was it all possible? Perhaps it was a midlife crisis, one in which he'd mistaken sex with a millennial for love.

Slowly, I moved down the stairs. I lowered myself onto the couch in the den, trying to stay rational.

Burke was confused. I'd sent him—willingly—into another woman's bed. He would snap out of it, he would. Skye had somehow lured him in, with her plump, youthful skin and ribbony hair and endless money, but I was Burke's *wife,* his partner of three decades. All I had to do was remind him of our love, our children, our future.

Twenty minutes later Burke came downstairs in sweats and a T-shirt, his hair dampened from the shower.

"Whatcha doin'?" He rubbed his nose. That disconnected glaze was over his eyes again, and I felt my stomach sink.

I shrugged. "Nothing. Come here."

He hesitated, then sat beside me on the couch.

"Maggie and I are going to make your favorite chili tonight." I turned to face him, inhaling the scent of his damp, clean skin. "But the kids won't be here for another hour. . . ." I reached for him, sliding my hand down the waistband of his sweats. My job was to remind Burke that he only had one wife, and it wasn't Skye.

For the next several minutes I let myself forget the reality that the man I'd been in love with for the better part of my life—the father of my children—had fallen for someone else. I let myself drift back to the old Burke and Heather, those two scrappy lovebirds who'd found their home in each other. As our bodies rocked into a steady, familiar rhythm, I swallowed the inevitability that Burke's mind was somewhere else and dropped wholly into my body—my body that still wanted him. *God,* did it still want him.

Then it was over, and Burke got up from the couch too quickly, and it was easy to tell that he'd only done what he had out of obligation. I loathed Skye more than ever, for her bewildering, unforeseen ability to sink her claws into my husband.

On Sunday, before Burke went back to his beloved *Goose,* I found another private moment with him so I could ask about his progress in proposing to Skye. I gritted my teeth as I watched his face fall in response. I didn't let him answer before reiterating the white lie I'd already told him several weeks earlier—that Hope's second-semester tuition was overdue, and that if it wasn't paid in full by the end of April, she wouldn't be able to graduate. We were running out of time. Yes, our cash-flow problem was grave, but I made it sound even graver.

By the end of the conversation Burke's face was stricken with fresh panic, just as I'd hoped. He said he'd already gotten Mr. Starling's permission for Skye's hand, and agreed to get the ball rolling on the engagement, and to work on opening a joint checking account with Skye so that he could start sending me money. I felt brittle and angry as I slid the diamond-and-sapphire ring off my finger and placed it in Burke's palm. It was all part of the plan—I knew they wouldn't actually get married—but still, the idea of Skye wearing my beloved ring sent venom through my bloodstream.

When Burke said he was happy to take a cab to the train station, I didn't object.

"So I'll come back in May," he offered. "For Hope's graduation. I'll get her tuition paid in time, Heather. She *will* graduate. I can't believe it. How did our kids grow up so fast? I guess they're not kids anymore."

I said nothing, attempting to lock his gaze. He glanced away, but I grabbed his hand.

"Look at me, Burke," I pleaded, swallowing my anger. "You know how much I love you, right? Your children love you. We're a family. Don't forget that."

He sighed, finally resting his eyes on mine. "I know. I just wish life could be easy, Heather."

"It can be, Burke. It *will* be. Eyes on the prize, okay?"

He nodded silently. He squeezed my palm, just once, before walking out the door.

I watched from the kitchen window as his taxi

pulled away, a mix of grief and fury crushing my lungs. For days, all I could think about was the phone conversation I'd overheard between Burke and Skye, and the dispassionate, empty way my husband had made love to me afterward, the lifelessness in his hands and eyes.

A few weeks later I received a text from Burke, a photo of my sapphire-and-diamond ring on Skye's finger accompanied by the words *Engaged. Opening joint account ASAP. Stay tuned.*

I had to run to the bathroom and hurl at the image, but afterward I felt okay. Things were on track. Burke would find his way back to me. And Skye would get what was coming to her.

Payments from Burke started coming in in April, $3,500 every two weeks, the sight of each cash deposit quickening the current of my blood.

Despite that the Big Plan was moving forward, I couldn't shake my resentment of Skye. I detested her, the woman who'd stolen my husband's affection, the same woman whose tantrum over a beesting had resulted in Gus's death almost thirty years earlier. The urge to cause her pain was thick and heavy inside me, all-encompassing.

And if anyone was in a position to maximize her suffering, to twist the knife in deep, it was me. I'd spent the better part of Skye's life watching her from afar, studying her every move with analytical obsession. I remembered the name Max LaPointe from her tagged Facebook pictures all those years ago; for some reason I couldn't shake the mystery of what had happened between them.

That's why, on a quiet Tuesday near the end of March, from the midst of my own, obsessive loathing, I logged in to Julia Miller's Facebook and crafted a message to Max LaPointe, pretending to be a potential employer vetting Skye for a tutoring position. I never knew what had happened between them, only that it clearly didn't work out.

I wasn't fully expecting Max to reply, but he did, and after only a couple of hours.

Sure, I know that bitch. She told insane lies about me that got me kicked out of grad school. Starling belongs in an institution.

I wrote the first email from "Max" to Skye later that night, half a bottle of red deep.

A little birdie tells me you're engaged. That poor, poor guy.

I figured that ought to give her a good scare. Maybe it would even make her OCD flare up, in front of Burke, I hoped. Soon enough my husband would wake up from his trance and remember that Skye was a mental patient, not the kind of girl he could ever actually love.

As promised, Burke came home the third weekend in May for Hope's college graduation. He seemed tense, but reasonably happy. The visit was quick, then he was gone again.

Throughout the summer Burke didn't provide much information about the wedding; I only knew it was scheduled for September 21 on Nantucket, and that Burke's plan was to skip out several hours before the ceremony, while everyone was getting ready and was distracted. He would aim for a midmorning ferry to

Hyannis, where I'd be waiting to pick him up. From there we'd drive home to Amity, drop the car—Maggie would need it—grab our suitcases, and cab to Bradley International. I'd already charged two one-way tickets to the Maldives on the Visa. Airfare from Hartford to the island of Hulhulé was exorbitant, but chump change in relation to the two million dollars that would soon be ours. As for that piece, on the way to the airport Burke would use his phone to transfer money out of his joint account with Skye and into a new account he'd set up offshore. Ideally we'd take more than two million, but that's the maximum amount you can send electronically, and even then there are multiple added layers of security. Burke would have no trouble answering his own security questions, so the transfer would be seamless. The Starlings would be so preoccupied and freaked out about the missing groom, they wouldn't notice the transaction until Burke and I were checked into the Four Seasons at Kuda Huraa.

I figured it would be nice for Burke and me to have a quiet moment to reconnect and recharge after the commotion of the past year, and the Maldives had been on my bucket list for ages, ever since I read a feature on them in *Travel + Leisure*. In the mindless hours I spent behind the Uber wheel, I would dream of the glittering turquoise ocean, white-sand beaches, and exotic web of sandbars and lagoons. And a private beach bungalow at the Four Seasons would be exquisite, a literal dream come true for us. After all of his hard work, Burke deserved a lavish taste of the luxurious lifestyle that real money allowed.

The Maldives would only be temporary; of all the countries without extradition, I didn't exactly imagine us settling somewhere quite so remote. And two million dollars wouldn't make us rich enough to stay at the Four Seasons indefinitely—not even close. We'd have to be strategic with our fortune, make smart investments so that it accumulated and lasted.

Regardless, we'd have to wait and see how things unfolded back in the States before putting down roots anywhere. Once we had a better idea of whether the Starlings were going to press charges—I was convinced there was a significant possibility that they'd be too humiliated to make the situation public—we'd be able to determine our next move, something that made sense for the kids. After all, we were doing this for their benefit, too.

Maggie still had another year of high school, which worried me a bit, but Hope had started a job at a communications firm in New Haven and was living at home, which brought me some peace of mind. She'd be there for her little sister while Burke and I figured out what to do.

The summer crawled by as I waited for the wedding to arrive. Though Hope technically lived at home, she spent most nights at her boyfriend Trevor's apartment downtown, claiming it was more convenient being closer to her office. I dragged Maggie on a few college visits, but the bulk of the summer she spent at her waitressing job or out with her friends when she wasn't working. The days alone in the house with an estranged husband continued to be long and dull. To make matters even more unbearable, Mrs. Lucas's cancer had come back with a vengeance, and this time it was terminal—the doctors were giving her six months to a year, tops. I'd been shaken when I'd heard the news. Sweet and sassy Mrs. Lucas, with the giddy way she laughed after half a glass of Cabernet and her love for old Audrey Hepburn movies, was the closest friend I had. And she was dying. I'd kept up my biweekly visits next door, but with her heavy medication and the constant presence of the nurses, spending time with Mrs. Lucas wasn't the same.

September *finally* came, the temperature cooling slightly and the edges of the leaves just beginning to turn. I realized, with strange indifference, that I wouldn't be here for the real blaze of fall, that I might never see autumn in New England again.

Burke and I hardly communicated the week leading up to the wedding, but I imagined he was swamped with last-minute details and, knowing him, emotionally drained. The morning of September 20 I sent him a text: *All good for tomorrow? I'll be in Hyannis by eleven-thirty.*

I waited all day and night for his response, which never came. I knew the rehearsal dinner would be followed by a welcome party, so perhaps the evening would run late. I drank three-quarters of a bottle of Malbec to calm my nerves and turned out the light at eleven, willing myself to get some sleep. But my mind wouldn't rest. I tossed and turned through the night, checking my phone every five minutes like a teenager, aching for a reply text from Burke.

I finally drifted off late, but I woke early, exhaustion burning my eyelids. Burke still hadn't replied, so I sent him a follow-up text: *Let me know . . . we're almost to the finish line*.

Hope was at Trevor's and Maggie still asleep when I got in the car at eight to head to Hyannis. I didn't leave a note; I figured if the girls weren't home when we dropped off the car later that day, I'd text them saying that Dad had surprised me with a last-minute vacation, and that we'd call when we got there.

Burke will text me when he wakes up, I told myself as I sped north on I-95. The day was pristine, the air warm but not humid and the sky a rich, cloudless blue. Poor Skye. What a beautiful day for your wedding not to happen.

Traffic was minimal and I reached the ferry terminal in Hyannis just before eleven. Burke still hadn't texted, and it suddenly occurred to me that he might have poor cell service on the island. I decided to call him, and his phone didn't even ring before going to voice mail. *Bingo*—there was no service. I'd worked myself into a frenzy for absolutely no reason. Surely Burke was en route to the ferry, if not already on one. Now I just had to wait.

I sat in the car all day, squinting at the passengers disembarking each boat. But none of them were Burke, and except for a call from Hope, venting about a fight she'd had with Trevor, my phone remained silent. My calls to Burke continued to go straight to voice mail.

I knew from stalking Burke and Skye's wedding website—www.burkeisskyehigh.com, are you fucking kidding me?—that the ceremony was scheduled for four. When four o'clock came and went, panic began to creep back into my bones. By the time the sun went down, I was in a state of pure, wrenching anxiety. I debated taking the ferry over to Nantucket myself, to find out what the hell was happening. Perhaps Burke had been caught making a run for it and was in trouble. But I couldn't bring myself to go to Nantucket. If there was a problem, and if Peter Starling saw me and recognized me, that could make things even worse.

The wheels inside my head spun rapidly, and when I looked at the clock, it was almost eleven. I'd been sitting in the parking lot of the terminal for twelve hours, and we'd already missed our flight to the Maldives. I googled the ferry schedule on my phone; the last boat of the evening had arrived in Hyannis at a quarter past ten. My stomach sank, a fresh bout of nerves trembling through me. I debated finding a nearby motel— somewhere to go to rest and think—when suddenly my cell pinged. *Finally*—a text from Burke.

My phone has been off all day. I'm sorry, but I couldn't go through with it, and I'm not coming home to you. I married Skye. I love her, and I'm happy. You know it was over for us a long time ago. We'll figure out a way to pay for Maggie's college. I'll always love and support you and the kids. I hope you know that.

The world tipped.

I felt as though I were witnessing Gus drown all over again, sputtering for air against the heavy quell of gravity while I stood knee-deep near the shore, helpless.

Though my entire body was numb with shock, I was

conscious that the short text I'd just read had changed everything. My life would never be the same, I knew as I switched to autopilot, starting the engine and putting the car in drive. Barreling south through the night, back the way I'd come, a new kind of wrath leached into my consciousness, wrapping itself around every sensation inside me.

It all boiled down to a single thought, primal and lucid.

No.

The word hammered through me—an echo, a heartbeat.

No. Burke wasn't going to get away with this. I would do every last thing in my power—whatever it took—to make sure of it.

Chapter Fifty

Skye

Heather answered my Facebook message promptly, as I knew she would.

I'm home in Westport for the weekend—I'm there a lot these days—and I've brought Lexy with me. I filled Lex and Iz in on everything over Christmas, and Lexy has insisted on accompanying me today. My dad doesn't ask any questions when I tell him we need to borrow the car to run some errands, and we're heading north on I-95 just after breakfast.

It snowed a few days ago and the highway is lined with gray slush, but the sky is a sharp, relentless blue. There's hardly any traffic, and we reach New Haven in just under an hour. I pull into the coffee shop ten minutes before our scheduled meeting time.

"Let me come inside," Lexy pleads from the passenger seat. "I'll just sit in the corner at my own table, I promise I won't say anything. You just—you *can't* be alone with her, Skye. She's a sociopath. She could be dangerous."

I shake my head. "Lex, it's a coffee shop. It's not like she's going to pull out a knife and stab me. Just stay here, keep the engine running. I'll text if something comes up, but I need to do this by myself."

"Okay." Lexy reaches across the center console and squeezes my hand. "I understand. Proud of you."

"I love you for being here."

I take a deep breath and get out of the car. I'm terrified, even though I know what I have to do. I've known it since last month, since my meeting with Burke at the Oyster Bar, where I felt it—some complex but enduring semblance of love—still between us.

Heather is early, too. I spot her instantly and feel fleetingly creepy, the way you do when you recognize someone from the person's social media. She's sitting at a table by the window, her hair pulled back. I can see the peppered gray roots wiggling their way into the bleached blond. Lines are etched into her forehead and around her mouth, but she's undeniably pretty, with her high cheekbones and big green eyes. She wears an oversize tomato-red sweater and black leggings with quilted boots. When she sees me, there's a flash of disgust in her expression.

"Do you want to order something?" She glances down at the steaming mug of black coffee in front of her. Her voice has a crisp delivery I wasn't expecting.

"No thanks," I say, though I'm craving caffeine. I just want to get this over with. I slide into the seat across from hers. My heart feels tight inside my chest, as if it were a towel being wrung out. The cafe is busy and most of the other tables are occupied, which gives me a vague sense of security.

"I'm surprised you agreed to meet me." I say this even though it's not true. In my Facebook message I'd written that I had some important information to disclose, off the record, regarding Burke's plea deal. I said a settlement for Heather was possible, given the emotional toil this whole ordeal had inevitably caused her. In other words, I'd used money as bait, knowing Heather would take it.

She shrugs. Even through her thick sweater I can detect the boniness of her shoulders. She's thin in the natural, waiflike way my mom was.

"Burke's a manipulative scumbag," Heather says evenly. "I'm sorry for all he put you through. I'm sorry for both of us."

"I don't think you're sorry, Heather." I make every effort to keep my voice even, though I'm flailing inside.

"Excuse me?" She tilts her head, and I notice the faint crust of mascara underneath her eyes.

"In fact, I know you're not sorry." I fold my hands across the table, my heart thrashing behind my rib cage. "I know you helped Burke. I know you were in on everything. How did you think I wouldn't find out that you worked for my mother? That you resented her and blamed her for your brother's death?"

Heather swallows hard, color rushing to her porcelain cheeks. "I have nothing to hide, Skye. I figured you might connect the dots. But the fact that Burke chose *you* to prey on was a coincidence. Life is full of them. There are a lot of shitty guys out there."

"Bullshit."

"That Max LaPointe certainly seems like a real scummy one." Heather shrugs again, a smile playing at the corners of her lips.

The air in the room goes still. I feel violated, exposed, as if I were sitting across from Heather completely naked. I inhale slowly, letting it all sink in. Confirmation of something I already knew in my gut.

"You really did your research on me, Heather."

"Yes. When I found out the identity of the woman who was sleeping with my husband, my curiosity was piqued."

"Oh, is that it?" I cock my head at her, suddenly boosted with confidence. "You were completely oblivious to Burke's scheme? I don't think so."

"Believe what you want, Skye. Doesn't matter to me."

"Why, because you think there's no evidence?"

Heather's eyebrows jack up at this, and I know I've caught her off guard.

"Look." I sigh, meeting her gaze. "My mom used to say that it's important to keep your side of the street clean. But I've realized in the past few months that maybe she didn't always take her own advice. That maybe she wasn't . . . the woman I thought she was."

Heather stares at me, the expression in her eyes indiscernible.

"I'm not going to go after you, Heather." I shift in my seat. "My lawyer is a shark and one of the best in the Northeast, and if I told him to find evidence that you collaborated with Burke, he'd dig something up in a matter of hours. Believe me. But that's not why I'm here."

Her eyes narrow. "What do you want?"

"I'm going to give you a choice, Heather."

"Are you, Skye?" Her tone is mocking.

"Yes. I think you and Burke fucked up, but perhaps so did my mother."

Heather's jaw tightens. "Your mother got away with murder. Literally."

"My mother should've made things right with you a long time ago. But she's not here—only I am—and I can't apologize for her. I can't justify her actions. I *don't* justify her actions. Speaking of, I know things about you, too, Heather." I pause, remembering what Burke said at the Oyster Bar in January. "I know that you spent a great deal of time and energy trying to emulate my mom. And it's funny, because for so much of my life, I've done the same thing. You and I have more in common than I ever expected. But my mother wasn't perfect, Heather." There's a block in my throat, and I swallow it down. "So, that two million dollars that disappeared from my bank account and magically landed in your neighbor's account weeks before she died? That two million I *know* you have? It's yours. Go do whatever you want with it." I let that sentence hang in the space between us, watch as Heather's eyes instantly glitter at the mention of all that money.

"*Or* you can return the two million and keep Burke. I'll work with my lawyer and get the charges dropped—as many of them as I can, at this point—and you can have your marriage back. It's your decision."

Heather's expression instantly hardens. I hold her stare, listening to the background noise of the coffee shop: clinking utensils, coffee beans grinding, the hum of a dozen different conversations.

"And why would you make me an offer like that?" Heather asks eventually.

"Because you deserve something."

Heather considers this. "Well, I can't have my marriage back." She snorts. "Seeing as Burke doesn't give a shit about me."

The moment between us is sticky and stretches on for several long beats. "I'm sure that's not true, Heather."

"He doesn't love me. Not anymore." Her eyes land on mine, a shock of emerald. "He fell in love with someone else, Skye. You of all people should know that."

I'm suddenly debilitatingly tired. There's a pain behind my forehead. I just want to get back in the car with Lexy and go home.

"I can't stay long," I say quietly. "Just choose. Do you want the money?"

Heather brushes a loose strand of hair from her temple and drains the rest of her coffee. Then she tilts her chin down slightly, just once. A nod. Her lips spread into a contained smile.

My answer.

I sit in silence as Heather signals to the waitress for the check. I'll let her leave the cafe first—the last thing on earth I would do is give Heather Michaels the satisfaction of watching me do my knocks.

"By the way, Skye." Heather stands, and she's shorter than I realized. "Your mother knew Burke. When I first met her, the two of us were dating. She never liked him, always said I could do better. She thought he was trash and that he was always going to be an addict, that he'd only cause me pain. Just figured you might like to know that."

A stream of sunlight spills through the windows and washes over Heather's face. But I can see her eyes—the enduring spite that lingers there, the quality of a person who steamrolls through life without due remorse. All too quickly, she is gone.

I stay for a few more moments, absorbing Heather's words. I let them land. I let them sting. Then I leave the cafe, and Lexy and I drive south in the yellow winter sun.

Chapter Fifty-One

Burke

I am numb. Empty. Brian Dunne says that based on his most recent conversation with Skye's lawyer, I'm looking at a longer prison sentence than anticipated, somewhere between five and eight years.

Somewhere between five and eight years. That isn't two years, which Brian originally mentioned as the cap. Two years was daunting, but fathomable. I survived one year at MCC; I could make it through two if I had to. But *somewhere between five and eight*? That's five to eight years of my life I'll never get back. Five to eight years I'll be absent from the lives of my children.

I think about how I could be in prison when Garrett gets married and starts having babies, my grandkids. I think about how Hope could marry that boyfriend of hers while I'm still locked up. I think about Mags, eighteen-year-old Mags, with her inquisitive eyes and fragile self-esteem—I imagine her having to explain to her friends that her dad's in jail, and why. I think about her graduation and the job interviews she'll go on and how she'll fall in love. And I think about me, sitting in a cell for five to eight years, missing all of it. I think about the year I already spent in jail, and all that I missed then—Hope's birth for God's sake.

According to Brian, the grand larceny charge is what's fucking me. Bigamy, surprisingly, is a minor felony that's essentially ignored in most criminal cases, but grand larceny is a grave crime, made graver by the high amount stolen and the fact that I'm unable to pay any of it back. The two million dollars is gone. A paper trail shows a mobile transfer I made to the bank account of a Georgina C. Lucas on October 3, the same Georgina Lucas who was our next-door neighbor for nearly twenty years. She died of lung cancer on October 28, three weeks later.

Like everybody else involved, Brian thinks I'm a piece of shit. I can just tell. After all, I stand by my guilt. I don't dispute the claim that I lured my dying next-door neighbor Georgina Lucas into helping me embezzle the money from the joint account I shared with Skye. I can't tell Brian that I've never had a conversation with Mrs. Lucas, or that Heather visited her multiple times a week. I can't admit to him that I truly don't know where the two million dollars is; he probably thinks I spent it on drugs or buried it in the woods upstate somewhere only I know the coordinates. Anything I can say to help my case will incriminate Heather. And I won't do it—I just won't. Garrett and Hope and Maggie will already have to live with the knowledge that their father is a fraudster who let them down. I won't let them think the same about their mom, too.

I wish I could talk to Skye, but I haven't seen or heard from her since our meeting in the city in January. I texted her a couple times since then, just to let her know I'm thinking of her, but she never responded.

Late February, the day of the plea hearing finally arrives. I wake early so I can make it to a six A.M. AA meeting at the rec center, which helps calm my nerves. Afterward I head back to Todd's, where I shower and brush my teeth and put on a clean suit, per Brian's directions. Todd has already made coffee and eggs, but I feel too sick to eat. He drives me to the train and the sky is white and a Frank Sinatra song that Grams used to love is on the radio, and I feel so sad I can't form answers to any of Todd's questions. We ride in silence.

When he slows to a stop in front of the station, I thank Todd for everything and climb out of the car. From behind me he calls something—something that might've been *Good luck, Burke* or maybe *You're a good man, Burke*—but it's a gusty morning, and his words are lost in the cold gray wind.

Chapter Fifty-Two

Heather

Dear Dr. K,

I got to work right away on my new plan to obliterate Burke, willing fury into fuel. Skye's Instagram stories—which I watched from an anonymous handle—gave me a glimpse into the new Mr. and Mrs. Michaels's Italian honeymoon. It was almost too much to take, but I stared at the app obsessively nonetheless, watching as they climbed the Duomo in Florence and moseyed blissfully through the Tuscan vineyards, stopping every ten minutes for a fresh pour of Chianti. Each snapshot was more idyllic than the last, and I counted the seconds until it would all be over, until Burke would plummet from Skye High to Rock Bottom.

Because he *would* plummet—I was going to see to that.

The idea for the New Big Plan came to me just a few days after the wedding, one evening when I was drinking wine in bed and staring at Skye's Instagram, seething. After Burke's text, my obsession with Skye had intensified, resulting in a daily journey down the rabbit hole of her online presence, which led me to visit burkeisskyehigh.com for the umpteenth time. But that night, I noticed something I hadn't before.

Though Burke had hardly told me anything about the wedding over the summer, I'd pried enough to know that he'd paid a bunch of opioid addicts from Langs Valley to act as his groomsmen, one of whom was our old friend Andy Raymond. On the wedding website Skye had listed her bridesmaids, including her maid of honor, Andie Roussos. That's when it clicked—the co-incidence of Andy R and Andie R. That was the light-bulb moment.

I could tell the story any way I wanted, Dr. K. I had plenty of information to work with—information Burke had provided himself in the early days of the Big Plan, when we were still teammates. Burke told me how he first lied to Skye in Montauk about being an alcoholic, and how he came clean during their ramen dinner at Ippudo. He told me when Skye treated him to the chef's tasting menu at Le Bernardin, and when they first said "I love you." He even told me, back in the spring—before he really started to drop off the face of the earth—that they'd chosen September 21 as a wedding date because Skye loved the Earth, Wind & Fire song and wanted it to be their first dance. Though I often had to pry the details from him—more at the end—he'd still revealed so much of their relationship to me over the past year. So many little snippets, precious moments. And I remembered all of them, because how could I forget?

So yes, the story was mine to tell. And I would tell it the way I wanted. I'd rewrite the narrative. I'd use my power to tell another version of what had happened—

the version I'd share with the world through Burke's electronic diary.

I worked diligently and around the clock, the days and nights blurring together as I composed Burke's eleven fictitious diary entries. I pictured Burke and Skye gallivanting around Italy and used the resulting pain as ammunition. I scrutinized my work, triple-checking every detail to make sure it all lined up, that the entries conveyed a believable version of the truth.

The special sauce behind the New Big Plan was that even *if* someone questioned the authenticity of the digital diary, Burke would still plead guilty. He would take the fall, and the last thing he'd ever do would be to take me with him. He would never, ever do that to our children. This was my armor.

Besides, Burke *was* guilty. He'd committed bigamy, willingly, and not on my watch. He'd made his own fucking bed.

By the time I'd finished the diary and decided it was bulletproof, Skye and Burke were a little over a week into their honeymoon. I'd watched them make their way from Tuscany to Rome, where they stuffed their faces with rigatoni alla carbonara and gelato. They'd since ventured down the coast, from Pompeii to the beaches of Positano, where one particularly sickening photo showed them kissing under a tree of lemons.

But reality would soon enough hit, I continued to remind myself. In five days, as soon as the lovebirds touched back down on American soil, I would leak the diary.

In another part of the New Big Plan, I'd still wind

up with the two million dollars. Luckily, I still had the information I needed. When Burke had first opened the joint account with Skye back in the spring—back when we were still in on the Big Plan together—I'd made sure he sent me the mobile banking log-in information as well as the list of security questions and answers, so I could keep track of it all. Not surprisingly, the moron hadn't bothered to change his Bank of America password.

Still, things were a lot more complicated now that Burke wasn't involved. I wasn't going to flee the country alone, so I had to figure out a way to effectively steal and keep the money without incriminating myself.

The idea unfolded rather spur of the moment. I'd been so preoccupied with writing the fake diary, I hadn't given ample consideration to the money piece. But then I remembered something, Dr. K. I remembered Mrs. Lucas.

Mrs. Lucas had taken a turn for the worse, I'd learned during my last visit almost two weeks earlier. I realized, with a pang of guilt, that I hadn't been to see her since. I'd been so consumed by my own devastation after Skye and Burke's wedding, I'd forgotten to check in on my dear friend.

Tragic as it was, recalling this was another lightbulb moment. I popped over for a visit that evening, praying I wouldn't find her already gone. Relief flooded me when the nurse answered the door and said that Mrs. Lucas was awake and lucid, and feeling okay. Better than yesterday.

"Mrs. Lucas." I smiled tightly, shifting my chair

closer to her bed, which was set up in the den. The nurses had left the room, and we were alone. "It's so good to see you. I'm sorry I didn't come by last week."

Her thin mouth curled into a frown. "You look unwell, Heather."

"It's been a strange few days, Mrs. Lucas." I sighed. "I actually need to ask you for a favor, and I warn you, it's quite an alarming ask."

The corners of the old lady's eyes crinkled. "Honey, they tell me I have weeks to live. A month or two if I'm lucky. Try alarming me after that."

I gave her bony hand a gentle squeeze. "Okay, here goes. I have access to two million dollars in a private bank account that's not my own. It's supposed to be my money—well, mine and Burke's, technically, but he's having an affair. I desperately need the cash, but I can't transfer it into my own account, and I can't say why. What I'm wondering is if I might be able to transfer it into *your* bank account, and then, well . . ." I pause, exhaling a thin stream of air. "I realize this is extremely inconsiderate of me, Mrs. Lucas, but I can't not ask."

"What is it, Heather?" Her brow raised, ever so slightly.

"I'm wondering if—if I do transfer you the money—you could leave it to me in your will."

Silence permeated the room.

"I realize this probably isn't something you're up for. Given your . . . situation. But if you are, I'd be eternally grateful, to say the least. And I'd give you a cut, of course."

Mrs. Lucas was quiet for several long beats.

"Heather," she said finally, her voice breathy. "You know very well a dying woman has no need for 'a cut' of anything." She raised her fingers in an effort to make air quotes.

"Well, it could be for your niece out in California. Something to leave her." Mrs. Lucas had never had children of her own.

"I'm already leaving Gwen everything I have," Mrs. Lucas croaked.

I said nothing, suddenly feeling stupid to have brought this up with poor old Mrs. Lucas. It was too much, too selfish an ask at this point in her fragile life. I would just have to figure out another way to get the money.

"Forget I said anything, Mrs. Luc—"

"I'll do it, Heather." Her voice was slow and husky. "I won't ask why, but I'll do it for you. You've been good to me in these last years of my life. You're a good person, Heather Michaels. I'm sure whatever is behind this comes from the heart. I'll have my lawyer come over tomorrow and make the arrangements."

"Oh, Mrs. Lucas." I leaned forward to kiss her hollow cheek. "Thank you. Thank you so very much. You'll never know how much this means to me."

"You're my friend, Heather." Mrs. Lucas's voice was a shallow whisper, and she squeezed my palm with the strength of a mouse. Pressure swelled behind my eyes, and I blinked back tears. Perhaps Mrs. Lucas was the only real friend I'd ever had.

Several days later, October 3, when the newlyweds were in Capri—fuck them—I logged in to Burke and

Skye's Bank of America account to make the transfer, using the mobile app on my phone. I knew I'd need to answer all the security questions to make such a large transfer, and luckily Burke hadn't changed those either.

A couple of days after that, during my visit to Mrs. Lucas's on October 5, I helped her log in to her own bank account, and my heart bloomed in my chest when I saw that the money—*$2 million*—was there. I'd done it.

The timing was perfect. An airport selfie on Skye's Instagram told me that the newlyweds were flying back to the States that evening (*Trip of a lifetime with my one and only—arrivederci, Italia! See you in a few hours, America!*).

I fell asleep that night to the image of Burke and Skye floating through the western hemisphere in first class, clinking champagne flutes in blissful ignorance of the hell that awaited them on the ground.

The morning of October 6 I woke at the crack of dawn. I felt invincible; it would be a day of green lights. I put on a pot of coffee and logged in to Burke's Gmail. I swear, the idiot never bothered to change a single password except his iPhone code.

I opened the carefully crafted email that I'd already drafted with Burke's fictitious digital diary attached to the message, and after triple-checking that it was perfect, I clicked Send. White-hot elation flooded my veins. Now all I had to do was wait.

Three weeks later, Mrs. Lucas would pass away peacefully in her sleep. A week after that, her executor would contact me and confirm what I already knew— that she'd left me two million dollars in her will. It would take a couple of months for the assets to land in my new, personal bank account, but they would, and then I'd be a millionaire—marginally, but a millionaire nonetheless.

The prize of the Big Plan turned New Big Plan would finally be mine. It would be enough. Enough to start over. Enough to help Garrett and Hope pay off their student loans, and send Maggie to the college of her dreams. Enough to invest in a decent-size place in Westport, one with central air and good resale value and maybe a pool. Enough to have a good portion left over to invest, a big chunk that would sit in the bank and multiply so that, one day, it might be enough to buy an even nicer house in Westport, one with a view of the ocean and a tennis court and enough bedrooms for all my future grandchildren—children who would grow up with even more possibilities at their fingertips than I'd been able to give my own kids.

Maybe one day I would join the country club—the glitzy one where Libby was a member for so many years. Maybe I'd take up golf. Garrett sometimes played golf with his buddies in Boston—maybe he could teach me.

That was another immeasurable positive, for which I would always be unthinkably grateful—I no longer had to run. I could stay here with Garrett, Hopie, and Mags and give them a better life. I no longer had to worry about whether the Starlings would press charges against Burke and me, forcing us to live thousands of miles away from our babies. The authorities would see that the money had been transferred to Mrs. Lucas's account, but they'd never be able to trace it further—

she'd wisely placed the assets in a revocable trust that could never become public record. Besides, Burke would take the fall for all of it. He would never let them dig deeper and link any of it back to me. The knowledge that Burke would protect me—for the sake of our children—had always been my bulletproof vest.

It continued to be too easy to know things from Instagram. I sometimes wondered if people understood just how much they exposed in the content they shared. I wondered if they were even vaguely conscious of the dangers of it. A picture posted was a behavioral pattern. A video clip contained background faces and voice snippets— information that proved invaluable to shrouded, invisible me. I knew when Skye got wind of the digital diary and the misdirected email to Andie. I knew because Skye stopped posting photos from the honeymoon and the wedding; she stopped sharing her enviable content because her life stopped being enviable. Soon her presence on Instagram seemed to have dropped off entirely.

Still, I knew that Skye and Max were at the same birthday party in November because from my anonymous handle I watched Lexy Hill's Instagram stories—@lexyblanehill posted incessantly—and decided it would be a perfect night to send Skye another chilling email from Max's fake account. I had to keep that girl on her toes.

The first week of December, a couple of men showed up at the house and asked me a bunch of questions about Burke, and about his relationship with our late neighbor Georgina Lucas. I kept my voice level as I answered the questions, my tone passive.

A month or so later, on a frigid January day, I was, as usual, alone in the house. The money from Mrs. Lucas's will was officially in my account; it had been for a few weeks. I put on my new Moncler parka and drove to the Chase branch a couple miles from my house, which had a recent FOR SALE sign staked in the front yard. At the bank, I approached the kind-faced teller and withdrew $2,000 from my account—the daily limit. A layer of fizz prickled my skin as I pocketed the white envelope filled with crisp bills and headed home.

It was the tenth day of my doing this, and I'd collected $20,000 in cash. A hefty sum, but a fraction of the two million that belonged to me. Two million dollars that, in one way or another, I'd earned.

I lay down on the king-size bed I now slept in alone. I took the $20,000—all of which I'd requested in twenties—and, because I could, sprinkled it around me and over me, let it fall like twirling snowflakes from the sky. I lay flat like a starfish, as if I could make snow angels out of the one thousand twenty-dollar bills that were finally mine. I closed my eyes and inhaled the sharp, chemical scent of money, peace washing over me like a warm bath. Hope tingled in the tips of my fingers.

If there was one thing Libby had been right about, it was that you've got to make your own future happen. I had finally claimed the one I'd always been meant to have.

The image of Burke's face caught in my mind— those telltale dimples, brilliant blue eyes. I let it pass.

Chapter Fifty-Three

Skye

The weekend before the plea hearing is scheduled, I'm home in Westport. I've just finished my first week at a new gig, an internship in social work at SCO Family of Services that I got through a referral of Kendall's. The organization provides a range of services to children and families across New York City and Long Island, and on any given day, I could be shuttling between three different boroughs, with infants in the morning and teenagers in the afternoon. It's strange to be an intern again, to be starting at the bottom, but already the work feels right. Much more so than book editing ever did, oddly enough. I'm realizing that the thing I liked most about working with Jan was the age group she wrote for, and the messages that she was trying to convey to them at a formative time in their lives. At SCO, I'm constantly reminded of how our childhood experiences shape us. I've started working on my application to the exploratory program at NYU's Silver School of Social Work, an option for students who haven't yet been admitted to the master's program, but want to learn more. If accepted, I'll start classes in the fall.

Winter has been long and lingering, but today is unseasonably warm, and I swear I can hear the faint chattering of birds. My father is putzing around and the boys are out with friends, so it's just Nancy and me in the house. She suggests we go for a walk, which is perfect, because I've been needing to talk to her.

After lunch we head to Aspetuck, Westport's local land trust, and Nancy and my dad's favorite place for an easy hike. It's overcast but the sun hangs behind thin clouds, and even though it's still February, I can feel the promise of spring on the horizon.

We walk for a while, our boots crunching through an old, hardened layer of snow.

"Nance," I say, after we've gone a little over a mile, "I want to tell you something."

"Yeah?"

"I haven't told my dad yet. I will. But I wanted to tell you first."

"Okay. Should I be worried?"

We reach the top of a small hill, on the verge of entering the woods. I pause and turn to face my stepmother.

"I'm not going to testify against Burke in the criminal case. And I'm going to tell Davis I want to drop the civil suit altogether." The decision has been cooped up inside me for weeks, marinating; it's a relief and a terror at once to set the words loose.

Nancy says nothing. Silence permeates the woods.

"What do you mean, Skye?" she asks finally.

I look up at the bare treetops against the clouds, their branches swaying in the light wind. In a month or so they'll start budding, and the forest will fill with green.

Early spring—the hope, the burgeoning life of it—is my favorite time of year.

"What you told me a few months ago, about choosing love even when it's the hardest choice?" I clip my gaze back to Nancy's. "I haven't forgotten that. And it's what I have to do. It's taken me a long time to come to this decision, but I just—ever since I saw Burke back in January, I've known. It might not work out—I mean, there's a good chance it won't—but if I don't do this, if I don't at least *try* to fight for the possibility of what we could have, I'll never forgive myself. And I'll always wonder."

"Wow." Nancy folds her arms across her chest, nodding slowly. After a few long beats, she smiles. "I think that is a difficult, and brave, and noble choice, Skye."

"I mean, the last I heard from Davis, he said he was almost positive Burke could get locked up for seven years. *Seven years*. I can't let that happen to Burke. He fucked up hugely, yes, but so much of this was Heather's doing." I shake my head.

"But, Skye—and I'm playing devil's advocate here—are you sure letting Burke walk is something you even have the power to do? I know it's in your control to drop the civil suit, but the *state* is charging him with grand larceny. That's a *criminal* charge."

"I know. But it's also contingent on my testimony. Burke had access to our joint checking account. If I don't testify, there's no way to prove Burke is guilty."

Nancy nods. "I see you've thought this through. He would still get time for bigamy, then?"

"I don't know." I stuff my hands inside the pockets

of my jacket. "Davis says it isn't a serious offense, so maybe not. But regardless . . . I know he's not innocent, Nancy."

"No, he's certainly not." She swallows. "But I understand where your head is in all this. And your heart. For what it's worth, I'm exceptionally proud of you."

"Thanks, Nance. For saying that, and for understanding. I hoped you would. I'm going to need someone on my side because Davis is going to hate me. So is Frank, the state prosecutor. They aren't going to get it, and neither is my dad."

"I'll talk to your dad." Her tone is decisive and warm, and I feel a weight fall from my shoulders.

"Also, I—I didn't tell you this, but a few weeks ago I drove up to New Haven and had coffee with Heather."

"What?" Nancy's hazel eyes grow wide. "Are you serious?"

I nod, my cheeks flushing. "I needed to talk to her. I needed to ask her some questions."

"Oh, Skye. I wish you'd told me. I would've offered to take you. How was it?"

"Lexy came with me and stayed in the car. It was . . . completely surreal." I don't tell Nancy that it was clarity that I needed, that I'd been craving. Even if I knew that I still loved Burke, even if I believed he loved me, I couldn't live with the uncertainty of knowing whether Heather would continue fighting for her marriage—or whether Burke would ultimately stay with her out of some misguided loyalty to his children. "But, Nancy, she said something at the very end of our conversation that's stuck with me, that I can't shake." I pause, remembering the disdain in Heather's eyes. "She said that my mom didn't like Burke. That she thought he was trash."

Nancy looks confused. "What do you mean?"

"My mom knew Burke a little, since he and Heather were together back in high school. And I guess she never liked him. She thought Heather could do better."

I watch Nancy absorb this, "Ah, So your mom didn't approve of the man you ended up falling in love with. That's what Heather is shoving in your face."

Hearing Nancy articulate it like this is both a relief— how come I never realized how much she just *gets* me?—and a dagger to the heart. "Right."

"But you know what, Skye?" Nancy uncrosses her arms, and her voice is firm. "It doesn't matter. Whether or not what Heather says is the truth, your mom knew Burke a long time ago. People change."

I nod. "It killed me to hear her say those things, but you're right. Plus, I've started to realize that my mom wasn't . . . perfect."

"Well, nobody's perfect. When people pass away, it's sometimes easier to pretend that they were."

"Exactly. I mean, for so long I've put her on this pedestal. Losing her destroyed me, and in response to my grief I've spent so much energy following her every footstep. But I don't think I can do it anymore. It's . . . exhausting."

"Skye." Nancy's gaze lands on mine. "Your mother might not have been flawless, but she was an *extraordinary* woman. She was loving and smart and charitable— all this I know from your father, from the way his eyes light up when he talks about her. And what I also know is that she *loved* you and Nate more than anything. The two of you—you were her whole world. And I know she would've been proud of you for chasing your dreams, Skye. Even if they weren't her own."

Sunlight cracks through the clouds then, causing both of us to squint as the hardened blanket of snow gleams and shimmers at our feet. The world is suddenly bright, and very clear.

Nancy's smile breaks into a laugh, and she looks at me knowingly. "I think it's safe to say, your mom agrees."

When we get back to the house later that afternoon, I go upstairs and open my laptop to Gmail. I need to share my decision with one more person before I act on it.

Email feels like an oddly formal way to communicate with my best friend, but what I have to say is too long for a text, and I'm not sure I could get it out over the phone. I craft the message to Andie, reiterating what I've just confessed to Nancy. I explain why I'm not going to testify against Burke, and that I'm going to drop the civil suit. I tell her that I believe Burke and I have a chance, and that, for better or worse, I need to see that chance through.

I click Send and feel the email disappear into the cloud, out of my control. A blade of afternoon light spears through the west-facing window by my childhood desk, illuminating the dust particles in the air. I wait.

Andie's reply comes a few hours later, after the sun has gone down and I've finished dinner with Nancy and my dad.

S,

When Burke was in your life, you were the happiest I've ever seen you. The two of you lit each other up—I meant that when I said it in my wedding toast, and I mean it now. To say that I have doubts about your decision—and about Burke—is an understatement. But if you believe that what you had was real, and that there's a fighting chance for you to get that love back, then I believe it, too.

I never told you this, but after everything fell apart in October, I reached out to your wedding photographer (I drunkenly got his card at the reception in case Spence ever proposes . . . FML). Anyway, I told him that things had gone downhill with you and Burke and asked him not to send you the wedding photos when they were ready. He said that he was almost done editing them and asked if he should send them to me . . . so I said yes. I don't really know why. I've looked through the whole batch a bunch of times, if you want to know the truth. I'm sorry . . . I just knew seeing them would destroy you. I promise I didn't show them to anyone though, not even Spence. But there's one picture I keep going back to, attached, that I thought you should see. It's

Burke's face when you were walking down the aisle with your dad.

Love always,

A

I reread Andie's words, staring at her email in awe. I'd completely forgotten about the wedding pictures, and that the photographer never sent them over. There's a warm glow behind my chest, and no matter what Andie and I have been through, no matter the stormy, tumultuous nature of our friendship, she is always the one who knows every last way to protect my heart, and that will always mean everything.

I open the photo attachment, and a black-and-white image floods the screen. Burke is standing at the front of the church, tall and handsome, hair combed back, hands clasped behind him. You can tell I'm walking down the aisle because the edge of my veil is in the frame. It's not a close-up of Burke, but Andie is right that when you look at the photo, all you see is his face. His gargantuan smile, the way it radiates, the way it lights up the tears in his eyes.

The following Wednesday, Nancy, my father, and I arrive to the plea hearing a few minutes early.

Davis is waiting for us in the courtroom, looking redder than usual and thoroughly pissed off, which isn't surprising given that I told him and Frank Monday night that I would not testify. I'm surprised Davis has even shown up.

"Frank is *not* happy," Davis growls.

My father shakes his head. He's angry, too, but having Nancy as my advocate has helped calm him down a bit. One day, I trust he'll be able to understand.

I've realized after this whole terrible process that the tragic day at the lake—the day Heather's brother drowned—was the catalyst for so much continued pain. If Heather could've found a way to overcome her anger—if she hadn't responded to her grief by so obsessively focusing on revenge—none of this would have happened. I don't want to be like her. I don't want to keep perpetuating this punitive cycle, even with the law on my side, because what's the point? I've found it in my heart to begin to forgive Burke, so why shouldn't I act on that? Why shouldn't I let Heather just keep the money my mom tried to give her in the first place? Don't we all deserve to move on?

Burke is already at the hearing, too, sitting next to a man I assume to be his lawyer. My stomach is in knots as Nancy, my father, and I follow Davis to the table next to Burke's, where the state prosecutor, Frank Bruno, is already perched. Frank barely registers our arrival, and I can't say I blame him. The minute we sit, he stands and approaches Burke's lawyer, and the two men step to the side of the courtroom, huddled in conversation. Cold sweat slicks my brow and palms.

The courtroom isn't like the ones you see on TV; the space is carpeted and far too small for the power it authorizes. I sense the familiar squeeze of my windpipe, the vibrations in my fingertips, that tell me I won't be getting out of here without knocking on the closed door. *One two three four five six seven eight; eight seven six five four three two one.* Already, it calls to me.

Instinctively I look at Burke, and he's watching me, his blue eyes bright as ever. I crave the sight of his dimples, but he doesn't smile, his mouth a thin line of concern. I know that Burke can see the panic that has entered my mind because that's the way love works. I know now that I still love him and he still loves me, and it isn't just because of what I learned from Heather, though her words ring inside my head: *He fell in love with someone else, Skye. You of all people should know that.*

I thought it would be different, somehow, seeing Burke in court like this, after nearly two months without communication. I thought it would be awkward or devastating or humiliating, or some combination of the three, but it isn't. Being in the same room with him is mostly just—relief. Cold water when you've been parched for hours. The feeling of coming home after a long time away.

Burke looks pale and tired, as he did at the Oyster Bar in January. But he's still as handsome as ever in his suit, the way it stretches the span of his broad shoulders, his black hair neatly combed.

The judge seems to be waiting for Burke's lawyer and Frank to finish their conversation, and the two men finally approach the bench. Frank's mouth is a thin line as Burke's lawyer whispers something to the judge, whose eyebrows jump. She gives a brisk nod, and the two men return to their seats.

The judge begins speaking, and I watch Burke's gaze shift to the front of the room. I'm so nervous I'm dizzy, and I grip the table for support.

"Burke Michaels." She clears her throat. "In a very surprising turn of events, the State of New York hereby has reduced the charge against you, from grand larceny to petit larceny. How do you plead?"

Burke opens his mouth to speak, then turns toward his lawyer, who whispers something in his ear. A few moments of silence pass.

"Guilty, Your Honor," Burke says, and the sound of his steady, familiar voice fills me with ease.

I don't have to look at Davis to know that he's the color of boiled beets.

"All right, then." A thoroughly stunned expression has morphed the judge's face. "Given that petit larceny is a class A misdemeanor in the state of New York, I hereby sentence you to a year of probation and a five-hundred-dollar fine. And with that, I'm pleased to say I'm taking an exceptionally early lunch. Court is dismissed."

Underneath the table, Nancy squeezes my hand. Relief drenches me.

I look over at Burke, whose forehead is scrunched. His lawyer's mouth is gaping. He leans in toward Burke and claps him on the back, obstructing Burke's face from my view.

"A year of fucking *probation*," Davis hisses, shaking his head at me. He snatches his briefcase and storms out of the room without saying a word to anyone, even my father. Frank Bruno follows in his wake.

The rest of us stand, and Nancy pulls me in for a hug. "That wasn't so bad, huh? You did the right thing."

Behind her, my father lingers. Finally, he steps toward me. "The rational side of my brain can't understand why the hell you're doing this. But there's another part of me that, well . . . I'm proud of you, Skye." His voice is stiff but I can tell that his words are genuine. I don't regret my decision, but I still can't bear how much pain this entire mess has caused him.

"You don't have to say that, Dad. I'm so sorry for everything I've put you through."

"No, it's true, I am proud. You followed your gut and you listened to your heart." He places a hand on my shoulder and squeezes. "Your mom always listened to her heart, too. If she hadn't, she wouldn't have ended up with me."

I smile. "Thanks, Dad."

From behind me, Nancy taps my arm. "I think there's someone who wants to talk to you, Skye."

I look past my dad's shoulder, and there he is, standing tall. I can tell he's working to contain his smile, likely out of respect for my father.

I pull my dad in for a hug, resting my cheek against his chest so that I can hear the strong beat of his heart. His good, good heart. "I'll catch up with you and Nancy in a few minutes, okay?"

My dad hesitates, then nods. Burke steps forward, and my father studies him sternly before turning toward the door. I cast Nancy a grateful look before she turns to follow him.

Suddenly, Burke and I are alone. I'm close enough

to inhale the familiar scent of his skin—soap and pine.

"Hi," he says.

"Maybe we should go outside?" I glance sideways toward the judge, who is watching us while she gathers her things from the bench.

Burke and I walk toward the double doors and out into the hallway of the courthouse.

"Skye." Burke's eyes are wild and wide. "What happened? Brian—my lawyer—said you let me go on the grand larceny? That you wouldn't testify? Why would you do that? Brian said I was supposed to get five to eight years. What's going on?"

I smile, a strange comfort filling me. The proximity of the man I've missed for so long—his strong, clean jawline, broad shoulders, shocking blue eyes—melts my body at the same time it steadies me.

"You didn't deserve to go to prison for that long, Burke. You didn't deserve to take the fall for everything. We both know that what you told your lawyer—and the judge—wasn't the true story."

Burke is quiet for a moment. We study each other's eyes.

"What do you think is true, then?" The air in the hallway is still, humming with uncertainty. "God, look at your face." He lifts an arm as if to reach for me, then lets it drop. "Skye, what do you think is true?" he whispers.

"I think you love me," I say finally.

"I do. You have no idea how happy it makes me that you know that."

"I think you did a bad thing, but I don't think you're a bad person. I think you can't tell me the full story of what happened, but I know I've figured it out. I knew that day at the Oyster Bar; I saw the look on your face when I asked directly if Heather coerced you into this whole scheme. I think you're an absolute *idiot* for even entertaining the idea, but I think you agreed to it because you didn't know how else to save your marriage. I think you didn't know how to acknowledge that there was nothing left to save. I think you and I fell in love."

Burke's eyes are wet and he nods slowly. "Do you still love me?"

I ignore his question. "I think Heather figured out that we'd fallen in love. I think that's when she decided to frame you. I think she wrote those diary entries; she set you up to take the fall alone. She knew you wouldn't bring her down with you, because of your children."

"Do you still love me?" Burke repeats the question, his voice a thin whisper.

"Yes."

"How is that possible?"

"Love doesn't just evaporate overnight, Burke. And, yeah, sometimes I hate you so much I feel like my head is going to split open." I pause, the contrasting emotions battling inside me, fighting for dominance. "I hate you for lying to me. I hate that there are all these things I never knew about you, like what really happened with your parents and where you grew up and the fact that you have *kids,* Jesus Christ. But, I mean, you're still *you.* I can't just *stop* loving you."

"Goose." Burke reaches for my hand, tears brimming his eyes. "I love you, too, but I—I still meant what I said in my letter. Love isn't always enough. What if it's not enou—"

"Look. You deceived me, you broke my heart, you destroyed me. But you also made me believe in a kind of love I never thought I deserved. You connected me with a part of myself I'd abandoned. You did that for me, Burke. And I don't know if we should be together, I really don't. I mean, I have this new internship in social work and I'm trying to figure out my career path, my next move, if I even want to stay in this city. And you need to serve your probation and figure out what you're doing with your life. We can't just crash back into each other, Burke—we need to fix ourselves first. But with that said, what I do know is that there needs to be the possibility of us, of our love. I couldn't just throw that away and live with myself. And you're a good father. Your children need you. Those are the reasons I couldn't testify. And I'm going to drop the civil suit, too."

"Really?" His voice is barely a whisper.

"Yes. And I'm not going to go after Heather, either. Neither will my father. I can promise you that."

"But—but what about the money? She took two million dollars."

"Burke, it doesn't matter. She can have it. If my mother did what Heather claims, she's owed that at the very least. My dad even said that they tried to give her money after what happened to her brother. Clearly my parents felt they owed her something." I don't tell Burke about my coffee shop meeting with Heather.

I don't know that I ever will. Somehow it feels like the kind of thing that Burke doesn't need to know.

"But it's two *million* dollars, Skye. I know how much your parents offered Heather, and it wasn't close to that. It's your family's money."

"It's my money. It's part of my inheritance. And, no, it's not an insignificant amount to give up. But for the chance to put the past behind us? The chance for you and me, for us . . . it's worth a lot more than that, Goose."

Tears run down Burke's face, and I feel my own eyes fill. Then he smiles—his biggest, most genuine smile that's nearly a laugh—and I watch those precious dimples deepen on either cheek.

"I hope you know how much I love you, Skye Starling. I've never loved anyone the way I love you." Burke blinks, his eyelashes thick and wet. "You're a miracle."

"But I still want an annulment."

He nods slowly. "That makes sense. Our marriage was never real."

I shake my head. "Besides, we were never ready to get married."

"No, I suppose we weren't." Burke's gaze pierces mine, cornflower blue. "But I'll tell you this, Goose. One day we *will* be ready. You may not know it, but I do. And when that time comes, it'll be the real deal." Burke interlaces his fingers in mine, and an electric current runs through my body. "What do we do now?"

"I don't know." I study every detail of his face, every little mark and corner that I've missed so desperately.

"Your dad is really okay with this?"

"Not entirely." I swallow. "But he'll get there. Nancy understands, and she'll help my father do the same."

"Nancy?" Burke looks surprised, but a grin plays at the corners of his lips. "You've been talking to Nancy about this?"

"Yeah. I'll tell you all about it later."

"Can you tell me about it now? And your new internship, I want to hear about that, too. Can we grab a coffee? If you're able?"

I nod, unable to suppress my smile. God, it feels good to smile again, to feel so happy that the joy bursts from your body, to feel so *free*. "I have lunch with the girls at two. But nothing until then. I took the day off."

"Lunch with the girls on a weekday? Did they . . . know what you were going to do today? At the hearing, I mean."

"I looped them in. They're a pretty supportive bunch, you know. Though it'll take them a while to forgive you."

"I could never blame them." We walk back down the hallway, toward our future, the open, unknowable road of it. "Hey, Skye?"

"Yeah?"

"Do you realize that when we left the courtroom earlier, you didn't do your knocks on the door?"

I stop midstep. I replay the scene in my head. Burke is right. I walked out without even thinking about my knocks. Without feeling any urge to do them. No compulsion seized me. How was it possible? Dr. Salam had always said that one day my compulsions might cease to exist—that they might stop serving their purpose— but I don't think I ever fully believed it. Until now.

"I didn't, did I?" I look up at Burke, and my voice breaks into a small laugh.

"No, you didn't." He leans down slightly, and for a second I think he's going to kiss me, and I know I'm not ready for that, and maybe he can tell, because he draws his shoulders back. "Not that it matters to me. I'll love you either way."

"I know." I look into his eyes. "I really do know that."

"Good."

"What if this is a new beginning, Burke?"

There in the hallway of the courthouse, my soon-to-be ex-husband extends his hand. "Hi. What's your name?"

"I'm Skye Starling." I touch my palm to his, and it feels like home.

"Nice to meet you, Skye." His grin is wide and bright. "My name is Burke Michaels."

Heather

New Canaan is so much fucking nicer than New Haven, you have no idea. I've been here several months now, and I'm telling you, this town is the dream.

Nicer than Westport, even, and I'm not just saying that to make myself feel better. I bagged the plan to move there—I had to, I realized after Skye confronted me in the coffee shop last winter. She claimed to know I was behind the Big Plan; she insinuated that her father knew it, too, after pinpointing my old connection to Libby. So as much as I'd been dying to move to Westport, as much as I loved the house I was about to put an offer on two days before Skye Facebook-messaged me—the master bath had heated floors—I couldn't go through with it. I couldn't live in a town where I'd fear the sight of Peter Starling's face every time I left my property. The Starlings were still Westport residents, and they hated me, and I needed a clean break from the past. A fresh start.

New Canaan is a quaint town twenty minutes west of Westport, a bit more inland, but just as wealthy. And the real estate market is better, too; according to my realtor, Anne, house prices in the area are low, and this is an ideal time to buy. Anne is a middle-aged mother of two who drives a Range Rover and invited me to join her book club. I already like the women here *exponentially* better than the T.J.Maxx–clad washouts of New Haven.

I closed on a great house here, a $1.1 million Cape Cod–style gem with two immaculate acres, four bedrooms, and—drumroll, please—a saltwater pool. That's more than half my Big Plan prize moola, but if you saw the newly renovated kitchen, with the Wolf twelve-burner and the soapstone counters and the black walnut floors, you'd understand why I had to make this place mine. Besides, real estate is an investment, and the best one you can make according to lovely Anne.

My days here aren't lonely, not even close. The girls are both living with me; Maggie's nannying for a local family before she starts college in the fall, and Hope broke up with Trevor and quit her communications job in New Haven. It wasn't fulfilling her, and she's thinking of pursuing an entirely different career. Maybe law school. She's having what she likes to call a quarter-life crisis, and right now we're just enjoying the summer together, sipping iced coffee by the pool and going for walks and having girl time. Garrett comes down from Boston some weekends; I can tell he loves spending time at the new house, loves the crisp new Matouk sheets on his bed and that he no longer has to share a bathroom with his sisters. All three of them are crazy about the house, and when they ask where all this money came from, I don't lie—I tell them sweet Mrs. Lucas generously left it to me in her will.

When the kids aren't around, I have my new friends, the ladies I've met through Anne and the book-club gatherings: Ginger, Helen, Grace, Fiona, Kerry, Adeline, Betsy. They are the same breed of women I knew when I was a young mom living in Gramercy; twenty-five years later, they haven't changed. They're older, yes, but startlingly well preserved and still immaculately groomed, with stylish clothing and careful makeup and expensive jewelry. They're well-mannered and charming and materialistic and a little bit bitchy, and they like me. They believe my story that my soon-to-be ex-husband made some bad financial decisions and cheated on me, and that I left his lying ass and moved here, and you know what? It's a version of the truth.

Here's something that will blow your mind: Burke didn't go to prison. How's that for a miracle? I almost wish I didn't know—I wish I could ignorantly and blissfully imagine him behind bars as I fall asleep at night—but I have to know these things; we're in the middle of a divorce. Burke, insanely enough, is still my husband.

The kids keep me updated on their father, too. They don't know the full story of what happened—the Starlings ensured that the local papers never even covered the plea hearing—but Burke did come clean with them about "having a relationship" with Skye. From what I gather, these days the kids think he's pretty scummy, but it sounds as if he's making a real effort, and they don't hate him. And that's okay. That's better. I wouldn't want my children to go through life hating their father—I'm not that kind of mother.

The news also never got wind of the stolen two million, and all Burke got was a year of fucking probation, so I can only assume Skye dropped those charges—what a doormat. I don't know if they're a couple again. The kids say Burke doesn't mention her, and Skye made her Instagram private, so I can no longer stalk her. Maybe they're back together. They're both so dumb, they probably deserve each other.

Besides, I have better things to worry about these days. About a month ago, Ginger called and said she wanted to set me up with her husband's single friend, a man named Paul.

"He's divorced and a sweetheart and he's *loaded*," she gushed to me on the phone. "Hedge-fund manager. And he's definitely looking to settle down again. And you're, like, ten times hotter and saner than his ex."

The evening of our scheduled setup I blow-dried my hair and slipped into a baby blue Milly dress I'd bought online at Saks. It hugged my body perfectly—fitted but not *tight*—and I knew I looked good. For forty-seven, I looked amazing.

Paul and I hit it off right away, his eyes glued to me throughout the evening, and after dinner ended, he invited me to stay for a nightcap. We got together again a couple of nights later and have been "an item" ever since. In a nutshell, Paul is ideal. Polite and interesting and successful, with a house four times the size of mine and a membership at the country club and a fifty-foot Hinckley sailboat on a mooring in Greenwich Harbor. And he doesn't have kids, which is perfect because I have zero interest in being involved with some other woman's children. I haven't introduced him to my kids yet, but I told the girls I've been seeing someone. They're supportive. "You deserve to be happy, Mom," Hope told me the other day when we were sunbathing on chaises by the pool.

Paul isn't as good-looking as Ginger first made him out to be. He's partially bald and he's not tall like Burke— I don't feel small and delicate in his arms—but I guess not every man is going to make your spine feel like a melting candlestick.

But Paul adores me, and there's a cap on the New Big Plan money, a very real cap, one that gets realer the longer I live in Fairfield County and realize just how quickly two million dollars can go. If I play my cards right, Paul has the power to take this cap away, to make it limitless. Something about him is so refreshingly *reliable,* too, the way he always has a nice bottle of wine breathing on the wet bar when I come over, the way his lavish house is permanently tidy, the kitchen stocked, how he always seems to have everything I need on hand. He's a provider, Paul is. He's nothing like my husband.

These days, living in Fairfield County, I think about Libby often. I think she would've approved of my house, the way it's decorated, with the white walls and beige furniture and faded Persian rugs and designer printed drapes.

Some nights I'm alone, when Maggie and Hope are busy and Paul is working late. On these nights I like to open a bottle of wine, a nice, light red, the kind I imagine Libby would've had on a casual summer evening.

I pour myself a glass and walk around the house, admiring the details of each room, inhaling the smell of fresh paint as I pace the sleek wood floors of my beautiful home, the home I've made for myself and my children.

Then I wander out onto the back porch—the wraparound that overlooks the pool—and watch what's left of the sun disappear, the tangerine melting into darkness. I stay out there awhile, until I'm well into the bottle and the cicadas are buzzing in the black, and on these nights I feel Libby. I feel the way we were together, sitting on her porch in Langs Valley, drinking good wine and talking about nothing and everything, the vivid memory of the hope that brewed inside me in those precious moments with her. And what I feel now isn't anger. It isn't vengeance. It isn't appreciation, or even nostalgia. But it might be fondness. It might be something like peace.

Acknowledgments

Endless thanks to my dynamite agent, Allison Hunter, and my brilliant editor, Sarah Cantin. Not a day goes by that I don't feel humbled to have the opportunity to write fiction, and I would never be where I am without the two of you, my dream team. Thank you for your dedication, your invaluable guidance, and your big, compassionate hearts—you have made this novel better in every way. I am lucky to call you my friends.

Joycie Hunter and Amelia Russo, thank you for your willingness and eagerness to read early drafts of this manuscript (and everything that I write)—your enthusiasm and feedback kept me peeling back the layers of Skye, Burke, and Heather's story.

Thank you to the extraordinary team at St. Martin's Press, who have rallied behind this book and worked tirelessly to send it out into the world. Especially: Jennifer Enderlin, Lisa Senz, Sallie Lotz, Olga Grlic, Katie Bassel, Marissa Sangiacomo, Naureen Nashid, Steve Boldt, Meg Drislane, Kerry Nordling, Kim Ludlam, and Tom Thompson.

Daniella Wexler, thank you for your early encouragement and indispensable feedback.

Sylvia Shweder and Josh Parks, thank you for sharing your knowledge of insider trading, courtroom procedures, and overall legal expertise. I am incredibly grateful for your advice and insight.

Brian Fink, thank you for so patiently and expertly answering my many questions on financial crimes and bank policies. You've been an immensely helpful brother-in-law.

To Elsie Swank, Emily Finnegan, and Hannah Thompson—thank you for reading with such sharp eyes and providing key feedback at the eleventh hour.

To all my wonderful friends and family who have been there for me and encouraged my writing—thank you. Thank you for showing up for me, for preordering my books, for recommending my work, and for every single expression of support and kindness. It means more than you know.

Thank you to the many people in the publishing and media industries who have helped my work reach a wider scope of readers, especially: Natasha Minoso, Karah Preiss, Jamie Blynn, Avery Carpenter Forrey, Crystal Patriarche, Taylor Brightwell, and Jason Richman. Thank you to the book bloggers and others who have shared photos, posts, tweets, and reviews—I appreciate each and every one of you.

To my readers, I am indebted to you. I will never be able to thank you enough for reading.

Mom, Dad, Charlie, and Ellie: you are my people—always have been, always will be. Thank you for celebrating with me in the light, and for helping me find my footing in the dark.

To Rob, love of my life—thank you for it all. Being able to wrap my arms around you after a long day of writing is the very best thing. I'll never know how I got so lucky.

Lastly, to my baby. When I started writing this book you were a dream; as I now write these words, you're soon to be a dream come true. Thank you for choosing me; I love you infinitely. The world is yours, and so is my heart.

Read on for an excerpt from

Can't Look Away

the next thriller from Carola Lovering, now available
in hardcover from St. Martin's Press!

Chapter One

Molly

Molly never would have gone to the concert in East Williamsburg if Nina hadn't dragged her there.

It wasn't actually a *concert*—not really—but one of those bars with a grungy back room where desperately-trying-to-make-it-bands played for free on the weekends.

Nina offered to buy Molly's drinks if she came with, because Cash was going to be there, and Nina was dying to sleep with Cash for the third time. And if Molly was being honest with herself—which she almost always was—she knew she had nothing better to do, and that if she didn't join Nina she'd sit at home in sweatpants and reheat Thursday's pad Thai, twisting her fork into the limp noodles with the festering knowledge that, on this perfectly good and possibility-filled Saturday night—the first one of the new year—she should be somewhere else.

At the bar, Nina ordered two tequila sodas and pretended not to notice Cash at the other end, drinking Bud Heavies with his cohorts, their laughs open-mouthed and dramatized and, in Molly's opinion, obnoxious.

"He texted, 'Come hang tonight,'" Nina whispered

anxiously, glancing toward Cash's corner of the room. "And he texted me the address, but is it dumb that I showed, Moll? Is it desperate? Do I look okay?"

Nina's chocolate hair fell in loose waves around her bare, bronzed-even-in-January shoulders—Molly would be forever jealous of her friend's perfect Colombian skin. Dewy makeup smudged the apples of her cheekbones, and mascara lengthened her already-thick lashes. In a crimson silk top and dark jeans, Nina—as always—looked like a knockout.

"You look amazing," Molly answered, ignoring her best friend's first two questions.

The bar was filling up and getting louder, a rising drone of voices saturating the space and clouding Molly's eardrums. She thought of the empty two-bedroom on Withers Street that she shared with Liz—they'd been roommates since sophomore year of college—and the pad Thai chilling in the fridge, and the twenty-five hundred words she hadn't yet written that were due on Tuesday. Molly wasn't into going out these days, not the way Nina, Liz, and Everly were. They'd all met at their small liberal arts college in Vermont, after which they'd migrated to New York together, the party vibe still very much their calling card.

Tonight, Liz and Everly were at some girl's birthday thing in SoHo, and Molly hated to leave Nina without a wing woman when she knew her friend really, *really* liked Cash, even though Cash was, in her opinion, immature and uninteresting and not remotely good enough for Nina. And besides, Molly possessed the self-awareness to admit that she *had* been in a bit of a rut, and she needed to make herself go out more, if only because "out" was the place where life happened, where inspiration and possibility had the opportunity to strike.

Nina ordered another round and closed her tab, and the bartender watched her as she signed her bill—the way so many men shamelessly stared at Nina—and winked.

Nina handed Molly the full tumbler of ice and tequila—no soda this time, just lime—and Molly felt the first sip of the second drink spread through her limbs, dense and pleasant, anchoring her more decisively into the night.

"I always forget how much I like tequila." One side of Molly's mouth curled effortlessly as she sank back onto the barstool.

Nina tilted her chin forward and smiled. "You're drunk off *one* drink?"

"I'm not drunk." Molly twisted a lock of her wheat-blond hair, drawing in a breath. "I'm sorry I've been lame lately. I've been so in my head. With the writing stuff. I'm glad you dragged me out."

"I'm glad I dragged you out so you could witness Cash ignoring me at the dirtiest bar in Bed-Stuy." Nina drummed her freshly manicured nails—a shiny eggplant color—against the bar top.

"We're not in Bed-Stuy, Neens."

"This far from the river, we might as well be."

Molly rolled her eyes as—suddenly—Cash appeared behind Nina. He slung one of his long, brawny arms around her delicate neck.

"Hey, girls." Cash smiled widely. Nina beamed, her eyes blooming with delight as if she were five years old and meeting Mickey Mouse at Disney World.

"You remember Molly? You met at Everly's apartment a couple of weeks ago."

"I think so?" Cash's thick eyebrows knitted together. "You're the writer?"

The question caught Molly off guard. "No, I'm just— I'm getting my MFA."

"In creative writing," Nina chimed. She knocked back the rest of her tequila.

Cash pursed his lips, confused.

"I'm just not sure what I want to do with my degree," Molly added quickly. "Maybe teach."

"This girl is my smartest friend," Nina crowed drunkenly, wrapping her arms around Molly's shoulders.

"What do you do again?" Molly asked Cash.

He opened his mouth to speak, just as the bar lights dimmed. Someone cleared their throat into the microphone.

"Ladies and gentlemen," a male voice bellowed theatrically from the stage. "It is my *absolute* honor to welcome my dear friends—friends who are more like brothers—the extraordinarily talented Danner Lane to the stage!"

The crowd cheered, the bar quickly emptying as dozens of twenty- and thirtysomething Brooklynites pushed their way toward the back room, toward the stage.

"There are a lot of people here," Nina observed.

Cash pushed his thick brown hair back from his forehead. "Have you heard Danner Lane's stuff? Jeb, one of the owners here, the guy who just announced them, is old friends with the Lane brothers. But they're honestly sick—they're on iTunes *and* Spotify now."

Three guys—all of whom appeared to be in their midtwenties—stepped onto the stage. One sank down behind a massive drum set, and the other two held guitars, positioning themselves in front of the drums.

"Let's move closer," Cash suggested. His friends were still at the bar, but he led the way toward the front, worming through the tightly packed crowd, Molly and an enchanted Nina in tow.

"They're brothers?" Molly asked loudly, glancing up at Cash.

"Those two are brothers." Cash stabbed his middle and index fingers in the direction of the stage. "Drums and bass guitar. The other one is Jake Danner. He's guitar and vocals. They all grew up together."

The Lane brothers looked similar, with wispy auburn hair and pale complexions, their frames lanky. But Jake was the one Molly couldn't take her eyes off of.

He was the color of honey—honey skin, golden curls that fell in front of his eyes as his fingers expertly plucked the strings of his guitar. When he looked up, Molly saw that his eyes were pale blue, and clipped right to hers, and she suddenly felt glad to be twenty-three and single, living in the greatest city in the world. Her mind—which had felt a bit dark and crowded lately—cleared.

Jake smiled broadly, and Molly felt a drop-kick in

her gut. Keeping his eyes fixed to hers, he spoke into the microphone.

"Hey, East Williamsburg." His voice was clear and perfect in pitch, edged with the slightest twinge of a Southern drawl. "It's Saturday night, and we're Danner Lane, and we're gonna play some music."

When the same thing would happen years later at Madison Square Garden—when Jake would find and hold Molly's gaze in the crowd, this time of thousands instead of seventy-five—it would be habitual for them. Danner Lane would be opening for Arcade Fire, and they would be rising in the ranks—soaring, making it— but Jake would still need Molly, his Molly, the one who tethered him to the ground.

In East Williamsburg, he opened his mouth to sing, the melody of a famous Elton John song filling the room, followed by the most exquisite voice Molly had ever heard.

And now I know
Spanish Harlem are not just pretty words to
say

Her life, Molly sensed in some deep, subconscious crevice of her heart, as Jake's eyes pierced hers, would never be the same.